THE WOMEN AT OCEAN'S END

Also by Faith Hogan

My Husband's Wives
Secrets We Keep
The Girl I Used To Know
The Place We Call Home
What Happened To Us?
The Ladies' Midnight Swimming Club
The Gin Sisters' Promise
On The First Day Of Christmas
The Guest House By The Sea
The Bookshop Ladies

THE WOMEN AT OCEAN'S END

FAITH HOGAN

An Aria Book

First published in the UK in 2025 by Head of Zeus,
part of Bloomsbury Publishing Plc

Copyright © Faith Hogan, 2025

The moral right of Faith Hogan to be identified
as the author of this work has been asserted in accordance with
the Copyright, Designs and Patents Act of
1988.

All rights reserved. No part of this publication may be: i) reproduced or transmitted in any form, electronic or mechanical, including photocopying, recording or by means of any information storage or retrieval system without prior permission in writing from the publishers; or ii) used or reproduced in any way for the training, development or operation of artificial intelligence (AI) technologies, including generative AI technologies. The rights holders expressly reserve this publication from the text and data mining exception as per Article 4(3) of the Digital Single Market Directive (EU) 2019/790

This is a work of fiction. All characters, organizations, and events
portrayed in this novel are either products of the author's imagination
or are used fictitiously.

9 7 5 3 1 2 4 6 8

A catalogue record for this book is available from the British Library.

ISBN (HB): 9781035906529; ISBN (XTPB): 9781035906512
ISBN (E): 9781035906505

Cover design: Leah Jacobs-Gordon
Typeset by Siliconchips Services Ltd UK

Printed and bound in Great Britain by
CPI Group (UK) Ltd, Croydon CR0 4YY

Bloomsbury Publishing Plc
50 Bedford Square, London, WC1D 3DP, UK
Bloomsbury Publishing Ireland Limited,
29 Earlsfort Terrace, Dublin 2, D02 AY28, Ireland

HEAD OF ZEUS
5–8 Hardwick Street
London EC1R 4RG

To find out more about our authors and books
visit www.headofzeus.com
For product safety related questions contact productsafety@bloomsbury.com

For Judith Murdoch, literary agent,
co-conspirator and friend.

'...and the truth will set you free.'

John 8:32.

Prologue

Galway, May 1957

Constance Macken wiped her nose with the back of her hand; her hanky was nowhere to be found and she wasn't going back onto the street to look for it. She'd had enough of Mickey Kane calling her names and making fun of her in front of the others. *The girl with no da.* Her mother called him the original invisible man. 'One minute he'd been promising me the earth, moon and stars and then quicker than you could say a baby Guinness and a chaser in the local pub, he'd hightailed it off to Dublin with the barmaid.' That wasn't much use to Constance, she could hardly go telling the other children that her father had run away and left them. She could scarcely admit it to Dotty, never mind anyone else.

The girl with no da. That's what they called her, but since news of her mother's good fortune was in the paper, it had become much worse. 'They're only jealous, you know that yourself,' her best friend Dotty said, but even if she was right, and Constance doubted it, that still didn't make things any easier.

Constance was small for her age, tiny, in fact; an easy target. At twelve years, she was still waiting to sprout up, but it felt less likely with every passing day as everyone in her class at school shot up around her. Her mother said she was like a little sparrow, not like her best friend. They were the same age and already Dotty Wren had developed curves and stood taller than any of the boys their age. Constance sighed now. Her mother talked about going away, leaving Galway altogether, and maybe that would be for the best. She'd miss Dotty though – for all she'd be glad to leave behind in this grotty little street, she'd miss Dotty Wren.

'There she is, boys.' Mickey Kane's thin voice cut through the hedges opposite. They must have slipped over the low wall at the side of Mr Wren's garage. They wouldn't dare come into Constance's garden, would they? 'Want it back? You'll have to come and get it, Constance.' Mickey's hand protruded through the thick privet, waving her handkerchief over and back like a sail swaying on the high seas.

'Give that here.' Constance shot to her feet. She was within grasping distance of the hedge when she remembered herself. The last time they caught her, they'd held her down and forced a worm into her mouth. She still remembered the taste, the feeling of it slithering about on her tongue; she'd almost choked through tears and trying to keep it from the back of her throat. In the end, to catch her breath, she'd had to swallow it. The humiliation of it was unbearable; even now, it was like a sharp whack against her gut, doubling her up in its unexpected intensity. If she allowed it to play out in her mind, she could almost be back there lying on the pavement, holding her breath until it felt as if she was going to drown under the weight of them. Their laughter had jeered in her ears as she'd tried to stand and straighten down her vomit-covered dress.

Later, she thought of what they could have done to her. It might have been much worse. The way Glen Howard looked at her sometimes made her shudder with a revulsion she didn't fully understand. She wasn't sure which was worse, that numbness of being reduced to something so vulnerable or the raging fear of where it could lead to if they picked on her again. They had pinned her down, sneered at her: that was the undoing of her; she'd been completely helpless.

She shot away quickly from the hedge.

'I don't want it back, you're welcome to it.' It was her best one, her mother would surely do a dance about it, but she didn't care. She had to sound as if it didn't matter, like Dotty. They'd never dare hold Dotty down or call her the awful names they called Constance. Of course, Dotty had two parents. Her parents were married. She carried no shame with her everywhere she went.

'And now, did you hear, boys, the Mackens are going up in the world. Lah-di-dah!' Mickey tried to sound posh. 'Probably be moving out of this dump too…' He stepped through the hedge, inching just a little too close to Constance for her liking. 'Will your da be coming back from England now he doesn't have to make all that money for you?' There was tittering laughter to that. Constance felt her cheeks flush. It was the lie she'd told once when they'd first begun to jeer her about her father. *Oh, he's gone to England to make money for us.* Simple as that and Constance had trotted the lie off because she had wanted to believe it.

'Probably, but...' she stammered, felt her lower lip quiver, a small muscle tighten in her jaw as if she was being wound up for fight or flight. She took a deliberate step back from the boys, who were jostling so much in the hedge that the whole border was moving in waves like the ocean.

'My ma says your mother probably made enough money on that book to buy up this whole street if she wanted to...' That was Glen Howard, an overgrown bruiser of a boy. Glen had sat on her legs when they'd forced the worm in her mouth. His big face looming behind the others, eagerly lapping up every moment of her agony, as if she was just another creepy-crawly he'd picked up off the ground to pull apart, limb by tortured limb.

'So?' Constance asked, placing one foot behind the other to move away from them. She could feel the path give way to grass beneath her sandal. She was reversing gradually towards the empty garden on the other side. It was her only hope. She'd never make it to her own back door. This was what it must be like to be set upon by a tiger or a bear and know that you were within seconds of mortal ruin. All those books she'd read, they never talked about how you could feel sick with fear. Sour bile rose up in her throat now, lodging just where she remembered the worm slithering down. *Holy God.* Her hands were sweating, thin clammy films building up between her fingers, her palms sticky. She thought her heart might explode in her chest. *Just breathe; outwit them*, because they would be on her in a flash if they thought she might try to escape. One more step. She felt the border behind her that separated the Macken garden from the one next door. Mr Morrison had died months earlier. His house stood empty, waiting for someone new to take it on. So far, no-one seemed to be very keen on becoming their new neighbour. The Kelly brothers, moving as one, stepped from the hedge. They looked around, appraising the Macken back garden as if they'd landed in a tantalising oasis. Constance did a quick calculation. There wasn't a hope she'd make it to the back door now. She was nowhere near as fast as the boys when it came to running. Hadn't she learned that to her cost last time?

The empty house next door loomed over her like a great big silent presence. All the windows were caked in dust and cobwebs hatched by a year's worth of neglect; it felt as if she was being watched by dangerous eyes.

There was no choice. She might just escape if she slipped through and hid in the undergrowth. From there, she could crawl along the side of Mr Morrison's old shed and press herself through the narrow gap in the fence further along so she emerged back into her own garden just opposite the scullery door. The only thing stopping her was the niggling sense of fear she had about Mr Morrison's ghost stalking about and keeping an eye on the place. Stupid. She knew it. But ever since the funeral – Dotty had insisted they look through the windows in the mortuary to see the old man laid out in his best suit – Constance had had nightmares about him. It was her first time seeing a corpse and she still hadn't gotten over it. Added to that terror, Mr Morrison never liked children. Certainly, he'd never been keen on Constance going in to fetch her ball if it strayed across the fence.

'All the money in the world doesn't change what your ma is…' One of the boys guffawed.

'Trollop.' They began the familiar murmuring chant that

they always teased her with. They hummed it, just enough to be heard, but not so loud that anyone who wasn't in the know would have had any idea what the taunt was. Constance gasped, tried to push down the ball of fear in her chest. Oh, how she despised them.

'Doesn't that make Constance Macken a little bastard?' Lickey Gillespie said and he pushed his glasses further up his nose, as if he'd just made a brilliant discovery.

'Little bastard. Little bastard. Little bastard.' The chant was menacing and now they were moving towards her in intimidating steps. They would fire into a sprint any second.

Be damned with the ghosts, she'd rather take her chances with dead old Mr Morrison than have to endure another worm slithering down her throat. Or worse.

She fell rather than turned back through the small gap in the fence. It was hardly visible and, from the other side, it looked as if she had just disappeared into thin air. Once beyond the fence, she realised there was a thin run, flattened along the centre of the hedges. Foxes. They raced about at night, calling out their strange coughing sound and wakening Constance so she tossed and turned and had to beat down nightmares about Mr Morrison's garden and what else might be living there.

Now, Constance dropped to her knees. The ground was wet and uneven here, ruptured with roots and bits of debris the old man must have raked to the side over years of clearing back for vegetables and fruits that were too bitter to entice any child to steal them.

In Constance's throbbing ears, the filthy chorus had grown louder, threatening. Her blood ran cold and icy. There was no going back now. The garden was more overgrown than last time she was here. She'd better not miss the gap to break away from the thick foliage, otherwise she would hit a dead end and be trapped for sure. She took a deep breath, pushed further through the hedges, scratching her knees as she crawled, avoiding animal droppings and hoping that none of it clung to her clothes or her shoes.

Once through the undergrowth, Constance crawled quickly along a narrow trail made by all sorts of nocturnal creatures she preferred not to think about. Evening was drawing in, the smell of woodbine sweet and cloying in the air. Probably her mother had forgotten about the time. Ideas did that to her mother. It was not a bad thing when other children were put to bed while the sun still shone brightly and Constance could laze in the garden or flop into a chair with a book and a glass of milk from the cool cupboard beneath the kitchen sink.

Behind her, she heard the boys move closer. She hesitated, her heart thumping in her chest, suddenly disorientated, she wasn't sure which way she should go, not without raising her head above the undergrowth. She started to move quickly. Maybe it didn't matter so much which way she went, if she could find somewhere to hide until they gave up.

Then she heard it. A noise, a mewling, it was a lonesome whine above the voices of the boys who scrabbled somewhere behind her.

It had to be a cat, hadn't it? Not some ghostly apparition of old Mr Morrison, giving his onions one last check from the spirit world? Constance shivered. *There are no such things as ghosts.* The nuns at school were adamant about that. *No such thing.* That's what Sister Consietta said. Although, the nuns were great believers in purgatory even if Sister Consietta wouldn't be drawn on where that was exactly. *Stop it.* Wherever it was, it certainly wasn't at the end of Mr Morrison's garden.

Two gardens across, she thought she heard Mr Wren's car being reversed into the little garage he had built at the back of their house. She was tempted to call to him for help, but she feared the boys would be upon her in an instant. Mr Wren was the nicest of all the grown-ups she knew, and Constance couldn't help wishing that he was her dad.

There it was again: a mewling sound coming from the end of the garden.

Was it coming from the old well? She was so close to it.

The well had been locked up years ago. You'd hardly even know it was there, thanks to the way the garden had outgrown itself over the last year. It was little more than a hole in the ground with a wooden trapdoor across it. No-one went near it usually, except if a winter storm flooded the gardens and it had to be pushed across to take the overflow. The timber cover was crude but effective in keeping out animals and children, until now, it seemed. The well wasn't used any more. All the houses along here had been built with indoor lavatories and kitchen sinks linked up to the city's main water systems. Her mother gave out often enough about the colour of the water some days and the fact that it turned her tea a dreadful shade of grey in summer.

Constance listened carefully, hardly daring to breathe; she tried to tune her ears unswervingly to the cries, above the drumming of her racing heart. It was definitely a kitten. He sounded pathetic. She heard him again; lower this time, a sort of keening sound.

Constance sat there for a moment, part of her afraid to break cover, but the howling felt like a knife twisting up in her guts and smothering out the fear of what she was risking. She couldn't leave the poor thing to suffer any longer. She seemed to be alone in the garden: the boys had not yet broken through the fence. A deep breath and she pushed through the undergrowth, looking up and down the garden all the while to check that it was safe. She ploughed on all fours through a sea of overgrown vegetables and weeds that were probably waist-high in places, thistles and briars scratching against her bare arms and legs as she went.

'It's okay, I'm coming,' she whispered under her breath. The well was little more than a hole in the ground. At some point, a rough frame had been placed around it, to define it by a matter of inches from the garden Mr Morrison had prized above all else. Constance wasn't sure she'd have been so brave had it been anywhere near the house. The old cover lay loose across the low frame. Constance crawled to it, slowly and carefully to avoid fox droppings and who knew what else was buried here in the neglected long grass. In the distance there was a sharp scream. Lickey Gillespie had been stung by a wasp; she watched him through the thick foliage. Only a few yards away, but it seemed they had forgotten about her, for now at least. The boys were moving away, towards Mr Morrison's empty house. They had spotted a slightly opened sash window which proved more interesting than torturing Constance, a mercy she was grateful for even if she didn't count on it lasting very long.

The mewling sound again made her push on.

Pushing the cover across was easy. Lying on her belly, gingerly she leaned over the edge. *Urgh.* Immediately the overpowering smell of putrid water caught her breath, making her retch. Now she wished she had her hanky.

The mewling was loud and echoey here, not the gentle sound that had whispered through the grass moments earlier. *Definitely a kitten.* Constance told herself sternly to forget her mother's warning that this place was filled with rats' nests. That had only been to put her off, why would rats choose here when there were far more comfortable places to set up home? Dotty maintained *it went down all the way to hell and if you got too close, there was a chance Satan himself could reach up and pull you in.* Well of course, Constance didn't believe all that nonsense either. After all, she had made her confirmation a year ago. She knew better than anyone that the road to hell wasn't down some smelly old hole in the ground. Reverend Mother Mary Ignatius said it was to be found most easily in the big cities, especially in the communist and atheist countries. You knew it because its road was paved with good intentions, not that Constance had any idea what that sort of road would look like.

She shivered in spite of herself. Perhaps she should wait for Dotty?

A pathetic whimper came from the darkness. There was only one thing for it. She would have to reach down as far as she could and try to grab it. The stench was getting worse the longer she was here, far better to move as fast as she could. Naturally, this was what her mother had complained about for years: *the foul-smelling constancy of it just when the days are good enough to open a window.* In winter time, it was like pulling a plug on an overfilling bath. Summer was a different story. If the days were fine as they had been for weeks on end now, the reek of dirty water would hang on the air and cling to clothes drying on the lines in the gardens all along the road.

That didn't matter now. All that mattered was— Silence. The sound of the cat's mewling had ceased. Oh God, had she killed it, made some part of the wooden cover splinter down and cut the creature in half? Constance scrunched her eyes up, afraid to peer over the edge, but she had to, she just had to get her courage up, move closer and peer down into its darkest depths.

She gripped the side of the well tightly, felt the dry slab burn against her skin. The outer rim was little more than a few rough bricks dug into the earth to save the whole garden from falling in. She had to force herself to look over the side, fully expecting to see nothing but black and the reflective circles of two pathetic dead eyes staring back at her from the bottom of the well.

'Meow.' It was faint, but by some miracle, the kitten was clinging onto a narrow ledge at the side. It was a little way down, but not so far Constance felt she couldn't reach it if she stretched.

'Shh, here puss, puss,' she soothed as she pulled the sleeve of her dress up further, leaned over the side and reached down as far as she could to grab the kitten. She hoped he wouldn't scratch her, but she braced herself in case, because regardless of how feral the creature was, she had to grab him and pull the poor sod to safety, it would only take a second, not enough time for him to do any real damage. Except, she couldn't reach him, not like this. His soft ears were just beyond her fingertips.

'Right,' she murmured, looking around her. She inched

closer, so close her belly was now balancing on the side of the well, her body almost at a right angle, so the blood rushed to her head, making her dizzy and sick all at once. *Bloody hell.* It still wasn't enough. She rattled off a quick Hail Mary – an insurance of sorts – then she steadied up, before stretching as far as she could. She reached her hands down, down, ignoring the pull on her shoulders; still she couldn't feel the animal near her grasp. She leaned further over, her head spinning as if she'd just stepped off a carousel; she was bent way across the edge of the rough wooden frame so its jagged splinters grazed beneath her belly button. Taking a deep breath, as if about to dive into the water, she reached as far as she could, feeling her muscles tighten all along her spine and down the sides of her body. One more stretch. Fur. She could feel it, soft, wet, downy beneath her hands. She grabbed the cat by his neck, yanked him up in a flash and swung him across behind her back, so he could land on the safe ground. Maybe not the gentlest rescue, but he was alive.

It was as she was swinging her arm back again to place her hand on the rim of the well that a crow screeched over her. It was so low, she felt the breeze of its flight almost lift her dress from her skin. The jolt caused Constance's whole body to jerk and before she knew what was happening she had lost her footing. For what felt like an eternity, she swayed back and forth, her head tipping further into the well, her hands before her face, she couldn't right herself around to grab the sides of the well to keep her balance. She tried to bellyflop her body backwards on the grass. On the second attempt, she thought she felt the earth beneath her as if she might have shifted her weight so she was safe, but then something silky and writhing brushed up against her – the cat, startling her – and she lost her purchase on the ground.

Falling into the well seemed to happen in slow motion.

Constance reached out, trying to catch onto something, perhaps another ledge just as the cat had. There was none. Something rubbed against her back: a rope against one wall. She grabbed it, wrapping her body around it. Her hands, covered with sweat, betrayed her by slipping too easily against the braids and losing purchase so holding in one place was impossible. The tighter she held on, the more the rope cut sharply into her skin, peeling it coarsely, which might have made her let go, but for the drop beneath. She slid down it, desperately fighting against fate and gravity; gripping hungrily to descend as slowly as she could, clinging to the narrowing shaft of daylight as if it could save her from what was clearly unavoidable. She wanted to scream – tried hard to call out for help – but her voice caught somewhere in her throat, her breath halted in her lungs, she was beyond making a sound, too petrified to do much more than hang on.

Inch by inch she slid down into the blackness, too engrossed in the task of holding on to think about what waited at the end. She must have fallen from the rope, but even years afterwards she wouldn't remember what had happened next.

Forty foot or was it yards? That was the first thought she had when she woke. She'd heard the grown-ups discuss the well a year earlier, but she couldn't for the life of her guess at just how far down she was. It was dark, but still, she could see the sky, just a glimpse far above her in the narrow well mouth. It was as much as she could make out and she lay for a long time staring at the clouds and sobbing miserably. She tried to think of a way out, but her head hurt, her body felt as if it had been broken into a thousand pieces and she was too scared to move much in case of what might be lurking in the shadowy walls above her.

Later, she remembered Dotty's father – Mr Wren. He must have been near his garage, but he wouldn't have heard her scream, not from two gardens up.

She tried calling for help, when she woke up later. By then, she had no idea if it was morning or afternoon or even how long she'd been there. It was no use. She stood up, reached round, searching the air above her head for the rope she'd clung to earlier, maybe she could climb back up again? It was no good. It was not there, it must have ended somewhere above her reach. There was only one thing for it. They would have to find her, maybe just like she'd found that kitten, maybe someone near the fence at the right time would hear her call. And so she began to call out, her voice quickly ascending to a frightened scream which only fed her terror. In the end, her voice grew hoarse and her sobs overtook her calls for help. She was lost down here in the darkness and soon even the slim shaft of light that penetrated from so far over her head began to fade.

Later, much later, she thought she heard them calling her. *Constance. Constance. Constance.* Her mother's voice had a strange musicality to it, as if keening her daughter's name. But Constance was too tired for any of it to register beyond a mere whisper. *I'm here. I'm here. I'm here.*

By the time night came in, she had fallen asleep as much from giving up as exhaustion or fear.

1

Pin Hill Island

Constance Macken

Pin Hill Island had always been a haven, not just for sea birds and undisrupted native species of everything from Irish hare to native Irish goat, but also for people. Visitors to the island often remarked on the prettiness of the place. In summer, the locals pushed the boat out with hanging baskets, a strident tidy village committee and a touching-up of the pastel-coloured houses that were a tourist's first impression as they disembarked the ferry. The overall effect was welcoming and comforting. Nothing bad could possibly happen here, could it? Maggie Macken, Constance's mother, must have recognised it the first moment she'd stepped on the, then, busy dock. Oh, that was a long time ago now – Constance and Dotty had been girls, glad to leave their old lives behind. Pin Hill Island couldn't have been more different from Galway and the narrow terraced streets they'd known. The island seemed vast by comparison, but it was only ten miles by eight miles. Sometimes Constance found it hard to believe it had been her home for almost seventy years.

Ocean's End, the art deco folly house her mother had purchased all those years ago, stood on the westernmost tip, between the only two villages on the island – well, you could hardly call Muffeen Beag a village, but no-one would ever say that to anyone who lived there. Muffeen Mór, on the other hand, boasted the vital conveniences any modern village needed. Snuggled beneath Pin Hill and at the top of a narrow slipway the locals grandly called *the pier*. There was a post office, a church (albeit without a resident priest these days), a supermarket, two pubs, a hotel, the cemetery, a ramshackle community hall, and a small school, which was fought hard for when Constance was just a girl. Later, she'd taught there for many years. Two of those years were more precious than the rest when her darling husband had taken up the principal's job. Oisin had fallen in love with the island soon after he fell in love with Constance. Sometimes, she found herself smiling wistfully when she caught a flicker of those hopes and dreams. A lifetime ago, now.

Ocean's End was as different from the terraced house they'd lived in in Galway as it was possible to be. A striking, two-storey white edifice, peering over a rocky cliff to the ocean below, it wasn't a huge house, not by today's standards to be sure. Over the last few years, there had been some monstrosities erected on the south side of the island, holiday homes for people who didn't really know the island at all. Still, Ocean's End felt far too big for one person, even if she did live here all year round. For a start, there were five bedrooms too many and a generous library Constance hardly ever poked her nose into these days. The windows, in their thin pencil-like frames, now seemed insubstantial, the flat roof a nod to a very different era and the once white paint had turned to a flaking red-grey, thanks to the constant onslaught of the sea below.

Still, when the sun shone here, it was glorious, like no other place in the world, though, for most of the year, the skies filled over with layers of incessant clouds that appeared to have no start or finish to them. The fields wore mists like cloaks wafting above the land as if suspended by some great puppeteer intent on hiding the best until he was quite ready to unveil the stupendous beauty of the place.

It would be weeks yet until the sun broke through the blanketing grey with convincing brightness that indeed, summer was on its way in. Constance knew many of the islanders preferred the winter. The place was left alone. It was an excuse to pull across the curtains early, drink hot toddies and pretend the mad world on the mainland no longer existed. Still, summer was the lifeblood of Pin Hill. Tourism was the only form of external income to be relied upon for many families. Constance loved each season as it came, but if she was pushed, she knew her preference was the summer. Her favourite day of the year was the one when she saw the first swallow shoot through the air outside the kitchen window and she noted it down each year in her weather journal, oh joy!

It was too early in the year to think of that today; the swallows would not even have thought of packing their bags for Ireland yet. For now, Constance would make do with robins and doves, huge grey crows and occasionally, on blustery days when the fishing boats could not leave the dock, a flock of seagulls landing on the rough grass outside her window in the hope of finding something to tide them over until the storms passed.

Constance shivered. She plugged in the little two-bar heater she kept beneath the kitchen table for those days when draughts found a way of catching you out in spite of the ancient Aga going at full steam. If she sat here long enough, it felt as if she was stepping into the hot sands of the Sahara and being warmed from the ankles up. If she could bend to take a proper look, she was certain there must be a blackened circle scorched beneath the table top, but what did it matter at this stage? It was only a table.

Really, she should be used to the cold. They'd left Galway when she was just a girl to live here at Ocean's End. And it wasn't as if the Atlantic was any more biting today than any other spring day. This was a different sort of chill. It felt as if a shadow had streaked across at her back, sending an icy frisson along her spine. She knew what it was; of course she knew what it was. Another of her dreams. It seemed that as age dulled her reflexes and slowed down her movements, it had a canny knack of switching up the velocity of her night terrors.

She'd woken at five o'clock, just as the rooks shook their feathers in the tall pines in the distance. Her nightdress soaked. *Heather*. That darling child she'd doted on so many years ago. And in that way that dreams can mash up all reality, the girl was reaching down into a well at the gate to Ocean's End. She was reaching down, down, and then scurrying at her back a badger flashed out of sight.

Dreaming of badgers was never a good sign. Constance

had cast the dream off when she woke earlier. She'd long believed that anything she dreamed of in black and white would eventually turn into a magpie and she'd just been thankful to waken before that final and familiar denouement.

Constance wiped the tears from her eyes. The last time she'd laid eyes on Heather was right here, in Ocean's End. They'd had an awful row, Constance and Heather's mother, Dotty, the sort there was no coming back from, it turned out. Heather had been tugged along in the slipstream of her mother's rage, tripping out the door and back to England once and for all. When Constance thought about that time, it still twisted sharply in her heart. In spite of the passage of so many years, that fissure in a friendship that should have been forever would always be a huge regret. So long ago. Certainly, life had trundled on. Over the years, Constance's mind had wandered down roads wondering if she should reach out to Dotty just one last time. *Perhaps it still wasn't too late? Silly old woman*, she told herself crossly, *of course it's too late.* As time trundled on, she'd imagined Heather, growing into a young woman, forgetting all about Ocean's End, or perhaps resenting it as much as her mother seemed to that day, or maybe, just maybe, at odd moments missing it and remembering Constance, still here, thinking of them both. At some point, Heather would have been packed off to university, her father would have seen to that, maybe she got married, had a family, made a good life for herself. Dotty was bloody lucky and she took it all for granted and maybe that was at the root of why Constance had lashed out so fiercely.

All of this was surely what her mother, Maggie, called

the mixed blessing of hindsight. Constance, older than her mother had ever been, could see it quite clearly now. There had been no daughter for Constance. Her chance to have a family with Oisin was cut short before they had celebrated their cotton wedding anniversary. Her own fault, of course, hadn't she been the one to bring him to the island. A man from County Laois, the most landlocked county in Ireland, and she'd dragged him to Pin Hill, to start their lives together. What had she been thinking? He knew nothing of island life. The sea he'd loved snatched him from her on a day that gave no suggestion of what it had in mind that bright and balmy morning he set off to catch some trout for their supper.

The fact was, Dotty Wren, or Dotty Banks as she was by then, had everything Constance could have dreamed of, a good man who adored her, a darling daughter and the hope of future grandchildren, family to pass things along to, to grow old with, one day.

Constance had never remarried. Island living meant there was a scarcity of men at the best of times; certainly, there was no-one who could take Oisin's place in her heart. It was as simple as that. It was strange, but to Constance, time had shaped Heather into another of those ghosts who drifted in and out of her thoughts while always at a distance.

This morning, for the first time in a long while, she knew that Heather was no ghost – that dream had made her feel alive in a way Constance hadn't felt in years. And she knew that for certain when she looked up and saw Oisin's face looking back at her from the photograph on the wall. She turned slightly away from his broad and happy expression watching her, smiling out from beneath a floppy fringe, holding up a small salmon, frozen in time from a happy day so many summers ago. She'd taken the photograph herself. Happy days, indeed. 'What would you make of me now?' she asked his image. A little old woman, hair whiter than sea foam, still thick and wavy, but pinned these days as well as she could manage it with slightly arthritic shoulders. Oisin would probably always know her by her eyes. He always said she had eyes that held the forest, even though there was little more than a sheltered copse at the centre of the island. It was too long; over half a century, years since they'd looked into each other's eyes. She turned away. It did no good thinking of things that you couldn't change.

This house was full of memories. When she turned back to take a fresh cup from the dresser, she found herself staring at a photograph of Dotty.

Oh, Dotty. She murmured that so familiar name like a prayer and, once again, she wondered if it was too late to reach out to her childhood friend.

In spite of their divide, some things bonded you beyond friendship, perhaps to eternity. Even with distance and time washing out what went before, they would always be bound together. Perhaps, if the world turned long enough, one day none of it would matter. Wasn't that a comforting thought to wrap up in on a sleepless night? But she wasn't doolally yet. The past was always there. Sometimes, it took only the aroma of wild woodbine to cast her back to *that* summer, when they'd swum in waters far beyond their depth and innocence was smothered utterly. That summer, in 1957, had been the start of everything, its fingers reaching through and clawing out the things that mattered most to Constance and perhaps to Dotty ever since.

All that time.

She and Dotty Wren had been like sisters. They were closer than sisters, at one point. They'd grown up together, essentially in the same house, but more than that, they'd saved each other. And for a while, Constance had truly believed that Dotty had been saved, but then, as the years went on, she could see it. Dotty had changed, the past was eating her alive and she was drinking just to stay ahead of it. Well, too often, without proper help, that was the way, wasn't it? Was it better or worse to destroy yourself or stand by and watch fate exact the price and more from you for your sins? An eye for an eye. Because Constance had always believed that had been her own lot.

Constance had watched as her future happiness was snatched from before her eyes, while Dotty set out to destroy the best of life before it could take root.

By their thirties, Constance's best friend had settled into what she considered to be an unsatisfactory life in Fulham. Dotty had married a man called Bobby, who was going to be an actor, until he ended up working in a factory. Their divorce was messy, their marriage over before it even got a proper chance. Dotty had wrestled with the fact that life had launched slowly, without fanfare, into a dull version of the dreams that had pushed her from the island when she was still a girl. Constance always knew she drank, maybe a bit too much; she struggled with her health – her mental health. There had been a breakdown, years earlier, when Heather was just a kiddie. Dotty insisted it was baby blues, but there was more to it than that. They both knew it. Some ghosts never rest. Then there were a few years when it seemed that things had settled down, or Constance hoped so, at least. Her own life filled up, she married and, for a while, the horizon dazzled. Until it didn't.

She smiled, remembering her friend.

It was Dotty who had come to her rescue all those years ago, and found her when everyone else but her mother had given up hope of ever seeing her alive again. Search parties had trawled every street and laneway of Galway. It seemed they'd looked everywhere else, but it was Dotty who, from her bedroom window, noticed something was amiss and thought to check the well.

Later, her mother told Constance, it took ages to get her out. Mr Gillespie and some of the other men from along the road had made up a pulley contraption and winched Maggie (by far the slightest of the adults) down to rescue her daughter.

Constance was hardly conscious by the time they got to her. Luckily, she was in need of little more than sustenance, rest and reassurance to be back to herself.

It seemed for ages afterwards all her mother could talk about was covering over that well. Someone needed to do it. *My daughter could have died down there*. If Maggie Macken said that once, she must have said it a hundred times.

Usually, the morning was Constance's favourite time of day. She'd realised it late in life, but once she did, she made the most of it by pushing through the back door sometimes even before her breakfast and scattering feed out for the birds who visited the garden earlier each morning.

She closed her eyes for a moment. The sea was calm today. She could hear it, just the background noise of the waves, washing in and out at the shore far below. No matter what it robbed from her, she had to admit it would never be any less splendid. In the distance she thought she saw a shadow lurk beneath the water. A shark or a whale? The sea was already a very dark grey thanks to pewter clouds blocking out whatever sunlight spring might have had to offer.

She squinted slightly, leaning against the scraggy wall. All of this fencing had been brilliant white once. A series of breakers crashed over the shadow, but after each had passed, she knew it was still there. There had been a flutter on the island for the last week or two, some pilot whales spotted off the southern coast. Constance hadn't expected to see one. Usually, the only time anyone on shore saw them was when they ended up beached in one of the tiny coves and, by then, it was too late to refloat them again. She stood for a while, watching the shadow hover, as if it was idling away the time and waiting for something better to come along – perhaps the 39B bus? That notion made her smile as she watched the shape in the water. It became clearer the longer she waited and when eventually it decided to flip its tail and raise its body to surface level for just a second, it was almost a relief.

Definitely a pilot whale, she was convinced of it, and even when it had swum away and was probably miles out to sea, she stood there, reflecting on the vastness of it all and yet, how insignificant her life felt within it. Eventually, she turned back to the house. She would make tea. Spend a little time writing in her weather journal and maybe later, if she was lucky, she might catch a glimpse of the huge whale again before the clouds creasing the sky against the top of Pin Hill swung back and unleashed a battering of rain against Ocean's End.

Constance pushed open the back door to let herself into the kitchen. Her home – Ocean's End. Her mother had bought it from a Hollywood film director that everyone talked about having lived here once. Actually, he'd only spent a week on the island after he'd had the place constructed. It was at the height of his success on the back of a movie remembered more for its stars than its plot.

Sometimes, Constance actually saw the place for what it was: a tragic relic of grander times. A vessel of little more than memory and nostalgia. At night, keeping time with the creaking boards and rattling pipes, she thought she heard the sound of voices, long lost, travelling across the years with snippets of conversations they'd never had a chance to finish. So many voices: her mother's, Oisin's, Dotty's and, yes, maybe even her own.

It would be kind to describe it as faded, but really crumbling would be closer to the mark. These days, Constance tried to contain her living to just two rooms, the kitchen and a ramshackle sitting room. They were both on the ground floor and so the leaks that grew larger each year were at least one storey up. Her bed was set in an alcove which had once been filled with a grand piano that her mother gifted to the local community centre. It had been a waste having it here when neither of them played and now her bed fitted snugly in the corner. In the mornings, if she pulled herself up high against her pillows, she could watch the sea crash against the cliffs of Mallory Bay in the distance. And always, she thought as she looked at it of her darling husband Oisin and asked herself if he still lay silent and alone beneath the waves.

Even then, when the unthinkable had happened, Constance knew, in some fibres knitted too deeply for her to pick apart, that losing her husband, in that way that she did, was nothing more than just wages for the sins of the past. She sighed deeply now. The past. She needed to wrap it up and put it back where it belonged but dreaming of Heather Banks had somehow unearthed those things that she'd carefully packed away for a long time now.

The sound of the stairs creaking in the hallway stirred her from her memories. How on earth could steps still fall heavily on stairs when no-one had trodden across them in months?

The truth was, Constance hadn't been brave enough to climb the stairs since early last summer. No reason why she shouldn't, aside from aches and pains she was trying to appease by staying put. When she'd last gone up there it was to check out a scurrying sound that she feared was rats, or perhaps a badger. It turned out to be a crow's nest begun on top of a French armoire in what had once been a guest room.

Thankfully, the crows had only managed to get in through an open window and not the roof, which would have been a total disaster. She couldn't begin to imagine the cost fixing the roof would bring to her door, far more than she could afford, that was for sure. Instead, she shut all the windows on the upper floors even though she knew it probably reeked of stale air; the risk of mould was preferable to sharing her home with a family of cawing crows.

This morning, while she waited for the kettle to boil, the

old clock in the hallway rang out the hour. It seemed to lose a minute with each year that passed. The postman would have been already, while she was watching that pilot whale. She was lucky. Jay Larkin called in regularly, if only for a short time. He collected her pension for her and paid her bills when she asked him to and he did both with an easy manner that never made her feel as if he resented it. That was island living – everyone looking out for everyone else.

Just one letter sat on the hall table inside the door, a bill by the looks of it. Jay had long given up leaving her post in the box at the gate to Ocean's End. What was the point when the door flew open in the gusting winds that surrounded the house for the winter months? So instead he pushed in the unlocked front door and left any letters on the hall table. If he had time, some days he'd sit in the kitchen and have a cup of tea with her, tell her about the football match or whatever big race he was hoping to place a bet on. Constance always made sure to have something fresh from the oven that he could take home to the kiddies. *You have them spoiled*, he'd say before making his way to the next house along the road where two German fishermen had settled a few years ago. They seemed content to live mostly off the rocky garden. In the summer months, they made what money they needed working in the village pub and supermarket. Occasionally, if time had weighed too heavily on Constance's hands and she'd baked far more than was decent to hand over to Jay, she wrapped up scones or homemade brown bread for her neighbours to enjoy. Two men on their own, she didn't expect either of them to be up to much when it came to baking, and better to share than endure a lecture from the visiting district nurse about her sugar levels and a fatty liver they couldn't really prove she had either way.

Constance looked at the letter, feeling that familiar stab of stress bite into her stomach. It was definitely a bill. Not today. She couldn't face it today. She tucked the letter in behind the vase with faded artificial flowers. Today, she would think only of happy memories with Dotty, not of people wanting things from her that she didn't have to give. And she definitely wasn't going to think of the last time she and Dotty spoke. It would be too much to bear to think of that awful time.

2

Heather Banks

Heather Banks had enough money in her current account to be anywhere in the world. The one place she didn't want to be was here, in her mother's house, checking out the contents of her mother's leaking fridge.

She had come as soon as she got the call. When she arrived, her mother's body was still lying in her bed in the cramped front room that they had turned into a bedroom for her a few years earlier. Heather had made sure her mother had everything she needed in terms of life's little comforts in the end, but always there remained that unbridgeable gulf between them. Dotty had never wanted a daughter; she'd made that plain too often from the very start.

It was strange, this silence that enveloped her now.

Two paramedics arrived to take her mother away on a stretcher to some part of the local hospital where visitors never went. Closing the door after they left with a soft click,

Heather had a feeling this house had never been so still before. Her mother had lived life with a radio constantly blaring in the kitchen and the TV switched to a low hum of endless soaps in the front room.

It wasn't just the silence that made the house feel out of kilter. There was something else and Heather had been aware of it from the moment she entered the house, but it took a little while to register. She was standing at the window in the front room when she realised it. She was staring at her reflection in the glass: an odd thing to see yourself when you least expected it. Time was catching up with her, fine lines etched around her eyes, her dark hair just that little more severe against her skin than when it had held its natural colour. Expensive colourists weren't always all they were cracked up to be, it turned out.

Then it hit her.

That was it. The windows had been recently cleaned, oh, they weren't gleaming but they'd been washed around the frames, the glass if not sparkling was grime free. The place was spick and span, as if her mother had been ready to leave, in that way that people tidy up before they go on holidays, making themselves so late they almost miss their flight. Heather stepped back from the window, turned to look around the room.

It wasn't just the windows either. The small chair was free from the mountain of clothes it typically groaned beneath. The floor was free of the pile of magazines and empty glasses and the obligatory ashtray filled to overflowing. On the bedside table a small tray held six bottles of pills and assorted medicines that she guessed at a glance had something to do with treating either stomach upset, constipation or diarrhoea. There was one glass of water sitting next to them, half drunk.

Water? Since when had her mother ever drunk water? At a push, she might wash down some aspirin with a glass of orange juice, but mostly Dotty Wren exhibited not just a disregard for contraindications but a scornful snub of any notion that she should curb her drinking or indeed her bitterness.

Heather moved to the kitchen, then climbed the stairs, ambling into each of the two bedrooms there and lingering for a while over the dull and faded familiarity of it all. As familiar as it all was – nothing very much had changed here in years – she felt as if she'd missed a step.

She knew what it was, of course she knew what it was, but she walked around the house once more, peering into drawers and cupboards as if to find a missing jigsaw piece that would somehow make the picture real. She even went out into the yard and checked her mother's bin. But no, not even there – she couldn't understand it, there wasn't an empty bottle anywhere to be seen. And suddenly, Heather wasn't so sure what she felt standing here in this place that was meant to be her home, but had never truly felt like it.

It (her mother's alcoholism, that thing she was never allowed to mention) had driven a wedge between them years ago. It had broken her marriage to a man who'd been a good father and a long-suffering husband, long after he was legally obliged to be one. Heather thought of her father now.

Bobby Banks was an actor, once. He told Heather he'd fallen for her mother and whatever talent he had took second and eventually third place behind their little family.

She'd always been a beauty. But when the hard realities of bills hit with the birth of their daughter, Bobby gave up on dreams of the stage and settled for a factory job, putting aside everything else for his family. Her darling dad had died three years earlier, in a small nursing home, with views of a river and the comfort of knowing he'd been as good as mother and father to a daughter who adored him. Dotty Banks was not a bad woman. She was, Heather had known all along, just a disappointed one who needed a crutch and found one she liked in a bottle. It seemed everything in life came up short for Dotty. Every glass was half empty. Every win was just a fluke and for every diamond she saw mostly the rough.

None of that mattered any more. For better or worse, Dotty Banks was her mother and, even if Heather was staring fifty years of age between the eyes, today it felt as if she needed her as she never had before. Automatically, she sniffed the milk carton before she flicked on the electric kettle for tea. A small note pinned against the fridge door caught her eye. Her mother had a podiatry appointment later today. Heather would have to ring and cancel it before the visiting chiropodist arrived at the front door. At this moment, she couldn't cope with having to talk to anyone and hear some stranger telling her empty lies that her mother would be missed.

She left a message for the podiatrist, explaining that her mother had died and that she had no need of her services any more. Then she made a cup of tea which unnervingly tasted just as tea had when she was a teenager living in this house. Was her mother still buying the same tea bags?

Perhaps the water pipes had so much lead in them that they gave everything a sort of peppery taste.

It didn't matter. She took the tea to the table and sat there for a while looking out at the back yard. It was a bleak rectangle of crumbling brick and peeling paint. Heather couldn't remember having seen so much as a robin outside her mother's kitchen window in all the years she'd lived here. Her mother always said, *what bird in their right mind would want to live in Fulham?*

It was all so different to the Chelsea flat she'd shared with Philip for most of their marriage. Heather had loved that ground-floor flat. It was her home for twenty years. She'd tended the little back garden lovingly, cultivating not just a sea of flowers in the summer but a year-round haven for city birds that visited from the park nearby.

The flat was sold now. For less than five minutes she had considered buying out Philip's share, but in the end, as much as she had loved living there, she couldn't imagine just carrying on alone. Somehow, the idea of it being just her there made how they'd ended up feel even more depressing. For the last few weeks, she'd been staying in a shoebox flat in Battersea. It was meant to be temporary, just somewhere to catch her breath; most of her belongings were in storage at this point. She was drifting, looking for something or somewhere to drop anchor. It was now obvious to her that apart from a mother who hardly wanted her near for longer than it took to say the rosary, there was nothing to keep her in this city any more. The only thing stopping her booking a one-way flight out of it was she had no idea where she wanted to go.

It was while she was thinking about the lack of birds in the garden that her phone rang. Her friend Ruth. Oh, God, she'd forgotten that she'd promised to meet for coffee this morning.

'Where are you?' Ruth sounded as if she was already sitting in the coffee shop with tea and croissants waiting for her.

'I totally forgot, I'm so sorry...' And somehow she managed to explain about the phone call from Carmelita, which felt as if it had been days ago at this point, but really, it was only two hours earlier. Her mother's carer had caught her just as she was leaving the gym. Heather had come straight over, taking the tube and then walking in the rain so Carmelita could let her into the house before she was due to go and visit the next client on her morning roster.

'I'm so sorry, is there anything I can do?' Ruth asked.

'Oh, God, Ruth, you have done more than enough already.' And it was true. Ruth was her best friend these days. She'd been the first to swoop in when word seeped through their circle that Heather's marriage was finally over. It was Ruth who'd come to court with her for the divorce hearing. It was Ruth who'd managed to get them both uproariously drunk afterwards in a Soho bar. They got so drunk that other patrons thought they were celebrating rather than mourning the end of a twenty-year marriage and a business partnership that had made Heather a very wealthy woman.

'Don't be silly, this is different and you're... well, you've already been through quite a bit this year so, just ask, if there's anything.'

'I think I might...' Heather started to say, but she wasn't

sure. After all, it was years since she'd stayed in this house, it was firmly her mother's house. It hadn't felt like home for so long she could hardly remember it ever feeling that way. 'I might stay here for the night, just...'

'Poor you, but it's completely natural, you need time to get your thoughts straight. It might be good for you to surround yourself with the feeling of your mother for as long as you can,' Ruth said. 'Still, if you need anything, you know where I am.'

'Thanks Ruth.' She meant it. 'And, I'm so sorry, for forgetting about us meeting up this morning.'

'Oh, that doesn't matter, you know me, happy to eat pastries for both of us...' With that she laughed that tinkling sound that somehow made Heather feel as if the world could be a lighter place if only you could change the way you looked at it.

It was one of those days that Heather felt she would always remember, not just because it was the day her mother passed away. It was a day she took to herself, to reflect on the absence of the woman she had tried to love more than she'd ever been able to. In spite of everything, Heather found it was comforting to sit in the little kitchen and remember some of the happier times they'd spent together over the years.

Some of the most vivid memories of her mother were those holidays they'd spent back on Pin Hill Island. Her mother had grown up there. She always spoke about it so wistfully. Secretly, Heather suspected she couldn't shake the dust from her shoes quickly enough to escape to London and follow her West End dreams when she was a girl.

As the evening drew in and the kitchen fell into a series

of unfamiliar shadows, Heather wondered if she should call Philip and tell him that her mother had died. Maybe not, what was the etiquette with ex-husbands and the passing of relatives who were no longer related anyway? Her stomach rumbling with hunger pangs pushed her from the chair and she reminded herself that they weren't connected to each other any more. Philip had started a new life. He could already be dating someone else. In London, a man with a fortune wasn't going to be single for very long. Heather wondered if he'd slip into a second marriage with some glamorous woman about town, or more likely someone much younger who would fall for his easy charm. The fact that he had just made a cool four million pounds from the sale of their flower shops wouldn't hurt either.

No. Philip was firmly in her past and, even if she was sitting here alone for the rest of her days, their time together had run its course. She knew that even if staying together might have been easier, it was no longer what either of them truly wanted.

There were half a dozen eggs in the fridge and, for a moment, Heather wondered at the idea of her mother cooking an egg for herself; perhaps that was one of those things Carmelita did when she dropped in twice daily to check up on things. Perhaps Carmelita cleaned too? It was the only likely explanation for the unfamiliar orderliness that had taken hold of the little house. Funny, but Heather could imagine her mother sitting down to a boiled egg some evenings with a triangle of toast on the side. Tonight, because she was here alone and suddenly ravenous and her stomach growled to remind her that she hadn't eaten since breakfast. She decided to make an omelette. There was salt and pepper, eggs and cheese. She toasted a slightly hardened heel of brown bread to go with it and settled down to the silence of the kitchen again.

She must have slept, sitting at the table on the club chair that had been her mother's favourite. She woke at nine to the sound of a car alarm pealing into the unheeding London chill from one or two streets across the back fence. As soon as her eyes shot open, she knew immediately she couldn't stay here. What on earth had she been thinking earlier? She gathered up her bag and took her mother's key from inside the front door.

It was only when she was standing out on the street, the night sky that familiar not-quite-black shade of London, that the reality of her situation actually hit her. She was cast adrift, completely alone in this city now. There were no foundations with which to fasten her to anywhere – she had no family, no husband, no business, and even her flat had strangers pinning their notes to the cork board in her kitchen. For the first time in her life, she knew what it was to feel truly lonely. She was alone, completely and utterly on her own. As she stood there, her head swimming, her heart racing in a skipping panic, she understood something that had never made sense before. Was this what her mother had felt? The aching desire to connect with something that made you feel not quite so empty? Had Dotty just needed to blot the world out and keep it at a distance removed enough to feel as if she was protected from it? Had that been it all along?

Heather felt herself stumble, her balance lost, making her swerve. The bricks were cold and rough against her back, but she only vaguely registered them. She fumbled for the key in her oversized bag and when her shaking hands managed to separate it from the jumble of other things she didn't need, she thrust it as quickly as she could into the door, pushing hard and tumbling back into the hall. When she slammed it shut behind her it seemed to echo into a vastness so deep she might drown in the silence. She felt herself sliding to the floor and then she cried as if her heart might break, uncontrollable sobs that she just gave herself over to, since she had no idea where they were coming from or how to stop them. She had neither the strength nor the will to try. Instead, she lay against the door and sobbed until it felt as if there were no more tears left in her.

3

Ros Stokes

Six months, Ros realised, was the longest she'd spent sleeping in the same bed since her mother died. That was four years ago. Strange, because she hadn't come to expect ever staying in one place for very long, much less having a place to call her own, what with the state of the rental market in Ireland being what it was. After her mother passed away and she could no longer afford to pay the mortgage, Ros's biggest priority was finishing out her degree. If she had to sofa surf through her finals, what did it matter? She'd promised her mother she'd graduate with her degree in environmental science and she'd kept her promise. Sometimes, she thought her mother had sent the ranger's cottage and the job on Pin Hill as her way of saying: *well done, darling, well done.* It was a nice thought. It made up for the occasional stabs of melancholy when she thought of all the things she was missing out on thanks to a few rogue lymph nodes and a diagnosis that came too late to do much more than let her sit by while her mother slipped away.

No point thinking of any of that now. Ros pulled her hair back from her face. The wind was in one of those moods when it couldn't decide on a direction and so her too-long red hair blew about her face, making it hard to see ahead of her. She pinned it up untidily with a grip from her bag. No need to preen. The only ones to pass judgement on her appearance were the wild goats and the gulls, who were much too busy catching breakfast to bother with her. With a sheer drop down a rocky face to her left, the one thing she needed was to know exactly where each foot was going to find safe purchase.

This morning, the views were as breathtaking as she'd ever seen them. She'd just walked along a track that ran from her cottage to Muffeen Beag, checking on several nests of sea birds tucked beneath the cliffs out of sight for the most part.

The nests were perfectly intact, hidden from view for the common walker. She felt a familiar swell of relief and gratitude within her that they were safe. She still dreaded coming upon one that had been vandalised by some brute who thought they didn't matter.

God, she shivered. She was doing far more than her job, far more than the other rangers would have done. Or was she simply making amends? Sometimes she wondered, when the memory of that night came rushing back to her. It was an accident. She hadn't set out to cause any harm. Not her fault. That was what her supervisor said and Colleen French had told her to remember that, no matter how bad things got. But heads had to roll, not Ros's obviously, she was just on placement, hardly even a bearing never mind a cog in the wheel. In the greater scheme of things perhaps early retirement was not the end of the world, or at least, that was the way Colleen had tried to paint it. Ros was vilified, of course, the silly girl who'd let slip the location of a precious eagle nest. It resulted in the nest being destroyed by a group of yokel farmers intent on believing that the arrival of the birds posed some threat to their livestock. It was her darkest secret; her greatest mistake. The guilt of it still made her chest constrict if she didn't push it from her mind in time. Being a woman didn't help either. She'd toyed with the idea of cutting off her long red hair, resorting to dungarees, but there was no covering over the porcelain fineness of her skin or the fact that her willowy frame belied a resilient hardiness that meant she could work as well as any man, even if she'd never look like it.

The sensible part of her knew it was wrong to tar all farmers with the same brush, but she couldn't help being wary of them for the most part. They should all be working together for the good of the environment, but too often Ros felt as if it was a them-against-us situation and so she set about her work mostly quietly, making sure to avoid conflict if she could.

It still rattled her. The sadness and waste of the destroyed nest, the shame of being at fault through silly naivety. There was no excuse, she should have known better. Then, when she graduated, she'd been aware that anyone looking too closely at her résumé would have known immediately that it was she who had been responsible for the destruction of something so precious. She had been the reason Colleen French had to retire and, of course, Ros knew what the subtext was – Colleen was a woman, she was soft, not able to do her job, compromised. In truth, it was shorthand for the undercurrent of male chauvinism that was the prevailing culture of a male-dominated profession. Ros still felt badly about Colleen; she'd been good at her job. She didn't deserve having to take the rap for Ros's mistake. The finish-up was, neither of them were exactly employable at the end of it, Colleen for having been in charge and Ros for having been the cause of her losing her job. No-one would want to employ the person who cost their boss her job, would they?

Stop it. It was a beautiful morning, she had the most spectacular view in the world all to herself. She should be enjoying it, not beating herself up over things she could not change.

Ros halted suddenly when she heard a strange sound rippling on the breeze before her. It took a moment to pin it down as a bleating goat. The island was full of them. Wild, they roamed about on land that was too scraggy and rocky to farm. Often, they feasted on weeds and wildflowers growing along the sides of the most winding roads, munching happily while motorists tried to navigate already narrow stretches around their reckless dining positions. She'd seen them at the top of Pin Hill the previous summer, when the ground was festooned with daisies and buttercups and all manner of other treats that the goats were happy to idle over for days on end. This goat didn't sound as if it was idling though; it sounded as if it was in trouble.

She found herself moving more quickly, while still careful to watch her step. One wrong move here and it was a good two-thousand-foot drop into the ocean beneath. But the goat had not fallen over the side, as she feared it might have, instead it was lying in a bunch at the end of the track. It must have fallen from the ledge that hung over the path. A tiny pathetic creature, its bones jagged beneath his shaggy body, it was only young. *How long had it been here?* she wondered. *How long more could it survive?* For a moment, she thought she was too late. The goat lay so still. Ros moved as quietly and gently as she could, hardly daring to breathe in case she frightened the animal. Then it bleated once more, much louder than she'd have expected, and the sound startled her so she screamed and found herself almost tripping over the rough surface of the road side. She steadied herself for a moment, trying to assess what the matter was without getting too close. That was the first lesson of conservation. *Don't go close to feral animals. Do not help them, unless you are absolutely certain that they need help.*

This goat, a young male from what she could make out, was obviously in trouble, otherwise, Ros knew, she wouldn't have gotten within fifty yards of him. She walked around the animal now. His head was low, short gasping breaths coming from his open mouth and his eyes closed. Perhaps dying, but then the animal looked at her, lifted his head and opened up those strange eyes, pinning them on her. Ros could swear later it felt as if the little fella was begging her for help. She bent down, put a hand on the creature's back, ran her palms over the animal to check for breaks. She found what she was looking for quickly. The goat was lying on it, what felt like a dislocated hind leg. Ros was no vet, but it didn't take a degree in biology to see this kid was in real trouble. The whole shape of the hip and back was completely distorted. She stood for a moment, moved to the side, knowing that her presence alone could be enough to cause too much stress for the goat.

She couldn't carry him back to the cottage. She didn't have a car and she couldn't think of a single person she could call to help her. It felt as if the seconds were ticking loudly in her head, when she heard the roar of what she presumed was a big four-by-four on the road winding up the hill beneath her.

This track ended at a locked gate. Beyond it, she could see farmland, stretching out and back up the mountain. It was good land, obviously cleared back and drained when that was the way farms were managed. Ten years ago, farmers were still clearing land, heedless of the wildlife they were evicting as the price for an additional acre for their dairy herd. Thank goodness things were now changing back again.

The vehicle, when it arrived, was one of those awful off-roader things, ancient and billowing black smoke behind it. Not a scat of road tax on it either, Ros noticed.

She stood out before the jeep, fearing otherwise the driver would run right over the injured kid.

'Hey!' the man shouted out his open window. 'What the...' He was looking behind her, trying to make out the crumpled goat on the road.

'Hey,' Ros repeated back to him, but she kept her tone determinedly friendly. 'Can you help me?'

'I... well, I'm just about to check on my ewes...' he said, but they both knew there was no passing her.

'It's just, I was walking along the clifftops and I found...'

'You shouldn't be walking along the cliffs alone. Not this time of day and not this time of year either,' he said grumpily, but he jumped out of the van and stalked towards the injured goat. He stood next to her for a moment and she couldn't help but register the sheer presence of him. It was not so much his size, although he looked like a man for whom physical hard work was a way of life; there was a definition about him that she'd never seen in men who spent their time in the gym. Hard to put an age on him, beards did that to a man, didn't they sometimes. Well, maybe not a beard so much as thick dark stubble; thirties, she figured, early thirties, at the very most.

'Do you want me to get rid of it?' he asked, looking about, as if this was something he'd done many times before. She could imagine him, hoisting the poor mite up as if he was no greater weight than a mug of tea. Definitely a tea man, she decided. How on earth had she not run into him before? She'd have remembered him for sure, his dark curly hair, unshaven ruggedness, but then, she reminded herself – farmers, she considered them a breed apart.

'NO, of course not. God, no. He's only got a broken leg, he'll be fine with a little TLC and a splint.'

'Oh, so you're a vet, are you?' He eyed her suspiciously. Everyone knew there was no vet living on the island now. There had been one, but he'd moved away years ago. These days farmers were reluctant to call a mainland vet, because the call-out fees alone were rarely worth it if they wanted to make a living off the animals they farmed.

'No, but I'm not stupid either.'

'You are if you think you can bring a wild goat home with you and make a pet of it.' He looked around; maybe the penny had begun to drop. 'Where's your car?'

'I don't intend to make a pet out of it, but I'd like to

get him back on his feet and release him as soon as he's mended. Better that than your solution. You'd probably throw him over the side of the cliff...' She paused: after all, she was hoping this man – bad-tempered and all as he seemed to be – would help her bring the goat back to her cottage. 'Actually, don't answer that, I'd rather not know.'

'It's called natural order. But I don't suppose someone like you would know much about that,' he said and he bent down to look more closely at the goat. For a minute, she thought he might do something terrible to it.

'I don't know what you mean by "someone like me", but I'm Ros Stokes, the local ranger here, filling in for Max while he's away. So, I think I might know a thing or two about wildlife...' *That took the wind from his sail*, she thought smugly. 'Will you help me or not?' She stood, her hand on one hip, not really expecting any help at all, but at least knowing she was the ranger meant he wouldn't drive his bloody jeep over the poor animal in an effort to *put it out of its misery*.

'Sure. I'll help you. My name is Jonah Ashe by the way,' he said, more on an out breath than with any great enthusiasm. 'But I will say, even if you know what you're doing, I guarantee you have no idea what you're letting yourself in for.'

'We'll see.'

'I have to check the field first, I have some late lambing ewes, then I'll take the pair of you back to the village, or wherever it is you want to bring him.' He stood up then and opened the gate to his field before stomping out of sight for almost half an hour. *What an infuriating man*, Ros thought, a typical pig-headed farmer, thinking that because she was a woman she had no clue. She was leaning against the bonnet of the jeep when she spotted him returning from the field. He looked nothing like any of the local farmers she'd met already. He was tall and angular, walking with a slight limp; his accent was west of Ireland but still not quite local. Mostly, the farmers here were all pension age or not too far off it. Younger people tended to leave the island. The only ones arriving were married couples intent on living their version of *The Good Life*, hoping to scrape by on a few acres and a dream of bohemian life that invariably involved some sort of crafting pursuit on the side.

'And you're sure you want to do this?' He looked at the kid on the ground. Ros had a feeling he was only asking because she was the ranger, otherwise he might have tossed the little fella into the ditch.

'Absolutely, if you'll just bring us back to my cottage, I'll take care of things from there.'

'You know he won't make it.' Jonah shook his head. 'Even moving him could cause enough stress to kill him before we get him into the truck...'

'I know what I'm doing.' She didn't, but she certainly wasn't going to admit that to this bloody know-it-all.

'You're in luck, mister,' he said as he walked around the goat. 'No other passengers, you have the back of the jeep all to yourself.' He went round the rear of the vehicle, opened out the drop-down door and took a length of tarpaulin, unfolding it as he walked. 'Come here,' he called to Ros. Between them, they unfurled it beneath the goat and managed to make a stretcher of sorts for him. For someone so gruff, she couldn't help but notice Jonah was surprisingly gentle in the way he moved the little goat. 'I don't want it touching the sides of the van, it's not good to have him too close to where I might have to place my own sheep or lambs.'

'Of course,' she wanted to say, she wasn't a dummy, she knew about diseases and how easily something could spread from one species to another. She wanted to say, 'Diseases go both ways,' but she didn't, because she needed to get this lift back to her cottage.

To break the uncomfortable silence, Ros tried to start some conversation as they drove. It was like squeezing sun out of December. He'd grown up on the island, left when he was a teenager and returned a few years earlier to take care of his uncle's farm when the old man fell ill. 'It was old age and self-neglect mostly, there isn't any proper treatment to cure a lifetime of that. He spent six months in hospital, but in the end, he just gave up,' Jonah said and maybe, Ros thought, she could glimpse a heart underneath that wax jacket and his serious expression.

'So you stayed on then?' she asked. They were speeding along, bumping over the uneven roads and each time they hit a pothole she winced thinking of the kid being bounced about in the back of the jeep. There hadn't been a murmur from him. She could only hope that Jonah wasn't right and the stress of being close to them hadn't finished him off already.

'My uncle died in the middle of lambing season, what was I meant to do? I couldn't just abandon the place, could I?' he snapped.

'Of course,' she said, almost regretting she'd asked. 'Anyway, we're here now.' She was never so relieved to catch a glimpse of the chimney pots of the cottage rising over the hedgerows in the distance.

After they turned in to the small yard behind the cottage, Ros raced in through the back door and pulled out a huge plastic bed that had been home once to Max's old German Shepherd. Jonah waited, talking on his phone while she set about tearing up newspapers and positioning the bed in a corner of the porch where it wouldn't be a trip hazard and still wasn't in a draught.

'Are you ready now?' he asked and there was no missing the impatience in his voice.

'Sure,' she said. She should probably be grateful for the help, but all she felt was a growing uncomfortable dislike for this stranger who seemed to judge her badly from the get-go.

Between them, they carried the goat and placed him gently into the hastily made bed. For his part, the goat seemed resigned to whatever might happen from here on in. She wondered if perhaps he wasn't drifting in and out of consciousness. His eyes, opening and closing, were no longer fixing on her, instead they had a faraway quality to them which she knew, even without any medical experience, could not be good.

Quite a lot of what Ros needed to take care of the kid she found in the old pantry in the cottage. Her predecessor, Max, had a supply of baby bottles with newborn teats, formula food which was still miraculously in date and a selection of worn-out pillows and old blankets to wrap him up and keep him warm. What she didn't have was the medical experience or confidence to go about resetting the goat's injury. That would take a vet, but she could take care of him and make him comfortable until the vet arrived.

When she walked into the kitchen, having heard the huge jeep execute a speedy three-point turn, she felt relieved to be in the quiet and comfort of her little cottage. Now she wasn't sure what to do first, whether it was better to light a fire and keep the kid warm – did he need heat? Or should she sort out food for him? She found the only thing she could do was sit on the stone floor and look at the little goat. He lifted his head slightly, angling it so when he opened his eyes he gazed at her, solidly, beseechingly. God, was it possible to feel your heart melt with a swelling of love for one beaten-up little animal? A little ball of sadness caught in her throat.

'You should still have your mother to look after you, but I'm going to do my very best for you, I promise,' she whispered and she traced her finger gently along the floor between them.

It was just silly to cry over a kid goat. Ros knew that even as the tears raced down her cheeks, but she wiped them away, realising she wasn't crying about the goat, this sadness was more deep-rooted than that. These were tears of connection; the fact that another living creature needed her and the only other time in her life that had been the case was with her mother.

Four years ago, sometimes it felt like a lifetime ago, but now it felt as raw and uneven as if she was still holding her mother's hand, praying for a miracle. She'd learned the hard way that miracles didn't come by prayer alone. Her mother's cancer had moved along at its own hectic pace and all the wishful thinking, positive vibes and holy rosaries hadn't a hope in heaven of saving her once it got a grip.

Other gamekeepers who had stayed here in the cottage had kept pets before her. There had been a succession of cats and dogs, two donkeys and a noisy cockerel, but no-one had ever kept a goat so far as she knew. Could you even keep a wild goat? She had no idea.

Not for the first time, she realised that she knew so little about wildlife in a practical way. Oh, of course, she had great textbook learning, but actually having hands-on experience – that was harder to find. Against the odds of losing her mother and keeping herself in college, she'd graduated with top marks, but it seemed her timing was off. There were no jobs in the Parks and Wildlife Services for people heavy on qualifications but light on experience. Self-doubt niggled at her heart, fearing she was not really up to the task she'd offered to take on at the end of last summer. Her predecessor, Max Toolis, had been diagnosed with cancer; she was an easy solution. Max had gone to stay with his sister in Galway while undergoing treatment. If he'd been the sort of man to offer his help had she needed it, she might have been on the phone to him every other day asking silly questions. Maybe it was lucky for her that Max was the opposite of that. She'd known that if she called him, he could easily have talked to the higher-ups and had her whipped out of the cottage before she had time to unpack her few belongings and settle in for the long winter.

Thank goodness for Google, that was all she could say at this point. It was down to online searches that she knew by heart both the English and Latin names of every flower and weed she came across on her daily walks about the island. For all she had learned studying environmental science, it was surprising how little she actually knew when it came to doing the job of a ranger. She had spent many long nights on her laptop with the crackling fire for company, learning as much as she could about the wildlife she was meant to be protecting.

Ros sighed, but she couldn't do everything alone. She'd need to get a vet to take a look at the little goat, set the bones properly. She rang the practice in Ballycove, which was the nearest to the island. It didn't take long to discover she was talking to the vet's wife, an animal lover too. Aida Bauer gave her great hope, telling her a story of how her husband managed once to save a baby fawn. 'Just keep him off his legs, plenty of fluids, and my husband will call next week, when he's booked to travel across for a herd inspection,' she promised.

By lunchtime, Ros had found several sites online with stories of how goats healed in the wild and went on for many years with bones that set well enough to carry them into old age. It bolstered her optimism. As the day wore on, she found herself smiling for no particular reason. It seemed there was no escaping the warmth that had begun to fill her heart since she'd picked him up and made the journey home. It was nice to have somebody – okay, a kid goat – to look after. It was terrific to think that she could care for him and make a small difference to another life on the island.

Her mobile phone vibrating on the table jolted her from her contentment. She recognised the number immediately.

'Keith? Hello. Ros here,' she said because she still didn't expect him to remember her name. Keith Duff was a middle-grade civil servant who'd somehow ended up in the Parks and Wildlife Service and couldn't wait to leave.

'Ros.' He said her name as if reading it from a clipboard.

She suspected that he did a double-take each time as if to check there wasn't a spelling mistake. She knew he thought she was as unlikely a candidate to be a wildlife ranger as Boy George was to become a cosmonaut.

'What can I do for you?' she asked. He would have no interest in the goat currently residing in her porch.

'Ah, it's more about what I can do for you, I think…' He cleared his throat as if he just wanted to get this phone call over with. 'I've had a call from Max Toolis, I don't suppose he's been in touch?'

'With me? No, not recently.' Max was the least likely person she had ever met to pick up the phone for a friendly chat. 'How is he? Is his treatment coming along well…?' Because even though he'd been a distant character when Ros had arrived here first, she hadn't disliked him. She assumed that he'd had his fill of students holing up on the island for the summer months and counting every blade of grass for post-doctoral work that would make no real difference to how Max would do his job.

'He's almost at the end of his treatment, so that's good news, I suppose.'

'Of course that's good news,' she said because it had been a very long road for the old man. 'And has he gotten the all-clear?' She found herself taking a deep breath; surely they wouldn't have put him through months of chemo and treatment just to tell him at the end there was nothing more that could be done for him?

'He says it's all done bar the shouting. So, I suppose that means they got the bugger cleared up. Of course, he's not the same man he was before.'

'But he could be, given time to get his strength back.'

Lots of people recovered fully, more and more of them, it seemed to her, these days. Ros felt that familiar ripple of sadness press over her again when she thought of her own mother.

'Well, it's neither here nor there, because he's applied to take early retirement.'

'Oh, that's unexpected.' She didn't mean to blurt it out, but when Ros had thought of Max returning to work over the last few months, she'd pushed those thoughts aside swiftly. The truth was, she didn't want to leave the island. Actually, she didn't want to leave this little cottage: it felt like home, even though it was always only meant to be hers until Max returned.

'So, I'm only letting you know as a matter of form. The thing is, we won't be advertising the position for a few weeks yet, because we have to wait until he makes it all formal. And you know the way these things go; for now, he's on the sick pay and sure, why would he give that up just to let the state have an easy time of it?' Keith made a sound that landed somewhere between a gassy snort and a laugh at this. Ros tried not to sigh, but the joke wasn't funny. 'Anyway, I suppose I'm just checking that you can stay on there until we find a permanent replacement? It'll take HR a while to get things firmed up enough to run an advertisement.'

'Oh, that's grand.' She had to level out her voice before she went on, but she was flooded with an unfamiliar wave of relief. It was as if she'd had some sort of reprieve from the inevitable. 'Of course, I'd be happy to stay for as long as you want me here,' she said and she found herself moving over towards the back of the kitchen and peeking behind the door to see a set of curious rectangular pupils staring up at her.

'Well, it's not forever.' Keith said this as if to assuage his own misgivings. 'So don't worry, you'll be away to carry on with real life before you know it, but it'll be a few weeks at least.'

'Weeks, months, honestly, there's no rush, don't worry about Pin Hill. I'll take care of things here,' she said softly and it was a physical relief when the phone went dead in her hand. She stood there for a moment, taking in the cottage around her, feeling overcome with a sense of tugging loneliness at the certainty of having to move on at some point in the future. It wasn't much of a place, not really. It was dated and cold and filled with other people's belongings, but then, since her mother had passed away and she'd had to give up their home, every place she'd stayed had been someone else's really. Here at least it felt as if this was just a little more hers than anywhere she'd been in years.

She made herself take a deep breath. It was ridiculous to be upset at the idea of moving on. After all, there was nobody on the island to keep her here, beyond a frail goat, and she would have to let him go in a matter of weeks anyway. Except... what was it? It felt as if there *was* something here to stay for, something more than just a job or people she could call friends. Pin Hill Island had somehow crept under her skin and into her heart, even though she'd known she shouldn't let it happen. It was already too late. This leaching sadness was all about having to move on eventually, when all she wanted was to stay here forever.

4

May 1957

Dotty Wren

Their home had always been different from the Mackens'. It felt, to Dotty at least, as if her parents had been bundled in rigidly one night while they slept and woke the following morning only aware of a certain tightness about them which they spoon-fed to Dotty so it was internalised long before she could decide to be any different. It materialised in unfinished sentences, in things not said, unlike the Gillespies who regularly had huge shouting matches from one end of the road to the other. In the Wren home, the important things were held on the in-breath, making every second on the kitchen clock tick more loudly, every sigh laboured with heavy consequence. Perhaps it had crept through the slightest open crack in a window, stolen silently and sat in a corner, casting invisible shadows across each of them. It wasn't in the walls or on the breakfast table. God knew, her mother did a good enough job scrubbing and polishing every surface of the house so, unlike at the Mackens', there was never a lingering smell of last night's dinner to be found. This wasn't just an aroma; rather it was stitched deeply into the fibres of them. It sat there, as easily in unspoken sentences as it did in meaningful glances; it crackled on the rustle of her father's paper as carelessly as it did on the vinegar tartness of her mother's gleaming windows. Three people, living together and all treading softly so as not to arouse something that silently threatened to swallow them; or at least that was how it felt to Dotty.

Dotty might not have been sure of how it came about, but she was pretty certain that it had something to do with her father. Norman Wren was a hero. Everyone said so, he'd fought for King and Country, although, as Mrs Price was quick to point out, it wasn't her King or her Country. Her mother, Sylvie, who hardly ever had a bad word to say about anyone, said quickly in low tones, *let you not be heeding Mrs Price*. He even had a medal for it. *Which is more than Albert Price has to show for all his years turning out for the IRA.* The medal – the African Star – was a heavy star with a crown on the front and 'N Wren' inscribed on its back. It sat in proud repose in the small glass cabinet in their front room. From what Dotty could gather, her father had been given it for being brave. *Or just for showing up*, if you were to listen to Mrs Price. Anyway, it didn't matter, the fact was that her father was different to every other father on their road. For one thing, he was older. For another, he dressed smartly, *dapper*, Mrs Price said, although Dotty wasn't sure this was a compliment. Unlike the other fathers along the road, her father worked in a shop, selling fancy men's clothes to *people who had more money than sense*, or at least that's how her father described it.

Her mother by comparison was not so dapper. She was country stock and hardworking, happy to have a house and a husband to be proud of and a daughter who was no bother. She was younger than all the other mothers on the road, although mostly she didn't look it. Unless they were going to mass, then she would wear her best woollen suit which cinched her tiny waist, smart black shoes and the precious silver clip against which her hair gleamed blacker than a raven's feathers. Each Sunday she carried a small bible in her hand that was well thumbed even though she could only read the short words. Still, no-one else knew that. Dotty noticed that people did a double-take when they saw her all polished up; it was as if she emerged from the grey shell of everyday life, a pearl just visible before the oyster snapped shut for another week.

'Beauty never boiled the pot,' her mother said when she caught Dotty staring at her reflection in the mirror that hung inside their front door. They were so different, Sylvie and Dotty, in spite of the fact that everyone agreed that they were *the spit down of each other*. If Dotty had been allowed, she'd have worn her mother's silver hair grip every single day. She'd decided early in life that she would not keep things for good when she grew up. She would be glamorous always, not just for mass or funerals or special occasions.

Maggie Macken was one of those women. Instead of a husband, she had a career. Just a few weeks earlier, she'd been in the local papers, her picture and her words. She was going to have a book in every shop in Ireland. All that tap-tapping had finally paid off, it seemed. Dotty thought she'd die of happiness if her picture was in the paper. Mrs Macken didn't care if the kitchen table was cleared after dinner, she couldn't give a hoot if her doorstep was covered in weeds and the talk of every other housewife on their road. She'd told Dotty there were more important things in life than caring whether the nuns approved of the length of your skirt or not.

For her part, Sylvie was never *sure* about Mrs Macken. 'Wouldn't trust her as far as I'd throw her, anyone's husband is fair game with that one', Mrs Price said in tones not quite low enough to escape Dotty's keen ears. 'You want to watch your Norman around her.' But that comment had sent her mother into a fit of hysterical laughter, the likes of which Dotty had never heard before or since.

That was the thing about being twelve, there was so much you heard, some of it you understood, but the most interesting bits always seemed to be held in the words that adults never actually said.

Still, her mother liked Constance Macken very much; far more than Lickey Gillespie or any of the other kids on their road. Of course, Constance and Dotty were practically the same age, although you'd never know it because Constance was tiny whereas Dotty had already grown breasts her mother encouraged her to hide beneath clothes that were too big. 'You don't want the boys making fun of you, do you?' she said once. 'Time enough you getting married when you're a lot older than I was', she said often, always hastily adding as if to confirm for herself, 'not that I would change a thing.' Recently, Dotty had taken up her parents' wedding photograph from where it sat on the glass cabinet and examined it. They were a striking couple, she with her wide eyes and thick black hair and he in his uniform, pressed and proud – he was older, quite a bit older when you looked properly. Sylvie looked as if she'd only just made her confirmation, but that couldn't be right because girls of thirteen or fourteen couldn't get married, not even just as the war was ending, no matter how different times had been back then.

That day, the day Dotty had looked at the photograph, had somehow tipped over the atmosphere in her home, even though she had no idea at the time that one simple thing could change everything. It was that photograph and the idea that really, there hadn't been more than a few years in the difference between her mother then and her now.

Her mother's wedding dress had been a simple lemon tea dress with a fitted bodice and a skirt that just passed her knees. It was still hanging in the wardrobe over a decade later, never taken out or looked at, never mind actually worn. Suddenly, Dotty had felt herself drawn to it. She raced upstairs, let herself into her parents' room and took it carefully from the wardrobe. Her mother had wrapped it up in a delicate weave of soft tissue paper, typically doing her best to keep it as near to pristine as possible. It took a few minutes to figure out a way to liberate the dress without damaging her mother's handiwork, but when she did, she held it before her for a moment. It looked exactly her size. It smelled faintly of her mother, but more of her father, whose overwhelming scent of silver mints and shaving soap travelled before and after him wherever he went. The fabric was like nothing else hanging in any wardrobe in their home; a softer, silkier version of her mother's best Sunday blouse, Dotty imagined it must feel like being wrapped up in a golden cloud. Suddenly, she was unpeeling her own clothes, letting them sit where they fell and slipping into the dress easily. It felt strange, grown-up, illicit. Incredible. She looked down the line of her body, bent sideways and leaned back, closing up buttons which she assumed had last been closed by her grandmother on Sylvie's wedding day. Oh, she could have stood there for hours enjoying the feeling of the fabric against her skin, it was so different to the layers of cotton her mother made her wear to stop the boys noticing her now firmly protruding breasts. She peered out over the net curtains on the window. There was nobody about. Her parents had gone to visit the graveyard earlier for a small ceremony in remembrance of a comrade of her father's who had not managed to win a medal. Indeed, he had not even managed to make it home to the graveyard, but there was a headstone and there would be flowers.

Dotty cast the idea of the sombre afternoon her parents would be putting in aside and raced down the narrow stairs to the mirror that hung just inside their front door. She stood there for a long while, taking in her own reflection. Her hair, shorter than her mother's, had the same shine to it. Her eyes, a little greyer, were just as wide. The dress fitted perfectly. She threw her shoulders back, pouted her lips to make a face that felt not quite as childish as her own. She looked grown-up, all grown-up, like a woman who could do anything in life, be anyone she wanted to be, have a great adventure if that was what she felt like doing. She felt, for almost a whole minute, that one day she could be the sort of woman Maggie Macken had become and that was thrilling to her then.

The groan of the front gate almost threw her off balance.

Her mother, pushing it out carefully, was, as usual, four steps behind her father, turning his key in the door. Oh God, Dotty thought, her mother would be livid. Though, she wasn't sure why she thought that, because her mother rarely got cross with her. Generally, they got along very well and if there was a reproach, it was issued with kindness and in gentle tones.

'Dotty?' It was her father's reaction that surprised her most.

'Sorry, Daddy, I was just...' She backed away from him, suddenly shy beneath his penetrating gaze.

'Well, well, well,' he said and he stood for longer than was comfortable for any of them, gazing at the dress that Dotty supposed must have the happiest of memories for her parents.

'Dorothy Wren, what are you wearing?' her mother whispered. Her voice, a thin streak across the narrow space between them, wobbled, a rogue nerve playing havoc with the corners of her mouth. Dotty could see her mother's face was ashen, as if she'd seen a ghost. 'Upstairs now, this instant. Take it off and put it back exactly as you found it.'

'Ah, now, Sylvie, sure you can see yourself, she's hardly a child any more, let her be, if she wants to be a grown-up...' Her father smiled and pulled Dotty towards him for a moment. 'Your mother's wedding dress, eh?' He halted and seemed to breathe her in, but Dotty was glad he was not cross with her at least.

'She's not a grown-up, Norman, she's just a child,' her mother snapped.

'I'm so sorry, Mammy, I didn't mean to, I just... you were so beautiful in it and I wondered...'

'Hmph,' her father said and then he held her at arm's length for a moment, his eyes carefully running up and down the dress, as if seeing it for the very first time. 'Dotty.' He said her name then, slowly, as if relearning it from a long time ago. It was one of those times when, in spite of the fact that she might look grown-up, Dotty knew that a lot more had been said in that one word than she understood.

'Go on with you,' her mother said and her voice sounded as if she had somehow been defeated once again in that narrow hallway that she spent so much time scrubbing clean. And somehow, Dotty knew that all the scouring in the world would never quite make things as spotless as her mother craved so deeply.

5

Constance

As always, it was a relief when the doves swooped into the garden to watch her fill the bird table. Constance found herself smiling, as if two old friends had turned up to stop her thoughts from wandering down dead ends that had nothing to recommend taking them. She had grated breadcrumbs the evening before while the bread was still at its freshest. It sat now, waiting for her in the little covered saucer.

Although the morning looked sublime, with lemony spring sun picking out green shoots and occasionally glinting on the puddle that Constance liked to think served as a bird bath, it was much colder than she had expected. She almost immediately regretted not taking the time to put her coat around her shoulders before she pushed through the back door. It wasn't so much the sea breeze, rather the temperatures must have dipped to below zero overnight, because now, she realised the path glistened with an icy sheen. She would need to move slowly, hang onto the rail that the bossy district nurse had insisted on at the end of the previous summer.

It was early yet. It felt as if she was the only person in the world, or at least on this side of the island, to be up and about at this hour. Constance adored the stillness of mornings like this, where even the crunch of a dead twig beneath your feet held within it the potential to echo as loudly as the ocean in the distance. She looked towards the small veranda that dipped out over the back of the house. It was the doves' favourite place to perch while they watched her divvy out their breakfast. She smiled up at them, noticing how fattened up they looked thanks to their ruffled feathers. Oh, but it was cold. She turned again and began to spread the crumbs across the table, separating them with her thumb when she'd finished so the smaller birds would have a shot at the leftovers. Usually, she stood inside the kitchen window and waved her arms about like a mad thing if she saw the big old crows come towards the table.

Today, the crows had begun to circle before she'd even turned on the path towards the house. 'Shoo, shoo,' she shouted half-heartedly at them, but only because she preferred the doves – somehow they stood for something nobler than the crows. Although, years of watching the crows dip in and out of her garden had taught her they were the more intelligent of the two breeds. You had to admire their determination to go at a thing again and again until eventually they managed to succeed. She watched now as they flew off towards the roof of Ocean's End, *humph, only waiting for me to disappear through the door and swoop, no doubt.*

She was too old to think that a fight she couldn't win was worth waiting for the freezing temperatures to chew easily through her clothes. These days, it took longer and longer to warm up after she got cold. It was much better to be sitting inside with a nice cup of tea and her shawl about her shoulders than to be out here inviting the chill into her bones.

It was only when she made it to the back porch that she realised the door had swung shut and locked behind her. And damn it, her house key was in the jacket pocket currently hanging on the hook in the porch. She was locked out. She checked her watch. A while yet before Jay Larkin arrived with the post. For a moment, she stood there, trying not to panic, but she was shivering and, with little more than her nightdress and her dressing gown for warmth, she would be in a terrible state if she had to stay out here for a full hour, and even then Jay sometimes got delayed until almost lunchtime.

Constance stood for a moment, trying to think what to do for the best. It was a good half-mile walk to the next house on the road. Those two very nice German men who had taken over the McElhinny house would not expect to see an old woman in her nightclothes on their doorstep when they woke up. Not that it mattered. She couldn't imagine walking half a mile on the narrow boreen in thin slippers, especially not today, when there was a slim coating of ice that could prove treacherous to her. She found her eyes skirting about the garden, trying to figure out the next best thing to do. There was nothing in the shed to keep her any warmer than standing out here, certainly no dry coat to throw across her shoulders or fire to stand beside.

She was still deliberating when she thought she saw a figure walking along in the distance. At first, it was hard to make out if it was a person or if the early sun was just playing tricks on her eyes against the hedgerows. Constance stood still for a long minute, concentrating hard, narrowing her eyes to get a better view and willing it to be a person walking towards her. Then, the movement slowed and she was certain it was a walker, coming along the edge of the cliffs – didn't they know how dangerous it was out there?

Constance shuffled further down, nearer to the fence, keeping one eye on the figure and another beadily checking out the path so she didn't add to her troubles by missing her step and landing on the broad of her back. It felt as if it took forever to walk a few short yards. How on earth had that happened – time had caught up on her. It seemed like only yesterday she'd have raced around this garden mowing the lawn and pushing back the weeds.

'Hello,' she called thinly and she cursed herself for the feeble tone that rang out when she spoke. Sometimes, she wondered if she'd put her own strong voice on a shelf one day and forgotten where she'd left it so there was only this old lady timbre left for her to use. 'Hello...' she called again as thickly as she could muster.

'Oh, hello?' The young woman with red hair turned and waved at her as if that greeting was as much as you were going to get away with when you lived on Pin Hill Island.

'Hello, I say, could you possibly help me?' Constance called again, slightly panicking now, in case the woman should decide to take off in the opposite direction – away from the mad woman in her dressing gown outside the crumbling old mansion.

'Is everything all right?' the stranger asked with a smile. Constance watched as the girl – because she was hardly in her twenties, or only just at most – easily jumped across the small border fence as if used to climbing up and down these cliffs all the time. 'It's very cold to be out here without a coat, isn't it?' she asked– there was no getting away from the fact that the temperatures were far too low to be hanging about in the garden in your nightdress.

'I'm afraid I've locked myself out,' Constance said and she felt very foolish indeed. 'Well, not locked myself out, I'm not entirely stupid,' she said, trying to make light of her situation, 'but it's the door, you see, it has a tendency to blow closed and I didn't think to bring my key. I only came out to feed the birds so...'

'Never mind, is there a window I can get through?' The woman looked up at the house. Constance could see, even from here, the only window that was even slightly ajar – and then not enough to allow access to the crows – was the tiny box bedroom window on the first floor.

'Do you mind climbing?'

'Not at all, in fact, I'd see it as a bit of a warm-up for tomorrow. I'm hoping to do the higher cliffs along the north-facing side of the island then.'

'Well, at least I have a ladder. That should make this a little less of a challenge than Malloy's fields.' And Constance led the young woman to the shed where she was certain there was an old ladder and they even managed to get a wire hanger and a thin blade in case it was needed to wedge the window open.

'Be careful, won't you?' Constance called after the girl as

she climbed quickly up the steps. It was only as she was near the window that Constance realised they really should have checked that the ladder was safe for use. Then, just as this thought crossed her mind, she watched as the girl pulled open the window and dived into the bedroom beyond. It seemed to take only moments for her to arrive at the back door and let Constance back into her cosy kitchen.

'Oh, you have no idea, I can't thank you enough,' Constance said, relieved to feel the warmth of the house bathe her as she pushed through the kitchen door.

'It was no bother. I probably should go back up and make sure that window is closed again as it was before, just in case you end up needing to use it another time...' And the young woman raced upstairs and Constance heard the bedroom door being pulled out on the floor above.

'It's basically closed, but with a little manoeuvring you won't be locked out again and I put one of the old pillows from the bed at the threshold to stop any draughts flying through the house.' The woman smiled at her as she walked back into the kitchen.

'Thank you so much, honestly, I don't know what would have happened if you hadn't come along,' Constance said and it was the truth, she might even owe this stranger her life.

'It was no bother, really, and anyway all is well that ended well, I'm glad I came along at the right moment. Now, I'll return the ladder and leave you to thaw out, shall I?' The young woman was smiling.

'Oh, but you can't just go like that... you must have a cup of tea with me, at least...' Constance said and she remembered the cooling fruit muffins she had left sitting on the table. They were meant to be for Jay, but today, it was a question of first come gets the spoils. 'Have you had breakfast yet?'

'Well, no, but I wouldn't want to impose. After all, you must be tired and cold after your ordeal.' The young woman smiled.

'No, that was no ordeal; sure, didn't you come along before the worst happened?' And then Constance told the girl that fears of hypothermia or maybe falling and breaking a hip had crossed her mind, but in reality, she'd only been locked outside for a few minutes.

'Maybe you should think about leaving a spare key near the back door or hidden somewhere in the garden.'

'I suppose I should, I really should,' Constance said as she switched on the kettle. 'You'll have a muffin? I'm sure there's some blackcurrant jam here somewhere...' She was searching for it in the cupboards. She found yesterday's brown bread too, still fresh, lovely for toasting. 'I bought the jam at the summer fair last year.' She held the jar up to the light; just the thing. 'I must say, Delia Bradley certainly knows how to knock out a decent pot of jam, it's every bit as good as if I made it myself.'

She placed it on the table, thinking of all the preserves she'd made over the years. These days she depended on village fetes and the opportunity to pick up other women's work to fill her larder for the winter months.

'We had lots of fruit bushes, back in the day, amazing really, considering how close we are to the sea, you know, but...' Her voice trailed off. It was all so long ago now. The girl smiled as she unfurled a huge scarf from around her neck, then she hung the cloche hat she'd been wearing on the back of the kitchen chair Constance had pulled out for her. 'We had blackcurrants here, strawberries, raspberries, plums too and even pears when the winter was mild, a full kitchen garden if you can believe it.' She nodded towards the walled-off area that had become overgrown years ago. It didn't do to think too much about how the briars, nettles and ivy had set about taking over what had once been such a joy to her.

'You're spoiling me,' the young woman said and she buttered a thick slice of the bread. 'Oh my God, that's amazing... oh...' She rolled her eyes. 'Honestly, I think that's the nicest thing I've had to eat in... like, forever.'

'Well, there's plenty more there for you, I bake far too much of it...' Constance smiled. The girl's enthusiasm was refreshing. With tea made in the pot, Constance sat at the table too. 'I can't place you?' she said then, looking at her. Even though she might lose track of some of the younger people on the island, generally she was able to put a surname to people. Usually, they resembled their parents and, more often these days, their grandparents and sometimes great-grandparents. That thought made Constance feel utterly ancient.

'Oh, sorry, forgive me, what terrible manners, here I am sitting in your kitchen, drinking tea, and we haven't even been properly introduced. I'm Rosalind Stokes, Ros for short, I'm what most of the islanders would call a blow-in. For now, I'm staying in the ranger's cottage while Max is having his treatment on the mainland.'

'Of course, Jay told me about you. You came last summer with a bunch of students and then, when they all headed back to college, you offered to take up the post to help out...'

Constance said, tapping the table because sometimes the little things she remembered gave her the greatest pleasure.

'That's it in a nutshell.' Ros smiled. 'And this is the famous novelist's villa, isn't that right, but you're not Maggie Macken, are you?'

'Dear me, goodness no, that was my mother – if she was alive now, she'd be heading towards a hundred and twenty years old. I'm not even nearly that age!' Constance replied. 'No, I'm Constance, just Constance,' she said with a little pride, because it was nice to hear a young person had heard about her mother.

'It must be a wonderful place to live.' Ros sighed and she glanced towards the huge kitchen window that looked out across the Atlantic. 'That's some view.'

'Sometimes, but you never forget, the ocean has two sides to it. It's picturesque all right but it's bleak and savage also...' she had seen both sides of it.

'In summer it has to be stunning from here.' Ros craned her neck to look out across the garden again. 'This place must have been wonderful for summer gatherings; I can just imagine it filled with people all talking about books and sipping champagne while the sun set.' She smiled dreamily and Constance wondered if they weren't both in similar boats even if the choppy seas had always convinced her that hers was the only single manned craft on the water.

6

Heather

It was the worst possible timing. Heather looked at the envelope on the table before her. She had folded the letter which confirmed her decree absolute and placed it inside. There was no point reading through those words again, she knew them off by heart now. *Final Judgement, marriage contract, set aside, altogether unconnected–* that was the bones of it. The divorce had been an age ago, her solicitor had only now got around to sending out the paperwork. He might not even have sent it out yet, had it not been for the fact that the second letter was far more pressing. Her mother's will; there'd be no surprises there, but still she couldn't open that today, there was only so much anyone could take in one day. Later. She placed it on the table, standing to attention, as if there was any danger she might forget it was there. Heather wiped a tear from her cheek. It was senseless to cry over something she knew was the right thing for both her and her now ex-husband.

Today, even if it made absolutely no sense at all, she wanted more than anything else the arms of her parents around her. It was ridiculous, she couldn't remember the last time her mother had comforted her; as a child, all of that had been from her father, a gentle bear of a man who smelled of cigarettes and hard work. Now, on the air, she thought she caught a whiff of lily of the valley. She found that comforting in a way: Constance Macken's scent.

Old Constance was probably long gone now and that gorgeous house they had by the sea. Funny, how she remembered it so clearly. Of course, if they were on Pin Hill, it was down to Constance to make everything better with a kiss and a hug. Suddenly, Heather craved a soothing voice and the feeling that she was unconditionally loved by one person in the world. It was crazy; she had never had a bond like that with her own mother. If anything, she always felt Dotty only tolerated her, never that she actually loved her. It was the drink, she'd always known it. As the years had crept past, Heather had found herself building up a relationship with her mother that succeeded best in short bursts, in steering conversations only through trivial topics and never making requests that required any real emotional support. It seemed to Heather that Dotty had long ago sunk into an all absorbing bitterness, so it was hard to last for much longer than a half an hour in company that required anything approaching kindness.

And yet, for all the shallowness of their relationship, today, with her divorce papers in her hands, Heather felt as if she needed her mother more acutely than she'd ever needed her before.

Except, of course, it was too late now. She couldn't even face going back to the house. The last time she was there had discombobulated her completely. She wondered now if her mother had known she was going to die. Certainly, there was a feeling of sparseness to the place, as if she'd tipped every bit of old rubbish that had always hidden in corners. There was no evidence of a lifelong drinking habit to be seen anywhere in the house. She'd rung Carmelita, who seemed to think she was bonkers. 'Bottles? But there are no bottles,' Carmelita had said in her broken English. 'Your mother hasn't taken a drink in almost a full year.' Heather couldn't understand it, her mother had finally given up drinking? That was something she had never expected to happen. Indeed, now she was gone, it probably would always feel as if someone had made it up; like a fairy story, she wanted to believe but it was just too fantastical to be true.

She gazed at her reflection in the window opposite. Forty-nine years of age. Lines across her forehead and creases around her eyes had etched themselves into her face without her noticing over the last decade. She hardly knew the woman staring back at her and, this morning, she felt every one of those forty-nine years.

She was too old to procrastinate. She needed to make a plan to get on with her life. It was official now. She was no longer married. Her business was sold. She had nowhere to call home, unless you counted the little terraced house she'd grown up in and, somehow, that had not felt like home in a very long time.

Desperate to find some anchor or direction, she made an appointment with a life coach, pushing aside the second letter from her solicitor for now.

A life coach, no less.

And after Heather had offloaded all her concerns and detailed as much of her life to date as she could, the woman just sat there and looked at her and said simply:

'So, it's time to make a plan. It's time to move forward.' And she had the audacity to smile as if this was somehow a ground-breaking revelation.

'Of course I need to move on,' Heather snapped impatiently, 'but the thing is, I don't know where to move on to next.' And she felt that familiar swell of emotion rise up in her, where she didn't know if she wanted to cry or kick something with sheer frustration. 'That's why I came here...' she said then, examining the woman as if she might give up some secrets just by close inspection.

'I think, deep down, you know exactly what you need to do next.' The woman smiled again and Heather only felt more infuriated with her.

'Actually, I don't, I really, really don't,' Heather said. 'That's why I came here, it's why I filled out that stupid bloody sheet and it's why I'm paying you over a hundred quid an hour to give me advice that I can actually use.'

'The purpose of today is not for me to tell you what to do, Heather, I explained this already. It's so you can uncover what it is that gives you most joy.'

'Oh, God, seriously...' And Heather realised she was going round in circles and this wasn't helping one bit.

'Seriously, if you don't know what to do yet, then just do what you have to and a path will become obvious as you move through life.'

And for that, Heather handed over a hundred pounds and stepped out into the spring sunshine on a London street feeling even more at sea than before. That was when she spotted the bookshop across the road.

It was just a door really, with a very narrow window to the side and a small sign on the footpath: 'Second-hand Books'. She was attracted to it immediately; since the divorce and selling the flat, she had found herself strangely drawn to other people's belongings. It was funny, because although she'd been a voracious reader over the years, she'd never been one to hold onto books. There hadn't been one bookcase in the flat over which to pick out what would be hers and what would eventually go in the huge crates that had finally taken Philip from her home and her world.

'Hello.' The old man hardly lifted his eyes from the paperback he was absorbed in when Heather walked into the shop. It was a tiny space, with books old and new in every corner. They were crammed to the ceiling on overflowing shelves and spilling out of boxes haphazardly placed on the floor, what little there was of it, and permeating everything the smell of old books: woody; vanilla; utopia. Heather inhaled it and thought she couldn't remember the last time she'd smelled that faint aroma since her childhood.

The old man left her to look around without interference. It was that sort of place, a small disorderly corner of London to browse and lose half an hour or maybe more, among books other people no longer wanted. He seemed oblivious to her and even that was strangely comforting. There was no real order to the place, no point coming in looking for the latest thriller, because it was unlikely you'd find it here, unless someone had dropped it in by accident.

Even the disorganisation of the place was soothing; Heather was quickly lost in shelf after shelf, picking up books she'd heard of and reading the fly covers. Some books she'd read and had forgotten about and others that just spoke to her from the spines or the slightly battered-looking covers. She picked up three paperbacks, not classics, but books that had been on her radar at some point but she had never managed to get round to reading.

'Ah, a good choice,' the old man said when she brought them to the cash desk.

'I've never noticed this place before,' she said as he rang up her purchases.

'No, most people don't. My daughter says I should call the books pre-loved, rather than second-hand,' he said.

'Oh no, I hate that term, much better to call a thing what it is. After all, if someone loved them that much, they'd never have parted with them to begin with, would they?'

'I don't know about that.' The old man looked at her now and handed her the little carrier bag with her purchases. 'I had a woman who called me up regularly looking for this book.' He bent down and took a battered-looking old hardback from under the desk. It looked like a library edition to Heather, but then she looked more closely.

'Oh my God, is that a Maggie Macken?' she asked, holding out her hand and taking it from him.

'You've heard of her?' The old man shook his head as if wonders would never cease.

'I know, what are the chances? She was a friend of my family.' It was the easiest way to describe the relationship between her and this writer who had died long before Heather really had a chance to get to know her.

'Her books are long out of print, I mean, the chances of picking one up are so slim these days...' The old man was talking as she turned the book over in her hand. 'But the woman who had been looking for a copy is mentioned on the dedication...' he said.

'Oh.' And Heather opened the cover to see the faded typeface that had long gone out of fashion. *To Constance and Dotty, may the friendship you share last as long as the sea is hitting the shore and remember that home is always within a whisper of Ocean's End. With love. Maggie.* 'Oh, my God.' It felt as if she had been gut-punched.

'All right, love?' The man was looking at her as if she was about to collapse right across his cluttered counter.

'I'm fine, it's just the—'She had to stop to catch her breath. 'It's just the Dotty in the dedication is my mother and she died just recently.'

'That's...' The old man scratched his head as if trying to figure something out. 'That might be the biggest coincidence I can put down in all my days here...' And he went on to explain that it was Dotty who had been ringing him up on a regular basis to find this very book for her.

'That's...' Heather felt the book like a tonne weight suddenly in her hands. The idea that she had arrived in this very shop and now had this very book in her hands. It sent a shiver down her spine.

'A gift,' the old man said. 'From me, for your mother and now for you.'

'I couldn't possibly accept it,' she said, but she knew she was going to buy it if he'd let her. She had no intention of leaving this shop without it; that suddenly felt as if it was the most important thing she could possibly do right now, as if it might somehow put something right in her world.

'Of course you can, it's not worth anything to me and I have a feeling you are meant to have it.'

'Isn't it rare, I mean, if it's out of print?'

'Probably, but no-one reads those old-fashioned romances any more, it's all about killing and terrorising you and giving you nightmares before you go to sleep these days.' Again he shook his head as if he'd never understand the modern world.

'That's really kind of you...' She looked around the shop and, before she thought about it, she blurted out, 'I don't suppose you could keep an eye out for any of her other books that might come your way? I'll leave you my card.' But, of course, she didn't have a card any more. 'Well, I'll leave you my mobile number, if that's okay?'

'I'll keep an eye out, but the chances of another of her books arriving in here now, well I'd say I was just lucky to get that one. It was in a box that some lady had found under her mother's bed, tucked away for years like guilty secrets.' He smiled kindly now.

And for the first time in weeks, even though she couldn't understand why it was, Heather felt as if she had something to look forward to. She pushed the door into the next coffee shop she came to, ordered an Americano and lodged herself in a deep armchair before sinking into *Never Lose Heart*. This was one of the last books Maggie Macken had written, but the publisher had listed all her others – twenty-four in all. Somehow, that was an unexpected source of comfort to Heather as she dived into the story.

7

Ros

There was an exhilarating splendour about this time of the day, Ros thought, inhaling the salty sea air deeply so it filled her lungs. It was first thing in the morning, before the islanders were out of their beds. Today she was walking along the western sea-facing cliffs, taking stock and checking on the populations of sea birds nesting in the cracks below the overhang. By now, she knew where every nest was; it was her job to check and conserve wildlife on the island. This involved everything from the birds in the air, to the fish in the sea, to the tiniest species of plankton that could be endangered in the event of some heedless human interaction that disrupted the local biodiversity.

Ros hitched up her long skirt and tucked it inside the thermal leggings she wore every day to keep her warm. Here, walking along the sea cliffs and occasionally having to scramble down the sides, she knew the value of having clothes that would hold freezing temperatures at bay. She pushed from her mind the warnings about always dressing for the possibility that she might find herself stranded overnight. The PhD students she'd travelled here with had all the gear – of course, if Mummy and Daddy were paying for it, why wouldn't they? Ros had her mobile phone, a rucksack with a few snack bars, combined with a growing knowledge of the land that was earned in all weathers with twenty thousand steps a day. Anyway, she was too young to think of dire consequences of that sort.

No, if Ros thought of the worst that could happen, she always figured those things had already spun out in her life. She held onto the notion that lightning didn't strike in the same place twice and even if it did in her case, it couldn't just keep on hitting the same ground.

The fact was that she'd arrived on Pin Hill Island by happy accident, more than by any real design. She had applied for what felt like thousands of jobs after she graduated with her degree in environmental science. It turned out that the environmental sector was a small one in Ireland. Everywhere she went, it seemed they'd heard about the catastrophe of the eagle's nest and of course they'd assumed she was responsible for a senior manager having to quit her job. So, she'd drifted for a while, from one meaningless thing to another, growing more afraid to aim for what she really wanted. That was the thing about having no roots. Without her mother, or indeed any family, she hadn't any particular place to be and no-one to answer to in almost four years. She had completed her final year in college, gone out into the world, screwed up and licked her wounds without anyone to fall back on.

And then she'd arrived here, half thinking that she might apply to go back to college and this would be a summer job, just something to tide her over and remind her what her degree had been all about to begin with.

Everything about the island had wrapped itself around her since the day she arrived. It felt as if she was meant to be here, after all half the country was screaming out for the want of housing and here she was, landed in a cottage all to herself for the whole winter. Admittedly, it wasn't the Rockefeller mansion. She'd had to learn to build a good fire in the ancient stove to combat the biting frigidness in winter. She even chopped up her own firewood. She'd taken easily to wearing extra layers to combat the random chills that seemed to haunt the place in unexpected niggling draughts. True enough, it mightn't be everyone's idea of landing on their feet but Ros had lived in worse. She'd surfed sofas of friends of friends for almost eighteen months when it seemed Dublin hadn't a flat to let within her price range, and at least now she was in charge of when the fire went on and what time the lights went out.

And she had the kid goat. It had only been two days but it felt as if he'd been with her forever. He was the last thing she checked at night, the first she raced to in the morning. She was happy that he was eating, or at least trying to drink the baby formula, but his leg was no better, in fact, if anything, he was making even less of an attempt to stand or move about. Already, it seemed they were getting used to each other. She'd given him a name; well you had to, hadn't you? George, mainly because her mother had adored George Michael. It suited him perfectly. *George the goat.* Her phone was filling up with images of him, he was so cute, she couldn't help it. She spent hours online, learning as much as she could about the native Irish goat and how to care for him, and now she knew it was best to release him as soon as he could walk safely.

Constance had been enraptured with the notion of George. Ros promised she could come and see him, but then it turned out that she'd never be able to walk as far as the ranger's house and neither of them owned a car.

'So, this farmer who helped you take him home?' Constance asked, almost as wide-eyed as the goat.

'I think he thought I was deranged. He was definitely the sort who would have believed it kinder to finish him off there and then and leave his body in a ditch out of the way...'

'Oh, well, that's farmers for you, I think they work off everything in the same way they do with their own livestock, it's all weighed up in terms of the chances of survival against the cost of it not working out if you call the vet. But aren't you marvellous to know what to do. I wouldn't have had a clue and I've lived here almost my entire life.'

Constance was a dear sweet thing. Sometimes, Ros felt a little sorry for her unlikely new friend as they sat there in her faded mansion. She had a feeling that apart from a new fridge freezer, nothing much had changed there in forty years or maybe more. Ros had even spotted iodine tablets in the cupboard when she'd washed up their cups and plates one evening. That first morning they'd met, she had been momentarily stunned when she climbed through the upstairs window. It was beyond shocking in its neglected shambolic state.

'Perhaps I could come back and oil that door for you?'

She wanted to come back again and check on Constance. God knew how long she'd been wandering about in her nightdress. Ros knew better than anyone what it was to pretend that everything was not so bad as it appeared. 'Maybe put a hook up somewhere outside so you could leave a spare key handy in case it slips closed on you again?' she'd offered as she'd been leaving. The truth was, she felt even those two things were a lot less than Constance needed. A blind man could see she was lonely as hell and maybe as much at risk of tripping over on those mossy paths as she was of locking herself outside and freezing to death.

'Oh, you can't be doing that, I'm sure it's far too much trouble to go to just for me...' But Constance couldn't stop smiling. 'Are you sure? You really wouldn't mind?'

'Not a bit. To be honest with you, once I've done my rounds, the time can drag a bit in that cottage by myself.' It wasn't strictly true, especially since George had arrived on the scene. These days she was actually relishing just mooching about or wandering down to the village if there was something on. She'd even gone to a few yoga classes in the community centre, although she still wasn't convinced they were her bag, but at least she'd made some friends. Now, she wasn't an outsider; when she went into the supermarket or walked across the marshes, she said hello to people and they knew her. It felt as if she was becoming one of them.

'That's so kind and...' Constance looked around the kitchen as if for inspiration, 'I'll tell you what, in return, I'll cook lunch for both of us...'

'Ah, you don't have to do that, there's really no need,'

Ros said, although she'd never turned down a plate of food in her life.

'It'd be my pleasure, you just let me know when you're coming up and I'll have something prepared for us,' Constance said and, as she walked Ros towards the door that day, it seemed that she looked a little younger than she had just an hour or so earlier.

Since there had been no more news from the mainland in terms of when the new ranger would be appointed, Ros put all thoughts of having to leave from her head for the next few days. She was on her way back from checking on an area of beach with a history of having stranded whales, when her phone rang. Well, she couldn't bury her head in the sand forever.

'Hah, so you're still there?' Keith Duff said – it was one of his default greetings when he rang her.

'Of course I'm still here; I filed my weekly report last night.'

'Oh, you did, did you?' It sounded as if he was looking around his desk for the online update that she sent in each week about various vulnerable sites on the island. She hadn't mentioned the goat of course, why would she? It would be something else he could lecture her on and she didn't need that. With a bit of luck, soon she'd be able to release George back into the same area she'd found him in and Keith would be none the wiser.

'Of course, how's life on the mainland?' she asked, stopping to admire the sea beneath her. It was breathtaking today, a mixture of coral blues and green patches under the unyielding greyness of the water.

'Like it always is, neither as cold nor as wet as over there,

I suppose.' It was another familiar refrain. 'Now, I'm not calling you to find out about the weather or to compare notes on island living, but I wanted to check in with you. We put up that advertisement for the ranger's job on the island and it's hardly a shocker but, of all the jobs going out there this week, it's the only one no-one has actually applied for yet.'

'Oh!' That actually came as a pleasant surprise to Ros, even if it sounded as if it was giving her boss heartburn.

'So, I'm just double-checking, you're grand with staying on there until we find someone to come along and fill the post?'

'Of course, I'm more than happy to stay for as long as I'm needed, I'm looking forward to seeing the...' She was going to say *spring hatchings*, but of course, he had already moved on.

'Thank St Blaise for that. My desk is already groaning with the amount of paperwork on it, the last thing I need is to be organising rosters for that place out of the boyos here. They're crosser than stickler hens when it comes to having to put themselves out.'

'Consider it a problem solved,' Ros said and she breathed an almighty sigh of relief. Actually, she felt like celebrating except she wasn't sure there was a pub open on the island on a Monday night this early in the year. And then, she thought, maybe she could take a bottle of wine to Constance Macken's house and they might have a glass each to celebrate what felt like a glorious reprieve.

8

Constance

'How lovely.' Constance was sitting at the kitchen table poring over an old photo album when Ros arrived and placed a bottle of wine on the table. She'd heard on the radio earlier that day that people didn't have photo albums any more, the presenter and his guest talking about storing photos on a *cloud* of all things and having a million images but nothing in a frame. Ocean's End was filled with photographs. They stretched from the first days here on the island, documenting many of her mother's great triumphs, and later, they catalogued that short time in Constance's life when it seemed as if everything had worked out perfectly. Pride of place in the sitting room, a faded photograph of her wedding day hung above the fireplace and on every surface stood some reminder of glorious memories of a past that had fleeted by too quickly. Her darling Oisin forever young while she carried on in Ocean's End without him.

There was a photograph of Constance and little Heather Banks, standing on the beach, with the sun glaring against their backs. Stupid, really, when she thought about it now, Ocean's End had become a catalogue of lives that had only passed through it, but even all these years later meant the world to Constance.

'Sorry, am I interrupting?' Ros was standing there now; had she asked her something?

'Not at all, I don't know when I last had a glass of wine. Of course, the cupboards here are bursting with booze, between sherry and brandy and all sorts of disgusting liquors, but it's not the same when you're here alone, there hardly seems any point. I generally stick to tea.'

'If they've been there a while, you might be better off.'

'You're probably right.' Constance watched as Ros took two glasses from the cupboard and poured them both a generous measure of white wine.

'Sauvignon. It's nothing fancy, but I picked it up at the supermarket on my way over.'

'It's fancy enough for me.' Constance sipped the wine. 'Oooh,' she said because there was an unexpected kick from it, but it was pleasant. 'So, what are we celebrating again?' because she couldn't remember hearing.

'Well, now that I'm here, it seems a bit daft really, but I got word today that there are no applicants for the ranger's job here on the island. I'm just so happy to know that I'm not going to have to leave yet.'

'Oh? But will you have to go when it's filled?'

'I'm afraid so, the only reason I can stay on is because I'm getting the cottage and of course the job... otherwise, I'd have to go back to the mainland.' Ros looked down at her hands. 'Probably back to Dublin again, look for my old job back.'

The truth was, it took quite a bit of probing to learn that Ros's mother had passed away just as Ros was finishing up her finals, a tragic event that had consequences reaching far beyond just leaving her alone in the world. There were financial repercussions too. For one thing, she could no longer afford the flat she'd lived in, nor could she continue with her studies, to pursue a master's or a specialism, which would have prepared her for a particular field of work.

'I suppose it makes me a jack of all trades and master of none,' Ros told her. Never a girl to sit still, she'd taken a job in a bar and when she learned her old classmates had secured work on the island to study an area of special conservation she'd offered to join them if they were short.

'Bar work must be a very different life to here, I'm sure.'

'It was...' Ros reflected. 'It was okay, I suppose, I didn't mind it, but compared to here, well, maybe I've been spoiled since I arrived, what with the house and everything. I love the job and being part of a small community, I really feel as if I belong.'

'Of course you belong.' Constance sipped her wine again. The taste was growing on her as was this young woman who had taken to visiting her every other day. Not only that, but when she came, she arrived with a bundle of energy and good cheer. In the short time they'd known each other Ros had unstuck her back and front doors, shaving down the winter swelling and oiling the hinges. She'd placed a hook beneath the ivy on the back wall to hide a spare key, so if Constance did get locked out, she wouldn't have to bend down and start scurrying under old plant pots. And just the other day, she'd finished scrubbing the narrow path that cut through the garden down to the very end.

Constance looked across at Ros, with her funny seashell earrings and the hat she wore when she went out walking, perched now on the corner of her chair; she would miss her very much if she had to return to the mainland. And then it came to her, in a flash, the most obvious thing.

'Why don't *you* apply for the ranger's job?'

'Me?' Ros looked at her for a moment, went to say something else, but sidelined the words, shifting her gaze out toward the back garden. 'I don't think I could, I mean, I'm sure you must need to have a lot more experience for it. They'd hardly go handing out jobs to just anyone, would they?'

'I don't know, they were content enough to let you do the job for the whole winter and it isn't as if they could even properly supervise you, is it? I mean, how long is it since anyone actually set foot on the island to see what sort of job you're doing?'

'That's a point,' Ros said slowly, but she looked as if her thoughts had raced to a place a million miles away. 'Still, I don't think I'd have a hope of getting it, not if…' She halted and for a moment it felt as if something of momentous importance hung wordlessly on the air between them. 'Well, you know…' she said, sounding a little sad, as if it was the story of her life.

'No, I don't know. Why wouldn't you get it? Haven't you got all the qualifications and from Trinity College, no less, and plenty of experience here on the island – they'd be mad not to give it to you, if you ask me.'

'I don't know, it's a lot of responsibility and really, they'll want someone with a bit more...'

'What?' Constance leaned forward because she couldn't imagine anyone not liking Ros.

'All the other rangers in the area are men, older. I'm not sure they'd want a woman taking on this whole area on her own.'

'Pah, those days are meant to be well and truly behind us. I'm sure it wouldn't just be down to silly ideas that are truly stuck in the last century.'

'I'm not so sure.' Ros kept her eyes glued to her hands, which played nervously now with the stem of her glass, and Constance couldn't overlook the feeling there was something she wasn't telling her.

'Well, I think you'll be bloody sorry if you don't apply for it. Jobs like that don't come up very often. Max Toolis was here for over twenty years, you don't want to be sitting in some desk job on the mainland waiting that long for it to come up again, do you?'

'I'd be a long time waiting, I suppose,' Ros murmured.

'I think...' Constance considered this lovely girl who'd shown her nothing but kindness since the first day they'd met. 'I think you absolutely have to... Otherwise, you'll regret it, especially if you just walk away and feel as if you didn't even try.'

'I suppose I'll think about it.' Ros sat a little straighter on the chair and raised her glass to her lips, then held it out to make a toast. 'To being brave and going for what we want in life.'

'I'll drink to that.' Constance smiled and she had a feeling that if Ros got that job, it would be good for both of them to have her here on the island.

9

June 1957

Dotty

A bellow of thunder, somewhere in the distance, made her heart jump. Dotty was looking out her bedroom window in Galway as her father and a few of the men who lived along the road worked in the sleeting rain to once more unfasten the cover of the well in Mr Morrison's garden.

'That rain is going to wash us away if we can't drain it out,' her father had complained earlier. True enough, their garden was currently under about a foot of water, which if she'd seen it in the newspaper she might have thought, *oh, goody, our own swimming pool*, but the reality was, it was mucky and murky and smelled of drains and dirt. So, her father had the brilliant idea that perhaps if they opened up the old well again, the water might drain away and run through, emptying all of their gardens of the dirty water that had pooled stagnantly until now.

The well had been sealed across after Constance fell

into it at the start of summer. Mrs Macken had insisted on it, not that Constance was ever likely to go near it again. She wouldn't even venture through the hedges into old Mr Morrison's garden to pick blackcurrants with Dotty, even though they were practically bursting out of their skins.

Dotty had a clear view from her bedroom window, and she now rushed upstairs to watch the men work the opening free. Constance had told her that when she fell into the well, she felt she wasn't alone. Dotty's mother said it was probably a grave to more unfortunate cats and rats than you could shake a stick at. Dotty pressed her face to the window, half expecting something grisly to float up to the top, finally freed from its watery grave.

Dotty watched, fascinated, as the men worked together, their hands buried in the brown water, their arms and backs twisting this way and that, until finally, her dad stood up, raised what looked like a huge crowbar above his head in victory, and Dotty shivered, even though she couldn't say quite why.

The men's laughter and backslapping were enough to tell her he had managed to prise it open. And Dotty looked away, suddenly not wanting to think about what might float to the top of that well or how easy it would be to end up at the bottom of it without a trace of you to be found.

It was a week later when the garden had just about dried out after the heavy flooding. If it hadn't been for the smell, Dotty thought it might be fun to pretend they were looking at a rainforest, to play make-believe that they were deep in the Amazon, somewhere far more exotic than St Patrick's Terrace in Galway. It might have been too, but Constance had gone to some island with Maggie for a week's holiday. You could see she was still pale; if Dotty had been hailed as a hero for finding her, poor Constance was still being treated as if she was convalescent from some awful catastrophe. In any event, the garden reeked of mud and dirty water, but Dotty had spent days cooped up inside and her mother had sent her out to get fresh air, which was not much fun on her own.

'Hey?' Lickey Gillespie called out to her from across the fence. For a moment, she thought he was in Constance's garden, but when she peered through the hedges there was no sign of him. 'Up here,' he called to her and when she looked up she saw him, sitting on the low roof of the shed in Mr Morrison's garden.

'What on earth are you doing up there?' she asked, but she couldn't keep the giggle from her voice, because as much and all as Lickey terrorised Constance, he could be funny. Certainly, life was never dull around him.

'Come over and see…' he called and he popped a fistful of blackcurrants into his mouth before walking to the end of the roof and sliding down the side then dropping to the ground. Boredom more than curiosity edged Dotty through the hedges. As she crossed Constance's empty garden she spotted the kitten, who eyed her lazily from an old pillow wedged beneath a makeshift cat cubby. She couldn't say he'd grown on her; she still blamed him for Constance almost dying in that bloody well and it was perfectly obvious he'd fallen on his feet as a result.

'So?' she said, eyeing Lickey with the sort of disdain she knew was the only way to handle him. 'I'm not climbing up on that shed if you think I am.' Her mother would kill her for one thing and, for another, she wasn't about to let Lickey know she was afraid to stand on anything higher than a kitchen chair.

'No, here, it's this, look what I found.' He went into the shed and she followed him. She'd never been in here before, but if she'd thought about it, there was hardly a surprise to see last year's onions hanging from the rafters and all of Mr Morrison's old gardening tools lined up against the walls. Lickey spun round now to face her, his eyes shining in the way they did when he managed to play a trick on someone. 'Here.' He pushed a bottle towards her. 'It's poitín.'

'It's not.' Although Dotty would hardly know if it was or not, because she'd never actually seen the stuff, far less had a bottle of it in her hand. She'd heard about it from her mother's people, who seemed to drink it by the gallon. It was one of the reasons her mother never really went to visit her family any more.

'It bloody is. Smell it.' He wrinkled his nose as if to show her how to get the best whiff of it. She put her nose over the bottle. It smelled sweet, not unpleasant. Uiscebeatha – fire water, that's what it was called – it seemed pretty harmless to Dotty.

'Go on, take a sip.' Lickey was watching her now, as if testing her in some way. They'd always had a funny relationship, a sort of mild mutual respect. He never picked on her and she never told anyone that Mrs Gillespie had once asked her mother for advice in taking stains out of her best sheets because Lickey wet his bed.

She wanted to taste the poitín. She really did, had always wondered about it, because her mother only mentioned it quiet tones. It was another of those things in her house that was mildly swept beneath the carpet. Her mother's family. Backward. Country people. 'Stocious drunks,' her father said once, but then he'd reached out and patted her mother's hand and said in a soft tone, 'no matter, better out of it, better here with me.'

'Are you scared?' Lickey's face had turned almost puce, as if he was expecting something extraordinary to happen.

'Course I'm not scared,' Dotty said and she upended the bottle, swallowing a huge slurp before she realised why they called it fire water. 'Bloody hell, Lickey,' she said between splutters. In that first moment, she thought she might die, the heat of it racing down through her was shocking. The sheer sweetness of it, pleasant and unexpected. Then a wave of abatement that washed from the pores at the top of her head right down to the very tip of each of her toenails with delicious ripples unfettering the boredom of earlier and the niggling worries that she couldn't quite put a finger on. Every fibre of her slackened, as if someone had come along and unknotted her. It felt sublime, as if she had submitted to a greater power, and it was heavenly. She sipped again, slower this time, breathing deeply the woody sweet aroma of it. She closed her eyes. Bliss.

'Here, come on, you can't have it all, there's only a small drop in the bottle.' Lickey pulled the bottle from her.

'I wasn't... I was just...' she said but a little part of her didn't want to see it go. It felt as if he'd wrenched something necessary from her. For a while, she sat in the little shed, enjoying the feeling of the alcohol in her system, watching as Lickey poked about the shelves, prodding things and picking them up and examining them. It didn't take long to finish the tiny drop of poitín between them, but at the end of it, Dotty knew one thing. She couldn't wait to be grown-up, to drink and smoke and have grown-up adventures. Wouldn't life be wonderful if she could always feel this bliss.

10

Heather

Heather couldn't remember the last time she'd finished a book within twelve hours of beginning it, but that was what happened with the copy of Maggie Macken's battered old paperback. It wasn't exactly high literature, but it was well written with an unexpected intensity that carried Heather along so she was invested in the characters to the final page. It was the setting too, painted with such a loving hand, the descriptions of the coastal village, drawn, Heather guessed, from the island where Maggie, Constance and indeed Heather's own mother had lived at the time it was written. Heather could remember quite vividly the beautiful art deco house overlooking the sea. When she closed her eyes, she was almost transported back to its startling form against the cliffs. She remembered clearly walking along the beach and looking up at it with her hand in Constance's hand; feeling happy – that way only children can, when there was no question about how long it could last. By the time she finished the book, she wasn't sure which she wanted more, to travel to the island immediately or to track down every book Maggie Macken had ever written.

She settled on the latter and by the following morning when she should have been getting ready for breakfast, she was still rubbing the tiredness from her eyes after an online search that ended up with nothing to show for it. Maggie Macken books were rarer than daisies in the desert, it seemed. This morning, since she didn't have a place that felt like a real home of her own or a job or a husband to answer to, she decided that she'd take a trip around the city's second-hand bookshops and see if she could track down any more copies.

Heather set off for the markets first but, as she had half expected, they turned up nothing. None of the booksellers had heard of Maggie Macken, much less carried copies of her out-of-print novels. It was as she was walking about Charing Cross that she noticed a small pop-up bookshop at the front of a coffee shop. It was little more than a table and a few racks and, if she was honest, the aroma of good coffee drew her in as much as the lure of the books. She was dead on her feet and suddenly realised it was late afternoon and she hadn't eaten anything since a slice of toast for breakfast.

'Ah, Maggie Macken, is it?' the woman on the bookstand said. 'I haven't thought of her in years, I read all her books, used to count down the days until the next one was due to come out. I worked in Foyles, back then, different days, you know, she was a real author –old-school, real class.'

'You met her?'

'Of course I met her, didn't I just say? Different times,

she would call into the shop and her publicist would be flapping about the place. One time I remember, it was a really hot day, the sort where you think we should all be having siestas, like they do on the continent.' She pulled the fleecy collar on her coat closer, because warm temperatures were quite a bit away for a few more months yet. 'She sent the publicity girl out to get us all ice-creams. The kid didn't know what Maggie meant and so she arrived in with just two ice-creams, one for each of them.' She cackled, a deep rattling sound that probably spoke of too many cigarettes over the years. 'Maggie Macken wasn't having that and she went out into the street and ordered them herself and there, in the middle of the shop, all of us shop girls were licking our ninety-nines and happy as clams. I loved her after that, honestly, she could do no wrong as far as I was concerned.'

'Do you ever come across her books now?'

'Nah. They're probably all out of print at this stage, but I've often wondered why they've never been reissued. I mean, you see the likes of Georgette Heyer and Agatha Christie and even old Conan Doyle gets more than his fair square yards in all the big shops now.'

'And they never have? Been reissued?'

'Well, that's up to whoever is in charge of her estate now… I haven't seen new copies of hers come this way though and, to be honest, if I picked up an old copy, I'd probably hang onto it.'

'If you picked up two, would you let me have the second one?' Heather asked.

'Sure, if you're knocking about.'

'Better than that,' Heather said and she gave the woman her mobile number.

'Perhaps we should set up a club? The Maggie Macken Appreciation Society?' The woman threw her head back and laughed at this suggestion, but strangely, Heather found herself wondering if it wasn't such a bad idea at all. 'You know what you could do?' the woman said later as Heather passed by her again, having drunk a coffee strong enough to make her head swim. 'You could contact her publishers, see if they have any old copies lying about or if... Well, you never know, it might make them sit up and take notice.'

'I might just do that.' Heather smiled and thought it was nice to feel as if she'd had something important to do for a few hours at least. And then, just as she was catching a bus back to the flat for the night, she thought about her mother's house. If there was anyone in London who would have a shelf full of Maggie Macken books surely it was her mother.

She was too exhausted to go looking for a tube connection or a bus to take her and so she sank into the first taxi she came across and was glad to speed across the city and watch the evening crowds dawdle on the footpaths as she passed.

The house felt even emptier when she pushed through the front door. It was desolate and chilly too. Perhaps she should have left the heating on at low? She'd switched everything off, fearing the chances of fire thanks to the dated wiring and the number of papers and soft furnishings in the house. Now, she shivered and the first thing she did was reach under the stairs and switch on the radiators throughout.

She stepped into what had been the sitting room up until a few years earlier, when her mother could no longer make the stairs and it had been reappropriated as a downstairs bedroom. Even though they'd hardly been close, the sight of her mother's empty bed, the old alarm clock on the bedside table and the walking stick leaning across the chair brought a knot of grief to Heather's chest. For a moment, it felt as if she couldn't breathe, such was the swelling of pain that pushed between her heart and her throat. She closed the door quickly. It did no good to think of what might have been. Their relationship was what it was, not because Heather had given up on it, but because her mother had pushed her away before she even had a chance to start.

She walked into the little kitchen, where a small bookcase had been squeezed behind the kitchen table after being evicted from the sitting room. Her mother's bed now stood empty along the wall that it had always leaned against. Heather switched on the light and pulled out the kitchen table so she could check the shelves and there, within a few minutes, she managed to find a dozen copies of Maggie Macken's books. They looked as if they had been read many times over. Had her mother returned to them again and again for the comfort they could offer? Heather understood what it was to return to a place, if only between the covers of a book. She had found such consolation in *Never Lose Heart* when she read it.

Suddenly, she began to pull them out, book after book, and they landed on the floor by her knees. She was feverish in grabbing them, each one faster and more frantically than the last, and now her eyes filled with tears and she wiped them harshly. Her hair was spilling into her face and it was hard to see what she was pulling out, what was being thrown on the ground. But she knew she wanted to read every single one of those books, to feel as if she was somehow closer to her mother or maybe to a world where everything was the way it should be. It was stupid of course. The world that Heather craved might never have existed. Still, she was desperate to catch hold of her mother, before it was too late. At this point she'd settle for drawing closer to the Dotty her mother had been before she'd sunk into bitterness and alcoholism.

Eventually, Heather slumped back on her knees, sitting on her folded legs beneath her. Suddenly, the hunger for something she didn't understand began to subside. A raging emptiness within her felt as if someone had pulled the plug from its power, so it ebbed from her, more like a bath emptying of emotion than a woman coming to terms with her grief.

She had no idea how long she sat there, touching each of those novels, carefully separating the Maggie Macken editions from other books that had once belonged to her father and one or two of her own childhood books also. By the time they were sorted through, she had three piles to lift up onto the kitchen table. There were too many to carry home on the tube. She looked around the dreary kitchen. Perhaps it was time to stop running away and thinking that the path she should take would somehow magically present itself to her if she kept moving.

Of course it wouldn't. She was an intelligent woman, she'd always known that the future was there to be chased or planned and then, when the unthinkable happened, to make another plan. And so, she sat in the club chair that had been her mother's position for years, picked up one of the paperback books and settled down to read.

By eight o'clock she was starving. She hadn't eaten since breakfast and the coffee she'd had earlier felt as if it had turned to acid in her stomach. There was a fish and chip shop just around the corner. It had been there for years, only the name over the door had changed, but any time she'd passed it, the aroma of fresh oil, salt and vinegar and cooking batter still smelled as good as she remembered from her childhood.

She set off with her bag in her hand. Ten minutes later, she brought her fish and chips home with her and a few groceries from the corner shop.

Later, much later, she sent Ruth a message. She was going to stay in her mother's house tonight. She appreciated the fact that for months now, her friend Ruth had watched over her as if she was a young duckling in her care, but perhaps it was time to start facing up to things. She needed to stand on her own two feet and she needed a purpose.

That thought struck a chord deep within her. Why hadn't she seen it before – she needed a purpose and now she knew it, it felt as if something shifted within her. She wouldn't find that shut away in a flat, moving from sessions in the gym to endless days browsing in bookshops. She needed to move forward. Her mother had passed away a week earlier, it was time to face up to things. She reached into her bag and took out the envelope that contained her mother's will. She opened it slowly, carefully, as if she could somehow preserve some part of her mother's presence by keeping it intact. She was wrong, it wasn't a will. It was just a letter, a short letter in her mother's handwriting. Strange, she recognised the script immediately and her heart tumbled over in her chest with an unexpected stab of loneliness.

Wednesday, 15th...

Dear Heather,

Today, I came across a photograph taken of you when you were just a small kiddie one summer long ago on Pin Hill Island. I've been thinking of the old place a lot recently, my age, I suppose, I've come to that stage where there's more to regret than to look forward to. Sorry, I'm trying to be more optimistic, more to remember – that's better.

I've been thinking about people too, about my parents, my mother mostly, buried so far away, about Constance and Maggie; probably all gone now. I don't expect you to understand this, Heather, I know it wouldn't have made any sense to me years ago, but I dearly want to be buried next to them all, not in some place where I'm just another faded headstone. When I die, I want you to bring me back to the island, there's money to pay for it in my account and you'll have the house, of course, but this is my only request.

Well, there's one other small thing. The little letter box, beside my bed; if by some miracle Constance outlasts me (that'll be down to all that fresh air and clean living!) that's for her. I want you to take it to her. There are letters inside, I'd like you to open them together, but not until I'm gone. I don't think I'm brave enough yet to face you both with all I have to say.

I know I have no right to ask, but I also know that you

won't refuse, you have too much of your father in you to say no!

Take care,

Mum.

Heather read the letter again, not entirely sure what to make of it. She could hear her mother's deprecating humour, but there was a clarity to the words that felt at odds with the woman she'd become over the years. And the letter box? She had no idea what the letter box was, should she remember it?

She got up from the table, walked into the bedroom and checked in the locker next to her mother's bed. There, tucked in on the bottom shelf, sat a long slender box, antique certainly – it looked Edwardian, maybe art deco. It was very pretty, a rich handsome wood with a black lacquered fanning leaf design across its top. It was locked and Heather turned it over. Surely there should be a key to fit it around here somewhere. And then she remembered, everything here would have to be organised and gone through, it was something she couldn't put off forever, especially now if she had to organise an Irish burial also.

Tomorrow she would begin to sort through her mother's belongings. It would be a step in the direction of her future and at least she had Maggie Macken's books for company if it all got to be too much to bear as she put things straight.

11

Ros

Ros missed the call to her mobile, so instead she opened her phone to a voicemail from her boss on the mainland. They were sending an environmental engineer across in the afternoon to take a look around the island. *Shane McPherson. This bloke knows his stuff. Make sure you don't let us down by saying something daft.* Apparently, if the visit went well, the island would be on the way to getting a green light in turning huge tracts of its unused land over to National Park land. There would be an application to the government departments and all sorts of hoops to jump through, but all they needed was for Ros to show the guy around the place, make a good impression and keep him away from any farmers who might be against the proposal. Shane McPherson would also check on the status of the water quality at the source of some of the streams. These tributaries, little more than a trickle in places, were vital to the wildlife on the island. They started in the mountains and traced across the island, washing through the marshy bogs and the hidden tree copse. Ros loved going down to the copse; it was home to a rich assortment of wildlife, from the microscopic to the majestic red deer that spent most of their time hiding among the silver birch and out of sight.

Shane McPherson. Ros tried out the name, but there was nothing even vaguely familiar about it. He was probably one of those middle-aged men who dressed in regulation ranger kit (in the vague hope that it made them seem outdoorsy) that sagged on the backside and stretched dangerously across their middles. That was what doing a desk job did to you. Ros just hoped he'd be fit enough to make the climb to the top of Pin Hill because it was a good two-hour trek and steep at the top. Certainly not a place you wanted to get stranded for the night, at least not until the temperatures rose a little.

He was due to come across after lunch, which gave her plenty of time to make sure that there was enough food in the fridge to feed him at least. The best the island ran to this time of year in fine dining was a pub lunch with a choice of either shepherd's pie or toasted sandwiches on a Tuesday. Life here was nothing if not predictable. She made up the narrow single bed in what doubled as an office and a spare room in the cottage. If they were going to climb Pin Hill, they'd have to do it first thing in the morning. At least the weather forecast for the following day was mild and dry. In spite of the fact that she was having an uninvited guest, she was actually quite looking forward to the climb to the mountain top. It was a few weeks since she'd been there and the views were spectacular, although she knew there wouldn't be a lot of time to take photographs or sit back and enjoy it.

'Hey?' A knock on the cottage door almost made her lose her balance as she was searching on top of the old dresser for a torch to pack in her rucksack for the trek. 'Whoa, careful there... you could fall.' She turned to see a man, dressed in regulation kit that looked as if it had been made to measure. Not a dumpy bottom or an overhanging belly in sight. This guy looked as if he'd walked off a *Vogue* shoot for rugged country living.

'Shane?' She had to check, because he was the complete opposite of what she had been expecting. This guy was young, well, thirties but good-looking, fanciable even, and he was smiling, which made a change from the likes of Max Toolis or Keith Duff or indeed moody Jonah Ashe.

'Last time I checked.' His smile was dangerously contagious. 'Do you get many men pushing through your front door at random hours then?'

'A few,' she lied, enjoying the banter. She stuck out her hand to him. 'Ros Stokes and you're early.'

'Early? I didn't realise there was an ETA.' He looked confused.

'Well, not that there was a time mentioned, but the ferry only comes across once a day at this time of year and that's when the tide suits, so not for another hour or more. So I just expected you a little later.'

'Ah, sorry, I came under my own steam,' he said.

'You swam then.' She was joking too.

'Very funny, I have a small boat; it was good to get a chance to take it out. Normally it's laid up until summer, but I thought, well, it'll give me a bit more flexibility about the job. I might even manage to get back a bit earlier.'

'So you're based close by?' She'd have expected him to be in Dublin – after all, how much work was going for environmental engineers in the sticks, well, that was unless they were attached to one of the big energy companies.

'I live in Ballycove.' He smiled.

'Sorry, I just assumed they'd sent you down from HQ, you know. I didn't realise that there were environmental engineers on staff locally.'

'I'm freelance, I do consultancy work, when I can get it and when I can't...' he shrugged his shoulders, 'I surf and sail.' He was making fun of her now. 'So, what's the plan? Can we start straight away?'

'Sure, we'll see what we can do about that for you, shall we?' She pointed to the kitchen table where she'd spread out a map of the island so they could agree their route. While he pored over it, she made tea and brought a plate of sandwiches she'd made earlier from the fridge.

'Ah, you shouldn't have gone to all this trouble,' he said.

'No trouble, it's my lunch too.' She grabbed a ham sandwich and took a bite.

Because he had arrived earlier than expected, it turned out that they could cover quite a bit of the lower-lying river locations for testing straight away.

'All on foot?' he asked as she pointed out a route that went mostly across country.

'Unless you brought a car on that boat with you, yes, it's the only way to travel over here.'

'There are cars though, I mean, the locals have to have

cars? It's a bloody big island if you wanted to walk from one end to the other.'

'It is and there are cars and tractors and even a helicopter when our local millionaire is at home on the southern part of the island.'

'It's a different world here, isn't it?' he asked. He had walked to the open half-door and was gazing out towards Pin Hill Mountain and the boggy terrain that lay for umpteen acres at its base. Mostly it was wetlands, marshlands and, really, the ideal spot to conserve as National Park land.

'It certainly is,' she said and she knew it wouldn't be everyone's cup of tea. She hoped that might prove to be a good thing when it came to people applying for the ranger job.

Shane had brought a kit bag filled with sample bottles and testing gear. 'They'll still have to go back to the lab, for the official seal, but at least we'll have a fair idea of things before we finish.'

'It's probably my imagination, or maybe the heights of wishful thinking, but I think the water is running clearer since I've been here. I've spotted any amount of river life on the lower stages of those rivers that were on the endangered list last year when we arrived.'

'You came over with the students?' He shook his head. 'So, that's how you managed to end up here. Have you finished your postgraduate work?'

'No, not yet. I thought I might go back, but it didn't work out that way.' There was no point going into the fact that she couldn't afford to do a college course when she had bills to pay and she was completely on her own in the world.

'So you just tagged along with some mates after they were talking about it in the pub?' He looked at her now as if he only half believed what she was telling him.

'I wanted adventure and I found it here in spades.' She bit her lip; she'd have to do much better than that if she went for an interview. She'd have to talk about her degree and find some reason to gloss over the fact that she'd spent the largest part of her life since graduation working in a bar. Somehow, she'd have to hide that the only real experience she'd ever had working in a job related to her degree before she arrived on Pin Hill. She knew, if the Parks and Wildlife interview committee realised how things had gone south with Wild Bird Ireland, she wouldn't have a prayer in securing this, her dream job.

'You found adventure on Pin Hill Island?' He was watching her now, as if reassessing what he saw. But it was the truth. She'd had the time of her life here, in the little cottage, making connections, and the place had quickly felt like home. Now, people like Constance cared about whether she turned up in the day and that was something Ros hadn't had in Dublin or anywhere else, not for quite some time.

Within half an hour, Ros had settled George for her absence and they were making progress quickly across the marshy fields and towards some of the many streams that flowed clear and fast towards the sea at the south-facing side of the island. Shane chatted easily on the way, telling her about his consultancy business, which sounded as if it wasn't very busy, and his real passion, surfing and the sea.

'Come on, we're nearly at our first location,' she said. For the next few hours, they worked hard to gather up as many samples as they could. She enjoyed pointing out places of interest around the island, places like Blackrock Island in the distance and the old castle ruins that had once belonged to Grace O'Malley, Ireland's most notorious pirate and, according to legend, the only woman known to have gotten the better of the first Queen Elizabeth.

'God, it feels as if we've been walking for a week, but I could keep on going,' Shane said as they turned onto the road that would bring them back to the cottage.

'It's like that here. The one thing that you need for this job is comfortable walking shoes…' Ros said lightly, but she'd learned the hard way with blisters and wet feet at the start.

'Well, in fairness you need a bit more than that now.' He had been eager to correct her earlier when she had pointed out some hedgerow plants with their Latin name. *Real rangers call them by their proper names; Latin is only for your final exams.* She tried to brush it off, but it stung, this way of letting her know that actually you needed more than a degree to do a ranger's job. His point was, she needed experience. She needed to be a person who belonged in the country, not one who grew up in a flat in the city.

They walked back to the cottage via the cliff trail. It was as stunning as on any day she'd walked it and she hoped that maybe they might catch a glimpse of basking sharks in the water. Ros thought that surely, if that went into a report, it would have to be another string to the bow of the island. They stood for a while, looking out to sea. The water was calm today. Shane had been lucky in travelling across; some days it was ferocious, reminding Ros of a wild beast, angry, roaring and hungry. The sound of the crows making their way back across the island to their nests after the day reminded them it was time to make a move for home.

'It's getting late. We should probably get an early night and set off first thing for Pin Hill?' He sounded eager to get going, whereas Ros could have stood there for another hour, drinking in the beauty of the place.

'Sure, I've got a lasagne in the fridge. We can heat it up and turn in for the night.' It was shop-bought, but it would do. Suddenly, no matter how long it had been since she'd actually spent time with an attractive man, she found herself wanting to get away from him for a few hours alone.

Ros realised she wasn't going to get her wish for that any time soon when they turned into the back yard of her cottage to be met with a parked and idling huge four-by-four jeep. Jonah Ashe was nowhere to be seen, but then, just as she pushed through her back door, he emerged from one of the tiny sheds that bordered one side of the property.

'You have bats,' he said as if she didn't already know it.

'Yes.'

'Don't they bother you?' He walked towards them, stopping for a moment to nod at Shane.

'No, not particularly. I mean, they're protected, we're lucky to have them here. No-one disturbs them – so long as you leave them be, they're happy to nest and I'm happy to have them,' she said, eyeing the door he'd pulled out tightly behind him. She marched across to open it slightly once more so the bats could emerge when the day had drifted into darkness.

'Pah! Protected. I never heard such madness. Bats are well able to survive in nature, how do you think they made it through for the last fifty million years?'

'Well, be that as it may, Ros is right,' Shane said. 'They are protected and anyone interfering with their nests would find themselves in trouble with the law if it came to our attention,' he added a little primly. It seemed whether Ros invited them both or not, they were following her into the cottage, when really, all she wanted was a bit of peace and quiet. Shane was hanging up his coat, now he turned, extended his hand to Jonah and introduced himself, making sure to mention his reason for being on the island.

'Good God, more of our land being taken over for swamp and bog,' Jonah muttered. 'I hope it won't interfere with my application for a wind farm?'

'I can't comment on that, but there are plenty of examples where the two aren't mutually exclusive, it really depends on where you want to situate the masts,' Shane said. 'It'll be down to compatibility with the site and, of course, your neighbours might have some say in things too.'

'What can I do for you, Jonah?' Ros stood between them. This was one conversation she didn't want to have to tell her boss had happened in her porch while her rescue goat lay half asleep in his bed at their feet.

'Oh, yeah, it's what I can do for you. I have the vet coming across tomorrow. I know it's probably not... well, I mean, let's face it, whatever chance the poor bugger has... but if you wanted, I could send him your way when he's finished at my place.' He didn't sound as if he particularly wanted to send anything her way, but it was how the island worked, you didn't waste a resource as precious as the vet if he was making his way across. 'Of course, it'll cost you, you do know that?'

'I think I can afford it,' Ros said, 'but don't worry, he was coming here anyway, I called him the other day, so...' She didn't add that she'd have paid all her wages to sort out

George if she had to. She bent down to him now, placed a hand on his snout, assuming that like dogs it was some indicator of good or bad health. Did she really need to check? He looked even worse than when she left him this morning.

God, poor George. His crate needed to be cleaned, his water changed, it had been a long day for him on his own. At least he hadn't tried to stand on that leg, chance would be a fine thing, he could hardly lift his head tonight, much less his leg.

'Did you expect him to be up and running already?' Shane had followed her to the porch and he leaned against the door jamb now, watching her. He wasn't an animal person especially, he'd told Ros when he'd spotted the goat earlier, but she thought you'd have to be made of marble not to fall for George.

'Of course not, but it's been a long day for him and he's going to need to have his bedding changed and…' She was lucky, Max Toolis must have bought the Sunday paper every week he lived here and he rarely recycled the old copies, so there were stacks of free bedding in one of the sheds outside. She began to fold in a layer around George now, hoping it would support his injury as well as keep him cosy.

'That doesn't look good.' Jonah stated the obvious. He had bent down next to her and was holding George while Ros pushed extra bedding around him and checked his injury.

'No,' she said quietly and willed him not to say what she knew he was thinking – that she should never have taken him home, that they should have put him out of his misery rather than prolonging it.

'A wild goat is never going to do well caged up, the stress alone...' Jonah paused. 'Well anyway, he's here now, I suppose.' He stood for a moment assessing the whole set-up. 'He's doing a rum job on that plastic bed, isn't he?' It was true, in his short spurts of wakefulness, George had managed to gnaw his way through the rim of the old dog bed she'd put him into.

'A strong antibiotic would go a long way,' Shane said from his vantage point in the doorway. Ros found herself being grateful that he was here, if only to act as a foil against the damning judgement of Jonah.

'Yes,' Ros said, but there was no getting away from the fact that George looked a lot worse than he had earlier that day. She took a deep breath. She would not let these men see just how upset she was, she wouldn't give either of them the satisfaction.

Once George was looked after and Jonah had charged out the back door to whatever was next on his agenda, she and Shane ate in near silence. Shane read over some report he'd pulled from his bag. Ros flicked mindlessly through her phone. It seemed her whole Instagram feed had room for nothing more than images of one soppy goat. It turned out there was an avid goat community on social media and now she was getting messages from people all over the world wishing George well. One girl, Aisha, from Germany owned a goat farm – Ros had been intrigued, because Aisha told her she hadn't a scrap of land, but her business was thriving. In fact, what she did was brilliant. She was responsible for herding a flock of goats from one mountain to another and, between them, the goats managed to clear the ground of enough growth so that there were no longer mountain fires in the region. 'See, George,' she told the sleeping goat that night, 'your appetite could yet be your greatest strength, if only you'd been born in Germany.'

As she closed her eyes that night, all she could do was pray that George would make it through the night. It was decent of Jonah to think of sending over the vet to her, even if he'd left unsaid that he thought she was foolish for taking George home and trying to patch him up.

The sun was pale lemon, picking out frosty webs and the dew still resting on the grass when Ros and Shane set off the following morning with a flask of strong coffee Ros had made up. It was hard not to feel in good humour as the day stretched out ahead. George, by some miracle, looked a little brighter before they left; maybe keeping the wound clean was going some way towards halting an infection.

Early morning birdsong, the rustle of wildlife taking cover as they approached and the sight of fishing boats bobbing out to sea in the distance lifted her spirits further. There had been many times when she'd set off walking and not returned until late evening, bringing a packed lunch and settling down to enjoy views so spectacular they still took her breath away.

They made the journey to the mountain top easily. At this time of year, the silvery rock was washed clean between scraggly clumps of wild grass and occasional clusters of heather and clover. Overhead, the sky had turned to an obstinate grey veil, diluting the sun as if determined to keep its lustre in the shadows. Ros expected the clouds to burst open at any moment with rain to wash the pink-hued walls that lined parts of the path.

'Famine walls?' Shane murmured and she presumed he wasn't asking so much as confirming.

'Yes, they litter the whole island, but in summer time, with the weather bright, they're fantastic when you look across the land and see them.' They were pink and mellow in straight lines going nowhere at all, but standing to attention all the same.

'It must be very striking,' he said and his voice was unexpectedly soft.

'I think so, but then maybe I'm just carried away on the notion of the place,' she said to cover over her embarrassment. They climbed the final hundred yards in silence. It seemed as if their long strides were in step most of the way and by the time they reached the summit Ros was ready to sit and drink some coffee to catch her breath.

'I think I understand now,' he said as they lay back against rocks that had managed to dry off in the morning breeze.

'What's that?'

'Why you called this place your adventure…' He looked at her. From here, the view across Clew Bay was amazing. Forty or more islands dotted the bay. Beyond the unfettered view it felt as if you were looking towards the end of the world. 'Yeah, that's what you said yesterday and I didn't understand. I just saw bogs and rocky fields, and then one of the men down at the pier said that there are days on end when no boatman worth his salt will even think about landing on the island.'

'That's very true.' They had been cut off for almost a week after Christmas. Ros thought it was the most glorious thing. Thankfully, she had Max's old chest freezer to work off. It had been packed up with fish and shop-bought bread and frozen berries that he must have spent most of the summer picking out of the hedges on his daily rounds. It was probably lucky he wasn't coming back; she had put a real dent in his supplies.

'And I suppose, when I think of adventure, you know, well, I think of trekking in Peru or doing voluntary work in some third-world country that welcomes Westerners who are happy to build homes even though the closest they've ever gotten to construction was a box of Lego or a three-D jigsaw puzzle.'

'Yeah, well, each to his own,' she said. That really marked out the difference between them. Well for some. None of that mattered now. At this moment, the only thing that concerned her was being here, in this rook's nest above the world, and she just wanted to enjoy the view. They sat there for a while in silence, both keeping their thoughts to themselves.

The actual work of testing the running streams took very little time, as she knew it would. They had already taken samples on their way up and the return journey to the cottage would be made on the east-facing side of the mountain. Over here, farmers let their sheep graze freely and you were as likely to run into a giant red deer as you might a herd of wild mountain goats.

'You've done a good job here,' he said as he took the final sample. The water was clear and there was evidence of thriving biodiversity with frogs, newts and even, in the lower reaches the previous day, salmon making their way back to breed.

'Thank you,' she said and, this time, she willed herself

to look him in the eye, because as much and all as she had enjoyed her time here, she had worked hard, she had given it her all. It had truly been a labour of love, but for that no less a demanding job at times.

'You're welcome,' he said and when he looked at her, for just a moment, she thought she saw something else at play behind his smile. Was he flirting with her?

They walked back to the cottage mostly in silence. Occasionally, Shane would comment on something he spotted in the distance, a falcon overhead or the waves crashing about a trawler making its way out to deeper waters.

'So, that's it.' He stood awkwardly by his boat later before setting back for the mainland. 'I mean, I probably won't see you around, you'll be finishing up soon and then back to city life,' he said and it felt as if he was asking her something, except she wasn't entirely sure what it was. As they stood there, she almost forgot about the fact that he had been so dismissive of her the previous day. For the briefest moment, she held her breath as a wordless tension sat between them and she wondered if he was going to lean forward and kiss her. Then the screech of a seagull broke the spell. Just as well.

'Hey,' a familiar deep voice called from along the pier. 'I've been looking for you, the vet's just finished on my farm. He's calling out to a sick calf over on the other side of the island, so he should be back at yours in the next hour or so…'

'Er, yeah, thanks…' Ros said, but she was completely discombobulated. What had just happened? Had Shane McPherson just been about to kiss her? She looked up at him now, distracted by Jonah Ashe, bloody nuisance of a man. 'Sorry, I better get back to George.'

'Hope he's all right,' Shane said softly.

'Fingers crossed,' she shouted as she backed away from him.

'Ros,' he called to her again, took in the space between them in a few long strides. 'Just... if you did find yourself over in Ballycove... um, if you fancied lunch or dinner or something, you know... give me a call, yeah?'

'Yeah, that might be nice,' she whispered, feeling her stomach flip because he was standing so close to her now.

'Do you want a lift back or not?' Jonah pressed the horn on his awful jeep.

'Sure.' Ros sighed. She didn't want to get in the car with Jonah, but it was a long walk back and she'd scaled a mountain already. 'I'm coming.' She rolled her eyes and Shane smiled as if they were sharing a joke just between them, before giving her a final wave and turning back towards his boat.

Ros climbed into the jeep with hardly enough time to fasten her seat belt before they were roaring away from the pier and out into the open countryside.

'So, that's the boyfriend, is it?' Jonah glanced across at her.

'No. He's a work colleague,' she said but she wanted to tell him it was none of his business what their relationship was.

'Just as well.' He shook his head as if confirming something.

'What's that supposed to mean?' she snapped.

'Well, he's a bit...'

'A bit what?'

'Smooth. Girl-in-every-port sort of fella. Not really your type, I'd have thought...'

'Excuse me?'

'Well, he's very,' he waited, as if trying to decide on a word, 'worldly, I suppose.'

'And I'm not?' What did he think she was, some sort of yokel like himself?

'I didn't say that.'

'You didn't have to and I'll have you know that we get on very well together and...' She felt her blood boiling. What right did Jonah Ashe have to go putting his oar in?

'I'm sure you do.' He shook his head and smiled to himself as if he knew something more than she did.

'What is it you're dying to say?' Was he trying to annoy her? 'Actually, no, I don't think I want to know, keep your comments to yourself. For your information, Shane McPherson is a lovely, professional guy and he's probably the only fella I've met since I've been here that I'd even consider going on a date with...' She could hear her voice rising, but there was nothing she could do to stop it. 'And, yes, if you must know, he did ask me out, but I haven't agreed to go on a date with him, just yet.'

'Hmph.' Jonah was staring straight ahead now, his features set in a mixture of cold fury and resignation, as if none of this was exactly news to him.

'But since you've already made your mind up about him, I'll take that as a positive sign, because I have a feeling that you and I will never agree on anything, Jonah Ashe.'

'No skin off my nose,' he said in a low voice that made it more than obvious he'd had enough of listening to her.

As they made their way back, bumping along the uneven roads, Ros's mind wandered across the water with Shane McPherson – maybe she *would* look him up and go for dinner with him. Why not? After all, he was attractive and interesting and, certainly, he seemed to love the countryside as much as she did.

12

Constance

The shrill sound of the phone ringing out made Constance jump. And with that, the old photograph she'd been looking at went flying and she watched as it sailed slowly to the floor. There was no time to pick it up, not if she wanted to make it to the hall table to catch the caller before they gave up. Constance had learned the value of moving more slowly a few years earlier, when she'd gone too fast and ended up in a tailspin and sprained her ankle in the process.

'Hello? Constance speaking...' She had answered the house phone in the same way for decades. Her mother had drilled it into her and, even if she thought about saying something different, it would probably take another decade to hammer it out of her.

'Oh Constance, thank God, you're there,' a voice Constance didn't recognise breathed, and yet, there was something in it that resonated with deep familiarity. 'It's Heather here, Heather…' Heather's voice faltered as if trying to remember her second name. 'Heather Banks.'

'Heather?' Constance felt her head begin to swim. Heather Banks. Dotty's daughter. Her body dropped rather than sat on the velvet-covered stool that was part of the telephone table. 'After all this time, Heather…'

It was as much as she could manage because, suddenly, she felt almost overcome and hardly noticed that huge tears of joy filled her eyes and were running freely down her cheeks.

'Yes, it's me, Constance.' And for a moment, Constance thought she could hear Heather on the other end of the line sob too; it felt as if a sigh of relief passed across between them.

'Is everything all right? How have you been? Oh, I've thought about you so often over the years and wondered…' Then she couldn't help it. 'And Dotty, I've regretted that argument every single day, I just…' It was the truth, but now, as the words tumbled out of her, all she felt was a relief to say them. 'Sorry, I'm just so happy to hear your voice and… how have you been, oh dear, I already asked you that but tell me anyway…' She was babbling, but it didn't matter.

'Oh, Constance, I've been…' Heather made a sound, a sort of mixture of a laugh and a cry. 'It's Mum, she's…'

'Oh no.' Constance knew already, maybe she'd known from the moment the first tear had escaped her. 'When?'

'Just over a week ago, I think, the days have sort of…' And it sounded as if Heather was searching for a calendar or a clock or something to explain.

'It doesn't matter. I'm so, so sorry, Heather,' Constance said and she was, really sorry, for Heather, but also for herself, because she'd missed the opportunity to put things right, not that she'd ever expected Dotty to let her, but there had always been that hope, lodged deep in her heart.

'It was peaceful, in the end, I think; she died in her sleep...' Heather was being kind, trying to spare Constance further upset.

'You're very good to tell me,' Constance said.

'I didn't even think, to start, but then...'

'I wouldn't have expected it, really, I'm sure you have a million things to think about.' And Heather sounded completely harried, too, not unlike Dotty used to sound when there'd been some small thing chewing on her nerves that she'd needed to get off her chest. Dotty was good at sharing the small things, the gone-off milk or the electricity bill that arrived on the wrong day, just as she'd spent all her money on a new coffee table. The big things she buried too deeply for her own good. Sometimes, Constance wondered if you could excavate a person – just how much had they all buried over the years?

'I'm... well, it doesn't matter how I am, the thing is...' Heather started. 'The thing is, I know this is going to come out of the blue, but she wanted to be buried on the island.'

'Oh.' It sounded like a squeak, as if a mouse had taken over Constance's voice. 'Really?'

'I know, I never saw that coming either, but maybe, near the end, things had begun to change with her,' Heather said softly.

'She wants to come home after all this time.' And once again, Constance felt tears fill up her eyes and flow down her cheeks. Strangely, she didn't feel sad, rather a rush of relief washed over her because Dotty was finally coming back to her.

'So, I was thinking I might go there in a week or two... I'm not sure of the dates myself yet, I mean, there are things to be taken care of here before I go...' Heather paused again as if she wasn't sure what had to be organised. 'And then, I haven't even thought about making arrangements over there, the plot for one thing and some sort of ceremony for another...'

'Don't worry about any of that, you can figure it all out when you get here. Father Rory will fit you in, we'll pick a day that suits and he'll be delighted to come across. It's not as if he's exactly run off his feet this time of year – mind you, come July and August, it can be a different matter...' Constance said. Everywhere filled up when tourists arrived on the island, she could only assume that went for the church too. Did people go to mass on their holidays anymore? She really wasn't sure.

'Oh, Constance, thank you, I couldn't think where to start.'

'Is it... I mean, is she already...? I mean, have you got Dotty's ashes there... with you?' Part of Constance didn't want to ask, because she liked the idea that Dotty was still pottering about her little house in London. Over the years, she'd imagined that house, a little like one from a sitcom on the telly, with tiny cosy rooms and the kitchen table always ready with a tea pot. Perhaps some geese flying up the wall and Dotty's umbrella leaning against a coat stand in the hall.

'Yes. All done. They called me this morning and I can collect them when I'm going. I thought maybe it would be nice, to spend a while on the island, but the hotel isn't answering their phone and all the bed and breakfasts are closed up for a few more weeks, so I think maybe I should stay on the mainland. Ballycove looks lovely, but I'm not sure if there's a ferry over or...'

'Don't be silly, you're not going to stay in some B&B, you're very welcome to stay here. I wouldn't like to be depending on the ferry across this time of year. It's okay in the height of summer, but really, if there's a storm or a swell, they mightn't travel across for a week at a time.'

'I couldn't impose on you like that, Constance. I'm planning on staying for a week or two... I really couldn't...' Heather sounded as if she was tossing over the idea of it and Constance understood, no-one wanted to be stuck with some silly old woman and not have an escape plan.

'Look, it's not The Ritz here, but I have a room for you. It'll be aired and you can stay for a night or two, just to get your bearings on the island and organise the funeral arrangements for Dot. Then, if you want to stay over in Ballycove, you can just book somewhere. I think that hotel opens all year round and it's very nice, much nicer than the one on the island, which is a bit grotty by comparison. You can travel around if that's what you'd like, but if you want peace and quiet and solitude, you won't find it any better than here at Ocean's End,' she said kindly. That was the truth of it: there was nothing for miles around except the sea and the calling gannets, gulls and whooper swans.

'Are you sure... I...' And even if she didn't say it, something about the urgency in Heather's voice sounded as if she needed to get out of London. Perhaps she needed the break away more than she realised.

'Of course I'm sure, I'd love to have you.' Then Constance remembered that she hadn't actually been upstairs in any of the bedrooms in ages and a sudden chill swept through her. 'Now, you might have to make your own bed and you'll definitely have to plug in the old two-bar electric heater to get the place cosy, but you're welcome for as long as you'd like to stay.' In spite of the sad circumstances for her journey, Constance was looking forward to seeing her.

'That's so kind, Constance, thank you. I'd love to stay with you and I'm not expecting The Ritz, don't worry, making up a bed is the least I could do. Actually, it'll make a nice change from packing things away. I'm clearing out Mum's house, before I go, so...' Perhaps that explained the troubled tone in her voice.

'Well, you just let me know when you're arriving and if there isn't a ferry crossing to suit, I'll ask one of the fishermen here to go and pick you up in Ballycove, okay?'

'Oh, Constance, you've no idea how much I'm looking forward to seeing you, I already feel as if I'm coming home,' she breathed with obvious relief in her voice.

'Good, I can't wait to see you too.' And she couldn't, because she had adored Heather as a little girl. They had walked for miles and picnicked on the beach most days when she'd come to stay. It had been Constance who had tucked her in at night while Dotty sat in Maggie's study and drank brandy and listened to stories of the glamorous London literary scene Maggie was part of when she travelled to meet her publishers. And Constance had relished every single moment with Heather. She would have kept her here, had begged Dotty to let her stay for school holidays and beyond, but Dotty was adamant that they were managing just fine.

'Oh, Constance, I'm so sorry,' Ros said when Constance told her about the phone call that evening. 'And you were best of friends?'

'When we were children, yes, but then, later, we had a falling-out, a terrible falling-out really, and after that Dotty made it very clear she wanted nothing more to do with me or with Pin Hill and so I never saw either of them again.'

That was how it had worked out. Constance had sent many letters, which were returned unopened, with just Dotty's familiar handwriting across the front. Eventually, sometime after her mother passed away, she'd stopped writing, had to face up to the fact that the friendship had died, and with it grew a huge regret for all that had been lost in its passing. They were so connected, far beyond any ordinary friendship; they *should* have been able to pick up the pieces from a silly argument. She still couldn't believe that Dotty was gone. It didn't feel real. But maybe when Heather came across and there was a ceremony, then, maybe.

Constance felt a tug once more at her heart; God, it had been a day filled with emotion. She'd cried for most of the afternoon at the news that Dotty was gone. But she'd made up her mind, she was not going to be miserable while Ros was here. She simply wouldn't allow herself to wallow for the next few hours.

'Here? She's coming to stay here? In the rooms upstairs?' Ros said then, as if she just realised something very important. 'But Constance, the room, it's...' She threw her hands up in the air. 'It's... You can't put anyone sleeping in there with the state of it at the moment.' And she shot up from the table.

'Hold on… what's wrong with it that a bit of heat won't put right?' Constance asked, because honestly, no-one had touched the room in years, it should be perfect, if a little dated.

'I'm sorry, I don't want to hurt your feelings, but it's damp and it smells of mould and…'

'Neglect?' Constance slumped into her seat.

'Well, let's say, it needs about twenty years of spring cleaning and a lot of freshening up.' Ros was too kind to say what they both knew: the rooms upstairs were probably in worse repair than the ones downstairs. 'Look, I'll just run up and open a window; do you have anything I can spray to cover over the…?' She cut her words short, perhaps trying to be delicate so as not to cause offence. Instead she walked to the kitchen sink and emptied out a basin, filled it with hot water and added a good measure of washing powder. 'I'll just spend an hour up there; if I open the windows for a few days, I'm sure the place will be right as rain.' She stood at the door for a second. 'I don't suppose you have an electric blanket?'

'An electric blanket?' Constance repeated, feeling a little stupid now; obviously she hadn't properly thought this through.

'Never mind, I'll see if we can't find one somewhere on the island to borrow for a few days until we can get one over from the mainland. We can make sure the bed is aired and if the place is nice and fresh, it'll be lovely.' Ros was still talking as she raced upstairs and Constance followed her out into the hallway, already feeling terribly guilty for having made the commitment to Heather without thinking it through.

'Not...' Constance broke off, but of course, she knew Ros wouldn't think of putting Heather into the room the crows had broken into.

'I thought perhaps the large room at the front?' Ros waited midway between steps.

'Perfect, the guest room, that'll be perfect.' Constance sighed with a small measure of relief.

13

Heather

A few days later, it was the woman from the pop-up bookshop in Charing Cross who messaged Heather with the news that she'd found a couple of Maggie Macken's novels among others in a box that she had agreed to take.

'Don't you want to keep them for yourself?' Heather asked, because the woman had seemed keen to pick up copies of her own.

'Some of these I already have, the rest are yours if you want them,' the woman said. 'It's your lucky day, but you'll need to come before lunch, because I'm off to the dentist in the afternoon.'

'Perfect.' Heather knew that even if the books were the same as the ones she'd unearthed on her mother's shelves, she was going to buy anything she could lay her hands on.

The stall was quiet, as Heather had expected, although inside the coffee shop seemed to be busy. It was, she could see, quite the place for gathering hipsters and the young and self-consciously upwardly mobile in the area. Through the glass door, she spotted a few pushchairs that looked more Rolls-Royce than casual stroller – wealthy wives with nothing to do but gossip and drink coffee. Heather remembered a time when the idea of having a baby seemed like a possibility. That was all a long time ago; funny, but even now, it still hurt in a dull sort of way when she thought about it.

'My son agrees with us, by the way.' The woman was packing one paperback after another into the tote bag Heather had brought along.

'Oh?'

'Yes, he thinks that they are ripe for republishing. He said any publisher worth his salt would be mad not to pay to get his hands on them, just to get them out into the world.'

'Your son is a fan?' Heather hadn't thought the books would be enjoyed by young men, but what did she know?

'No, I'm sorry to say he's not, he sticks to crime and thrillers, but he's a literary agent and he's always on the lookout for something he can help make into the next *big thing*.' The woman put her fingers up to make air quotes as she said it and she smiled fondly. 'He's always been the same, mad about books and a born salesman – he's only starting out, but he's already making a name for himself.'

'You must be very proud,' Heather said and she wondered again what it must be like to have a child and watch them grow into the person you had hoped they would become. 'Well, you never know, maybe he'll discover the next Maggie Macken and we'll all be queuing to buy her books in Waterstones when they come out.'

'You really are a fan.' The woman handed over the bag of books to her. 'These must have been stashed under a bed for a few years, certainly, sealed up, they're like new,' she said proudly, flipping over the pages of one she was keeping for herself. There was time to spare, it was the one thing Heather had too much of these days, and she found herself telling the woman about her own connection to the books, that her mother had known Maggie Macken and she'd been best friends with Constance for years. 'Oh, well, now, there's a real connection.'

'I'm going to see her soon to...' There was no need to tell this woman about the fact that she was returning to bring her mother's ashes to their final resting place.

'Oh, what I wouldn't give to be going on a little holiday.'

'Well, it's not a holiday exactly...' Heather began.

'What's not a holiday exactly?' a familiar voice said from behind her. She turned to see Philip, standing there and eating an apple as if he was out for a day trip and had all the time in the world to loiter about second-hand bookstalls. Of course, just like Heather, her ex-husband probably had too much time on his hands. When they'd sold their chain of flower shops, he'd had even less of an idea of what he wanted to do with himself than she had, if that was possible. The one thing they did know was that it was a sweet deal and they'd be crazy not to take it. Perhaps they'd both been relieved that their ties were completely severed; even if the divorce had been amicable, who wanted to go to work and face their ex day after day?

'This one, she's only off to Ireland, isn't she? Hobnobbing with the literary crowd too, by the sounds of things.'

'Hardly,' Heather sighed, because the way the woman

put it made it sound a million miles from the reality of what she was facing on Pin Hill Island.

'Ireland, eh?' Philip said, and the tone of his voice held a mixture of surprise and disdain. He'd never been a man to seek adventure outside his immediate postcode.

She looked at him now, taking in his overall appearance, and she realised she might easily have passed him by in the street if she hadn't been paying attention. He'd put on weight and there was that thing where you saw someone out of their normal context and somehow they looked different. He'd gotten older without her noticing it and she found herself putting her hand to her hair and wondering if he thought the same about her. Philip had changed. Then, maybe she only really remembered how he looked from years ago. Living and working with each other for so many years, they'd become almost invisible to each other long before she realised it.

'Heather.' A second familiar voice emerged from the path. Charlotte Turan – she hadn't seen her since they'd sold on the shops. Charlotte had intended to stay on, hoping to become manager once the new owners took over.

'Charlotte, oh my goodness, fancy seeing you here too, it really is like a reunion of…' And then, something dawned on her. Charlotte and Philip, together. Together, walking along on this street – what were the chances that could be just a coincidence?

'You look well,' Charlotte said, dragging her coat closed and unsuccessfully attempting to cover a medium-sized baby bump.

'As do you.' Heather tried to find firmer ground. It suddenly felt as if she'd stepped off the edge of familiar territory and she looked from Philip to Charlotte as if they might pass her a life ring. 'And you're both...' she started. She was vaguely aware of the woman on the stall moving away from them, obviously tuning into signals that must have been as loud as sirens to anyone passing by their little unexpected group.

'Together,' Philip said and he had the good grace to look embarrassed. 'Sorry, I should have said something,' he began, but then he looked between the two women, one the past, the other obviously now the future. After twenty years of marriage, Heather could read him like a book. He was torn, between apologising and gushing; he truly had found the most awkward position between rock and hard place. She wanted to tell him he should have told her, but pride wouldn't let her utter the words.

'And you're...' The most basic but crucial words seemed to evaporate from Heather. It felt as if the fundamental ability of speech had deserted her when she absolutely needed it the most.

'Having a baby.' Charlotte smiled. It was the sort of smile that Heather had always pinned down to a certain smugness that pregnant women managed to hold over their childless sisters. 'Yes, isn't it wonderful news, we're over the moon.' She let her coat fall open again, as if it was a big surprise and bound to make Heather's day.

'Well, that's...' Oh, God, she thought she was going to be sick, right here across Charlotte's obviously expensive coat and shoes. 'Congratulations.'

She didn't want to know when the baby was due or what they were going to call it, or whether they had moved in together or any of the finer details. Suddenly she just wanted the path to open up and swallow her. But at the same time a little part of her knew that later in the day, or maybe in a few weeks or months, it would drive her nuts that she hadn't asked. 'I'm surprised you didn't give me a call, to let me know, Philip,' she managed to say through gritted teeth.

'Well... I did think about it, but Charlotte said...' And there it was. He was still a *yes* man. They'd been together for some time before she realised she had married a man who was happier to do what he was told, far more than ever leading the way. He looked across at Charlotte. She was one of those forgettable people who passed through the florists, except, she never passed through. She'd stayed on and worked in the Covent Garden shop for five years. She was still as clueless about flowers when they sold the shop as she had been on her very first day. Her true calling to the business had always been the ability to talk rich clients into spending more money than they had intended to. Looking at her Miu Miu coat and Celine trainers, it seemed she hadn't lost her touch. Heather wondered if they'd have so much in common after she'd spent Philip's nest egg.

'And when are you due? You must be so excited.' Heather turned towards the positively preening Charlotte, who was hanging onto Philip's arm proprietarily.

'Oh, we have a little ways to go yet, but yes, I'm really looking forward to it.' She sounded as if she was about to launch into telling her about the shopping they'd obviously been doing for the baby, because it was only now Heather spotted that Philip was carrying a bag from La Coqueta. Even Heather knew that their babywear was out-of-this-world expensive.

'Surely not that long, unless you're having twins.' And

Heather heard her own laugh, but it was high-pitched, nervous, yes, maybe even a little hysterical.

'Please Heather…' Philip said, clearing his throat as if he somehow held the higher ground here.

'Right… I didn't mean…' Heather breathed, but it felt as if the air had been pulled out of the whole city around her and she might drown if she didn't make one final gasp. 'So…'

'You aren't on the WhatsApp group, are you?' Charlotte shook her head as if this was some terrible oversight.

'Sorry?'

'We set one up, well, I set it up, just to keep everyone in touch, you know, all the gang from the shops. I'll add you to it…' she promised, as if it was the one thing that would settle everything.

'That's Charlotte, always organising everyone…' Again, it sounded like an apology.

'Aww, darling,' Charlotte said and she reached up to kiss him. Inwardly, Heather shuddered.

'Well, I hope it all goes well for you both,' Heather said. And it was a confirmation of sorts: there was nothing more to keep her in the city. She looked back at the woman on the stall who had been listening from afar.

'So, I'll see you when you get back, yes? From that big event you have in Ireland.'

'Oh, I don't think I'll be back again for quite a while,' Heather said but she wanted to run behind the little bookstand and throw her arms around the woman for being everything that Charlotte was not.

'So, you *are* going to Ireland, I did hear you right at

first?' Philip said, trying his best to disentangle himself from Charlotte, but she was like bindweed, clinging to him.

'Yes, I'm going to Ireland.'

'Ireland? Oh dear, what's in Ireland, apart from leprechauns and shamrock?' Charlotte laughed at her own bad joke.

'Quite a lot as it turns out.' Heather hoped she managed to sound a little mysterious, even though her stomach was turning over with a million butterflies. 'My new start, for one thing, and I'm really looking forward to it,' she said before stalking off with as much dignity as she could muster.

God knew how she made it back to her mother's house in one piece. She really wasn't sure how she managed it, because even though she didn't cry, it felt as if the very core of her had been mined away and she was just hollowed out, like an empty sarcophagus pretending to be a real person. She moved from street to street as if on automatic pilot and, all the while, all she could think of was, she was going to Ireland.

As she sat in her mother's cramped kitchen later that evening, she remembered childhood summer holidays spent on Pin Hill Island. It seemed an awfully long journey back then, but she'd been just a child and it had always been worth it. She remembered too Ocean's End, the big art deco house overlooking the sea. It was all so glamorous and luxurious. She wondered if, like so many things, it might have shrunk or faded from the memories that played out comforting and welcoming in her mind's eye as darkness crept in over London.

Later, much later, she was still livid after meeting her

ex-husband and Charlotte; there was no making sense of Philip moving on so quickly. She pushed the idea of the children they might have had from her mind. If only they had been on the same page at the same time. She had to remind herself, she wasn't in love with Philip any more. She hadn't been for years. Even still, no matter how hard she tried to think her way past it, there was no getting away from the sense of complete and utter betrayal she felt now.

The following morning Heather woke to the sun streaming in through the kitchen window. She was starving: it had been too late to go and get something to eat the night before when she realised she hadn't thought of dinner. It felt as if the hunger pangs in her stomach were telling her something. She knew it was time to start moving forward, even if she didn't know where forward was. She tucked the notebook from beside her mother's telephone on the hall table into her handbag, before letting herself out the front door. Coffee, she needed coffee, she would go and have breakfast in the first café that looked as if it served a half-decent brew. Then, she would make a list of what she needed to do to tidy up her life in London before she brought her mother's ashes back to Ireland.

14

Ros

It felt like a strange relief to Ros when she sent off her application to the HR department. At least now it was out of her hands. Constance was right, if she didn't apply, then there was no chance of getting the job; worst-case scenario, she ended up not getting it, but at least she'd have tried. She had mulled it over a million times. On paper, she was more than qualified to take on the ranger's job – if anything, she was overqualified. Her honours degree was several points above the basic criteria outlined in the job spec. Admittedly, she'd had to shave off some of her previous relevant experience, but as Constance was quick to point out, hadn't she just spent the last year doing the job? Surely that was more than enough experience to qualify her to apply? So, with the unwitting help of Constance, she had smudged over the fact that it was entirely her fault that a senior manager had to resign. She was lucky they hadn't taken criminal proceedings against her for negligence or worse. She shivered; could they have done that? She wasn't sure, it was unlikely, but one of those irrational fears that crept up on her now and again. Even now, she felt sick when she thought of the damage done with one stupid conversation to the farmer who owned the land where the birds were nesting.

'I think you might have inherited your mother's talent for creative writing,' Ros murmured once she and Constance had agreed on the body of the letter.

'Oh no, nothing creative about it, that's all true – you've done a great job, probably more than Max Toolis managed in all the years he spent here on the island.'

It was at times like this that Ros was crippled with guilt. She should come clean, with Constance at least – tell her the truth of the terrible damage she was responsible for in the past. All the saved wild goats in the world couldn't make up for the guilt she felt about it.

'I don't know about that, but I do know that I've loved every minute of it and if I did some good, well, I've had a lot more in return. I never understood before what a labour of love was, but now...' Ros knew it wasn't just the work she'd done for the Parks and Wildlife Service, but the little jobs she'd taken on around Ocean's End had given her a great sense of satisfaction also.

'Well, with that letter and your CV, they'd be crazy not to give you the job.' Constance squeezed her hand and got up to pop the kettle on again. Darkness tramped slowly across the fields and neither of them had anywhere else to go, so, very often, after Ros had spent a few hours in the afternoon setting the place to rights, she would sit here until late. It seemed they never ran out of things to chat about. Sometimes, she wondered at how their friendship had come about. Though they'd only known each other for a matter of weeks, Ros felt as if they'd been connected for a lifetime. She wondered fondly too, as she watched the old woman rummaging about for homemade shortbread biscuits in the tin, if this was what it felt like to have a grandmother you loved deeply. She'd never had that. It had always been just her and her mum.

When she set the biscuits out between them, Constance sighed. 'The lock on the bathroom window came off in my hand this morning,' she said with a sort of resignation that was out of character for her.

'Hardly the end of the world, I'm sure we can find another one to replace it with. Max Toolis has a shed filled with everything from old taps to chair casters, there's bound to be something we can use.'

'We both know, if I keep going the way I'm going, the place is going to fall in on top of me soon.' Constance didn't need to add the fact that upstairs the smell of damp and must and mould had to be unhealthy to live in, but Ros had thought it from the first day she'd broken through that open window. She was doing her best to put one room to rights for the arrival of Heather Banks, but really, the whole house was in need of a lot more than just scrubbing and polishing.

'Look, I can have a look at the roof too. I mean, it's easy to take a walk across it and see if there are leaks, at least you'd know that it was weather-proofed,' Ros said, although she'd never fixed a roof in her life. Then again, she'd never rescued a kid goat either and she wasn't doing a bad job of that. At least he was still alive, if not exactly up and running. 'I mean, there can't be all that much to it, just a bit of patching up. I'm sure there's going to be some sort of how-to video on YouTube if I look it up.' It was a flat roof, how hard could it be?

'Ah, Ros, I really appreciate the offer, but I'm not even sure if the roof is safe to walk across. For all I know there could be enough water lodged up there to drown in and God knows how strong the structure is to carry even a little thing like you.'

'Well, I could just take a look...' She knew there was a spiral staircase leading up and onto the roof. Probably, when it was built, the idea was that you could just walk up there and look out across the ocean. 'I'd actually love to get a look at it. It must have an extraordinary view.'

'Oh, it did have, I mean, in the summer, my mother and I...' Constance said with a tinge of sadness in her voice. 'We would have picnics up there and sunbathe when the weather allowed.'

'That sounds idyllic.' And Ros couldn't decide which part sounded lovelier, sitting with that backdrop of the Atlantic washing in beneath you, the sun on your skin, or the idea of having someone you were so close to that you could just spend hours on end enjoying their company in the sunshine.

'Those were happy days.' Constance murmured. 'But they were a very long time ago and no-one has been up on that roof in thirty years, or twenty at the very least,' she corrected. 'I couldn't let you up there, who knows what it's like now, you could fall right through it. I'd never live with myself if I was the cause of you falling from that height.'

'Not if I go up through the stairs.'

'I'm not sure that door even opens any more and if there is a lake of rainwater up there, you'll never push it out.' Ros could see even the thought of anyone going up there worried Constance. 'Oh, don't take any notice of me, I'm just weary of it all. Maybe I've buried my head in the sand too long already, sometimes it feels as if between us – me and the house – we're both just hanging on to see the other out.'

'Ah, Constance, wait a few weeks. When the sun starts to shine and warm everything up and the flowers are out, you'll remember why you love living here so much. Everyone feels a bit jaded after the long winter months.'

'You know you're better than any tonic; wise beyond your years.' Constance smiled.

'Ah yes, so I've been told. I'm an old soul at heart,' she said softly, because in the last few years she'd had to learn to be her own mother and grandmother.

That evening, on her way back to the cottage, Ros had to drop into the supermarket to pick up some basics. Shane McPherson had finished off her carton of milk in one long glassful before he left for the mainland and what was life without a cup of tea before you left the house in the morning?

It was this thought that forced her through the doors of the supermarket, in spite of the fact that she saw that familiar jeep parked up against the path outside. If it was for something like chocolate, she could have done without, but maybe, if she skipped down to the cool aisle quietly and made her way out quickly, with change ready to pay, she might avoid him.

It was not to be, unfortunately. The door swung in violently just as she laid her hand against it to push, almost sending her tripping over herself across its threshold. She managed to right herself in time to catch the trace of a smirk on Jonah Ashe's lips.

'Ah, it almost feels as if you're following me.' He held the door open for her and the only good thing she could think was, at least he was leaving. 'How's the—'

'He's fine. Improving.' Or at least he was still alive, still hanging on; it was as much as the vet had promised for now.

'Well, that's something, I suppose.' He looked towards his jeep meaningfully and she thought perhaps he was wondering if she wanted another lift back to the cottage.

'Mustn't keep you,' she said, swinging beneath his arm, as he continued to hold the door open.

'Are you sure you're…' He nodded towards the jeep, perhaps expecting her to come out loaded down with a week's worth of shopping.

'No, no, I'm in a bit of a rush actually,' she said and she nodded towards old Mrs O'Brien, who was idling around the chocolate display at the register.

'Is that fella bothering you?' Mrs O'Brien asked moments later when she'd picked up a carton of milk and chocolate she definitely didn't need from the display.

'Ah, no, he's…' Ros knew, as an outsider, it was better to pick your words carefully about the other islanders. From what she could tell, most of them were either related to each other or had been friends for years. You couldn't say a word without danger of putting your foot in it.

'Well, between me and you now,' the old lady leaned

forwards, lowering her voice, 'I'd give *him* a wide berth.' Then she put up her hands as if stopping Ros saying a word. 'No, no, I know, he's easy on the eye, I was young myself once, I remember what it was like to see a man with a good pair of shoulders and eyes you could swim in, but there's been a bit of talk about him doing the rounds, recently.'

Easy on the eye? Ros felt she would rather drink curdled milk than admit to anyone she found Jonah Ashe attractive at this point.

'No, no, I wasn't...' Ros tried to get a word in, but Mrs O'Brien could be deaf when it suited and was known to enjoy a juicy nugget of gossip.

'He was married, see?'

'Well that's not exactly...'

'Oh, I know, it's modern times and even the visiting rector is onto his second wife, but here's the thing. Jonah Ashe married one of those lovely Lucas girls from Ballycove, you must know them; their mother owns the dress shop. Lovely girls, the eldest of them was a model at some point. All very glamorous, tall and elegant and tanned as walnuts the lot of them, all married well.'

She halted then, as if she'd just stepped down from a lovely dream. 'That is, they all married well, except the poor girl that married that ne'er-do-good. Too easy on the eye, that's his problem, and of course, when they are that good-looking, there'll always be temptations.'

'So, he met someone else?'

'From what I've heard, she was working away as a nurse, came home after a night shift and found him in their marital bed with some floozy. No-one in the village could understand what on earth he was thinking, when he had such a lovely girl...'

'Well, who knows how people think.' Ros placed her change on the counter, then pushed it closer to the old shopkeeper, who seemed to have clear forgotten that she was meant to be taking payment for the carton of milk and the bar of chocolate she'd just rung up on the register.

'You be wise now, don't go falling for him. He's over here, running old Johnny Ashe's land as if it was his life's calling, when everyone here knows he's only running away from all the trouble he made back on the mainland.'

'Huh, they might say the same about me,' Ros said under her breath, because even if she hadn't left behind a wronged spouse, she certainly had escaped to Pin Hill Island and maybe she, too, was hiding from reality.

Eventually, she managed to pay for her groceries and walked back to the cottage deep in thought. Her head was somehow filled with the information Mrs O'Brien had passed along, and wouldn't make room for anything else. It felt as if that uneven feeling she'd had about Jonah Ashe made more sense now. After all, what sort of man moved to a place like this and contented himself with falling into the life so recently vacated by his recently deceased bachelor uncle? Yes, Ros decided, she'd definitely be giving him a wide berth from here on, if she could manage it.

It seemed to take an eternity from the closing date of applications for the Parks and Wildlife human resources department to come back to her. The email arrived just as she was sitting down to lunch in the cottage. It pinged through loudly on her phone.

'Oh my God, OH MY GOD!' She called Constance immediately. 'I can't believe it. I have an interview.' And as soon as she had said it, that crumbling feeling began to grind away at her insides – of course she got an interview, she'd basically lied on the application form. She hadn't mentioned Wild Bird Ireland or the dreadful damage she'd been responsible for there.

'Why wouldn't you have an interview! I told you, they'd be mad not to give you the job with bells on.' Constance said as if there had never been any question about it.

'Oh, my…' The enormity of it suddenly hit Ros.

'What? What is it?'

'It's just…' She couldn't put it into words, she could hardly think of it without wincing. 'I suppose, it's just nerves, there's so much riding on this one interview.' And that was true too, because she so desperately wanted to stay on the island, in spite of the fact that, deep down, she really didn't feel as if she deserved to.

'It's not the great political debate of the century. I'm sure they'll just ask about what's on your CV and maybe…' Constance raised a finger, as if plucking thoughts from the air. 'Where you see yourself in ten years? Isn't that one they always ask?' she settled on. Then she said, 'Of course, you can ask your best friend Google, he hasn't put you wrong yet.'

'There's a big difference between learning to bottle-feed a kid goat and actually being able to blow your own trumpet when you're nervous as hell.' Ros was grateful for the seemingly unlimited faith that Constance had in her.

'I'm sure there's no difference at all worth talking about and you won't be nervous, you just have to be yourself and they will love you,' Constance said with more confidence than Ros felt.

'I'm not so sure about that,' she said and she meant it. The vibe she usually got off Keith Duff had always been biting impatience at best. Not once had she felt that he actually saw her as anything more than a gap in a fence that had to be closed permanently at some point.

'Keith Duff is just one man in probably hundreds working for Parks and Wildlife,' Constance said airily. 'You just need a chance to shine, that's all. Between us we'll have you well prepared for that interview. Maybe you could ring up Max Toolis and ask him for tips, or what about that McPherson man who visited, maybe he'd...'

'Oh no, I couldn't ask Shane.' Not after that moment on the pier when it felt as if they might be about to kiss. The last thing she wanted was to have him think she was ringing him up as an excuse so he'd ask her out on a date. Nor did she particularly want him to think that she hadn't the professional confidence to go for an interview without turning to someone who wasn't even in the job for guidance. Had she been crazy to apply for the job in the first place? Her gut was telling her now she hadn't a snowball's chance in hell of getting it, regardless of how wonderful Constance thought she was or how much she tried to bolster her confidence.

15

July 1957

Dotty

It was in the house in Galway; it was an evening like any other. Dotty had raced downstairs when her mother called her from the front sitting room in a voice that bordered on an impatient scream.

'Help your father, will you, there's a good girl,' she said distractedly. 'He's in the kitchen, sorting out that leaking pipe at last.' Her mother was hanging wallpaper. All day long she'd been in there, with lengths of paper and paste and climbing up and down on kitchen chairs and then wiping the sheets into place. Now, she was red-faced, exhausted probably. It was her first time doing it and, even though she refused to give in, Dotty knew matching up the intricate pattern was driving her mother to the edge of reason. Earlier in the day, Dotty had been drafted in to help, but quickly her mother had run out of patience and sent her outside, claiming she was only getting under her feet.

'Come along, Dotty,' her dad called from beyond the kitchen door. 'Best leave your mother to it.' He was wearing an old pullover, so it seemed he too had been enlisted in this vicious midsummer clean that had grown into an overhaul of the downstairs of their house. 'I'm fixing that leaking pipe your mother has been going on about for the last few days,' he said, although he hardly needed to tell her, because the contents of the cupboard beneath the sink lay emptied out onto the kitchen floor. 'Will you go find me a spanner?' He nodded towards the door beneath the stairs where her mother kept everything they hardly ever used.

Dotty pushed in the door. She hated this cupboard; it was dark here and smelled of the remains of last winter's turf bags, which everyone knew were full of earwigs and beetles. Gingerly, she began to feel along the shelves for something that might be a spanner. Her fingers traced lightly across each shelf before her, her eyes scrunched up, her breath held, trying not to think about spiders and creepy-crawlies.

'Dotty, are you coming?' he called again. 'I need that spanner now if I ever want to get this job done for your mother.'

She felt beads of sweat race from her palms. She loved her father, she really did, but sometimes she couldn't push aside the feeling that something was amiss. She'd never felt the back of his hand in punishment, but with his eyes he could undo her in an instant.

'I'm trying to find it,' she called back.

'Oh, for goodness' sake,' he said and she heard him struggling out from beneath the sink. Next she knew, he was squeezing beside her in the tiny cupboard. Her mother was oblivious to the search for a spanner, completely caught up in matching up the gauzy flower design of the wallpaper across the hall.

'Isn't this a tight squeeze?' Her father's whisper sounded strange, as if it came from a variation of himself Dotty did not recognise.

Suddenly, Dotty felt herself shoved into the back of the cupboard, as her father behind her pulled the door closed quietly but firmly. Fear and panic gripped her, it was as black as if her eyes were tightly shut. She opened them wide, but there was only a sliver of light from beneath the door. More than that, she sensed a danger in the darkness. Her father pushed up against her, hard and sweating; Dotty thought she would be sick and then he whispered in her ear, 'shh, it'll only take a minute.' He was groping at her dress, fumbling with his own clothes. She was gasping for breath, the air so stale that it was suffocating, she couldn't breathe.

She tried to scream but found her voice stuck at the back of her throat, panicking she stamped her foot on his, heard him gasp and felt him crumple away from her. In a flash, she slipped out around him, rushing to her mother in the sitting room. The devil himself could not have persuaded her to go back into that hallway again until she heard him take his coat from the rack and shout in through the door that he'd *finish the damn pipe another day*, he was going to the pub.

16

Heather

Heather looked around her mother's house and couldn't help but feel that now she had almost emptied it, the emotion was not one of satisfaction or even loneliness, but rather disappointment. Perhaps she had expected to feel too much. The reality was, Heather had spent years of her life mourning the loss of her mother into the depths of a spirit bottle; her actual passing was almost an anti-climax by comparison. Dotty had slipped away from her years ago. Oh, they spoke once a week on the phone. Heather rang her, every Thursday evening at seven thirty. A perfunctory five minutes of enquiring after each other's lives, which always felt as if it was an intrusion into her mother's bland routine of soap operas, game shows and constant vodka top-ups. Strangely now, her death felt as if someone had only closed the door long after she had left the room.

Maybe, back on Pin Hill Island, Heather thought she might feel more – she wanted to feel more, she wanted to feel something, because at the moment, all she felt was numb.

There was very little left in the house now. Just the fitted kitchen and appliances and a small box of keepsakes that she had put aside because she knew they should mean something, but she really wasn't sure what she should do with them. She had kept all of her mother's copies of Maggie Macken's books. Those, she had packed up carefully and placed with her other belongings that she'd committed to long-term storage when they'd sold the flat. The tote bag now in her arms contained little things that reminded her only of her mother. There was the funny little wooden box for Constance, she'd left that on the hall table, she mustn't forget that, she reminded herself now. Perhaps Constance could tell her more about it when she gave it to her, maybe she'd have a key. Heather had searched the house looking for it and she was convinced now: it was not here. She kept out a few pieces of jewellery and an almost empty bottle of her mother's favourite perfume, the aroma of which brought Heather right back to her childhood. She didn't suppose her mother had worn it in thirty years, and yet, somehow, it evoked happier times when it had seemed as if they were just like every other family who lived along their little road. After all that, there was quite a bit to carry, the box, her bag, her coat over her arm because the day was warmer than expected. Just before she left the house, she placed her door key on the bottom step of the stairs. Somehow, perhaps overtaken by unexpected nostalgia, she completely forgot about the ornate letter box her mother had wanted her to take to Constance. And there was no going back for it then, even if she did remember it.

Once outside, she looked up, as she pulled out the front door. The estate agent had already hung a 'For Sale' sign. This house had been in the Banks family for many years, her father's aunt had owned it, once, but it was time to let it go.

The click of her seat belt on the half-empty plane to Knock airport felt almost like a punctuation mark. Despite the early-morning sleepiness of the other passengers Heather couldn't help but feel that this was not the end of a sentence, but rather the start of a new paragraph. She couldn't dare to hope it might even be the opening of a new chapter.

She hadn't been in Ireland since she was a child and her memory had been one of a long ferry journey, followed by a succession of buses, trains and finally a fishing boat ride to the island; all of which probably added up on both ways to being as long as the holiday itself. Looking back, she supposed it was as much a pilgrimage as a holiday to her mother. It was a sweet filling to the otherwise dreary sandwich of life that was busy streets, red-brick houses and buses that always ran late. Strange to think of her mother going back there now, to be buried in that little graveyard on the side of a hill, because really, so far as Heather knew, all in all, Dotty had only spent a handful of years on the island. Teenage years too, a time when she had felt the place was far too small to contain her dreams. She'd left just after finishing school for bright lights that dazzled more from afar. Showbiz had given her a sum total of two chorus line parts in a decade before she'd married and settled in that little house in Fulham. Sometimes Heather wondered, would her mother have been as well off staying on the island, would she have been any happier? In hindsight, it was mainly pride that kept her from moving back after the divorce. Couldn't face the disapproval, that's what she'd said once, and it had seemed so odd to think that her mother had ever cared what anyone thought of her.

This time round, the flight took just over an hour. From there, it was a bus ride to the coast, albeit via the scenic route. Heather had a feeling that they stopped by every little village along the way to pick up and drop travellers who for the most part were pensioners making what they could of their free travel pass.

It was pleasant, being driven along, eavesdropping on the conversations around her and drinking in a landscape that felt a million miles from London. Here, it was green fields that ran as far as the eye could see, cut through with wonky walls built of stone and held together by wildflowers and weeds. In the distance thick clouds lounged on military green and grey mountains with the promise that beyond them the sea lay, vast and waiting.

Ballycove. She remembered it well from when she was last here and now it seemed as if it had somehow been held in a time warp. Everything was smaller, fresher, a gleam of modernity catching the light from under the squatting cottages and the tall Georgian houses on the hill. There were obviously new roofs, solar panels and wind turbines off in the distance, but at the same time, there was a feeling of familiarity about the place that she couldn't quite quantify.

'Ye'll have to wait for the next tide, I'm afraid,' an old man bent over knotted nets on the quay told her.

It was too early in the season for the regular ferry trips across and Constance had organised for one of the local fishermen to meet her and bring her over.

'You can go for a wander round, if you want. There's plenty to do in the village, a nice bookshop and, of course, the hotel is open, if you fancy lunch,' Finbar Lavin told her, when he pulled up to the pier just after her. He looked as if he'd spent his life at sea, his face was fresh, washed clean by the salty winds, and his eyes were as clear as a summer's day. If it was possible to make your mind up completely about someone, Heather thought she liked him, she would feel safe in a boat in the very worst of waters with him.

'Thanks, I'll do that. When will we be ready to go...?' She was conscious the man didn't need to be out on the water as darkness drew in, better to make the journey earlier than later.

'About two hours, I have a little business to attend to first, plenty of time for you to get a bit of grub to keep you going.' Finbar smiled at her and raised his hand before turning back to his boat. He was scrubbing down the deck, clearing away any waste from his early morning catch.

It was pleasant to wander about the village. Heather took him at his word and dropped into the local bookshop, where she picked up another of the Maggie Macken books that she had assumed would be impossible to find.

'Ah yes, I think the previous owner, he had boxfuls of those novels stored everywhere,' the woman at the counter said. 'It seems every housewife in the village devoured them, over and over, but then they're of an age.' She was American and far more elegant than Heather remembered anyone being in Ballycove. 'Joy Blackwood.'

Heather introduced herself and they chatted for almost half an hour. She had a feeling that if she came here very many times, she and Joy would surely become firm friends.

The trip across to the island was colder than she remembered from her last visits. In the little fishing boat, about halfway across the bay, Finbar placed a huge oilskin jacket over her shoulders. Her teeth had begun to chatter and they'd laughed when she'd tried to convince him that she was hardly cold at all.

When they reached the island, a girl dressed in a coat that surely belonged to her granny introduced herself as the official welcoming committee, Ros Stokes.

'Well, when I say committee,' she smiled then, 'Constance sent me, to make sure you made it back okay.'

'You can't mean to tell me you expect Heather to walk from here.' Finbar shook his head as if there was no way he was having that. 'Come on, the pair of ye,' he said and he hoisted Heather's bags across the back seat of an ancient jeep that smelled of a combination of sea air and dog hair. Heather had a feeling that the dominant aroma would always depend on whether the windows were opened or closed.

'Constance is so looking forward to seeing you.' Ros leaned forward so she could chat to Heather as they bumped along the uneven roads.

'I'm looking forward to seeing her too. It's strange, but I hadn't thought about this place in years and then with my mother...' Heather said and she wondered if perhaps she should have made it her business to visit the old woman before this. Until that moment, the notion had never entered her head; after all, Constance had been her mother's friend – until she wasn't any more. With Dotty, even reaching out to her could be enough to cause a rift that could go on for months between them. 'These last few days, I've felt as if Ocean's End is drawing me back.' And she glanced back towards the largest of her cases, the one she'd packed her mother's ashes in. Perhaps she'd needed to get out of London more than she realised. This journey felt as if it was inching her heart open wider with every mile she travelled. 'I'm *really* looking forward to seeing her too,' she said again and she smiled because she really was. 'I worshipped her when I was a kid, she was such a force of kindness.'

'Join the club,' Finbar said. 'Every kid on the island adored Constance, for all the years she taught at the local school, you won't hear one bad word about her.'

'She's, ahem...' Ros bit her lip, perhaps trying to pick out the right words.

'Not as young as I remember her?'

'Well, yes, probably and the house – Ocean's End – it's...'

'I adored it as a child. It was so different to where we lived in London.' It wasn't just the house; it was Constance more than anything. It was having bedtime stories and hot chocolate in the little tent they'd made in the garden from old sheets hung across a broken fence.

'If it's a while since you've visited, it's probably not quite what you remember,' Finbar said softly. He'd turned off the engine, waiting while a farmer herded what felt like an unending line of sheep before them from a field on one side of the road to a similar field on the other side.

'Constance showed me a photograph of you both when you were last here, the house was in the background and, well...' Ros wavered. Heather assumed she was trying to pick her words tactfully. 'She's on her own, you see, there's no-one to help with the upkeep. A place like that takes quite an amount of maintenance to keep it standing. I don't suppose that there's the money to do much either so the house has fallen into...'

'Disrepair?' Heather smiled. It was kind of Ros to prepare her for the worst, but she knew that too much time had passed for things to be as she remembered them. Hadn't she had the biggest reminder of that with her own mother passing away and having just had to empty out their little house in London?

'Well, that's a kind way of putting it, but I suppose, if I tell you that there was a crow's nest being built in one of the bedrooms upstairs at one point, it might give you a better idea of what to expect.'

'Oh, poor Constance,' Heather said and she immediately felt guilty. It was one thing to have accepted that there was little she could offer her own mother beyond the practicalities of keeping the roof over her head and some sort of comfort around her, but she knew, in her heart, all Constance would have asked for was an occasional phone call and she would have offered a listening ear and so much more in return. 'I should have kept in touch,' she said quietly now.

'I think she would have liked that, but it's never too late to start,' Ros said.

'Okay, we're off again.' Finbar pushed the gear stick

forward and turned over the engine. They barrelled along the road and soon he flicked on the indicator and the jeep turned down into the familiar avenue leading up to Ocean's End.

Heather watched as the house peeked over the land, revealing itself inch by inch as the jeep rumbled closer. The chimney stacks, when they were visible, looked somehow more shrunken than they had before. Heather remembered them as huge gleaming white beacons against blue skies. Today they were little more than ashy squats, the blackest one puffing smoke towards a gloomy sky. The house, as it emerged from the overrun garden, had not so much lost its lustre as fallen into the sort of shabby neglect that made you suspect it had been abandoned years ago.

'Come on, she'll have the kettle boiled a thousand times over waiting for us.' Ros giggled as she flung open the doors and reached in to take out Heather's bags.

'Oh, Constance.' It was all Heather could manage. She was still sitting in the front of the jeep, hardly able to pull herself onto the path, so broken was her heart at seeing what the place had fallen into. She waited for all of a minute until the front door pushed open and the familiar shape of Constance Macken emerged from the darkness beyond.

'You're here.' The old woman stood a moment, smiling towards the jeep.

'Constance.' It was hardly a word, but when Heather breathed it, it felt as if every fibre in her being somehow relaxed. 'Constance.'

She flung open the door of the jeep and leapt from it, onto the overgrown gravel path, racing towards the woman who had meant so much to her when she was young.

'It's been too long. I'm so sorry, I should have called or

written or something...' And then, tears were moistening her eyes as she buried her head in Constance's shoulder and neck and she was overcome with a feeling of love and belonging such as she'd never really felt before.

'Don't be silly, I'm just glad you're here now. Come on in, pet.' All the while, with her soothing voice, it felt as if Constance was comforting Heather, with pats on her back and the very essence of lily of the valley coming from her clothes and even her hair.

'I never thought, I never realised...' What? Heather knew what, she knew exactly what – she had missed this place, even though it had only been the stem of a memory, from the very root of her childhood, she had missed this place, as others miss a loved one. 'I'm so glad to be back here, Constance, so glad.' And she knew, it didn't matter if the whole house fell down around them, she was just glad to be here.

'Don't be fretting now, I have tea in the pot and sure, doesn't that always make things better,' Constance said in that lovely soft accent and Heather felt herself carried along between her bags and her baggage and Ros and Finbar and of course Constance into the welcoming embrace of Ocean's End.

17

Ros

Heather proved a godsend. That's what Constance called her and Ros, although she'd never been one much for gods or angels or saints, thought Constance might be right.

It was Heather who supplied the smart suit that Ros wore as she waited to be called into the interview room. It was, she realised, the first time she'd ever had to wear a suit for an interview. Before this, she'd fallen into jobs. Her first job, with Wild Bird Ireland, had been a lucky break – she had ambled up to a table on careers day at university, struck up a conversation and ended up falling into an internship of sorts starting the week after she graduated. Her last job working in a busy city centre bar had simply been a case of spotting a notice in the window and asking for the job. So far as she knew, in both cases, she'd been the only applicant. This thought didn't exactly bolster her confidence for today, but in an effort to be optimistic, she had to admit that at least she was the only candidate sitting here and waiting for an interview. In fact, there was only one chair placed in the corridor outside the interview room.

She suspected the room was used for everything and anything, but someone had stuck a foolscap page on the door with sticky tape, grandly asking for 'Quiet please, interviews in progress'.

She'd been sitting here for almost half an hour now, waiting for someone to call her in, afraid to take the notes from her pocket that Heather and Constance had helped her to write up for the interview. They'd been bloody smashing, both of them, really. Constance so wanted her to get this job, sometimes it felt as if she wanted it just as much as Ros did herself. As for Heather – well, she probably had more experience interviewing people for jobs than any number of old hands that might be wheeled out to grill her today.

And Ros knew she would be grilled. Because even if she'd done a brilliant job, it was fairly obvious, the more she talked to people, there had never been a female ranger in this neck of the woods. Certainly, there had never been one stationed on any of the islands in the history of the state. From what she could see, thanks to the website, female rangers mostly ended up in desk jobs. They were to all intents and purposes glorified secretaries and administrators.

When she'd told Max she was applying for his old job, he'd nearly choked on the cup of tea his sister had handed him. It wasn't that she was underqualified; Max's only qualification for the job was that he'd worked for a few years with inland fisheries and he'd had a yearning to get away from it all. Island life – or maybe it was more reclusive life – suited him. He told her he'd been the only applicant for the job. That was twenty-five years ago. Now the ranger's job was better paid, it meant graduates with all sorts of experience would be interested in the post. 'Apparently,' he told her with some amusement, 'there's a fella over in Ballycove who spent the last twenty years working with a foundation to save the Indian tiger. He's come back to Ireland because his kids are ready for college and his wife has had enough of hot weather to last her a lifetime.' Well, she'd never be able to compete with that. She knew too, the added bonus of a free cottage thrown in made it even more attractive.

Ros sighed; she loved everything about the role and not just the cottage. Although she had to admit that having a place to call her own was a sort of heaven she'd never dared to dream she might experience. The job was challenging at times, but it was fulfilling in a way she'd never imagined work could be and she adored the island, everything about it, from the people to the landscape. She loved it in every season. Even on those days when the rain felt as if it might cut slices from your skin, she loved watching it dance on the water in the distance. She had friends here, good friends, chief among them Constance. In fact, maybe because they had no-one else, Constance felt more like family than a friend, like a great old aunt you were particularly fond of, while still feeling that intense bond of something that went deeper than just the blood running through your veins.

Constance was a one-off. She lived like a poor church mouse and yet always had something *in* for when Ros called to visit. It made her feel as if she couldn't do enough for her.

Clearing a path or making up the room for Heather coming to stay seemed such small things in return for the deepest friendship she'd ever experienced in her life.

She found herself smiling as the door opposite opened to reveal a familiar face.

'Shane?' she managed and felt her cheeks go red. For a second she felt as if she'd lost her balance, trying to figure out if he was interviewer or interviewee. But there was an air about him, unmistakable: he was here to impress. 'You applied for the job?' She couldn't quite believe it. Why on earth hadn't he mentioned anything when they'd talked about it on the island? And then, suddenly, her next thought – if she herself was overqualified, Shane was overqualified with bells on, she hadn't a snowball's chance against him.

'Yeah, sure, it seems like a nice job and you weren't sure you'd go for it, so I thought...' He managed to look embarrassed. Then he remembered where he was and looked back towards the interview room behind him. 'I think I'd really enjoy the work and make a big difference, so of course I had to apply.'

'But you're...' Ros wanted to say a consultant, a freelancer, an environmental engineer. But of course, all of those things meant nothing and everything if he just wanted a place to put down roots and make a living each week that didn't fluctuate depending on when clients chose to pay him.

'Perfectly suited to the job?' he smiled and she felt as if she was just giving him an opportunity to impress the interviewers within earshot even further. 'I know, but I just feel a real connection to the place. I want to be a part of restoring it to what it could be with a little care.'

'Oh, well...' She wasn't sure what to say. Later, she would try and find something positive about sitting there like a rabbit caught in headlights and the best thing she could come up with was that at least all thoughts of that near kiss had deserted her. The embarrassment she might have expected to feel had evaporated in the face of almost certain defeat.

The nerves Ros had struggled with earlier multiplied when a woman appeared in the doorway behind Shane. Sonia Mellet introduced herself. She sashayed her way into the middle chair behind a long table that was serving as an interview desk. On either side she was flanked by two old codgers who looked as if they'd been dug out of a locked cabinet from the cold war. At the end of the desk, Keith Duff shuffled papers as if he'd lost his lunch money and it was long past his dinner time.

'So.' Sonia fixed Ros with an even stare. 'You've been filling in the ranger's post for the last couple of weeks?' She glanced at the CV before her, but her voice softened as she murmured her name. 'Ros?'

'Weeks, well actually it's months, really, I'm there since the start of last summer, so nearly a year in fact...' she said, and if the temperature was freezing in the atmosphere from the end of the table, she found herself warming to Sonia – two women together in a male-dominated industry.

'Yes, about that...' One of the older men, Tom, looked at her now. 'Well done, I've read some of your reports, you've done a fair job, considering...' He sniffed loudly.

'And so I suppose, we're on to your education and suitability for the post. You seem well qualified for the job?'

'Yes,' Ros answered and began to expand on her degree course and elements of it that she thought most relevant to being a wildlife ranger.

'Won't you get lonely, out there on the island?' the other older man – Captain Jeffers – asked. 'You're from the city originally?'

'I am from Dublin. But I don't have family there any more. My mum died, before I graduated, and there had always been just the two of us, so…'

'That's unfortunate,' Tom murmured.

'I think what Tom means is that we're so sorry to hear that,' Sonia said.

'Thank you,' Ros said, because it was what you were meant to say.

'The big question is, of course, why you didn't follow up your degree with work in the field you were so well qualified for…' Maybe Sonia thought that this had to do with her mother's death, maybe not, but she looked up, pulled her lips into something that was a thin smile. 'You chose to work in a bar after you graduated, right up until you came here?'

'No, that's right, I suppose I sort of fell into it, I had debts to pay and…' Ros was so thankful to see that Sonia seemed to be already moving on.

'Hmm, everyone is trying to make ends meet these days, but from what I can see, young people still have enough for fancy coffees and overpriced bagels,' the captain murmured.

'And what do you think you bring to the job of ranger then, Miss… Stokes?' It was obviously Tom's question to ask.

'Well, I'm efficient and…'

'We're not looking for an office cleaner.' Captain Jeffers sniffed again.

'Sorry, Ros, what he means is, we'd like more of an idea of what your personal qualities might mean in terms of broadening the post. You know, making more of it than any of the other applicants?' Sonia said. It was obvious she was from HR, keeping everyone on an even, legal keel.

'Erm, yes, yes of course. I was only saying about being efficient, because I think it's important, especially if some emergency was to crop up, like a pollutant in a river or something along those lines. You need to be proactive, getting things moving along as quickly and properly as possible.'

'Quite right too,' Sonia agreed but she hadn't lifted her head from the scoring sheet before her. 'And is that it?'

'Of course not.' Ros hadn't meant to snap, but at least it made Sonia's head pop up and seemed to waken up the other two old sods as well. 'I've already shown that I'm good at writing up detailed reports. I've worked hard to keep habitats both monitored and safe. I've carried out additional work, taking samples and checking them too, and sent back any results that I've had.'

'To be fair, she's done all that, probably better than Max Toolis ever managed it, if the truth were told.' Tom threatened to break into a smile at Ros and it gave her some small measure of encouragement.

'And?'

'Well, if I'm successful at this interview, I've already been talking to the local primary school teachers and they're willing to have me come into the school regularly to talk to the children about conservation and about the wildlife and habitats on the island and how important it is that we keep them safe.'

'Good to get the kids involved,' one of the older guys murmured again.

'And, I've set up a beekeepers' group. We're hoping to start our first hives this year. We have six members and the plan is to set up communal hives in the grounds of the old monastery – we have permission and...'

'That's a great idea.' Tom was positively beaming now.

'I thought so, it took a few months over the winter, to get people together and on board. There was a big educational part to it all, you know, helping people learn about how to take care of the bees and what to look out for, but we should be getting the hives across in the next week or two, everyone is really excited about it.'

'Hmm,' Sonia murmured, but at least that led to a large tick on the page before her, which Ros hoped was good news.

'And, of course, I've done quite a bit of work on the cottage, you know, cleaning it up, clearing around it. I would hope to set up a kitchen garden, maybe revive the old vegetable patch, have a go at encouraging some of the native flora and fauna to make it more attractive to some of the local wildlife. And...'

'Hmm, it's all very admirable that you're trying to live sustainably but...' the grumpier old boy, Jeffers, sniffed.

'The food I'm producing will be going for the most part to the local meals on wheels. It'll mean people are getting organic produce and, hopefully, it'll encourage more people to cultivate a small patch in their gardens.'

'That all sounds very promising...' Sonia said. 'You've

heard that there are moves to convert a large tract of the island into National Park land?'

'Yes, I'm very excited about that, of course it'll mean more work.' It was work Ros would enjoy.

'How's that?'

'Before it happens, there will be quite a bit of bringing the islanders round to the possibilities for the island if we're successful. At the moment, all the farmers will see is a loss of common grazing areas and restrictions around what they can do, I know that change isn't always welcomed with open arms.' She smiled warmly at this. 'But I do feel, that with a little work, plenty of dialogue and a plan that involves the islanders, a National Park on the island will be great for the residents as well as the wildlife.'

The interview continued, and they seemed to talk for an age about how to bring the islanders on board, but Ros had thought a lot about it and, really, she felt she'd made some good points by the end. Points that could be actioned easily and make the transition as smooth as possible.

'Right, well, that's all well and good, but I think it must be almost lunchtime.' Keith Duff leaned back on his chair, made a big thing of checking his watch and then folded his arms behind his head and actually man-splayed. Urgh, if Ros had thought before that she couldn't like him any less, she had been wrong.

As she was leaving the building, Sonia caught up with her. 'Well done.' She squeezed Ros's arm.

'Thanks, but I'm not very hopeful.'

'Why not?' Sonia swung round to look at her.

'Because there are no female rangers and you can see for

yourself, in this area, well, it's less likely to happen than maybe anywhere.'

'Do you really want this job?' Sonia asked.

'Of course.' Ros sighed. 'Honestly, I've never wanted anything more and I think I could be good at it, I think I could make a real contribution.'

'Then it's even more important that a woman gets it, wouldn't you say?' Sonia smiled and winked at her before heading towards a Mini Cooper parked just outside the gate.

18

Constance

Constance had never imagined she'd have to make a phone call like this, but it was the very least she could do for Dot. True enough, she wasn't exactly the most regular church-goer on the island, but then, no-one expected someone of her age to walk halfway across the island every week, essentially a ten-mile round trip at eighty-plus years of age. She smiled, thinking that age sometimes turned out to be a dispensation once you got so far along.

Of course, she reminded herself as she picked up the phone and dialled the phone number to what had once been the priest's house, times had changed. After old Father Hanratty died a decade earlier, there was no priest to spare for a small parish, particularly when vast parishes on the mainland were being chunked together and ministered to by men who in many cases were long past their sell-by date. In place of a parish priest, or even a curate – who were rarer than hen's teeth these days – they had a parish administrator. He took care of everything from booking masses to scheduling the priest's *online* diary (if you don't mind) so the priest could fit in funerals and weddings alongside his work on the mainland. Finbar Lavin managed the parish on a daily basis, from making sure the church doors were oiled to printing out the weekly parish bulletin. He'd even had a go at tuning the old pipe organ and he'd made a fair job of that too, by all accounts. Of course, that was only his part-time job. Finbar was an islander, a true islander, and so he was as happy on the sea as he was on the land.

'Ah, Constance, is it yourself that's in it?' he said and she could imagine his eyes creasing with a broad smile as he spoke. She'd known him from when he was a boy and taught him in the local school when he was old enough to attend; she'd always had a soft spot for Finbar. Back in the day, a group of the kids from around the island would come to Ocean's End each year and pick the fruit trees that neither she nor her mother had time to tend. There was always too much fruit and they only stayed their best for a very short time. Constance hated to see fruit rotting on the tree, especially when the local kids had such fun gathering it up. 'What can I do for you?'

'I'm afraid, as you might have guessed, it's not a wedding I'm after, so...' It was a joke between them. When Finbar was a boy of no more than seven, he'd asked her to marry him and at the ripe old age of thirty-eight Constance had solemnly promised that one day she would. They'd laughed about it many times over the years. 'It's my friend Dotty, I don't know if Heather mentioned her, when you brought her over? Her mother?'

But why would she? Heather had taken the urn carrying her mother's ashes from a large suitcase and placed it wordlessly on the hall table.

'She and I were the best of friends, but...' There was no point going into all the nonsense that had kept them apart for years. 'Well, she'd like to be buried here, Finbar, and I'm not sure what we need to do to...' Constance wondered, did everyone hedge around the language of death and funerals or was it just her?

'Of course, of course, I'll help you in any way I can,' he said and she felt as if he'd reached out and taken her hand affectionately in his. 'Would she have liked to be buried here in the cemetery or was she hoping for something a little less formal?'

Constance knew Finbar's own father had had his ashes buried at sea. That was forty years ago now and it had been the talk of the island for weeks, probably years afterwards. Fortunately, his mother, Mary Lavin, took other people's opinions in her stride and perhaps she had the only solace a young widow could have by knowing that her husband's wishes had been granted.

'No, nothing too flamboyant, but I suppose I'll need to talk to Heather. I think she might like to be buried with her own mother. Of course, if that isn't possible then...' Dotty's mother was buried alone, her father – well, that was another story and Constance knew it wasn't one for today either. 'You see, her mother is buried in a single plot, I suppose she assumed that Dotty would be buried in London.'

Constance had bought her own plot years ago. It wasn't a morbid decision. It had happened quite out of the blue. She'd been sitting next to her mother's grave and realised she knew exactly where she wanted to be buried. The old graveyard had a few ragged-looking yew trees – it was hard to grow anything much on this side of the island – and was perched on the side of a hill with magnificent views but little in the way of shelter. However, favourable placing close to the scant remains of a famine wall had allowed a small oak to take root and, that day, it had seemed to stand some chance of survival.

Constance had stood next to it and looked across as clouds chased their own shadows over the hills opposite. In the distance, the village – roughly a dozen buildings snuggled together – looked lovelier than she'd ever seen it before. Far off, she could see the glint of evening light hit off the Atlantic as the tide turned and waves rolled with frothing vigour towards the shore. She'd imagined being buried here meant she could always keep watch over her husband, lying somewhere out there in the vastness.

The following morning she'd marched down to the parish priest's house with two hundred pounds in her pocket and purchased a plot big enough for two. Not that she had a sinner to share it with; the sea had taken her husband and never given him back. At the other side of the graveyard, her mother rested beneath a tall, old-fashioned Celtic cross and a poem from her own collection. It seemed wrong to be buried next to her mother. As if she was somehow pushing in where she was no longer needed, and a single plot, well, it was just too tragic for words, wasn't it? The old priest had smiled and taken her money. He'd marked off her plot on a book held in the parish office and probably pocketed half the amount for a gambling habit he'd never hidden as well he had imagined.

'She'd be welcome to be buried in my plot, if that's okay with Heather either,' Constance said and, for the first time since she'd bought the plot, she actually felt a shiver run through her. There was no longer any question, but she would be ending up in there at some point and that time was surely drawing closer with every day.

'Heather? The English woman? I thought she was London through and through?'

'Ara, Finbar, she's one of us really. Didn't I just tell you her mother lived here at Ocean's End and she spent almost every summer as a young girl walking along that beach with me. Surely you must remember her?' Although Heather probably could be a year either side of Finbar.

'Now you say it, I think I do remember her. It's funny, I'd all but forgotten your summer visitors from all those years ago,' he said, but it was a long time ago, no reason why he should remember. 'I'm sorry to hear about her mother, anyway. I could call up, if you wanted, or if you'd like to pop over to the church here we can have a chat and maybe Heather could decide then where she thinks her mother would prefer. I can collect you both this evening after dinner, if it suits?'

'Are you sure it's not too much bother?' Constance asked, but of course she knew that for Finbar, nothing had ever been a bother. He was a man who covered a lot of ground every day; although he worked hard, he'd never be a millionaire in terms of material goods, but maybe he was wealthy in more important ways that mattered.

'Of course not, I'll be expecting a cup of tea though,' he said, laughing as they ended the call.

Constance stood for a little while in the hallway. Dot's

ashes still sat on the hall table. It seemed an incongruous place for them and so Constance picked up the urn, which was heavier than she'd expected, and carried it through to what had once been a grand reception room. The window looked out across the bay and to the north and south at either end.

'Here you go, Dot.' *She'd like it here*, Constance thought, it was always their spot. They'd sit here often and watch as the nights would draw in and Dotty would dream of the bright lights of London and the glamorous lives they were both going to live. *Ah, well, best-laid plans.* Constance had made it as far as teacher training college, where she'd met Oisin. They'd been a match from the very first moment; the fact that he was charmed by Pin Hill only sealed the deal. Looking back, she was pretty sure that if Dotty had found any glamour in London it was fleeting.

The rain outside was meant to skirt by the island, but for now, it beat against the house with the ferocity of a gale. Constance went back to the kitchen and pulled out a drawer in the dresser. She ran her hands around the back of it, until they came across the old candles she kept there. There were too many blackouts on the island to take a chance on being left in the dark for days on end.

There was no need to light one yet, but somehow, there was a sense of ease in knowing it was here with a box of matches nearby if they were needed.

19

August 1957

Dotty

Danger had not always skulked in dark corners or at least if it had, Dotty managed to get through life until that day beneath the stairs blithely unaware of it. Now, she wondered if in fact it had always hung in the air, like the cobwebs under Constance's bed that she didn't realise were there, until she did, and now she checked each night with an old duster attached her mother's hardly used broom.

Dotty sighed; she'd rather have had the spiders. She chewed her fingernail, pulling away the raw skin so it hurt and bled and she had to wrap it up in her hanky. A new habit, she hardly knew she was doing it until her mother scolded her. 'Really, Dotty, I can't think what's got into you.' It seemed to be a constant refrain since that day when they'd come home to find her in the lemon dress. Something else had slipped between them into an invisible crack that Dotty could not quite locate, as if her mother had guessed at secrets Dotty did not want to share and maybe more: that they both knew the truth of what lurked at the very centre of their family.

Dotty exhaled, cursing herself for being so melodramatic. There was nothing else, just that day beneath the stairs. She had to get a grip of herself, it couldn't be what she thought; her father was a good man. He had a war medal, after all. And there had been nothing else, no other sign that he was a bad man. At night, Dotty lay in bed, listening while her parents shut up the house for the evening. Her mother's quick step on the stairs, followed by her father's slower, considered pace. Sometimes, he would linger at her door, as if about to say goodnight, and her imagination went into overdrive. Would he try to turn the handle? Would he try to push his way past the chair that she'd wedged behind it because she was afraid? He never did, of course he never did. It was silly. Dotty by name and dotty by nature, wasn't that what Sister Benildus said about her all the time. Dotty knew with the sensible part of her brain she was being childish, just a loopy kid, making up danger where it never existed in the first place.

But then, her father would switch off the electric light in the hallway and the house would plunge into darkness. She would suddenly be overtaken by panic, it felt as if she was drowning in grim shadow that went on forever, stealing her breath, quickening her heart, emptying her very soul. Sometimes, she just sat there and touched her face to feel if the tears that fell from her eyes were real, because she couldn't be sure if they were hers. It felt as if this life suddenly belonged to some other girl, who looked like her and sounded like her, but she was somehow less than she had been before that day her father had tried to…

At odd times, she found herself touching other things too, as if to confirm that they were actually solid things to be relied upon: the crimson petals on her mother's roses, the spine of a book, the sharp edge of the kitchen knife. It felt as if she hadn't slept properly in ages, afraid to close her eyes, she sat up in her bed, her elbows propped on the pillow, her palms beneath her chin to keep her head supported. She was going mad and she had to remind herself it was for no good reason. *Her father would never...* She'd never been truly afraid of anything in her whole life – well, maybe she'd been a bit afraid when Sister Benildus talked about the raging fires of hell and it being like trying to squeeze a camel through the eye of a needle to get into heaven. Honestly, she'd pinned her eyes narrowly on Dotty when she said it, as if she already knew what lay ahead for her. She'd never been afraid of Sister Benildus, not like Constance was, but then all the nuns made a thing of Constance just because her father was away.

For all their great resemblance, Dotty thought she couldn't be more opposite to her mother. Sylvie Wren was one of those women who thought every problem could be fixed with a good mop and a liberal dose of elbow grease. The house was empty now, her mother gone to the shops to pick up sausages for tea. Dotty was sitting in the kitchen; the dripping tap was the only aberration in her mother's drive for perfect neatness in their home. Dotty liked the sound of it or perhaps she liked its predictability. In the utter silence it seemed to fill the whole street with its steady rhythm. It was nice, having the place to herself. She was curled up on the armchair in the kitchen, satisfied after having searched through the kitchen cupboards that her mother had not hidden some treat that she might nibble at, when a noise outside made her stir.

Probably that plague of a cat from next door. Constance had it trailing about the place after her all the time, well, he could bloody well stay on her side of the wall and be content with that. A light shower had cleared and through the open window the aroma of her mother's sweet peas drifted pleasantly on the evening air.

'Well, this is a nice how do you do.' Her father appeared at the back door, as if out of nowhere, and Dotty roused herself with a start. She must have fallen asleep, because the clock above the range said it was an hour later than she expected. 'Has your mother not got the tea ready yet?'

'She's getting sausages, she thought you were…' Even from the opposite side of the kitchen she could smell a strong odour of alcohol. He must have visited some pub on his way home. Her stomach churned, reminding her of the last time her father had been close to her and smelled of drink.

'It's been a bloody hard day and the least a man should be able to expect is a bit of dinner on the table when he arrives home. I swear to God, if I had to spend another hour in that bloody shop today, I think I'd have rammed Jem Hannon's measuring tape down his throat.' He shook his head. Her father hated his job and never tired of talking about how much everyone there annoyed him.

'So, she'll be gone a while,' he said, pushing out the scullery door behind him and leaning against it with emphasis.

'No, she'll be home soon,' Dotty said, her voice giving away the fact that she was trying to convince herself of that as much as him. 'Any minute now, I'd say…'

'Not too soon, I hope.' He was smiling at her now. 'What say you and I play a little game?'

'I don't like games.'

'This is a new game, you haven't played it before, it's only for us.' He began to loosen his tie and moved slowly towards her. 'Let's see, I'll take off my tie and you...'

'I...' Dotty was frozen, for one awful second an ice age had stolen into her very heart, terror transfixed her. The sound of one of her mother's planters crashing from the wall outside startled both of them it seemed, because her father turned towards the window. Just for a second, it was all it took. Suddenly, Dotty knew, it was time to move. She jumped from the chair, slipped behind her father's back and hurled herself through the back door before he had a chance to call her back.

There was only one place she could think to hide. Mr Morrison's shed. Lickey had lost interest in it after pilfering anything that caught his eye. Dotty was out of breath by the time she pushed through the rough wooden door. She bent over double for a moment, trying to calm her breathing and her racing thoughts. And then, she started to cry, fat tears racing down her cheeks so fast she thought she might drown in them. She searched around the little shed, not prepared to admit what she was looking for, but knowing, deep down, that if she came across another bottle of poitín she would glug down a huge mouthful to numb the pain. There was none. No surprise, Lickey and his mates had taken anything worth taking. Just one sip, she thought, would have made this bearable. Just one sip.

20

Constance

The sound of the back door being pushed in woke Constance with a start. She opened her eyes to see Heather returning from her walk along the beach, soaked to the skin, of course. Constance had assumed she was in the village. She brought with her that vital aroma of sea air and salty freshness.

'You look as if you had a good bracing walk.'

'I forgot how cold it can be here, especially when it decides to turn to winter in an instant.' Heather shivered, but Constance thought she looked as if someone had switched her on in the few days since she'd arrived on the island. That lacklustre deadness that had lurked behind her eyes and the city grey that no make-up could cover over on her skin had been replaced by a glow that took years off her. Constance didn't ask what had been weighing Heather down in London, but it was very obvious that being here on the island was healing whatever had been crushing over her before.

Constance told her about the phone call with Finbar.

'The guy with the boat?'

'The one and same.'

'Is he a priest as well?'

'No, of course not, but he takes care of the church and looks after the parish administrative tasks. There wasn't a rush to take it on when they needed someone, but Finbar offered and somehow the diocese found money to pay him after a year or two. Now, there are a few around the place who wouldn't mind the job, but the fact is, the best man for the parish has managed to find himself in it.' That was the truth as far as Constance could tell it.

'So, is he a lay minister? Can he do a ceremony and, you know, say a few official words, so Mum's... on the path in the right direction?' Heather raised her eyes towards the ceiling, the obvious implication being she'd like to hedge her bets towards heaven if at all possible for Dot.

'You don't have to worry about that.' Finbar was at the door. 'And yes, if you'd prefer I can do a humanist ceremony. I mostly do weddings.' He looked at Constance, smiled impishly. 'The young ones are all for humanist services. We get lots of weddings here on the island and I thought, well, since they're coming across anyway, why not offer my services rather than have someone travel over with them for the sake of an hour...'

'I'm not sure which she'd prefer, my mother wasn't exactly the most devout woman,' Heather said diplomatically. 'But still, she never mentioned not having a church service.'

'Whatever suits. I can pencil in a time for the priest on

the mainland and he'd only be too happy to do the funeral. Are ye bringing across her remains or is it a question of an urn?' Finbar asked.

'She's in the front room, on the windowsill,' Constance said and then, when she actually thought about Dotty perched on the windowsill, she had to laugh, because at their age, there was nothing less likely than either of them wedging themselves up there again.

'Did someone say tea?' Ros was standing at the door. She halted when she realised that Finbar had come over to discuss the funeral arrangements.

'Come in, come in, don't be daft, you're not going without telling us how you got on.' Constance grabbed her arm, pulling her through into the kitchen. Ros looked as knackered as Constance had ever seen her. She frog-marched her to the kitchen table and went about making a pot of tea and placing homemade brown bread on a plate with butter and jam and a few biscuits to finish up.

'Oh, it won't take long to tell you. Let's just say, I was as prepared as I could be and we'll have to wait and see.' Ros plopped into the chair, obviously relieved to have it over with. 'Actually, maybe a bit better than expected, one of the interviewers might even be especially rooting for me.' She told them about Sonia and their chat after the interview.

'Well, that's as much as you can ask for; let's keep our fingers crossed, eh?'

The spin out to the church was actually lovely. Constance hadn't visited her mother's grave in the longest time and she hated to think how much longer it was since she'd stood in St Brendan's.

'You have the church looking lovely, Finbar,' she

whispered to him as they stood in the vestry. The place was a combination of gleaming brass and heady beeswax.

'Ah, go on with you, you know well I have plenty of help in the winter time.' It was true, some of the other fishermen were always happy to lend a hand when the sea turned back their boats with storms that would cut even the hardiest into pieces.

'Help or no help, I've heard that you're doing a fine job,' Constance said softly and she wandered out towards her mother's grave and stood there while Heather and Finbar made the arrangements for Dotty's funeral service.

21

Heather

'That sounds perfect,' Heather said as she and Finbar walked out towards the graveyard, where Constance was standing at Maggie Macken's grave. It hadn't taken very long to agree the details and at least she felt happy that now, finally, she was doing something that her mother couldn't but be pleased about.

'Oh, Constance, this is...' She looked up at Maggie Macken's headstone. It was a fine column of carved granite with a verse etched into the stem: *Listen for me on the autumn breeze, see me in the showers that fall across the hillside, sit by me on a summer's day in the shade of an old yew tree and remember that I have loved and lived and let you not cry that I remain only a whisper on the morning dew.* 'It's beautiful.'

'She wrote it especially. I think she was inspired by Yeats, but of course, it's a much longer pilgrimage to make, off the mainland, so really, no-one has ever sat here in the way she might have hoped,' Constance said a little sadly.

'I think anyone who does would be moved by those lines,' Heather said and although she was here to bury her own mother, something pulled at her heartstrings, because without Maggie Macken, neither of them would have any connection to this place. Suddenly, she was overcome with a feeling of deep gratitude to the woman for dragging her family out of Galway to this place all those years earlier, and she said as much to Constance.

'Oh, I don't think there was any dragging involved. Your grandmother was happy to come. It was hard times to be a single parent and the city was no place to raise a child on your own,' Constance said. 'My mother knew that only too well.'

'They must have been close? Maggie and Sylvie?' Heather asked later that night. Her mother never spoke about her own parents. It was as if Sylvie and Norman Wren had only existed as mere shadows, so long before that they hardly counted any more. It was a shame. Heather wanted to know about them and Constance was now the only one who could tell her. They were sitting on deckchairs that Ros had resurrected from somewhere and set up near the back door. From here, you could see right out to the crest of the horizon.

'I think they both just had a terrible shock, after the well and all and…' Constance hesitated, perhaps realising that Heather had no idea what she was talking about. 'Hasn't your mother told you the story of how we became so close?'

'No, I just assumed that you grew up together here,'

Heather said, reaching to the ground and picking up the bottle of red wine before topping up both their glasses. 'I'd love to hear it.'

'It's not my favourite story to tell, but anyway, it's how we ended up here, so I suppose, if you're interested, you should know it. We had been living in a little house in Galway, on the road out of the city towards Salthill. Apparently, it's what they call an up-and-coming area now. Dotty and her parents lived next door. Your grandmother was a great cook, far more a homemaker than my mother; it's a pity you'd hardly remember her, I'm sure.'

Constance sighed now, as if thinking back was almost making her tired. 'Anyway, the house on the other side of us had a wilderness of a garden and an old disused well at the end of it. As small girls, Dotty and I were thrown together while my mother wrote and hers kept house. I hated it there. The other kids along the road would tease me, but they wouldn't dare if Dotty was nearby. Your mother had the courage of a lion. I didn't see it at the time, of course, only later when I realised.'

Constance's gaze drifted off and there was a moment when Heather thought she might say something, but she simply sighed and then smiled before beginning again.

'One day, I was in the garden and some of the boys broke through. I knew I was for it if they caught me and I made my escape through the fence. Anyway, I ended up falling into the old unused well.' She sipped her wine before going on. 'I must have bashed my head, but the next thing I remember was waking up and everything was dark. I mean, the sky was full of stars, but I was down so deep, I could only just make it out. I was missing for days.

My mother told me there were search parties sent out all across the city, they didn't realise I was just a few hundred yards away. Your grandmother thought they'd never see me again. My own mother was afraid to think at all. She walked the streets with a photograph of me, showing my face to strangers, hoping that someone had come across me. And then Dotty, by some miracle, found me. I'll never forget her voice, calling my name. *Constance, Constance, please if you're down there, let me know.* I thought I must be dreaming it at first. I mean, I was down there days, two long days and nights. I was probably in shock, certainly fatigued beyond measure and most likely dehydrated too.'

'Oh my God, Constance, you poor little thing, so young, you must have been terrified,' Heather said and she reached out and stroked Constance's arm. The bond between her mother and Constance made sense now. How devastating it must have been all those years ago when it severed; she could understand how an experience like that could draw them together in a way beyond normal friendship.

'Ah, I gave them all quite the shock. My mother feared I'd never be quite the same again.' Constance's lips lifted into a wry smile and, for a moment, Heather had the strangest feeling that there was something very important she was holding back. 'She had just signed her first big publishing contract. We'd come into more money than she had ever dreamed possible and she thought that getting away from Galway might help me recover. She was right, of course. With a bit of minding and a good rest and moving away from that place, I suppose I was fine, mostly.'

'I can't imagine. But, after that, you all moved here?'

'My mother brought me for a holiday. We stayed in the

hotel. It was going to be just a holiday. Of course, while we were here, she heard that Ocean's End was up for sale. Your grandfather took off, a few weeks before we were due to leave the house in Galway. That was another huge shock to everyone, poor Sylvie just being abandoned like that with a daughter and no way of making ends meet. So, when we were to pack up our lives my mother convinced Sylvie to come with us and the rest, as they say, is history. She offered her a job, keeping house and a small cottage in the garden for both of them. It must have seemed like the perfect solution.'

'And my grandmother?'

'She probably found it different at first, but she was happy here, certainly, there was never any mention of going back. We were all as pleased as each other to get out of Galway, I think. At the time, a husband just doing a moonlight flit, well you can imagine, lots of tongues wagging about her at every turn and I'm not sure Sylvie could even afford to go on living there. She'd never really had a job, so the offer of staying here was probably the answer to all her problems.'

'My mother told me that her parents divorced,' Heather said.

'Oh, did she indeed?' Constance smiled sweetly but she looked as if she could have bitten her tongue off. She made a little noise; probably best to change the subject. 'Actually, the more I think about it, I think your grandmother loved it here. Do you remember the cottage in the kitchen garden?'

'Why, yes, I had completely forgotten about that...' Heather said then. How could she have forgotten that? Her mother bringing her along, showing her the window that had once been her bedroom, Heather standing on her tippy-toes to try and make out anything buried in the darkness within.

'You'd hardly notice it now. It's completely grown over, of course.' Constance looked down towards the end of the garden. Ros had cleared a path so you could walk all the way to the border fence. On either side, she'd cut back as many of the high brambles as she needed so there was a view of the sea beyond. To the left, there was the remains of the walled-in garden, smothered beneath a thicket of weeds and brambles.

'Of course, it was through the kitchen garden. I must go and take a look at it, one of the days when I'm here,' Heather said softly and maybe that was the moment. As the sun dipped lower in the sky, a little part of her thought that life would be wonderful if she never had to leave this spot.

She'd been here just over a week when the parish priest came across to perform a ceremony to bury her mother. It didn't feel like a week, it felt somehow as if she'd been here her whole life. She and Constance had slipped into an easy routine that pulled her back to a time she'd long forgotten. Back then, when she came to visit with her mother, she had dearly loved Constance. They'd always just clicked, of course, she could see it now, Constance took an interest in people. Young or old, it didn't matter, she just loved to spend time and she listened, really listened to people. Heather could see it with Ros and with Finbar. It was obvious they both adored her. She even managed to weave her magic over the parish priest, who almost missed the boat ride back to the mainland, so intent was he on chatting to Constance when they sat drinking glasses of Guinness after the funeral lunch that had only been attended by the three of them with Finbar and Father Rory.

'It was a beautiful ceremony, probably the nicest funeral I've ever attended,' Heather said and it was true. 'Thanks, Constance, and you too, Ros.'

'There's no need to be thanking me at all,' Constance said in that plain way she had of speaking. 'It should be the other way round, if right was right.'

'You should be thanking me?' Heather didn't understand.

'For bringing Dotty home to me, of course,' Constance said softly.

'And I was just glad to be here for you,' Ros said, sipping her Guinness. She still hadn't finished her first glass and Heather thought she'd never met a young woman like her. 'The readings were beautiful.' Ros had been quiet the whole time, as if the funeral had brought back memories of some sad time in her short life and she couldn't quite shake off the melancholy of that time before.

Strangely, Heather realised that her mother's funeral had not been a sad one for her. Rather, it felt as if Dotty was in some way coming home, which was strange because Constance was quite emphatic that when they were young girls, Dotty couldn't get off the island quickly enough. Now, all Heather wanted was to hear stories of what her mother's life had been like on the island all those years ago because, somehow, the woman Constance remembered seemed to be a much nicer person than the woman Heather had known.

Finbar lent his jeep to Heather while he ferried Father Rory back to the mainland. That way she could drive

Constance home, and he told her to hold onto it until he called her, he wouldn't need it for a day or two at least. Heather was slightly taken aback. In her whole life in London, no-one had ever just handed over their car keys just like that.

'You seem to keep forgetting, you're not in London any more, Heather,' Constance said gently and Ros only smiled and nodded. Maybe it was some part of the reason why Ros wanted to stay on the island so badly.

'Keep reminding me, I'm very happy to be here with you both,' Heather said softly, because she couldn't imagine feeling this sense of ease if she'd just buried her mother in some dreary London cemetery.

As the sunny day sank into an overcast grey evening, Constance confided to Heather she'd prayed for dry weather. There was some local old wives' tale about it being unlucky to have rain hit a coffin before it went into the ground.

'It can rain all it wants now,' she said after the final shovelful of clay had been patted into place on her mother's grave. Watching that had probably been the hardest part for Heather, but it was the way things were done here and she just had to accept it was what her mother would have wanted. So they'd stood silently by the graveside while two local men went about tucking her mother into the earth as if making up a hotel bed for her, with the utmost care and efficiency.

Yes, island life was completely different to anything she had ever experienced in London and Heather thought that none of that was a bad thing at all.

22

Ros

'You're doing far too much.' Constance worried about her and, while this made Ros feel a bit guilty, she had to admit she actually loved it, too. It had been a long time since anyone had cared enough about her to worry that she was eating enough, or that she was warm enough or that she was working too hard.

'I like to be busy and I'm hardly breaking my back. I mean, Heather is doing every bit as much as I am.' And that was the truth. It was Heather who had cleared a path through the long grass to the door that had sealed the kitchen garden off for years, probably.

'I'm just working out of curiosity; I remember only a shadow of what it was years ago...' Heather smiled.

'The garden?' Ros asked as she leaned on the spade she was using to hack away at the briars.

'No, silly, I'm sure that's well gone. I'm interested in

looking at the cottage,' Heather said and Ros hated to admit she hadn't even known there was a cottage tucked away inside the garden walls. But then, the walls were high, probably to keep the winds at bay, otherwise even the hardiest of plants would struggle here. The whole place was not only overgrown but sealed off too, with a door at either side fastened by ivy as much as any lock.

Once Heather had explained that the cottage had been where her mother had grown up, Ros was intrigued. She had come along today with every intention of washing some of the grey out of the faded creamy carpet on the stairs. 'It was white, once,' Constance corrected her. She wasn't even sad that it had slipped from pristine white so completely. Ros had gasped when she'd seen photographs of the house from its heyday. The comparison between then and now made its current condition even more pitiful. The whole place sagged with a sort of tragic melancholy. It was as though it had long ago accepted the fact that its time was marked on some wall and it was just slowly marching towards the inevitable, but Ros couldn't bear it, she couldn't let neglect and reduced circumstances win out.

'Oh, don't worry so much about it, sure indeed who is looking at it anyway, except myself?' Constance shrugged and Ros knew it had to bother her, but she was too proud to make a fuss.

'Right, well, if you can live with it for another while.' Ros grabbed the gardening gloves that had become her own these last few months. 'I'm going to help Heather cut through some of that jungle,' she added before making her way into the garden.

Heather was glad of the help. Ros knew, if there was one

thing you could depend upon on the island, it was that the rain would fall again, and maybe a day scrubbing that stairs carpet might be better spent when the weather was not as decent as it was today.

With the two of them hacking through the weeds, it didn't take long at all to clear a path to the faded old door that had long since cut off what Ros supposed was an even greater wilderness beyond. But regardless of what might be waiting for them on the other side, they pulled the door out eagerly and Ros held her breath as she peered into the tangle of growth beyond.

Sure enough, in the far corner, a squat building sat. Constance had called it the cottage, but even covered over by briars and nettles as high as the roof, it was obviously a miniature, single-storey version of Ocean's End. There was the flat roof, the flaking white walls and windows that sat in frames as thin as knitting needles. Ros had seen bigger garden sheds. From the doorway, the overgrown paths were somehow just about discernible beneath the flourish of weeds, but it was almost lunch time and, if Ros was hungry, she suspected Heather was famished. Her stomach had begun to rumble just before they pushed through.

'I so want to see inside,' Heather said, but then her stomach growled again. 'Let's have lunch and then we'll clear a path over. It would be nice to have Constance with us when we look inside, don't you think?'

'We couldn't do it any other way,' Ros said and she meant it. Even if there wasn't a lock on the door, which she assumed there probably wasn't, opening up the little cottage again would be something Constance would want to be there for.

Ros arrived back at the house to find several texts and a missed call on her mobile.

'Popular?' Heather smiled and she handed her an icy cold glass of water.

'Hmm,' she said because the missed call was from Jonah and the texts were from Shane. She opened the first text. *Hey, just wondering if you've heard from the interview panel?* The second, *It was really good seeing you.* The third, *Fancy dinner this week?*

'Everything all right?' Constance asked.

'Yeah, fine, I think I've been asked out on a date,' Ros said and she wasn't sure how she felt about that. After all, there was no denying the chemistry she felt for Shane, you'd have to be made of marble not to fancy him, but bumping into him at the interview felt a bit… she wasn't sure, but something had been off with him. She told Constance and Heather how she felt.

'Well, you can always turn him down,' Heather said.

'But you like him?' Constance asked.

'Fancy him. A different thing altogether in my experience,' Ros said wryly. It was true. She had yet to strike the right balance with any man, find one that she liked *and* fancied, not as easy as you'd think, it turned out. Then again, she hadn't exactly been looking all that hard.

'Don't judge him on just one thing,' Heather said then and that was unexpected because Ros would never have taken Heather for a romantic soul, unless it was between the covers of a Maggie Macken novel.

'Let's eat. Jonah Ashe can definitely wait until we've finished eating our lunch.'

Lunch was already organised, of course, Constance had

cut up what remained of a chicken cooked the previous evening for dinner. They ate it with fresh bread and dark red tomatoes. Constance slathered pickle across hers and licked her fingers as she finished up the last slice on her plate. Then, they sat outside the back door of Ocean's End, watching the gulls dive and soar in the distance as they circled a fishing boat making its way back to the pier.

'It's so long since I stood in that little cottage,' Constance said. 'If I'm honest, I've hardly thought about it in twenty years. It was tiny back in the day, just a kitchen, a bathroom and two bedrooms hardly big enough for single beds and a dressing table each.' She smiled and shook her head. 'I remember my mother saying that it had been built originally as a house for the gardener who lived here, a single man, and then, of course, to make way for mother and daughter, they had to divide the original bedroom into two. When I think of it now, they were probably little more than cupboards really.'

'I'm sure they were lovely,' Heather said softly, and even Ros knew that sixty years ago, any child in Ireland who had a bedroom to themselves was an exception, rather than the rule.

'Of course they ate here, in the kitchen, we all did, mostly. Your grandmother was a superb cook. It was just the four of us and we all ate together, there was no upstairs downstairs or any of that nonsense at Ocean's End.'

'I can't imagine there would have been,' Heather said softly, because of course the girls – Constance and Dotty– had been friends, equals, regardless of what their mothers earned or how famous Maggie Macken had become over the years.

From the west, a blanket of silver-grey clouds rolled in to cover the sun and Ros thought the reprieve from the warm rays was welcome. 'We should get back to it. We could have it cleared out by the end of the day.'

'Ah now, come on, you're killing yourselves, the pair of you, I can't let you keep on working like this, honestly, I feel as if I'm really taking advantage,' Constance called after them as they returned to clearing back the path.

'It won't take much longer,' Heather said and she was right. Hacking a narrow path to the little cottage was easy enough. They only needed to make it wide enough to walk along it in single file, but they widened it out as they went, so they could easily link Constance down to the end and be sure that she wouldn't fall or trip or lose her balance.

By five o'clock they had reached the front door of the tiny house. It was every bit as tragic-looking as Ros had expected. The paint had not so much peeled away as expired, giving up its dying breaths even as Ros traced her fingers around the old knocker. The door was down to the bare wood with only a scrape of red paint here and there to point you towards some idea of what it might have looked like back in its heyday. The walls had been whitewashed too; the chalky lime, although grey and greened up with moss, cracked and fell off against Ros's hand when she rubbed it over to get a sense of the place.

'Let's go back and get Constance to come down and look at it with us,' said Heather.

'Yes, let's, and maybe...' Ros gazed back up at the house again. It looked as if it had been abandoned for forty years. 'We'll need light, our phones are probably best, no point lighting candles or anything that might catch fire on a stray cobweb.' Because she absolutely expected the place to be filled with thick and clingy cobwebs, and damp from ceiling to floor and even damper in the corners.

'You can't have cleared it back already?' Constance said and she began to fill the kettle automatically when they came into the kitchen.

Ros nodded. 'We have, it wasn't as bad as you'd expect, but we thought you might like to see inside with us. We can open the door together.'

'Oh, I don't know, it's a long walk and what are the paths like…?'

'Don't worry, we have them well cleared back and plenty of space for us to link you on either side.'

'I'm sure I won't need linking,' Constance said quickly. Ros smiled. Constance hated the idea that anyone would think she was in any way dependent on other people. It was why she insisted on baking each day and plying everyone who came through the door with her hospitality. She wasn't giving in that she couldn't take care of herself and anyone else who needed it also.

They made the walk slowly and carefully down along the path. It felt to Ros as much like a pilgrimage as it did a walk to see the little house. From the outside, it looked sad and tragic and she assumed that inside would tell a similar tale, but it was part of Heather's history. Ros had made her mind up that she would ignore the cracking plaster and rotting wood she absolutely expected to find inside those grimy windows and tired curtains.

'Actually, it's quite…' Ros surprised herself, because she'd never seen anywhere quite like the inside of the cottage. *Quirky* was the only word she could think of

– a tiny art deco bolthole that with a liberal application of elbow grease could be the perfect getaway or refuge, depending on which you needed. Of course there were spiders and cobwebs and it looked dated, but there were dried logs stacked in an orderly pile next to the stove, cups, saucers and plates neatly displayed in the sideboard and two chairs pulled in at the table, which had an empty vase upon it, just waiting for someone to pop freshly cut flowers in it. The cottage had the air of a place that someone had tidied up before leaving and closing the door behind them with a firm click and a resolve to return at some point, not yet specified.

'I'm pleasantly surprised, I have to admit.' Constance smiled and she placed her arm around Heather's shoulder, squeezing the woman and perhaps thinking that the place would have some greater resonance with her than with either herself or Ros.

'It's cute,' Heather said, 'and I think I remember being here as a child.'

'I'm not sure that you ever stayed here. When you came over, I generally put you both up in the main house. Your grandmother refused to move out. This was her home, but you can see the bedrooms are tiny. Monks and prisoners probably have bigger cells.'

'Oh, but they are connected, how lovely must that have been,' Ros said, pushing through the door between the two bedrooms. She stood for a moment, looking at the narrow bed that she guessed must have belonged to Heather's grandmother. It was an old-fashioned cast-iron bed, larger than a single and yet not quite a double. Like the rest of the cottage, it was a study in straight lines, there were no affectations beyond the flashes of brass at the four corners.

The whole place was very much of its time and in keeping with the design of Ocean's End. At the foot of the bed there was a folded patchwork quilt. It looked hand-sewn. On the table next to the bed was a black and white photograph of two young girls, one of them she recognised as Constance and the other had to be Heather's mother – she was the spitting image of her daughter. The dressing table had been cleared, apart from a long thin comb and a paperback novel. In the corner, there was a tiny fireplace, cast iron and painted white – or at least, Ros assumed it had been white, a very long time ago. There were cobwebs and dust and signs around the windows that they let in plenty of draughts, but it was charming too. Perhaps it was its size, but she imagined that with a fire in the grate, it would be like a womb on a night when the winds howled up from the ocean beyond the garden walls.

'I'm glad we came here,' Heather said. She was standing at the end of the main room, a sort of sitting room/kitchen that was hardly big enough by today's standards to be either. 'I wasn't sure what to expect, but it's lovely to see it. It's the strangest thing, I have no memory of her, but I feel as if my grandmother is still lingering here, in some small way. Maybe it's the fact of her apron just left hanging on the hook there and the idea that…'

She reached out and touched the tap, turned it on and waited until water scraped along the pipes and spat into the sink in a few brown-coloured splashes. 'She must have turned this tap on a million times when she lived here,' Heather said softly.

'Probably ten million if I knew her,' Constance said. 'She was a devil for washing her hands at every turn. It was as if it was schooled into her from an early age, if her hands weren't busy chopping or mixing, they were underneath the flowing water. She was such a lovely woman,' she said sadly and it was clear that she, more than any of them, felt the weight of ghosts who had left here long ago, breathing in the heavy air from across the miles of time.

They stood there for a while, picking up little bits and pieces and examining them. Heather spent ages looking at a picture on the wall of a couple that Constance supposed were her great-grandparents. Eventually, the screech of a lone bat swooping about the garden reminded Ros that they needed to walk back to the house. As gorgeous and all as this little cottage was, it wasn't worth risking Constance tripping on the path in the dusky evening light. As they picked their way carefully along the path, each of them seemed to be lost in their own thoughts.

'If only we could turn back time,' Constance said to no-one in particular after they'd eaten steak and kidney pie that Heather had picked up in the supermarket earlier that day.

'Oh, my, wouldn't that be just marvellous,' Ros exclaimed and clapped her hands together. 'But maybe we could in a way. You know, bring that little cottage back to life and...' She only realised after she spoke that the idea of it really made her feel quite excited. 'I mean, even if it was just to have it as a place to keep guests, there's something very special about it. Don't you think so, Heather?'

'I suppose. But let's face it, I'm biased. All I could see were traces of my grandmother.' Heather smiled and Ros thought the day had relaxed her in a way that somehow softened her out even more than all the walks she'd gone on along the beach over the last few weeks. 'I was curious to see what it was like, but yes, it would of course be amazing to bring it back to its former glory.'

Ros suspected Heather was too diplomatic to say what they all knew – the sort of work that was needed on that cottage would cost a fortune. Probably, Ros reckoned, with a few quid, you could bring it back to a feasible standard to live in it, but it would cost a lot more to make it into a place people would want to stay.

'I'm sure there must be good money to make here on the island in summer holiday lets…' Heather said as if her mind was drifting.

'Are you joking?' Ros asked. 'There's an absolute fortune to be made, there's never enough space for visitors in the summer and the local hotel charges premium rates.'

'Ah, yes, well, they have to make hay while the sun shines. No-one wants to come for a holiday here in winter, in case they get stranded and can't get home again for days on end,' Constance said.

'Still though…' Ros could feel something like an electrical current racing through her brain. Constance could make something of that little cottage; they could help her, with some of it at least.

'I'm afraid I can't see myself letting the place out, even if I did have the money to invest in it now,' Constance said in that voice she used when she was tired with not just the day, but the whole world as well.

'I know you don't want to hear it, Constance, it's been a long day, but Ros could have a point,' Heather said gently.

'Of course she has a point, but I don't have the sort of money needed for work like that. Over here, Heather, they make you jump through hoops before you can even hang a B&B sign outside your door, you have no idea.' Constance rolled her eyes and maybe Ros understood. 'Look, I'm too old to want to learn new tricks; I just want to live out my days in peace and not have to worry about the roof falling on my head,' she snapped and with that it felt as if all the good humour of the day shattered apart at the same time.

'Sorry, of course, I'm sorry, I just got a bit carried away. Forget I said anything.' Heather's cheeks reddened and she turned away.

They were all silent for a while, thinking over the day. It had been a wonderful day, so much hard work with something worthwhile achieved at the end. It seemed a shame that Constance was happy to let it fall back into weeds again for the next forty years. Ros had a feeling that being in the cottage had meant a great deal to Heather.

'A penny for them, Heather?' Ros asked then, in an effort to revive the earlier light atmosphere.

'I'm just thinking of your mother, Constance,' Heather said. 'And that verse on her grave, the idea that she would have liked her readers to remember her...'

'I've often wondered if it isn't why a lot of writers write, to be remembered.' Constance said.

'In that case, Constance, it seems to me you have things to think about. Somewhere like this, it has to be the sort of place that people –I mean, like, Maggie Macken's fans – would like to visit?'

'How do you mean?'

'I know it sounds a bit daft, considering it's way out here

on the back step of Europe, but I was reading about Agatha Christie and her house, Greenway? At least, I think that's what it's called. Well, people – readers and writers – come from all over to visit it.' She smiled. 'A bit like Graceland for sleuthing fans.' She started to laugh, perhaps a little embarrassed at the notion of it all.

'Except no-one has read my mother's books in years,' Constance said.

'Actually, that's not strictly true.' Heather smiled mysteriously and Ros leaned forward because she suspected that they were in for a very interesting conversation.

It was late by the time Ros left Ocean's End that evening. The moon was creeping across the sky, while in the west the sun's final rays stretched for one last stroke across the waves. She stood for a while on Distiller's Hill, reputedly a spot where poitín was made many years earlier. The solitude was soothing until she saw a familiar figure in the distance.

'You know those blasted goats have every decent fence on the island destroyed.' Jonah Ashe came stalking towards her as if he had more on his mind than just passing the time of day. 'I rang you, did you not see the missed call?'

'Oh, no…' It was a lie; she'd completely forgotten about calling him back. Well, maybe she'd successfully managed to forget about it, until now.

'I don't know what the point is in having you here if you're not going to look after the place.'

'Excuse me, I do look after the island, but it's not my job to take care of your fences.'

'Just as bloody well it's not, I suppose,' he said gruffly and he stood next to her now, his eyes narrowing as he looked at her. She could see he hadn't shaved in a few days; he looked like a man who hadn't slept and was in a filthy mood because of it.

'Nor am I the keeper of the local goat population.' She did, however, technically have some responsibility for their wellbeing, in so far as they were a native species to the island and as such needed to be protected. Perhaps, if it was necessary to stop them doing damage to the island, then she supposed it probably was her job to intervene in some way. Although, having lived with George for a short while, she wasn't sure she'd fancy anyone's chances in talking a goat out of eating all around him.

'Well, if you're not going to take some responsibility for them, I'm not sure what your job is exactly. Surely it's more than wandering around the cliff edges, sightseeing?'

'That's not what I do…'

'Isn't it? It's all you appear to do when I see you,' he said. 'Those bloody eating machines have drilled their way through a thousand euros' worth of my fences in the last few weeks. Between them and the red deer, who knock through the dry walls on a regular basis, I spend more time mending fences than I do looking after livestock these days.'

'I'm sorry that you've had a run of it.'

'Yeah, I'm sure you are,' he said and he shook his head. 'It'd be a lot better if you did something about the stampeding deer and the marauding goats and spent less time being sorry.'

'Seriously?' she said, but he was walking away.

'I've a good mind to report you for not doing your job

properly,' he shouted back at her and that one threat was enough to make her cold to her very core. Whatever chance she had of getting offered the job of ranger permanently, there was no way they'd let her have it if there were complaints against her.

23

August 1957

Dotty

Constance's pale white face staring in the dusty shed window made Dotty jump.

'What on earth are you doing here?' She ran to the door and pulled back the old logs she'd stashed up against it.

'You mean, what on earth are *you* doing here?' Constance put her arms around her. 'I saw you through our kitchen window. You raced across our garden then slunk through the hedges and I...' She looked around her for a minute, taking in the shed for the first time. 'I thought maybe Lickey Gillespie or some of the boys were chasing you, so I came to help.'

'You came to help me? From Lickey?' Dotty felt the tears rise up in her once more.

'Sure,' Constance said as if it was the most natural thing in the world when they both knew that Lickey Gillespie put the fear of God in her. Wasn't it half Lickey's fault that she'd ended up falling down the well in the first place? 'Didn't you save me from the well?'

'I know, but that was different, Constance. I didn't actually do anything, just had a feeling and came looking. But you and Lickey Gillespie…' Dotty was touched beyond any measure she could possibly try to put into words.

'So, if you weren't running from Lickey?'

'I wasn't running from anyone,' Dotty said and she dropped Constance's hand. How could her friend understand what had just happened? How could she explain it to anyone, it was just too disgusting to put into words. Even thinking of it made her feel as if she was somehow… dirty.

'Well, you were running as if the devil himself was on your heels.'

'Ha ha, very funny.' Dotty dropped to the blanket she'd spread across the floor of the little shed. 'You'll have to tell me all about your holidays, I'm mad with jealousy,' she said, pulling Constance down next to her. Anything to take her mind off what had just happened in the kitchen with her father, or what might have happened if it wasn't for that cat.

'Dotty.' Her father's loud knock on the door sounded like an earthquake tremor rumbling against her heart. She grabbed Constance, pulled the old rug over them both to hide. It was disgusting, smelled of mould and earth and something sour, but it was better than being found. Then, as if her guardian angel was standing over them, her father moved away and she heard his footsteps, moving along the path.

'Mr Wren.' Constance fought her way out from under the rug. She looked from the door to Dotty.

'Shh.' Dotty pulled her over, covered her mouth roughly. 'Don't say a word.'

'Is it a game, do you mean we have to hide?' She began to giggle. Oh, God, he would definitely hear them now.

'It's not a game, Constance, he's...' Dotty whispered but she couldn't think how to put it into words. 'He tried to do things...' And even just admitting that much felt like it opened up a fault line in her.

'What sort of things?' Constance was too stupid to understand, or maybe she was just lucky.

'Like Sister Mary Benildus says, you know, with a boy, but it's not meant to be until you're married and it's not meant to be with your...' That was it, she started to cry, hungry tears stealing away the last dredges of her resolve. Within seconds her body was overcome with sobbing that threatened to choke her. 'You know...'

'You're saying...' Constance couldn't quite get a grip on it, but Dotty watched as her expression gave way to understanding of some sort. 'Grown-up things?' She waited for a second. 'Sinful things?'

'So, now you know.' *Oh, God. Now what?*

And then Constance shook her head, pulled the smelly rug over both of them.

'I'll help you, Dot, don't worry, I'll help you,' Constance whispered.

A second later, Dotty's father pushed the door in easily. 'There you are, I want you at home now,' he said in a voice she hardly recognised.

'I'm not going.' Dotty's voice wobbled. 'I'm not, what you did, that day, it was wrong, what you want is a mortal sin and I'm not going home... not for that, not ever...'

'Silly girl,' he said and then he caught sight of Constance. 'What nonsense to talk, has she been filling your head with nonsense too?'

'Dotty never talks nonsense, Mr Wren, she's...' Constance's voice was as thin as paper, but her eyes were defiant.

'Don't tell me you're as bad as she is,' he said and then he took a careful step back outside the shed, looking around as if to check if anyone was about. 'I'm not having this, Dotty, you're coming with me now and you'll do as you're told.' He reached down and grabbed her arm, pulling her to her feet and dragging her out the door while she screamed and writhed behind him.

'No, no, no, no.' She was hysterical now, hardly able to see straight, fear ripping through any bravery she'd ever managed to store up in reserve.

'NO! Mr Wren, no, you're hurting her, can't you see?' Constance was crying and racing along beside them, holding onto Dotty for dear life. 'No, I won't let you...' Then in a move that surprised all of them, probably Constance herself more than any of them, she moved forward, planting herself before them.

'Out of my way, you silly child.' He reached out an arm as if to swipe at Constance.

'NO!' With a deafening screech, loud enough to waken the dead, let alone the neighbours, Constance was on him, knocking him off balance. In the confusion, Dotty fell backwards, shocked at the savagery of her normally placid friend. 'Run, Dotty, run,' Constance called to Dotty, while she railed at him, thumping his chest, attacking him like a mad thing.

In this surreal moment, as Dotty sat on the ground, slightly dazed, watching Constance, it dawned on her that this anger was coming from so much more than just saving her best friend. Her dad was getting every beating that Constance had never been brave enough to give to Lickey Gillespie and his friends. It was the ultimate retort to every time the nuns made her feel small because she had no father. It was all that anger, coming flooding out of her in one furious ball.

'Constance Macken. Stop it, this minute, stop it.' Mr Wren tried to fend her off, but she was livid, beside herself with rage and fear, and Dotty doubted she could stop even if she wanted to. Constance pummelled his chest, kicking and lashing until he managed to manhandle her and push her to arm's length, then she bit and flailed until they were at the rim of the old well. Suddenly, he grabbed her and lifted her as if she was nothing more substantial than a rag doll he might throw aside.

Dotty would never know how or what propelled her, but she ran at him. Felt her legs drive her towards him with no plan in mind but to save Constance. Her father was about to drag her to the well, Dotty was certain of it. She pulled Constance back, lying with her weight against her to haul her to the ground. Sheer gravity worked in their favour and her father lost balance and before she knew what was happening, she watched as Constance turned, threw herself against him, so he bent in two, before falling backwards. Another push – Dotty this time – making him sway uncertainly. His left foot tripped up the right as he went back, back and to the edge of the well.

Dotty knew what was going to happen; a premonition,

just moments in advance. If the well hadn't been there, her father would have fallen on his backside, but as it was, he didn't realise it and maybe he'd expected to feel the earth save him. In those moments it was shocking and grotesque, even if some remote part of her knew she could stop it. She pulled away, as she glimpsed a thin white shiny shin; long dark hairs, exposed for one awful moment so intense she could convince herself later that she had seen each individual hair from root to tip. Then his eyes, bulging out in his face, as if the whites had grown too large for his sockets; wide, registering what was happening, as they glided past her into the dark of the well. Did he scream or shout or call for help? She couldn't remember. All she remembered was the sound of him falling and a horrible crunching splashing noise when he reached the bottom.

'Oh God,' Constance whimpered. What on earth had they done? Her face was chalky white, and Dotty thought she might faint, but she gasped for air for what felt like a long while with her eyes pinned on the blackness of the well beneath them. 'Oh, Dotty, what have we done?'

Dotty knew her father was dead and, if he wasn't, he would have drowned in the water that surely lay several feet deep at the bottom of the well by the time any rescue got to him.

'Can he swim?'

'I...' Dotty felt as if she was frozen to the spot.

'Can he?'

'I don't know. It's...' Dotty's mind raced in a thousand different directions. They would go to prison. They would be carted off and locked up and that would be the end of the pair of them. That was if they were lucky – could they be hanged for killing him? Dotty shivered; how long had they been standing here?

'We have to do something,' Constance said then.

'What? What are we going to do? Tell someone that I've just murdered my own father?'

'You didn't murder him, Dotty.'

'I wanted him to die and I was the one who… who… who…' She started to shake, the reality of what had happened actually beginning to hit her now, making her tremble, visions of what would become of her raced through her brain. *They hang murderers, don't they?* Or they'd send her to prison for life – she couldn't go to prison, she just couldn't.

'Come on, we'll tell them it was an accident, he slipped and fell.'

'But he didn't slip though, did he? And what if he tells them we tried to… You don't know him, Constance, you don't know what he's really like.'

'What do you want to do, so?' Constance looked at her. They hadn't time to waste and, suddenly, it was impossible to think clearly.

'Constance?' Mrs Macken's call wafted into the evening air from the garden next door. 'Constance, come in now, it's getting too chilly. Where are you, Constance?'

'That's it,' Constance said, closing her eyes tight, perhaps willing herself to have some sort of divine inspiration. 'Okay, we'll tell my mother, she'll know what to do for the best.'

'What do you mean, what to do for the best?'

'You know, the best thing to do so we don't get into too much trouble.'

'We can't tell her everything, she'd never believe us, not about the…' Dotty looked away and, of course, they both knew she was right, who'd believe that her dad would want to… 'Oh, Constance, I'd die if anyone knew what he…' Dotty started to cry again.

'It's okay, I know what to do,' Constance said. 'Wait here a minute.'

She snuck along the hedging, leaving Dotty in Mr Morrison's back garden staring at the well. In no time, she was back carrying the small bag Norman Wren carried his sandwiches in each day, his cigarette case and his wallet. She dropped the items down the well. Then they pulled the cover over the top, as much as they could together. He was already dead, Dotty was sure of it.

'We never, ever say a word about this to anyone, no matter what happens; we didn't see a thing today, yes?'

'Not a word, not ever.' Dotty took Constance's hand and the pact was made. Maybe not sealed in blood, but it was made in the most compelling spirit of all – fear.

24

Constance

It was the same every year on the second Saturday in May. Constance woke with a start from a nightmare that was as real now, some fifty years after it had spun out into reality. There was the sound of water: not gentle, rippling waves hitting the shore at your feet, this water was hungry, gnashing, pounding against the side of a small red fishing boat. There were screams, but they came later, with panicked shouting and a sense that the only thing worse would come when there was no sound at all.

It was a beautiful day. Sun shining, high in a clear blue sky, the vista in the distance shimmering with the promise of heat that would not dissipate until fireflies lit up the shrinking night. Constance imagined Oisin, walking barefoot along the pier, the concrete warm beneath his feet, maybe sandy residues sticking against his toes. She had made him tomato and corned beef sandwiches, with bottles of diluted lemon and barley water, filled the night before and stored in the cool box of the fridge so they would melt slowly, last longer too.

From the moment Constance had taken him to Pin Hill Island, he had been in love with the sea. She had fallen in love with him at university, both training to be teachers, their lives stretching out before them, or so they thought. Funny, but when not one but two jobs came up on the island, she thought it was a sign they belonged here, together. Her future panning out so perfectly, she couldn't have asked for anything more.

How were they to know?

That terrible morning, along the pier, all the big trawlers had set out to sea before the dawn had cracked open in the sky across the mainland. There was nothing to sway Oisin from that trip, not so much as a whisper of a breeze, even the shipping forecast had predicted nothing more than mild swells some two hundred miles out to sea.

Constance had long ago made peace of sorts with the fact that she'd never have the answer to exactly what had happened that day. For the most part, she just ached for Oisin. These days, as her own life was drawing slowly to a close, there was something like comfort in the thought that perhaps he would be waiting for her.

It was this thought, dug up after the rigmarole of clenched muscles, unspoken cries and tears staining her cheeks while she slept, that made life bearable once more.

The second Saturday in May. The same dream every year, only, with each year, she knew as sure as grass was green that she was drawing nearer to being reunited with him once more.

This year, somehow, the heaviness that usually weighed her down did not feel so oppressive. She knew why that was. Despite the fact that Dotty had died, there was life back in Ocean's End again. Having Heather and Ros here, of course it didn't dispel what happened all those years ago – she wouldn't want that, she wouldn't want Oisin wiped out completely – but somehow the sadness this year was diluted.

There was something else too. This time, in the dream, Constance was in the boat alongside him. Instead of standing on the shore, helpless and distraught, she was terrified, but she felt Oisin's arms encircle her. She would not have this dream again, she knew it; by next year, they would be reunited. She felt it in her bones. And maybe, she was grateful for that.

25

Heather

Heather stood on the pier, gazing across in the direction of the mainland. Although her morning walks were getting earlier, it seemed that she still could not quite manage to get here before the rising sun. Funny, but in London, the beginning of each day was marked with the sound of her alarm clock, the bleat of breakfast news and the hum of traffic, a background noise to every second of her life then. These days, the sound of a car approaching made her stop what she was doing, because islanders always made sure to pass the time of day before moving on. It was still too early for tourists, but probably everyone knew exactly who she was anyway, because it was such a close-knit place, a new face would instantly be news to share.

There were no cars today. It was that in-between time. It was those few hours between the trawlers setting off to work for the day and the life of the village taking shape for business as usual. The only other person busy for miles that she could see was the guy with the coffee van everyone called 'Surfer Dude'. Heather now knew his name was Jake.

He waved at her now, energetically, as if calling her over, as if he needed her. One morning a week earlier she had helped him to set up his coffee van. Jake didn't do much more than protein bars in the way of actual food, but he made a very fine cup of coffee, especially if the sea air had whipped around you long enough to make you appreciate the simple aroma of a decently brewed cup of something warm.

'Hey,' he called to her. 'You're up early, couldn't wait to come and have the best coffee around, I suppose?' He was joking, but already he was spooning beans into the grinder, getting ready to serve up any arriving customers.

'That must be it,' she said and she leaned against the truck, reluctant to take her eyes off the glittering sea in the distance. 'Go on then, make us both a cup, on me,' she said, reaching into her pocket and placing coins enough for two cups and a small tip. Usually, he never charged her for the first cup, but she made a habit of placing the price and then some into his tip jar when he wasn't looking. Not that he needed it, probably. Ros told her that Jake was a solicitor in Dublin. His surfer dude coffee van was only a summer holiday project. He loved the waves, loved the island, but probably there was nothing to anchor him here, not properly, so the coffee van gave him some sort of purpose, she supposed. She'd asked him about it, a few days earlier.

'It's just different, y'know?' he'd said, squinting up against the sun. 'My colleagues at the firm, they think I'm mad, but when I'm there, I'm good at my job. I enjoy the law. It's just a balance. I'm not sure anyone should bury their head in law books all the time. The sea rejuvenates me and...'

'The coffee van?'

'Without it, what would I do? Surf all day?' He shook his head. He was hardly forty; sometimes Heather wondered why he hadn't married or settled down with some nice young woman or man – she had a feeling it could be either – but she'd never voiced any of those things. 'I enjoy the van and meeting customers; I've had some of the funniest moments, right here, serving up a frothy white or a simple black.' He'd smiled at her.

'Purpose,' she said now, surprising herself that her thoughts had brought her back to the present moment so succinctly.

'What's that?' he said, placing her Americano on the counter before her.

'Purpose, that's what the van gives you when you're here – otherwise, you'd just drift.'

'I guess so. I hadn't thought about it, but probably, yeah.'

'You're lucky,' she said and sipped her coffee. It was divine, strong and hot and exactly what she needed after the walk across the clifftops from Ocean's End.

'How's that?' He shrugged, but she had a feeling he knew exactly how lucky he was.

'Well, I owned, or rather we owned, a string of flower shops in London.'

'Wow, I didn't know that,' he said, coming out to stand next to her, and they ambled over to the low wall and sat on it. This was one of her favourite places on the island, just before people arrived, to linger here and look across with the rising sun on her back.

'No? God, I thought everyone on the island knew everything about everyone!' she said. It was not an unpleasant thought. 'Anyway, when we decided to divorce, we agreed to sell them on...'

'I'm so sorry, but if it's any help, from the legal side of things, it was probably the right thing to do.' Perhaps Jake understood more than she gave him credit for.

'It definitely was. I mean, we didn't have an acrimonious break-up or anything like that, but it was just time...'

'Still, not easy. Divorce is bruising, no matter what the circumstances.'

'The thing is, I was at peace with all of that. I mean, until my mother died and I realised that Philip had moved on, I was happy, you know? I was drifting, but happy.'

'I'm no expert, but they say, after a divorce, the best thing to do, for a while at least, is to take time. This is a good place to heal,' he said as if he knew what he was talking about.

'It is, I can see that, well, I can feel it.' The sea was rippling, the current turning, changing before her eyes and, on the surface, the water fighting hard, waves against tide – perhaps there was something to be said for letting go. 'I had a therapist in London.' How ridiculous that seemed now, thinking of the amount of money she'd thrown away on something that, really, was here all along, if only she had looked. 'But now I see it.'

'What's that?' Jake drained his coffee. There were people arriving, surfers setting out their boards, struggling into their wetsuits, his first real customers of the day.

'I need purpose, that's what I've been looking for, all this time, a purpose.' It was not, as Heather had supposed for so very long, making a success of the flower shops, nor was it in being married to Philip, neither was it having a baby that never managed to materialise. She needed a purpose within herself that would anchor her to wherever life took her.

'Wise words.' He looked at her now. 'Do you still think you have to *go* and find it?' he inclined his head, as if it was a trick question.

'Maybe not,' she said, because suddenly, she knew the answer, it had been here all along, right here, on Pin Hill Island, in a little corner on the edge of the ocean, where all the best memories of her childhood had been carefully stored away.

For the rest of the morning, she thought long and hard about that conversation on the pier. She thought about it as she cut back brambles and briars that had taken root along the perimeter walls and, with each one she pulled, it felt as if she was somehow pulling back the weeds in her own life. It was cathartic. And the harder she worked, the clearer she felt.

'Max Toolis said that you could be no nearer to God than in your own garden,' Ros said gently, placing her hand across Heather's to pull her from her work and her thoughts. 'Still, I don't think even God would want you to miss out on lunch, would he?'

'No, and I'm fit to eat a horse at this point.' It was the truth. Soon after, sitting in deckchairs at the back of the house, Heather told Constance and Ros about her conversation with Jake.

'Jake?' Constance looked from one to the other.

'Surfer Dude?' Ros clarified and then she explained to Constance about the man with the coffee van that only opened for half the year down on the pier.

'So, I think that's it,' Heather said, licking her fingers of mayonnaise and melting butter now that she'd finished the last of the sandwiches Constance had made for them.

'You'll just keep on clearing back my garden until you find a purpose?' Constance smiled.

'That's it, if you'll let me,' Heather said softly.

'Let you? I should be paying you, if right was right, but...'

'Aren't you putting a roof over my head, feeding me like a king and, at the end of the day, I'm getting more peace of mind here than I was when I was handing over a small fortune to that life coach in London.' Heather shook her head. She leaned back in the chair, closed her eyes against the sun, which was as high in the sky as she'd ever seen it. A little later in the year and today would be a scorcher, but as it was the temperatures were still being reasonable and the sun simply broke through enough to warm her bones but not to call halt to her work in the garden.

'It's almost two o'clock,' Ros said suddenly. 'I should be getting back to George.' And then she was racing out the door and promising that she'd ask Finbar if she could borrow his jeep to bring Constance to her cottage to see the goat one day soon.

Ros had only been gone for five minutes when there was an almighty crash at the front of the house and Constance and Heather looked at each other wide-eyed, both knowing it couldn't be good.

'Come on, how bad can it be?' It was as good as Heather could do to dampen down the worry in Constance's eyes. She passed Constance, sidestepping her as they made their way to the source of the noise. Whatever calamity awaited them, at least she could jump out of the way more quickly than Constance.

'Oh dear.' It was all Constance said. Nothing, it turned out, had crashed to the ground. The noise had come from the rooftop railing: a thin steel band that ran around the semi-circular side of the house was hanging, as if someone had just unfastened a hair tie and let it loose.

'I don't think we should stand too close to it,' Heather said, guiding Constance towards the front drive. From here, it was easy to see that the iron had rusted, to the point of being almost thread-like, jagged straws of it only just holding on to the remainder of the handrail above. The wall, at least, had not been damaged, but the winter winds would surely make it crash against the side of the house with such force that the plasterwork was in danger of cracking and that was the least of the damage it could wreak.

'I suppose I'll have to get it taken down, properly.' Constance craned her head, to try and get a better look from this safe distance. 'I mean, I'd never live with myself if it fell down on someone's head.' She was shocked, Heather could see it.

'It mightn't be as big a job as you think?' Heather said, but the more she looked at the front façade of the house, the more glaring the ugly gap seemed.

'I don't know much about building, but I know that out here on the island, there's no steel engineering works and that railing is going to have to either be very carefully repaired by someone who knows what they're doing or completely replaced.' Constance shook her head sadly and levelled a look at Heather that said she knew about this, there was no point trying to sugar-coat it. 'I've lived on this island for a long time, Heather, I know better than most, getting raw materials out here is a job in itself. Every inch of steel would have to come by boat. Then there's the bringing over and back of the men to do the work and we both know that any decent craftsman is rushed off their feet, they won't want to take on a messy job like this.'

'You don't know that for sure,' Heather said mulishly. 'You really don't...'

Again, she felt that strange tug at her heart. It was something close to love and heartbreak for this old woman who meant so much to her. She'd begun to think that their relationship had been set together when she was a small child. Constance had always made her feel loved, far more than her own mother ever did; even to a child, it had been obvious, all that love.

'Constance, don't be cross with me, but I have money...' She put up her hand to stop Constance from interrupting her. 'No, listen to me now, I mean, I have a lot of money.'

Heather had never whispered a word to anyone since four million pounds had been deposited in her accounts after the sale of their business and flat in London. Until now, there had been nothing she wanted to do with it; somehow, it hadn't really hit home, all that money, it seemed unreal, like zeros in her bank account that were somehow removed from the reality of her life. Suddenly, she could see a way to make things right for Constance; maybe it would go some way to making her feel better too.

'I'd be happy to get it fixed for you,' she went on. 'I really would, it's the least I can do, after all, I've been staying here for weeks now, intruding on your kindness, and you won't even let me...'

'You've filled the fridge and every cupboard in the house with enough food to feed an army if the island was cut off for months. For goodness' sake, Heather, don't be silly, I can't let you go spending your money on a house that's falling down.' Constance squeezed Heather's hand. 'Hush now. We both know it is... I mean, I mightn't like to admit it to anyone else, but let's be honest, the railing is only the ribbon on the cake. The whole roof needs to be replaced probably and there isn't a window that doesn't let in breezes from every angle in the winter.' She smiled then. 'I'm certainly not going to stand by and watch you throw your money into what is effectively a bottomless pit. Dotty would never forgive me and neither would you. Some day, when whatever little nest egg you have is all gone, even then Ocean's End will continue to need work, let me tell you.'

'You're wrong, you know; I wouldn't be sorry,' Heather said, but she knew that if they were going to do anything about that railing, standing in the garden while Constance caught a draught wasn't going to make any difference to it.

'Sometimes, I wish we could make time stand still and you could see how truly elegant this place was once,' Constance said dreamily. 'Sometimes, when I close my eyes, I pretend it's still beautiful.'

'Of course, I remember it from when I was a child, and Constance, it's still beautiful...' Heather was about to reproach her when the glint of glass from the bookcases in the study caught her eye. She'd been in there, of course. Constance had every single edition of her mother's books stored away in beautiful art deco bookcases. Floor-to-ceiling shelves filled with books translated into many languages rested gently undisturbed, probably for years before Heather arrived, behind glass doors with a rich diamond pattern marking out the cherry walnut and elm of the frames. Heather had been giddy with excitement when she'd first found them. She was solidly working her way through reading the full collection. There were so many novels and a few unpublished plays and manuscripts that Maggie had held back for various reasons of her own.

'Constance.' Heather cleared her throat, but still her voice sounded a little high-pitched with excitement. 'What if you could pay for the work yourself, would you do it then?'

'In an ideal world? Of course, why would you even ask that?'

'Well, I mean, you think you would, but you know, really, making the house sound and safe and secure, it would mean a lot of inconvenience. Like you said, builders over from the mainland. It would mean a lot of coming and going.'

Heather knew Constance would love that, forcing cups of tea and brown bread on big working men who were only hoping to get their jobs done and be back on the mainland with the high tide.

'Oh, Heather, if that's all that was putting me off, I think I'd manage. I could even move into the little cottage, couldn't I? If I won the lottery...' Constance sighed then and it was good because anything was better than that feeling that all was lost.

'I think, maybe, there's a chance you could afford it,' Heather said and then she steered Constance inside the house and towards the room that she rarely ever entered but where she had preserved her mother's works as carefully as any museum might.

26

August 1957

Constance

Constance could sense it: a strange thing, this nervous sort of excitement between the women, calling into each other, whispering over garden fences. Of course, her mother had never been a woman to spend her time out scrubbing the front step or hanging clothes on the line, so to engage her in the latest drama, Lickey Gillespie's mother had taken to dropping by for afternoon tea. She would sit at the kitchen table, demolishing whatever confectionery was available and drinking tea while trying to get Maggie to contribute to the gossip that currently swirled around the street in relation to the whereabouts of Mr Wren since his disappearance.

'He's done a runner, if you ask me,' Mrs Gillespie said under her breath, as if Constance might not hear it just because she lowered her voice a fraction. 'Always too smooth, that one. I always said, Norman Wren was too smooth for his own good. He's the sort that could have a whole other life tucked away with a wife and family in some part of the country you'd least expect.' She sniffed, because there was nothing surer than the fact that her own husband was far from smooth, the last person anyone would want to marry, aside from Mrs Gillespie, it seemed. 'A grown man doesn't just vanish, does he?'

'No, I suppose not, but still, it's going to be very hard on his wife and daughter.'

'I suppose *she'll* have to get some sort of work now,' Mrs Gillespie said as she popped a corner of shortbread into her mouth, making a job of licking her fingers of sugar.

'Maybe I could ask her to do some ironing or...' Constance's mother looked around the house. As usual, it was a mess of books and odd items thrown about at random.

'It'd be something, I suppose, but she'll need more than pin money if they're going to put a dinner on the table every day.' Mrs Gillespie's eyes narrowed slightly, perhaps gauging just how much had been earned in the big book deal that had been pushed to second place now that the gossips had Mr Wren's disappearance to satisfy themselves with.

'Of course, maybe I could ask her to do a little tidying too...' Maggie murmured. Constance's mother had never bothered too much about keeping house, even less so over the last week or two since she'd had word from her publishers that they had managed to sell her rights into America. 'Still, I hate to think of them struggling.'

'I don't think they're struggling yet, so maybe give it some time,' Mrs Gillespie said, reaching for another square of shortbread. She stopped suddenly, as if struck by divine inspiration. 'Good God, he wouldn't have done what you did a few months ago, m'lady.' She turned around in her chair and pointed an accusatory finger at Constance.

'What's that?' But Constance knew exactly what she was saying.

'That old well is still open, isn't it? No-one ever got round to closing it after the floods. It might be worth shining a torch down there.'

'Urgh, I hope not.' Maggie shuddered.

'I'll get my Dan to have a look later,' Mrs Gillespie said and Constance shivered. But in spite of the growing panic rising up in her, Constance made up her mind that she'd have to tag along behind Mr Gillespie, just to be sure of what he found.

It was light until well past bedtime these evenings but thankfully it was early evening when she heard the men gather in the garden next door after their dinners were eaten and the women were left to clear up the dishes and sort out the younger children for bed.

'You shouldn't be here at all.' One of the older men tried to talk Constance out of tailing him down the yard. So she fell back a little, but stuck close enough to hear them speak.

'Ah, now, girleen, go home, you don't want to be down here with us now, do you?' Mr Gillespie said when he spotted her skirting behind them.

'I want to. I knew Mr Wren probably as well as any of you.' That much was true, at least. 'He bought us ice-cream, when the weather was warm.'

'Oh, aye, he was a great man for the kiddies and the ice-cream.' One of the men guffawed before stubbing out his cigarette with an undisclosed anger that didn't really seem appropriate to the job. The man hardly looked at Constance, but he stomped ahead, probably hoping for a quick look and then to drag the door back over the old well again.

Constance delayed just as they got to the well. She had the strangest feeling that maybe Mr Wren wasn't down there any more. Ridiculous, of course. She looked around, felt the bristle and sting of midges against her arm and neck. It was still bright. Guilt bruised something along her spine so she almost expected Mr Wren to appear with a condemning smile from behind the overgrown blackcurrant bush that grew up at the side of the well. What if he *wasn't* there any more? Suddenly, her heart began to race. *Stop it*. He was dead. But what if he wasn't? What if he'd managed to grasp onto that rope that was too high for Constance to reach? What if he was somewhere in the garden, waiting to push her in if she stood too close?

She thought she might be sick, feeling a tightening stricture somewhere between her stomach and her throat as if she couldn't breathe and yet there was too much air: cold, stabbing and accusatory. She had to fight the urge to run back to the safety of home, wrap herself up in the huge goose eiderdown on her mother's bed and hide there until this was all over. Except, she couldn't just run away. She couldn't move. She was stuck, as if turned to stone, like that poor woman in the bible that Sister Consietta talked about. Or was that a pillar of salt? Salt would crumble on the spot, wouldn't it? Constance wished she could crumble now, into a nice dense pile on the ground and then slip away unseen.

Nonsense, of course. Mr Wren was not going to appear from the dead – he was hardly Jesus and more than three days had passed anyway, she told herself. Still, she felt uneasy, so much so that she began to shiver, her heart racing, and then, as if struck from above, an epiphany: Constance was not afraid of finding Mr Wren. She was afraid of the questions that would be asked if they *did* find him.

Mr Gillespie's voice made her jump.

'I said, I can't see a blessed thing down here, can you run back to the house and get me some sort of light?'

'A candle?'

'Anything at all will do.' He was waving his lighter around the top of the well, but even from this distance, Constance could see pushing back the darkness with such a slim flame would be like holding out an egg cup to gather all the sand in the Sahara.

She raced back to the house and grabbed a bundle of candles her mother had left in the scullery so long ago probably no-one remembered they were there any longer.

'How long is he gone?' one of the men said and Constance wasn't sure if he was talking to himself or to her.

'Just over a week today.' Mr Gillespie lit one of the candles, held it out towards the centre of the well. Constance held her breath, maybe even her heart stopped ticking for a moment; or at least, that's what it felt like.

'We're going to have to organise someone to go down there.'

'What?' Constance said a little too loudly. 'No, no, you can't do that, it's...' She heard her own words break off, as if falling from a cliff. 'Here, let me look.' She made a bit of a show of leaning across, looking down, concentrating hard, although her eyes were firmly closed. 'No, no, there's nothing down there, only a tiny drop of water, nothing at all.'

'But there's a smell, Constance, and I'm no expert, but I know what that stink is coming out of there, it's…' Mr Gillespie rubbed his chin. 'Not good.' He stood up again, pulled the door back over the well. From there, he stalked back across the garden and soon he had gathered up a huge rope and some lengths of wood. It took no length of time for them to set up a pulley, as they had probably done when they managed to rescue Constance.

'Who's going down?' said Mr Blackwell, a huge bear of a man who would surely snap the rope in half by the looks of him.

'We're all far too heavy. The only one we could ask to go down before was Mrs Macken,' one of the other men said. It was true, Maggie Macken was a tiny woman just like her daughter. She would be easy to lever up and down, certainly more so than any of the men.

'She won't be keen on going down there again,' one of the other men said.

'I'll do it,' Constance said before she had a chance to think properly and even as she said it she felt sick to the pit of her stomach but there was nothing else for it. She couldn't risk her mother finding Mr Wren, lying at the bottom of the well with his lunch bag and cigarette case thrown in on top of him. 'I'll do it, I don't mind. I'm lighter than anyone and I've been down there before. But you have to be sure to pull me up when I say…' she said and she tried hard to keep the wobble from her voice.

'Are you certain, Constance? It's a long way down and especially after you falling in there and all that. I mean you don't have to, no-one expects it.' Mr Gillespie's voice sounded different suddenly. He was looking at her now in a way he'd never looked at her before, as if weighing her up and she somehow measured to be a much bigger person than he'd realised.

'Of course I'm sure. Dotty is my friend and Mr Wren was always lovely to us.' It almost stuck in her throat to say it, but she remembered all the things the nuns said about talking ill of the dead. Whatever else happened, she didn't fancy coming face to face with a dead man after having just blackened his name. Bad enough she was half responsible for him being down there in the first place.

'It's a very brave thing to do,' one of the other men said solemnly. She smiled, a watery smile, because she knew she wasn't brave. Far from it, she was going down that well not because she was brave but because it was the only way out if she wanted to save her skin, and Dotty's too.

'Come on then, I don't want to be coming up when it's dark,' she said, taking off her cardigan and folding it neatly on the grass.

'Constance, are you absolutely sure about this?' Her mother came racing down the path towards her just as Mr Gillespie was fastening the thick rope around her waist. He had wound it already beneath her bottom in a way that she supposed would feel like sitting in a chair when the ground went from beneath her feet.

'I'll be fine,' Constance said with a lot more courage than she really felt. 'I have a candle and Mr Gillespie promised to bring me back up as soon as I call out.' And for all of that, there was a great big part of her that wanted to unfasten the ropes that held her and run as far away as she could from this bloody well and Mr Wren and everything that had gone on before.

Then, before she realised what was happening, one of the men lifted her into the well and held her there while the others gathered up the rope, tight and taut. They formed what looked like a one-sided tug-of-war team ready to gently feed her down into the darkness.

'Your candle, lassie, don't forget, you need to hold it away from you, you don't want to get burned,' one of the older men said. He handed her his lighter, a scratched silver thing that smelled as if he'd just replaced the flints, then he patted her on her head as she was lowered. 'Watch out for rats,' he said softly, and if she hadn't been scared to within an inch of breathlessness, she might have screamed so loudly they'd have had no choice but to pull her back up instantly.

The rope moved slowly and she was tempted to tell the men to hurry, but a part of her was too afraid to risk any sudden noises or movements. For all she knew, there could be anything down here now or worse – although, what could be worse than the man you helped to murder? She pushed thoughts of Mr Wren from her mind on that slow journey downward, but he intruded on her in flashes in the way he'd set upon both her and Dotty in the garden that terrible afternoon. In her memory now, there was something of the wolf about him, but of course, he was just a man – even if he was a very bad man. He was just a man.

She clenched her eyes closed. She didn't want to remember. The gentle sway of the rope, over and back, had a rhythm similar to that of rocking a cradle for a small child. *Don't think*. She leaned into it, tried to concentrate on the image of those big arms and hands holding her safely in place. Nothing was going to happen to her. She was going to be fine. She'd get near the bottom, shine her candle so they could see just a few feet above where Mr Wren was lying and then she'd call to them to pull her up again. Perhaps she'd tell them there was some smelly water down here and then maybe that would be the end of it. A badger? No-one liked badgers – they still had the repute of TB attached to them. This old well could be locked up again and forgotten about.

It took forever and still, before she knew it, she could sense she was near the bottom. Would they remember how far down they'd sent the rope before?

She knew it, before she saw it or felt it.

'STOP!' she screamed.

'Are you all right, Constance?' Her mother's voice cut thin and clear through the gloom and Constance wanted to cry out. *No. No.* She wasn't all right, she'd probably never be right again.

'I'm fine,' she said and then as quickly as her trembling fingers would allow she lit the candle and held it in her own shadow, careful not to let the light escape too much. She didn't want the men at the top of the well to see any sign that Mr Wren was here.

Actually, it took a bit of figuring out the dark around her to realise that he was underneath her dangling feet. The water levels had risen and so all that was visible was his hand, lodged in against the side of the well, his bag propped up against it, as if he might pick it up at any moment and be on his way again.

Against the other side of the well, as if watching from a step above, there was a streak of black and white. Constance reached out. She couldn't help herself. It was soft and wet and cold. A magpie. He'd been caught up in some sort of netting and now his remains seemed to dangle midair, suspended from where the net caught on jagged stone. From the looks of him, he'd been down here longer than Mr Wren. She moved the candle around to take a closer look, some sense of having been close to the bird before swelling up in her. Had she leaned against him when she was trapped down here? The candle moved slowly, across his glossy feathers; a thin ribbon had become knotted around his toes. Constance's hair tie. She'd been wearing it that day. Had she rested her head against this poor creature? Had this been the comfort she had felt with her? She reached out to touch his wing, as if to thank him, but when it moved, she realised behind it was a bed of insects, slowly devouring the creature in a tidal frenzy. Poor Mr Magpie. They would start on Mr Wren next, probably; a horrible thought.

'Take me up,' she screamed then. 'Please, bring me up.' She had started to cry and even if she tried to figure it out, she'd never know if she was crying for the poor old bird and how pathetic he looked here at the bottom of the well, or for herself. Not once did she shed a tear for Mr Wren.

No sign. Absolutely, no Mr Wren. Only the rotting carcass of a badger.

Once she told the lie, to her mother and all of those men, that was it. She realised she was taking a quantity of blame on her shoulders that she couldn't share with Dotty.

By the time they pulled her to the top of the well she was shivering, not cold, but icy in other ways.

'Oh, darling, that was so brave.'

'Nothing?' one of the bigger men asked.

'No, nothing,' she shivered.

'Are you sure, because I could have sworn I…'

Mr Gillespie said but he sidelined whatever he was going to say next when he caught her mother's eye.

'I'm sure. There was a dead badger in the water, he must have gone in when the floods covered over everything, he was…' Constance scrunched up her eyes, tried hard to push away the image of Mr Wren's hand forever down there in the darkness. 'Decomposing, but it was definitely a badger. Horrible.' She shivered again.

'Well, that's that, I suppose,' one of the men said and she knew, with the way they all shook their heads, the well would be covered over now, the magpie and Mr Wren left to rot in peace.

'Oh, darling, come on, let's get you back to the house. I'm so proud of you.' Her mother bundled her up. She'd brought down a huge blanket from the chest at the top of the stairs.

'I'm fine, really, it was…' But when she looked up towards the Wren house, she saw Dotty standing at her bedroom window, tears streaming down her cheeks, and their eyes locked. She waved at her friend and nodded. She wanted to tell her all would be well, but a little part of her doubted that, even if she didn't dare admit it to another living soul.

27

Ros

The call came when Ros was stretching down the side of one of the small tributary river banks, trying to push back some moss which was covering over what looked like a clump of green figwort. She'd have to take a photograph with her phone and check it against the app she used to confirm if she was correct. If she was right, it was a great little find. She hadn't seen that particular plant growing along this stretch of the river before. It was not exactly endangered, but it was too easily overpowered by hardier plants like willows and alders which had colonised river banks all across the mainland. If it wasn't for Constance and Heather, the phone buzzing would just be an inconvenience. She crawled back onto the damp grassy bank and flicked the screen into life.

'Ah, erm, Ros?' Keith Duff, as usual, seemed to be checking he'd gotten her name right.

'Of course.' She sat up, reaching into the inside breast pocket of her waterproof jacket. She'd been here long enough to look out to the ocean for incoming weather rather than putting her trust in the meteorological services. She pulled out a small, slightly battered notebook and a pencil, because with Keith you never knew.

'Can you talk?'

'Well, I'm not exactly in the middle of a big stockholders' meeting, if that's what you're asking. I'm sitting on the side of a river called Abhainn Bán, looking at what I think is a new growth of green figwort.'

'Right, well, whatever about that, you're sitting down at least.'

'I am,' she said slowly, because people only said that when there was bad news, didn't they? 'It's the interview, isn't it?'

'It is. You didn't get the job, Ros, no point sugar-coating it, you're a big girl.'

'And, why…' She realised she'd better clarify. 'I mean, what let me down at the interview, was it because I was a woman?' She had to ask; she knew from the few team meetings she'd attended she was the only one. And there had been comments, the sort you'd expect from stupid men. *Out there, cut off on the island, a woman on her own. A girl, really.*

'Oh, God. Of course not, that would be…'

'Sexist? Illegal?' she finished for him.

'It would. It would, no, no, you can't say you didn't get the job on the grounds of…' His voice had dropped, as if even mentioning the word was too much for him.

'Sexism?'

'Well, yeah, but no, no, no, no.' He cleared his throat, perhaps hoping that was an end to it and she would toddle off and make life easy for him.

'Why didn't I get it, so?' She felt suddenly sick with disappointment.

'Someone more experienced turned up for interview. We offered him the job yesterday evening and he accepted it this morning.'

'He?' So, Shane McPherson, who'd been on the island for less than twenty-four hours – she had already known he'd probably get it, why on earth did she feel so upset now it was official?

'Now, I hope you're not going to be awkward about this... just because he's a man. Shane got the post because he was the best man... I mean, candidate on the day.'

'I'm not being awkward, but isn't it good practice to tell me where I went wrong at the interview, in case I apply for something else with the Parks and Wildlife Service?'

'Oh, right, well, you know, there's a lovely little maternity leave coming up here in a few weeks, part-time hours. It might suit you if you enjoy surfing, now there's no cottage but...'

'So, it would be office-based?' The irony was, she couldn't type to save her life, was very dodgy at taking messages and keeping files in order was something she feared would bore her to death. 'Anyway, that's grand,' she said, swallowing down her frustration. There was a huge lump opening up in her throat and while she might like to drag the old boy over hot coals for a little longer, actually, there was no point. She definitely did not want him to hear her become a sobbing mess. 'So, you'll let me know when he's arriving on the island? I presume you'll want me to stay until he comes and I'll have to organise a new place to live and a job and...' That was it, she was about to cry.

'It'll be a while yet and... Ros, there is that little job here. I'm sure that we can find you something to tide you over, if...'

'Hmm, thanks for that, must go, the rain is coming. I'm going to get soaked here and I still haven't gotten a good look at that figwort to be sure,' she said and she hung up the phone before collapsing into a spasm of despairing sobs. What on earth was she going to do now? She couldn't leave the island, she just couldn't, it was the first time she'd ever felt as if she had a real home, the first time in so very, very long.

That evening, Ros felt so low she knew, no matter how much she wanted to, she couldn't just put on a brave face and go to Constance's house and pretend that it didn't really matter. It did matter. It mattered very much to her. She felt as if the idea of leaving was like cutting out some vital organ. It made her breathless, the fact that she would have to go and live somewhere she knew now she'd never belong. Pin Hill Island was her home. All right, she wasn't born and bred here. She didn't have any actual family, but she had Constance and now Heather and the fact was they were as close to family as she had in the world.

That evening, she stayed in the ranger's cottage, snuggled up with a throw she'd bought in the Christmas market several months earlier. She curled up on the sofa and watched as the sky turned from grey, to shadow, to charcoal to black. She sat there with a bottle of whiskey that Max Toolis had bought before he left and never gotten round to opening.

Well, he was unlikely to come back and claim it now. The taste stung her lips but it warmed her mouth and down all the way to the very centre of her empty stomach. Over the course of an evening where it felt as if time both dragged and stood stock still, she got slowly, miserably drunk.

At some time after ten, she heard the unwelcome sound of a rumbling jeep turn into the back yard. Bloody Jonah Ashe, it had to be him. She listened as the driver pulled to a stop and the handbrake squeaked noisily. There was an odd silence for a moment, as if the driver was holding his breath just as Ros was – perhaps he sensed this would not be a good time for a sparring match with her. Then she heard the jeep door creak open, imagined she heard Jonah cross the yard, although in reality, there wasn't a sound, but then a loud thunk, as if something hit the door. Silence, for a full thirty seconds. There was no knock on the door, no calling out of her name, no signs that he had actually come to see the person who lived here. Just one excited bark and Ros imagined that black-and-white collie that sometimes travelled with him leaping about with excitement because his master had returned to the jeep. And then she heard the engine roar to life, the sound of the jeep being turned around on the gravel and growling once more onto the narrow road that led away from the cottage.

A half-empty bag of feed nuts, suitable for ewes and lambs. That's what he'd left against the back door of the cottage. Part of Ros wondered if perhaps he was saying sorry for their argument the last evening she'd met him, another part of her couldn't help but wonder if it was the wages of guilt – had he reported her to the Parks and Wildlife Service for not doing her job properly? Was Jonah Ashe responsible for her losing out on her dream job? That thought made her even more upset and then angry. How could someone be such a complete and utter bastard? But of course, a man who'd cheat on his wife wasn't going to have very much in the way of a decent character when it came to other things in life either, was he?

She wallowed for a whole evening and made a silent vow that the following day, she would get up and start all over again. She had done it before; she'd just never actually wanted to do it less than she did now.

28

September 1957

Dotty

If Dotty lived to be five hundred years old, she'd never understand how she got through the next few weeks after her father ended up in the well. It helped that their house took on a completely different shape, as did her mother. Perhaps her mother thought the change in Dotty herself was down to some sort of terrible grief at losing her father. Well, she was wrong about that. Dotty was simply petrified that anyone would find out what had happened in Mr Morrison's garden.

That first evening, Dotty made her excuses. Belly ache. Too many gooseberries and a mild reproach meant she could hide in her room for the night. She didn't sleep, how could she? Instead, she sat up in bed, listening to every floorboard creak, every stroke of the old poplar tree branches outside against her bedroom window. Her mother didn't sleep either. She heard her pad up and down the stairs several times over the course of the evening. Her father had stayed out before. If there was an occasion, or sometimes for no occasion at all, he could stay out until the early morning and then stagger noisily to bed with only the muffled sounds of her mother trying to mollify him quietly for what remained of the night.

Dotty knew she couldn't stay hidden forever, but the next few days shot past her as if they were unconnected images taking place around her, just beyond her reach. Search parties were organised; her mother watched the door silently, as if there was some chance he would walk through it at any moment. It felt as if every neighbour on the road sat in the front room drinking tea and talking about it being such a terrible to-do.

No-one, not one person, asked Dotty if she knew anything of her father's whereabouts. Not even her mother. Which was strange, because her mother asked just about everyone else, she even went to the local garda station with Mrs Macken and reported him missing.

It was a week later, maybe longer, when Dotty heard the doorbell ring. Time had taken on a new form in their lives; now it was measured out by ticking seconds on the clock, she couldn't possibly hope to calculate those into days or even into hours sometimes.

Mrs Macken. Again. At least she did not come bearing awful dinners that they could not face and did not want to eat. Her mother brought her into the front room where they sat for a small while. Mrs Macken would not drink tea and refused cake, which was probably just as well, since Mrs Gillespie had made it and Dotty wouldn't have put it past Lickey to spit in it if he knew it was being given away.

It had always been the way, Dotty wasn't sure why, but as soon as adult voices dropped to a whisper, you could be guaranteed it was then the interesting things were being said. Mrs Macken and her mother spoke in whispers that afternoon, but thankfully, they were *both of an age where they couldn't bear not to have fresh air slice through a room*, so the door was left ajar. At first, from her vantage point at the top of the stairs, Dotty feared that maybe Constance had let the cat out of the bag. This thought occurred to her often and, when it did, she felt bile rise uncomfortably in her chest, a thin layer of sweat oozing from her palms. This time she had to fight hard to stay exactly where she was, rather than bolt out into the wet afternoon. It was better to move closer to the open door, try and pick up what was being said.

'It's just a thought,' Mrs Macken said softly.

'But that's just it, I can't think… it's all so much. I mean, Norman has always been the one to decide these things and…'

'But Norman is not here, Sylvie, and you're a grown woman, you can make your own choices. For goodness' sake, you can't tell me he decided everything.' There was a taut silence then. 'Sorry, I just… I didn't mean…'

'No, no, you're right. I shouldn't have let him, but…' Her mother began to weep quietly. 'It's just, it's always been like that. I was so young when I married him, only just sixteen, and he took care of me. You know, I'm not like you, I can't just go out and make a life for myself, you've no idea where I came from or what…' She seemed to gather up her words for a moment. 'Well, no-one expected very much for any of us, put it like that. I was the only one of my family to get away, the rest of them are all...' She didn't say it, but maybe she didn't need to.

'Simple farming folk?' Mrs Macken was being kind.

'*Stocious drunks*, Norman called them and he was right, my parents just didn't really...'

'None of that matters, Sylvie. You are not your parents, you don't have to live like them and you don't need Norman Wren to make you a better person. You are just fine as you are.'

'I'm sure he'll come back, it's just...'

'We've checked everywhere, the hospitals, the guards. Sylvie, you have to do something, you can't live on fresh air and Nellie Gillespie's leftovers.'

'God, they're awful.' Sylvie giggled; it was a strange sound because, suddenly, Dotty realised, her mother rarely smiled, she hardly ever laughed.

'I know, I'd rather starve.' Maggie was laughing too. 'So, will you think about it?' There was silence, a long silence, and Dotty was on the point of bursting into the sitting room to ask exactly what it was her mother had to think about.

'I probably should ask Dotty first.' Her mother hesitated.

'Or you could tell her, see her reaction and if she doesn't like it then maybe figure out another solution.'

'Just tell her?'

'Yes, Sylvie, just tell her. You're in charge, remember. Even if Norman Wren walks in that door this minute, you always have to be in charge of what's best for you and what's best for Dotty.'

'Oh God.' Sylvie began to cry.

'What is it?'

'I never realised I could...'

'Look, whatever has gone on, this could be a fresh start. We're leaving for Pin Hill Island in two weeks, now, you can come with us, keep house, we'll give you a fancy title and there's a cottage, you'll have some money and it's safe. You know what it's like here as soon as you are a woman without a man. They'll turn on you as quick as milk in summer. And you're young and far too pretty, probably even worse for you! They'll all be expecting you to have designs on their husbands.' Mrs Macken's expression changed, as if the very idea was ridiculous.

'I could be a housekeeper?' Sylvie declared with a shot of surprise. 'I could have a job and my own money?'

'Not a lot of money, probably to start, but enough, and you'll have the cottage and you'll both eat with us, so...'

'You're very kind... offering me this, you didn't have to...'

'Far from it,' Mrs Macken said softly. 'It's the least I can do, and anyway, it'll work out well for us too. I'm a terrible cook and I can hardly manage to keep the small house here in one piece. I'll never manage a mansion like Ocean's End.'

'I suppose, we'll be going up in the world,' Sylvie murmured.

'It'll be an adventure,' Mrs Macken said and it sounded to Dotty, at least, as if it had been agreed. They were moving to Pin Hill Island with Constance and Mrs Macken and she breathed a sigh of relief. She couldn't get away from this place – and the idea that her father lay dead at the bottom of the well in Mr Morrison's garden only yards away – fast enough.

29

Constance

It was all such a long time ago and yet it was one of those things that left a mark that stained every memory Constance had of that time. It was, she knew as she woke up first thing in the morning, the reason why her life had turned out as it had. Some people had pivotal moments, you read about them in the Sunday papers – *the day I won the lottery* or *the day my hair fell out* or *the day I met my husband*. Constance knew, or at least she had convinced herself over the years, that the day she and Dotty had orchestrated the death of Mr Wren was a pivotal day that had stained every single joy and happiness in both their lives from that day on.

Dotty had spent her life sabotaging happiness by turning her back on it and drinking down the guilt. Constance had found that even if she faced life head on and did her best to put things behind her, the price of that afternoon was always going to be exacted on the trading account of her life. God had snatched away her future that day he'd upended Oisin's boat and seized her husband from her. She always knew, deep down, that it was the price of Mr Wren ending up in that well – she'd paid not just on the double but many times over with that one moment of loss.

'Good Lord, Ros, you look as if you've been up all night,' Constance said when Ros walked through the kitchen door that morning.

'Well, I might as well have been. I'm hungover, if I want to admit the truth of it,' Ros said a little sheepishly. 'Stupid, I know, it's the classic loser way to drown your sorrows, right?' She dropped into a chair at the table and seemed to immediately regret the sudden movement, scrunching her eyes up with the discomfort of it.

'Drowning your sorrows? Come on, it's not the end of the world,' Constance said gently, but she flicked the kettle on and began to root in the cupboards for some herbal tea that might make Ros feel a bit better. Except she wasn't sure whether to offer hibiscus or ginger, mint or camomile, because it was hard to know if Ros needed settling or soothing or just to have her whole system shot through with something that might put the colour back in her cheeks.

'Just tea from the pot is fine,' Ros said as if understanding the indecision of her movements.

'Tea, so. I suppose, you wouldn't fancy a bit of a fry-up? I have sausages and eggs.' She broke off her words, because Ros had turned from deathly white to a sickly greenish white. 'Never mind, tea it is.'

They sat for a while, watching the wind whisper through

the grass in the garden outside. Already, it seemed that the pathways they'd cleared over towards the kitchen garden were being swept across with encroaching dandelions and docks determined to re-establish their lost territory.

'So, I'm guessing that…'

'I didn't get the job. They gave it to someone else. I was just fooling myself; I was nothing more than taking up a space on the interview list so they could offer it to someone else.'

'I'm so sorry, it really is their loss,' Constance said, because there was no missing the fact that Ros poured her heart into that job.

'Well, it doesn't matter now anyway. The job is gone. They've asked if I can stay on until my replacement arrives, so I suppose there is that. It'll take a few weeks for him to get himself organised to move over here and then…' She shrugged.

'Oh, Ros, let's not think about all that just yet.' Suddenly it all seemed so final and it hit Constance like a bolt to her chest. Ros would be leaving and she realised how much this girl had come to mean to her. If there were markers in her life, certainly in this, the final chapters, the before and after meeting Ros point stood outside her everyday experience. Before Ros had come along that morning and rescued her from the cold, she'd been to all intents and every purpose very much alone. The only person she really saw regularly was Jay, who did far more than any postman on the mainland would. Apart from that, there were occasional visits from the district nurse, calling in to check up on her. It was just that – a check-up where Constance felt as if she was on stage, acting out a part so there would be no question that she could no longer cope with living on her own. Ros had, in a very short space of time, come to mean so much to Constance. The news that she would be leaving the island to be replaced with some stranger only made the fondness that Constance felt for her all the clearer.

They sat for a while in silence, the clock ticking, the tide turning in the distance, the lonely call of a curlew somewhere across the water beyond the only punctuation marks between them.

'What will you do?' Constance said eventually.

'I'll stay, for as long as I can, I suppose.' A tear raced down Ros's cheek. She didn't have to tell Constance how much the island or the little ranger's cottage meant to her. Constance had known that from the very start. Leaving here would be like ripping off a limb or, worse, maybe her heart out. 'Then, they've offered me a post on the mainland, but it's in an office, covering for some woman going on maternity leave...' She shrugged again.

'Well that's... I mean, if it was over in Ballycove, couldn't you travel across, stay here on your days off, maybe...' But of course, a maternity leave was for a matter of months and they both knew when winter came travel would be difficult, especially if you factored in the unreliable ferry times.

'It wouldn't be the same and anyway, there's the cottage and...'

'Stay here, at Ocean's End. There's plenty of space, well, that is if you didn't mind the crows in the eaves.' Constance tried to laugh to lighten things up. 'Could you get a job here, on the island?'

'Ah, Constance, we both know there are no jobs here on

the island. And even if there were, sure, there's nowhere to live. The cottage was my home, the first real home I've had in years.'

'I know, I know, but I'm thinking about the hotel. Maybe if you asked them for a job, I mean, you know your way round a bar and they might let you have a room. It's not as if they are inundated with people applying from the mainland, it's all kids on their school holidays and…'

Of course, they both knew the hotel would pay a pittance and any room they had free was rented out to make as much as they could over the short season when trade was booming with summer visitors.

'There's no harm asking, I suppose…' Ros smiled sadly and she sipped her tea, which was cold now.

'Come on, I'll make a fresh pot.' Constance took the cup from her hand and rinsed it out. She stood inside the kitchen window, looking out across the sea and noticing a fishing boat bob up and down on the choppy waters in the distance. Her mind began to wander, back to a time long before she'd met Ros, maybe even before she'd come to live here in Ocean's End. She thought of Dotty and long summer days and whispered things that had made her eyes grow wide. Suddenly, she remembered the things that friends do to keep each other close and, as she set the pot of tea on the table between them once more, she reached out to hold Ros's hand. 'We'll think of something, I'm sure we'll think of something. Between us, we'll figure something out.'

30

Heather

By some miracle, Heather had slipped the card from the woman on the bookstall into the back of her wallet that day in London and only remembered it was there a few days after she arrived on the island. Heavens knew why, but instead of throwing it in the bin, she'd stuck it into the corner of the mirror on the dressing table in her bedroom at Ocean's End. She laughed when she spotted it there, laughed out loud, because what were the chances? The morning had been spent in the long room that had once been Maggie Macken's office. It was a magnificent room, faded now of course, but you couldn't fail to notice the elegance beneath the smothering decay. It was a beautiful room, one wall lined floor to ceiling with glass-fronted bookcases. Thank God for the fact that the books were protected from the dust and mildew of the place, because although they showed visible signs of age, each of the books was still in good enough condition to take down and read and, yes, catalogue before she made a formal or maybe informal approach to someone in the publishing industry.

Constance had been dumbstruck. She'd repeated the idea to herself several times, whispering it as if the fairies might hear it on the breeze. *My mother's books? Republish?* And then she'd spun around in a movement quicker than Heather had imagined her capable of.

'But how would we do it? I mean, would anyone want to read them at this point, surely they are... well, they're of an age,' she said and her voice had trembled as much with fear as with any sort of optimistic trepidation.

They had the conversation, over and back, the notion of a writer who most people had forgotten, and of course, Heather knew only too well that this was true. It had been a surprise to her when booksellers had remembered the Macken books; more often than not younger shop assistants had no clue to whom she was referring when she'd searched in London. But that didn't mean that readers wouldn't enjoy them and, Heather argued, didn't readers deserve the chance to experience them, too? She herself had found them to be a complete escape from her worries and misery when she'd sunk into them after her mother's death. There was no reason why other readers would not feel the very same.

'I can't see the harm in trying, can you?' She didn't labour too much on the fact that some writers never truly went out of style. There were so many of those who sold perennially, albeit in specialist bookshops, but their legacy lived on in adaptations and special editions and all sorts of forms. Truthfully, once the excitement took hold of Heather it had kept her wakened for most of the previous night. She'd tossed and turned and flicked through her phone in the darkness, looking at other writers whose books still thrived through careful management of their estates. Why not the same for Maggie Macken? Why shouldn't Constance reap some reward and maybe they could talk a publisher into enough to secure the house around her, at the very least.

Heather spent a sleepless night, high on the excitement of a project that had ignited her imagination in a way she'd never dreamed possible. She could see that the whole legacy of Maggie Macken's life's work could be developed into something far, far greater than the books she'd written. In her mind's eye, she saw not just the special editions sitting on tables in Hatchards in London and The Strand in New York. Beyond that there was the potential for movie tie-ins, for serialisation and maybe, one day, for a writers' retreat right here on Pin Hill Island. What a wonderful way to bring visitors to the island when everything else had shut down! Certainly, the hotel owners would be thankful of the business. God knew, but from what she'd seen, Ireland was teeming with creative writing teachers, why not make the most of it, if they could. It would mean not just that Constance would have enough money to make the house secure, but maybe to bring it back to its former glory too. Constance would finally have the satisfaction of knowing that she'd secured her mother's memory for quite some time to come, which they both knew had always been important to Maggie Macken.

All of these things, racing around Heather's brain, had chased her from her bed before five in the morning. The silence was bliss and she had walked into the kitchen and made herself a cup of tea, which she drank in the garden, watching as the sun came up from across the bogs and scattered sparkling shards slowly across the water. A light wind played among the wildflowers in the garden and when she craned her neck to look along the island's coast, she could see the trawlers making their way out to sea for the day.

Later, looking along the wall of books, Heather knew she'd need some sort of system. They needed a catalogue and then, once she had sat with Constance to agree a plan going forward, she would contact that bookseller she'd met in London. She placed the card in the centre of Maggie Macken's desk. Emptying the desk of the mountain of discarded rubbishy paperwork that had amassed there over many years had been her first task. Now that it was clear and she'd found an unused notebook and pens, she sat looking around the room. It was elegant – more than that, it was inspiring. Heather smiled; she could see why Maggie Macken wrote so many books here, sitting at this desk. A little shiver of excitement reached up her spine at the idea of it.

She took the card in her hands again – Bea Hardiman. The woman on the bookstall had scrawled her name across the top of her son's business card. The son, Gregg, worked as an agent for a company called Bookpress – she had looked them up. They were impressive, to the point of being intimidating, but Gregg was a junior agent and hopefully hungry to build up a list of his own. Some of the senior partners represented writers' estates. Heather had never heard of most of them, but at least it meant they would be open to considering an estate like Maggie Macken's, or maybe they'd point her in the direction of someone who might be interested.

Cataloguing the books didn't take one day, it took four. And Heather worked tirelessly, hardly taking time to eat and only going for a walk to clear her head as night fell. Constance came into the office that first morning and offered to help, but Heather had already set up a system of sorts. She didn't say it, but the only thing she needed help with was clearing out the rubbish that had built up in the office, taking down the cobwebs, cleaning the carpets of the build-up of years' worth of dust.

A day or two later, she came across some shoeboxes, filled with letters that Maggie had kept tidied away in an alcove beneath the window ledge. When Heather opened them, she could see some were filled with fan mail, but some had more personal correspondence, things that related to not just her finances but also the little notes and cards that were a postscript to a life.

Folded in a drawer, Heather spotted a letter from the guards. It halted her in her tracks. It was a letter about her own grandfather – they were contacting Maggie in relation to any information she might have regarding his whereabouts. Norman Wren had never been found, remaining an open-ended question, and now Heather wondered if in that question was the answer to her mother's emptiness.

Heather lifted up the boxes and carried them into the kitchen. She placed them on the kitchen table in front of Constance.

'You still want to help?' she asked, because it was one thing to go through Maggie Macken's professional outpourings, but quite another to go raking through things that Constance might prefer to keep private.

'Oh, my, I had forgotten that these were even in the house.' Constance shook her head. 'To tell the truth, after my mother died, I just closed up that room. I couldn't face it.' She smiled sadly, but then her eyes brightened as she lifted the lid on the first box. 'Actually, now, I think I might enjoy a walk down memory lane,' she said. 'I'll start it after lunch. Ros is in the garden, she's tackling the ivy today.' Constance rolled her eyes, because maybe she knew that without someone like Ros here all the time, the ivy would eventually choke everything in its path. 'We're having pizza for lunch, Ros picked up a huge one in the supermarket on her way over here this morning. We'll eat outside, around one, I'll give you a shout,' she said then, carefully taking out the letters at the top of the first box.

The woman on the bookstall – Bea – remembered Heather well when she rang.

'I can't believe that I'm ringing you,' she said once the woman stepped away from the sound of traffic. Heather had a feeling she had a cup of coffee steaming in her gloved hands.

'I can. Certainly, if you've found a whole set of the books and... why wouldn't you see if something can be done about managing the estate?' the woman said. She'd told Heather she was madly jealous of her, how she'd love to sink into a chair and read one Maggie Macken novel after another, until the whole collection was finished.

'If your son can hook us up with a publisher, that's exactly what you'll be able to do.' Heather winked at Constance, who was sitting in the wingback chair opposite. Ros was crouching down on the fender before the fireplace. They were all eager to see if something might be done to resurrect the Maggie Macken legacy.

'Well, what's stopping you? Give him a call, tell him you were talking to me. I mentioned the books to him weeks ago, but I can fill him in on them more if you want to talk to him first. I'll lend him my copies so he can get an idea of the books,' Bea said and she sounded almost as excited as Heather felt. 'The only thing is, I have to warn you, much and all as I might love to see them in print, he can't take every client who contacts him, you know?' She was trying to prepare them for disappointment.

'It's okay, I've read the numbers.' They were depressing. 'They get sent thousands of manuscripts every year and their agency sometimes picks only one or two to represent.'

'Yes, it's a tough life for anyone wanting to break into it, but that doesn't mean you shouldn't give it a shot and I'll be rooting for you on this end,' Bea said in that jolly way that had meant so much to Heather that day she had run into Philip and Charlotte, when Bea – a virtual stranger – had come to her rescue when she'd needed it the most.

The phone call to Gregg Hardiman went straight to his voicemail. Heather left a short, business-like message.

'You should have mentioned his mother,' Constance said when Heather put the phone down.

'Seriously, Constance, have a little faith. He's going to want to take this on not just because his mother tells him to, but because it's absolutely worth taking on.'

'Hmm,' Constance said and Heather wanted to reach out and put her arms around her and tell her not to worry.

Of course, she knew that securing the services of a literary agent, never mind actually getting to the point of having the books republished, was not an easy ride. But, what was it they said, if you're not in, you can't win? Well, Heather had every intention of doing her best to make it happen, if she could.

It must have been the longest seventeen hours in the history of mankind, but the following morning, Heather's phone rang. She was alone in Maggie's study when it burst into life and almost gave her a heart attack. She had already catalogued the novels and now she was working her way through a box filled with short stories, all stapled together, with rusted edges holding each story in place on thin and faded paper.

'Hi, Heather?' said the voice on the other end of the line.

She didn't recognise the number, but when she'd seen the London code and her stomach flipped, she'd known it had to be Gregg Hardiman. Although, of course, in the next split second she realised it could have been anyone, from Philip to any number of estate agents she'd left her name with when she had been thinking of buying a new flat after the sale of their lovely home.

'Yes, that's me, hi…' She paused, afraid to hope that it might be the call they were waiting for.

'It's Gregg, Gregg Hardiman, you rang me yesterday on my mobile. Sorry it's taken me until now to get back to you, but it was back-to-back meetings yesterday and…' He waited a beat. Time was money. 'My mother is very excited about this writer you are trying to relaunch. Maggie Macken?'

'Yes.' Was she trying to relaunch her? That made Heather

seem as if she knew what she was doing, and truly she had no idea about anything to do with publishing.

'I read *The Island Home* last night, I think we should talk...' he said and maybe he continued to speak after this, but Heather was too excited to hear much more, apart from bits of sentences that had words like *rights* and *publishers, book fairs* and *international agents.*

'I'm actually helping her daughter.' Heather needed to explain. 'Maggie's daughter? Constance Macken. She owns the whole estate, but she's quite elderly. I can't see her wanting to travel to London, to sign contracts or...'

'Oh, don't worry about that, Heather, if we end up signing with the right publisher, they'll travel to the ends of the earth to make sure that everything is just perfect. I have a feeling that the Maggie Macken books could find a home sooner rather later.' He asked for the full catalogue and anything they had on hand relating to her old agency or her old publishing contracts. As luck would have it, only the previous evening, among the papers in one of the boxes Constance had been going through, she had come across a pile of documents that Maggie had tied together. Each and every contract that she had signed over the course of her career had been carefully filed away.

'I can email them to you,' Heather offered, because it was just a question of scanning them on her phone and scooting them off. 'I can have them with you by tomorrow...'

'That's a lot more than I expected,' he said. Even though he sounded young enough to be just about leaving school, she had a feeling that Constance would like him. If he was anything like his mother, Heather liked him already. 'I'll ring you as soon as I get a look at them, yes?'

'Perfect,' Heather said and she danced all the way to the end of the garden, where Ros and Constance were watching huge gannets fly back towards land from their morning's fishing on the water.

31

Ros

Heather had advised Ros not to turn down the job offer on the mainland immediately. Instead, she encouraged her to keep her options open – a true businesswoman, she was so wise; Ros was grateful to call her a friend.

And it was a good thing she hadn't turned it down, because it was increasingly looking like her only option. She had tried everywhere on the island she could think of – as she had guessed, the hotel would be employing the same kids it had the year before and they hadn't any spare rooms to give out anyway. She'd tried every single little business on the island. There was nothing she wouldn't turn her hand to. In the end, one of the bars offered her a few evening hours, but not enough to live on and there was, she had to face up to it, nowhere to rent even if she did decide to stay.

'You know you're welcome to move in here.' Constance had said it more than once. Ros would have loved to stay with Constance and Heather, but without some sort of proper job, she'd feel as if she was just hanging around. It was all very well doing odd jobs about the place, but if Constance came into serious money, all those jobs would be done in a day or two, with a crew of workmen who would bring in big machinery and sort out not just the garden, but every corner of the house too. And anyway, she wasn't that brilliant at maintenance jobs really: every little task she took on, she had to learn to do from YouTube. It was amazing what you could learn though. She'd fixed in a pane of glass, replaced a kitchen tile, cleared away the garden with Heather's help, mended the crazy paving, so many things she'd never realised she could do. Now, she'd done them and the place looked so much better than it had that first day she'd arrived.

'Two weeks. He'll be here in two weeks.'

She'd had an email arrive in her inbox as she'd been coming back from a rewetting project that had been started a few years earlier. Today, she recorded that a number of pairs of birds that had been all but extinct on the west coast of Europe had returned for a second year's breeding. There were, in spite of her own worries, still reasons to be optimistic about life, she told herself.

'So, I'll have to have everything moved out by then.' Not that she had much, not really, but since she'd come here, it amazed her that for the first time in her life, she had purchased things like her own pillows and a really decent frying pan. She had a collection of wildlife books and a painting by a local artist of Ocean's End, in its glory days. She'd bought the painting – a set of two – at the church fete, giving one to Constance and keeping one for herself. It was momentous, the idea that she'd actually bought something to hang on a wall, as if there was a feeling in her soul that there could be a semblance of permanence about her home here on the island.

'Anything could happen in two weeks,' Heather said brightly that evening as she dished out lamb stew into bowls for dinner.

'She's right, you know what they say, *tell God your plans...*' Constance was doing her best to be jolly, but they all knew Ros had tried everywhere she could think of on the island for work and there was nothing going.

'I'm going to email tomorrow and tell them that I'll take up the maternity leave cover, at least it's a job.' She'd be able to pop across to the island on her days off, well, while the ferry service was on a regular timetable at any rate. 'I'll have to think about George too.'

George was a real worry. He'd rallied somewhat, but he still couldn't put weight on that leg. Sometimes Ros looked at him and he was as bright as a button, but this morning he seemed to be at death's door. She wasn't unduly worried though, he'd had days like this before and he always rallied. She was certain now he was going to be just fine.

'Oh, George, I don't mind him coming here, although I'm not sure that I know very much about rescuing goats...' Constance smiled.

'Perfect, I can help, if you'd like,' Heather said. It was kind of her, because Ros suspected she knew even less about rescuing animals than Constance.

She was wrong about George. The following day, he was no better. If anything, he looked as bad as he had on that first day. The infection was obviously back, his eyes were completely glazed and he was barely breathing. The breaths he did take were jagged and shallow and even though she sat with him for over an hour, there was no improvement. She tried everything she could think of to get him to sip some water, but he wasn't having it. It was as if he'd given up. When he did look at her, just once about five minutes ago, his eyes fastened her with a stare of resignation and it felt as if he was trying to tell her it was time to let him go. Still, she tried to make him as comfortable as possible. He could be all right. She was willing it more than believing it, but miracles did happen and they very rarely happened to disbelievers.

She was bending over his bed when the sound of that bloody jeep turned into the yard once more.

'Glad I caught you, I was just up at the little grotto.' Jonah jumped from the jeep, then reached back in to take out a small cardboard box. *Oh, God, hopefully not kittens.* The little grotto, built around a small trickle of water that somehow managed to crack through the rocks even in the driest weather, was dedicated to St Deirbhile. Apparently, she was a good woman to visit if you needed help to see – from what Ros could gather, that *seeing* could be either related to your eyes or your understanding. Unfortunately, over the last year or so, there had been three occasions where kittens seemed to have just been left there. Ros felt her anger rise with Jonah. She wasn't the bloody ISPCA, just because she'd rescued one goat, she couldn't possibly set up an animal sanctuary, especially not if she was meant to be leaving in two weeks.

'What?' she snapped and instantly regretted it when she saw his reaction.

'Sorry, I just thought...' he said. 'If it's a bad time...' He began to retreat to the van. And then of course, she thought, well if it was kittens, what was someone like Jonah going to do with them – would he be the sort of man who'd do the unthinkable and drown them in a barrel without even looking for homes for them? She suspected he might be, especially if he was the sort of man to leave his wife and report Ros for not doing her job properly.

'Okay, what it is it?'

'If it's a bad time, I can come back,' he said, turning to look at her now.

'I might not be here when you come back.' Not strictly true, she had another two weeks, but still, wishful thinking. Not seeing Jonah Ashe would be the only good thing to losing this job.

'It's Japanese knotweed. I've been careful with it.' He put his hand up before she could begin to lecture him about trailing it across the island. He lowered the box for her to peer inside.

'It is Japanese knotweed, it's from up at the well?' That was unusual, there were outbreaks of this vicious weed in a number of spots across the island, but Ros had helped treat those last year. They'd marked them off so people couldn't trail them just anywhere, but of course, you couldn't do the same for wild animals. *Oh no.* She knew what was coming next. The deer herd that moved around the island constantly.

'He's still here.' Jonah peered around the doorway behind her. 'He's...' He didn't have to say it. It was fairly obvious now. George was dying, right before their eyes.

'Oh, George.' Ros fell to her knees again, vaguely aware that Jonah had dropped to his also, right next to her.

'Did he finish the antibiotics?'

'Yeah, they cleared up the infection too, or they seemed

to. It's just yesterday he fell back into himself, but...' She felt a huge lump rise up in her throat. 'It's happened before, you know, one day he's fine, the next he's at...' She was going to say *death's door*, but now, she didn't want to jinx things. He *could* still be okay. He *could*.

'Maybe between us we could make him more comfortable.' George had begun to shiver. Jonah stood up and went to his car. In a moment, he was back with a battered old sleeping bag, which he handed to her. Then he was placing those two huge sunburned hands beneath George's fragile body and raising the little goat from his bed with such swift gentleness, with such tenderness, that Ros had a feeling George didn't even realise he'd been moved. She went to work very quickly on pulling out the used bedding that had bundled up beneath the goat. *Oh God.* As she took it out, she saw, in the folds, tens and tens of small fly larvae and white insects that surely meant Mother Nature had already sent the call-out that George was not much longer for this world. Even so, she spread the sleeping bag evenly around the bed for him. At least he would have comfort for the time that was left. She bundled up the old newspapers, pushing them outside the back door, she could sort them out later, but for now, she placed her palm lightly on George's head. She loved this little creature so much.

'He's not in any pain, that's good, isn't it?' Jonah said next to her and his voice was hardly recognisable.

'How do you know?'

'I don't think he's fully conscious,' he said. 'Sorry, I hope that's not too upsetting, but if he was suffering or stressed, he'd make a lot of noise. I've seen them with little more than a foot stuck between two rocks, easily sorted and you'd think the world was crashing in on them.' They both tried to laugh and, maybe, there was some lightness in the fact George wasn't vocalising any pain. Instead he gave one almighty shudder and Ros knew he was gone.

'Oh, no,' she said, trying to stifle a sob.

'I think that's it. He's gone,' Jonah said softly. 'But you did everything you could, more than anyone could have expected...' he added and she found herself looking into his eyes. And for a moment, she felt her breath catch in her chest, because she could swear there was something more there. Something more than just that grumpy, argumentative husk she normally came up against. This was a very different man to the one she thought he was: there was compassion in him and maybe even a little emotion at George's passing. 'I'm sorry, I know you were very fond of him,' he said hoarsely.

'I was,' she managed, but she knew, even if she kept the wobble from her voice, her lips were finding it hard to stay in a straight line and so she bit her lower lip in an attempt to keep the tears at bay, but in spite of that, they sprang from her eyes, raced down her cheeks. 'It was silly, I knew the odds, but I thought maybe...'

'No. Not silly at all,' he said and he put his great big arm around her and pulled her towards him in a hug that felt as comforting as she could imagine anything being as she sat hunched there over the little kid goat.

Between them, they buried George in the front garden. There was a free patch, just next to a holly tree that had perished a few years earlier but remained standing, still providing a place where small birds perched occasionally. They dug in silence, wrapped George up in the sleeping bag and laid him gently to rest before covering in his grave again. The whole process was completed within a few hours and when they'd patted in the earth above the mound Jonah turned to her.

'I don't suppose you'd have a cup of tea going? I'm absolutely parched.' He smiled at her and she realised then she was half baked herself; they'd been working in the full heat of the day's sun and her throat felt as dry as the Sahara.

'Of course, I should have offered, I just…' She was all over the place, her mind and her emotions all a jumble, with losing George, and now, he really was gone. She would miss him so much.

In the little kitchen she ran the tap for a minute before pouring out two pint glasses of fresh cold water which they matched each other in gulping down. She felt much better for it.

'Right, tea or something stronger?' She took down the remains of the whiskey bottle she'd opened when she'd heard the ranger's job had gone to someone else. Max Toolis wouldn't be coming back for it and she didn't particularly want to leave it for Shane McPherson.

'You've twisted my arm. Go on,' he said and she poured them both generous measures which they took outside with their pints of water. The doorstep at the front of the cottage was wide enough for two to sit and warmed by the afternoon sun. They sat there and sipped while looking across at the little mound where George would be sleeping from now on.

'Thank you,' she managed, because Jonah might be a philanderer and he might even have reported her to the Parks and Wildlife Service, but he'd been kind to her today when it really mattered.

'I didn't do a lot. To be fair, the reason he survived as long as he did was all down to you,' he said and he clinked his glass against hers.

'Fat lot of good it did him.' She shook her head, but when she leaned back against the doorframe and thought about it, she was glad she'd picked George up that day and, for all his faults, she was glad that it had been Jonah who had happened to come along first. Because really, he had helped her every step of the way to save the little goat, first by bringing them back here, then helping her to set up a bed for him, making sure she knew the vet was coming, leaving the feed and, even today, he could have said, *I told you so*, but he didn't. Instead, he'd given over a perfectly serviceable sleeping bag when it was painfully clear there was no chance he'd ever get it back and then he'd spent the last two hours making sure that the little goat was buried in the perfect spot. He was not, it seemed to Ros, all bad. And that was something of a revelation.

32

September 1957

Dotty

Dotty did not have the shoes for island living. That was her first thought on arriving on Pin Hill Island as she looked up and down the windy pier they had hoisted her up to from the boat. More to the point, she didn't want the kind of shoes that would be sensible to have for a place like this. Dotty's shoes were black and shiny, with a T-bar running up the centre of each foot. Her mother had bought them for her especially, they were half price and it took her a full year to grow into them. She had no intention of growing out of them any time soon and every notion of wearing them as much as possible while they fitted her as well as they did.

Did everyone on Pin Hill Island wear either boring brown shoes or wellington boots?

It was not that she didn't want to come; in fact, when she heard her mother agree to it, she'd almost wept with relief, for back in Galway, every time she looked out her bedroom window, her eyes wandered across the gardens to the well at the end of Mr Morrison's. She just hadn't thought about the reality of it being an island. Lickey Gillespie had told her it was as backward as anywhere in Ireland, had they even heard of electricity over here? Much less the television! 'Oh, what does Lickey Gillespie know about anything?' her mother had said quickly. The decision had been made – even if the bishop himself had asked them to stay, her mother was set on leaving Galway.

It was no good thinking of all that now. They were here. The journey over hadn't exactly been a pleasure cruise, and Dotty knew her mother couldn't wait to set foot on dry land.

'Here.' Her mother handed her the small suitcase that Dotty had been forced to cram most of her belongings into for their move from Galway. Her mother had been in a state of distraction for weeks. 'Finding yourself deserted by your husband of fifteen years will do that to you,' Dotty heard her say in a low tone to Maggie Macken. Her mother was trying to keep the reality of their situation from Dotty, but failing miserably. Her father hadn't called Dotty 'Key-hole Kate' for nothing. As an only child, she'd always known far more about things she shouldn't than they (her mother especially) realised.

'Here indeed,' Dotty said and she looked around her. Here – Pin Hill Island – couldn't have been more different to their home in Galway than if Maggie Macken had decided to buy a house on the moon.

'Dotty!' An excited screech made everyone on the pier turn to see Constance Macken racing along towards them. 'I can't believe you're here at last,' Constance said and suddenly Dotty was gathered up in an excited hug by her best friend.

'You look different.' Dotty stood back a little and inspected her friend. Constance had grown taller, more than that, she had lost that wan and waxy appearance from her cheeks, looking brighter, bigger, better somehow.

'Oh, I don't know about that. I'm still wearing the same old dresses and I'm still the same old me.' She shrugged her shoulders. 'But I've got so much to show you, I can't wait for you to see Ocean's End and the beach and our new school and—'

'Okay missy.' Dotty's mother placed a hand on Constance's shoulder. 'First of all, you're going to bring us to where we'll be staying and I'm going to make us all a lovely pot of tea. My nerves are shattered after that boat.' She shuddered. It was her first and, she had declared, her last time on a boat, she wasn't a fan of the water.

Mrs Macken had organised a man to collect them with his horse and cart and even though it meant more jolting about, the girls climbed into the back of the cart and Mrs Wren sat next to the old farmer at the front. It was a day of firsts for Dotty. First time on a boat. First time in a cart. First time on the island. First time seeing Ocean's End. Whatever the other misgivings she had about leaving the city, or the idea that there wouldn't be any clothes shops or cinema to visit, Ocean's End proved to be breathtaking enough to make up for it.

Dotty stood beneath the house, staring open-mouthed at its striking appearance. She'd never seen a house like it. Certainly, in the little terrace that they called home before this, there was nothing like it. Of course, Constance had mentioned it was pretty, but pretty didn't come close.

All the dreams that Dotty had harboured about running away and becoming a dancer or an actress or something fabulous felt as if they slowly imploded while she was standing there, because aside from the bright lights and the glitz and glamour of a life on stage, what she really wanted was to live like this.

And here she was.

Her worries left behind her in Galway.

A fresh start. She should try to remember that, she decided, as Constance pulled her inside to have tea with Mrs Macken before they settled in to their cottage in the grounds.

'It's so cute, I'm a little jealous, but Mammy says, if your mother doesn't like it, you're both welcome to live here with us.'

Dotty could hear her friend speaking, but she was too overawed to really pay much attention now they were inside the house. She was dazzled by the white carpet on the stairs. White carpet? Their old house had been covered in linoleum. She wanted to reach out and stroke the carpet – it looked so soft. The staircase twisted and turned away from her up towards the top of the house; it seemed to call to her to explore the upstairs. In the kitchen, she could feel her mother judging the Formica-topped table – her mother took great pride in the state of her own tablecloths.

It was strange, being shown around the island by Constance, as if their lifetime roles had been reversed. Always before this, Dotty had felt as if she was the one in charge, the older, certainly the taller of the pair. But it was nice too; because the locals made such a thing of her, she felt like a movie star. The girls gawped at her shoes and, she knew, the boys gawped at her breasts. Some things didn't change, even if there was a choppy sea to part the present from the past.

In the cottage, her mother insisted they'd be fine there; it was just the two of them. From the moment she sat on the single bed in the narrow room they'd made up for her, Dotty sighed. There was a finality to the place, as if the idea of being at the edge of the world had drawn her up full stop and somewhere, beyond this place, the demons that had haunted her before were finally frozen in their tracks.

It was wet. The way people talked about it, perhaps, Dotty figured, that they expected sunshine long into autumn. She didn't know what to expect, her mother said *that was farmers and fishermen for you, they lived by the weather*. She supposed that must be so, but what good was sunshine to her when she spent her days sitting in a classroom anyway?

School was no less boring on the island than it had been when the nuns had droned on endlessly for hours. Here, the boys and girls were all thrown in together, it was two more years after primary school and then you were free. Dotty couldn't wait for that.

For as long as she could remember, she had ached to be grown-up and earning her own money and smoking cigarettes. She wanted to be Tracy Lord in *High Society* and if she couldn't quite manage that, then becoming a dancer or an actress seemed like the next best thing. She was pretty enough, everyone said so. She could dance and she was fairly certain that there couldn't be all that much to acting, it was just playing make-up, as far as she could see.

'There must be something else you want to do with yourself?' her mother said time and time again. She'd given up trying to teach her how to knit a sock or make a trifle. 'Look at Constance, there's a girl with a sensible plan.'

'Mammy, we both know I couldn't be locked up in a room with thirty snotty children for an hour, much less the rest of my days. You said it often enough to me over the years: just because someone else is doing it, doesn't mean I have to follow suit.'

'Oh, Mrs Wren, I'm not sure I'm all that sensible,' Constance said, hardly taking her eyes from the pan she was scrubbing. The two girls had been given the job of cleaning up after dinner each evening. It wasn't a job either of them enjoyed, but Constance always offered to scrub the pots, so at least Dotty could hope to keep her nails in good shape.

'There's nothing wrong with sensible, it's good to have a plan,' said Dotty's mother. Sometimes, Dotty wondered if they hadn't managed to get their mothers mixed up at some point.

'Oh, I don't know about planning or how far that gets anyone. Look at my life…' Maggie Macken dropped a cup into the sink. 'I'm a terrible advertisement for best-laid plans, but things worked out all right in the end, don't worry so much.' She had a way of making it feel as if everything would be fine. And it had worked out well for Maggie and Constance. 'I could have wallpapered the whole house with the number of editors who wrote to tell me they didn't want to publish my book. I was twelve years writing into a void before the books found a home. Even your father had given up on me long before I would have ever thought to give up on my dreams to be a writer.' She smiled and patted Constance's back as she said it. Then she turned to Dotty. 'You mustn't give up. If you have a dream, you have to give it a go,' Maggie said as she wandered off back to her study again.

'Oh, I don't know, it's all very well...' Dotty's mother muttered.

1960

But behind it all, sometimes, Dotty thought, if only she could be a little bit more like Constance. As the following months bled into years, it seemed that even though they remained close, somehow they grew to be quite opposite.

Constance, with her books, walked around the island like the Pied Piper of Hamlin with an entourage of young children who she seemed to adore, although Dotty couldn't see the attraction. For her part, Dotty had started to smoke, with some of the older kids. They'd mitch off a little early, walk the long way home, cutting across the empty bogs, and sit with their feet dangling above brown streams, feeling disillusioned with everything from school to home to this damned country that seemed to be going backwards more with every day. Dotty yearned to be in London, in the bright lights, anywhere but here, where the silence was oppressive and there was no getting away from who you were and who you'd always be if you stayed. Eventually she struck up with one of the older boys, someone she knew her mother would definitely disapprove of: Eddie, a would-be mechanic, was eighteen to her fifteen. He hung around with some of the other boys, always good for bringing along a few bottles of beer and, occasionally, a bottle of spirits he'd come across as payment for some job or other.

It was at the harvest dance, their last year in the local vocational school, that Dotty realised just how much her life had begun to spiral away from Constance's. She'd been looking forward to it for ages; they both had – she and Constance. They'd picked out their outfits weeks in advance; she'd even talked her mother into buying her a pair of kitten heels, sent over especially from the haberdashery on the mainland in her size. They were going together, Constance and Dotty, but Constance had agreed to sell tickets to raise money for a new veranda at the school, while Dotty planned to meet Eddie there. There would be refreshments served, tea and cake and sandwiches, but Dotty had other plans.

'Come outside for a while with me,' she wheedled Constance before the ticket-selling got going. God, Constance was dressed as if she was going to a church meeting; sometimes Dotty despaired of her friend, even if she still loved her like a sister.

'But I really should...' Constance made a face.

'Oh, for once in your life, live a little.' She dragged her out a side door away from the gathering eyes of the local priest, who was there to make sure that everything went with the right measure of decorum. There was no easy escaping the morality police here; if she cut out a side door alone, some old busybody would come looking for her before too long. 'Come on, I want you to meet Eddie.'

'Eddie? Eddie who?'

'My Eddie, of course...' Dotty wasn't sure he was actually her Eddie, but they had become something of a pair, meeting up, sitting in his old banger and giving out about the world as they saw it. Eddie couldn't wait to leave the island, although sometimes Dotty looked at him and wondered what was keeping him here. They left the hall to see only one car parked up. A beaten-up old thing that Eddie had rescued a few months earlier.

'Hey?' Eddie looked from Dotty to Constance as if it was a question, rather than a greeting.

'You know Constance, Eddie?'

'Sure, from the big house?' He hardly looked at Constance.

'Hello Eddie,' Constance said a little stiffly and Dotty could feel her silent judgement in the air. Just about everyone thought Eddie was a bad lot. All right, so he'd stolen some money from the garage and they'd fired him and maybe he'd gotten into a few fights over the last few months, but that was Eddie. Dotty liked that he had an edge to him.

'Is he your boyfriend now?' Constance turned to Dotty and, honestly, Dotty wished the ground would open up and swallow her – there had been no mention of boyfriends or girlfriends between her and Eddie.

'What? No, yeah, I mean...' Dotty shrugged her shoulders as if such things were far beneath her.

'Here, have a drink, Mary.' Eddie held out the bottle for Constance.

'I'm not Mary and no thanks, I don't drink alcohol.'

Oh, God, Dotty watched in horror as Constance moved

her fingers up to the pioneer pin they'd been given when they made their confirmation back in Galway.

'Jesus, she's a bit uptight.' Eddie grinned and swigged from the bottle. 'Here.' He held the bottle out for Dotty and she copied him, feeling a glorious wave of release as the liquid hit her throat.

'God, I was gasping for that all day.' She giggled, the heat of the drink warming her, making her feel almost whole again.

'Dotty?' Just her name, but the way Constance said it, it was full of reproach.

'Oh, come on Constance, live a little.' Dotty wiggled her hips slightly, but the rough ground underneath her feet made her almost fall against her friend.

'Are you all right? Come on, it's time to go back in.' Constance began to pull on her arm.

'Oh, Holy Mary, is it time for the rosary already?' Eddie was mocking Constance now.

'I'm not Mary and we're going back inside now.' She looked meaningfully at Dotty.

'You go, I'll be back in a minute,' Dotty said. Drinking with Eddie made her feel reckless, alive in a way she'd kept tightly wrapped up for years.

'Yeah, that's it, you go back to the prissy party, Mary,' Eddie jeered.

'Don't be like that, she's my friend,' Dotty said, but she sipped from the bottle once more, slowly this time, feeling a delightful warm infusion send comforting waves along her spine.

'I'm not leaving you here...' Constance said.

'Oh go on, I'm fine, I'll be back in five minutes, just go,'

Dotty said then, in that way she had to let Constance know that no amount of coaxing was going to get her anywhere on this. It had been like this all summer long, both of them heading in opposite directions and now, it seemed, they stood on a precipice of sorts. Still close, they'd always be close, but each choosing roads to take them on different paths.

'Fine,' Constance said and she turned and walked slowly back towards the dance hall. Dotty slipped into the passenger side of Eddie's car and settled down to have some more of the whiskey before any of the other boys he hung around with showed up to help them polish it off.

33

Constance

It's strange how memories could flood you at any time so you almost felt as if you were drowning. Except Constance knew the past was so long ago now, the worst it could do was taunt her with memories from so far away they might have happened to someone else entirely. She would not drown in them at this stage in her life. And yet, they could absorb her, snatching the present moment away so she had to reach out from behind them to catch up.

'Constance, are you okay?' Heather was looking at her strangely. 'You've hardly touched your breakfast?'

'I...' She looked down at the plate before her. 'My appetite seems to have vanished these last few days, I'm not sure why that is...' She smiled. If she'd been here alone, would she even have noticed? She wasn't sure, oh, but what a lovely thing to have someone close by who cared. 'I'm sure it's nothing.' She batted her hand. 'And anyway,

Mr Crow out there won't be sorry if I pop extra crusts on the bird table.'

'I thought you were getting the sun but...' Ros was looking at her also now.

'That's it, of course, who has a big appetite when summer comes? It's salad weather...' Constance said. 'I'm never ravenous in summer time, not like when it's cold outside and you need food to warm you up.'

'Do *you* think she looks a little jaundiced?' Ros turned to Heather now and there was no missing the concern in their expressions.

'No, it's just the sun, probably just the sun,' Heather said, but for the next few days, Constance felt their gazes upon her in odd moments. Sometimes, she tried to force an extra forkful of food into her mouth to convince them that she was fine. And she was fine. Oh, there were niggling pains and aches, of course there were – but she'd made it this far without a replacement joint and with most of her teeth. A few twinges, backache, stomach ache and nausea were surely par for the course.

It was a few days later that she caught sight of her reflection in the hall mirror. It stopped her in her tracks. She had lost weight. A lot of weight. When had that happened? She'd never been one to think of her figure. She'd never owned weighing scales, not even in the kitchen. Her whole life had been measured out in cups and handfuls – never had she thought of anything in ounces, pounds or stones.

When Constance looked out to see the district nurse on her doorstep the following day, the first thought that crossed her mind was that Ros must have asked her to pop by.

A little part of her wanted to be cross but, the truth was, it was far too long since anyone had been close enough to her to care about her and so, instead, she just felt lucky that she had two people in her life who wanted to make sure she was well. She welcomed the nurse over the threshold as if she was an old friend. She had nothing to hide. She was perfectly healthy, wasn't she?

'No, no, nothing out of the ordinary,' Avril Duignan said cheerily. She was new to the job, had taken over only a few months earlier from Sheila Deere, a sourpuss of a woman who thought elastic bandages were the answer to every problem. This young woman was a breath of fresh air by comparison. She arrived in smart exercise pants and didn't come loaded down with a big medical bag. Instead, she sat and drank tea and chatted as if she had all day to listen to you. The last time she was here, instead of bandaging Constance wherever she could, she'd given her a head massage and honestly, by the time she'd left, Constance had felt as if a weight had been lifted that she hadn't realised she'd been carrying.

While on the one hand she couldn't help liking her, at the same time you never knew with district nurses. There was always that chance that one slip and they'd have you booked into the nearest nursing home so they had one less call on their list.

'So, how have things been? I must say, the garden looks wonderful.' Avril stood at the kitchen window looking out while Constance switched on the kettle. It was another thing Constance liked about this new nurse: Avril didn't take over. She waited to have a cup of tea put in front of her. It didn't seem to matter if it took a while and she didn't care if it was strong or weak, hot or lukewarm, she was just happy to sit and listen and sip her tea.

'I've had a friend staying over, so we're going through some of my mother's old papers and, of course, Ros comes over regularly. She's taken on the garden as if she's got a personal vendetta against the briars and the moss.'

'It certainly looks a lot less hazardous for walking to the end. I see you've still got the bird table going.'

'Yes, well, the way I see it, they're used to being fed here. Why on earth would I just stop because the sun is shining?' Constance replied easily, but the fact was, the birds in the garden had been her only company for too long to just abandon them now.

'It's good to have things you enjoy, we all need that.'

'Yes, well, I do wonder about Ros…'

'Maybe she just loves gardening. I don't think there's much of a patch up around that old cottage that she lives in, is there?'

'She won't be there for much longer, I'm afraid.'

'Oh, no, she's not leaving the island, is she?' It was the big fear; people here held onto each other as tightly as they could. News of a new baby on the way was greeted with far more enthusiasm than it warranted in other places. It went back to the 1940s. At that stage, people left the island in droves. They were dark times, apparently. For a while, the population went down to less than a hundred. It had taken a lot of work and pestering of the mainland politicians to get schools reopened, a nurse stationed here and even a phone mast erected at the top of Pin Hill Mountain.

'She's going to have to take up a job over with the Parks and Wildlife Service on the mainland. I'm afraid she'll be leaving in a matter of weeks.'

'That's a shame, I'm really sorry to hear it. She's such a part of the place, you know, it's funny how some people seem as if they've been here forever.'

'I think she feels that way too. She doesn't really want to go, I mean, she's putting a brave face on things, but I can tell...' Constance said sadly.

They chatted for a while about the comings and goings on the island. The little coffee shop next to the church which had been closed since old Jackie McHale passed away two years ago was getting a facelift. Rumour had it that Jackie's granddaughter was coming back to the island to try and make a go of the place all year round.

'Which will be fantastic,' said Avril. 'Really, I mean, it'll be lovely to be able to drop by and sit for a while. They plan to do lots of fancy coffees and homemade pastries.'

'That's good, the island needs it,' Constance said because every new venture was welcomed as heartily as a new baby. 'She'll do a roaring trade with the community centre crowd.' Jay told her that there was something on in the big hall every other day of the week, yoga and women's groups and art classes and all sorts. 'It'll be great for bringing people together, even the men, with their men's shed – whatever they get up to there!' Although Jay explained it was organised to get older men out and meeting people, they whittled wood and played cards or draughts and probably gave out about their wives.

'I think some mysteries are better left unsolved,' Avril said. She was lovely company, light and funny, and they chatted away happily for another while and then she looked at Constance and smiled. 'Listen to me, I'd talk for Ireland. How have you been, apart from having your garden done over so wonderfully?'

'I've been great, actually...' Constance really had enjoyed the last few weeks. She told Avril about Heather and Ros and the fact that in spite of losing her best friend from childhood, it felt as if Dotty had sent two more her way to make up for the loss.

'It can take a bit out of you, all the same though, can't it? Losing someone like that, it knocks you sideways whether you know it or not,' Avril said wisely. And maybe it was the depth of kindness that seemed to emanate from the woman, or just the fact that it felt like such a long time since Constance actually thought about how she was, or maybe it was that overhanging feeling of guilt that seemed to come up in her more often these days, but Constance began to sob. Huge big shaking sobs that emptied her of tears and made her feel as if her whole core was falling down to the floor in spite of her.

'Ah now, there, there...' Avril said, wrapping her arms around Constance's shoulders. 'It's funny how even the smallest of words can open up the biggest of craters,' she said softly, 'but better out than in, isn't that what they say, no good carrying your worries around the place, then you really will be needing a nurse.' She was making a joke and Constance was thankful for it.

'The truth is...' Constance began to say. 'On top of all that, there have been aches and pains and I've noticed that...'

'Aches and pains aren't always such a bad thing,' Avril said softly.

'No, no, I expect they are par for the course once you get to my age, but…' Then it spilled out of her, the fact that she knew she'd lost weight, she had no idea how much, but once she'd spotted it in the mirror that day, she started to see it clearly at odd times, noticing how spindly her shins had become, how papery thin her hands suddenly were, and then she'd realised that even sitting in her favourite chair was no longer comfortable because it felt as if it bruised against her bones. 'That can't be in my imagination, can it?'

'Of course it's not. Let's see.' Avril went to her car, brought in her weighing scales and helped Constance up to see if there was anything to worry about.

'You're very light. I mean, you're at the stage where I'd almost be thinking…'

'It's not that I don't eat well, I have a healthy appetite and I cook all my own meals and…' Constance paused, realizing perhaps she didn't need to make excuses around her independence for Avril. 'Perhaps I could take Complan or some of those energy drinks you see advertised on the television these days?'

'Well, I think we can find something more palatable than that.' Avril smiled. 'But we're going to have to look a little deeper here. We can take some bloods, get them run through. They won't tell what's wrong, necessarily, but they'll tell us if something isn't right, how would that do you for now?'

'When will we know?'

'I can get them to the mainland this evening, but it'll take a few days for the lab to check them and then get the results back.'

'Would it show if it was something…?' Constance hated how her voice sounded so thin and frightened. 'Serious?'

'Now, listen to me, Constance Macken – you are in great health, you've lived a good life. If there's something amiss, getting checked is the most important thing you can do. Would you consider a full check-up if I booked it?'

'In a hospital?' That knocked her for six.

'Don't worry, it's just a precaution, you haven't properly been checked over in years. I mean, apart from blood pressure and the occasional visit to the GP when he holds a surgery on the island, when was the last time you had a good checking over?'

'Oh dear, between ourselves, I haven't been to the GP in years, and as to being checked over,' she rolled her eyes to heaven, 'I've been lucky to be healthy enough not to warrant it.'

'Well, I think there's your answer. This is probably something of nothing, but you need to get properly checked out. I'm going to make a call, see if we can't get you booked in for a full MOT. You won't know yourself at the end of it, it'll be like a little holiday for you.'

It was no good putting it off; Constance had a feeling that even if she dug her heels in and refused to go, between Avril, Heather and Ros, she'd be coaxed into it anyway.

'You know,' Avril said later as she tidied away everything, 'this is just a thought, but you could ask Ros if she'd like to be your carer.'

'My carer? But I don't need a carer; I couldn't possibly...'

'No,' she smiled and put up her two hands in a sign of peace, 'hear me out now, there's a government payment. It's not huge, but she could have a part-time job as well. I know it's probably unorthodox, that your carer is also your gardener, but I'd be signing off on the papers and I'd be happy to think you had someone close by, if only to give you reassurance,' she said softly.

'So, she could stay here and the government would pay her to live on the island and...' The tears threatened to well up again. 'I'd love that, I really would if it was something that Ros wanted...' Constance felt suddenly overcome, flooded with fears that had lived at the back of her mind for years when Sheila Deere had been visiting here as the district nurse. 'You know, I was always afraid of getting older, not being able to cope. I thought the district nurse would want to ship me off to a nursing home and lock up this place behind me.'

'Oh, Constance, why on earth would we want to do that? No, I'm all about community nursing and care. No-one does better in a strange environment than they do in their own home, but you need people around you, if only to sit down and have a chat with, that's as important as any blood test.'

'And Ros could stay here and get paid, if we did this?'

'Not a fortune. But if she is living here,' Avril looked around the house meaningfully, 'then even better. Certainly enough to get by on, especially if she was happy here on the island.'

'That's... I never realised that could be... well, it's good to know.' Constance cleared her throat. She couldn't help but feel it might be exactly the lifeline they both needed.

'It's really not very much money, I mean, she might like to have some other project as well, she's very young to settle for a social welfare payment, but maybe think about it.'

'Thank you, I'll mention it to her and then we'll see what the tests bring back, eh?' Constance would mention it to

Ros, but she decided she would wait and make sure that all those bloods were clear first of all. The last thing she wanted was Ros hanging about because she felt she had no choice; far better to have her here without it feeling like an obligation. And the bloods would be fine, of course they would, she was as tough as old boots, wasn't she?

'Right you are,' Avril said, fastening up her bag. 'Gosh, I don't know where the days go to, I really don't,' she added, making her way out the door and leaving in her wake a much more optimistic old lady than she'd found.

34

Heather

Heather had been sorely tempted to shirk off with Constance and Ros to see if they could spot the sharks, but the lure of Maggie Macken's office and archives was too strong. In the end, she had to work hard to convince them that she was actually going to enjoy her morning pottering about in the office.

To be fair, she had already sent across the full list of Maggie's published books. She didn't tell the literary agency that the published work was only a drop in the ocean of the papers that were still to be sorted. Maggie Macken had by any standards been a prolific novelist, but it surprised Heather to learn that she had also penned notebooks filled with poetry and a great many number of plays for both the stage and the radio.

Regardless of what Constance decided to do with Ocean's

End, there was no denying that Maggie Macken had left a huge cache of intellectual property in the office.

Heather stood now in the centre of the room. A few days earlier, Ros had insisted on cleaning out the chimney. Surprisingly, thanks to the fact that at some point many years earlier a nest had blocked up the top of it, it was actually a much easier job than they had expected.

God, but she loved it here. The thought came to her out of nowhere, but really, once it settled on her, she knew it was the truth. It was a combination of the place, the people, the house and of course the work. Maybe it was a connection too with her own mother. After all, she somehow felt closer to her here than she had in a very long time indeed.

It was with that lingering notion that she was brought sharply back into reality with the pealing sound of her phone ringing out. It was a London number, she noticed, before she answered.

'Hi, Heather Banks?'

'Yes?'

'Hey, it's Wesley McVeigh here, I'm...' But she knew exactly who he was. He owned the literary agency that were currently debating taking on the Maggie Macken estate.

'You're Gregg's boss?'

'Well, I wouldn't say... we work together, sure...' He paused. 'You've really caused quite the stir here with the Macken estate.'

'I'm only the lackey.' She smiled.

'We're very interested in representing the estate. Of course, we'd need to meet with the current owners, but I think I can safely say we could do great things with this.'

'The owner is Maggie's daughter. She's not here at the moment and I'm not sure she's going to be up for flying over to London, but I can certainly put it to her, or maybe she could give you a call when she gets back?'

'If she's Maggie Macken's daughter, I presume she's not a young woman.' He was being diplomatic.

'She's a very youthful lady of a certain age, if that's what you're asking, but she lives here in the house where most of the books were written. It's on an island off the west coast of Ireland, so it's quite a trek. I don't know when she was last in London, to be honest with you.'

Actually, Heather had a feeling that the furthest Constance had ever travelled was as far as Dublin and that was many moons ago, but that was neither here nor there. If they were really up for sitting down and having a chat, they could just as easily come here, couldn't they?

'Your outlining submission was very impressive,' Wesley said and it sounded as if he was thumbing through the pages as he spoke.

'It's easy to be impressive when you're talking about Maggie's books.' It probably helped that she'd read most of them too and, unlike people who actually worked in publishing, she could spend all her time on just one submission.

'It really comes across on the page that you know them inside out, your passion is...' He delayed his next words as if praise did not come easily from him. 'Well, I'm a long time in this business, and I suppose I see so many people who just view these estates as a job, rather than a passion.'

'Thank you.' It was a compliment and Heather found herself blushing. It had been too long since anyone told her she'd done a good job. 'I adore the books. I've read quite a few of them at this point and there's a family connection, so perhaps that makes me more invested.' Actually, what was making her really invested was the idea that if they could make something of the estate, it might be the saving of Ocean's End and peace of mind for Constance.

'So, this is not your job?'

'Oh no!' she exclaimed. 'I'm just here on holiday. I live, well, I lived in London and I'm sort of between things, you might say.' It was the truth, she had nothing else to do with her time at the moment.

'Well, if you haven't already thought about it, you might consider it,' he said.

'Consider what?'

'Working on the estate, you know? These things have a tendency to become monsters if they aren't managed from the start. Of course, we'll do our bit here, with contracts and as much as you want, but the most successful estates are managed on the ground as well.'

'I don't understand.'

'Well, you know, you could think about setting up a board of trustees to support the estate. It means making decisions about how to move forward, keeping a second eye on contracts and royalties and any other opportunities that might come our way.'

'I think that would be a conversation you'd need to have with Constance. Really, as I say, I'm just the bottle-washer,' she answered.

'It's not something that has to be set out immediately, at any rate, but these are conversations that need to be had. We're talking about a potentially very valuable estate and if, as you say, Constance Macken is of a certain age, then there will be questions on any publisher's lips as to what happens when she's no longer here,' he said. His voice was soft, perhaps he was trying to be delicate, but Heather simply did not want to think about a time when Constance was not shuffling about the kitchen in Ocean's End.

By the time Constance arrived back from her trip with Ros, Heather felt as if her head was spinning with possibilities for the future of the Maggie Macken estate.

'Ooh, it sounds very posh when you say it like that,' Constance said when Heather had relayed the phone call with Wesley.

'So, what does that mean, a board of trustees?' Ros asked as she went about potting up some slips she'd taken from the garden earlier in the day. 'Will Constance have to give her rights over to people she hardly knows?'

'No, not at all. It's up to Constance to decide what it is she wants to do, but Wesley's point was that there will be quite a bit to manage on the ground in terms of royalties and contracts and making decisions about the future of the Maggie Macken brand. He thinks a good publisher will want to see that there's long-term continuity when it comes to managing the whole thing.'

'What she means is, Ros, I'm a little old lady and I won't be around forever.'

'Stop it, Constance, don't say that,' Ros said softly.

'Sorry, Constance, but yes, that's sort of what he was saying. For a publisher, especially if they offer a big advance, this is business. It's about investing in something with an eye on the return.'

'For us too, though,' Constance said thoughtfully. Then she looked from one to the other. 'Oh, come on now, we all know I've had a good innings, but I won't be here forever. My mother, on the other hand, her work could go on for decades yet, for generations, and that's what she always wanted. Isn't it what we all want?'

'I suppose,' Ros said begrudgingly, as if the having of one meant the sacrificing of the other.

'I for one would sleep a lot more soundly knowing that everything was sorted out once and for all.' Constance smiled at Ros and then turned her attention to Heather. 'Let's get the ball rolling, shall we?'

35

Ros

Ros headed back up to the cottage after her walk, taking the long way round so she could enjoy the evening sun glittering on the incoming tide. She halted abruptly when she spotted a huge billy goat standing on top of the old dolmen at Riley's Hinge. It took a moment to figure out what she was looking at, the goat in profile struck such an arresting sight. Then, one after another, more goats came into sight, until there were six she could make out. The falling sun, a glowing sky, the whisper of something approaching a breeze through the long grass and the image of that huge goat would stay in her memory for a very long time. She was officially, she decided at that moment, not just a fan of dear George, but of every single wild Irish goat that lived on the island.

When she eventually pushed the back door into the

cottage, she decided she might as well get the worst over with. She emailed the HR department and told them she would be very interested in filling the maternity leave on the mainland if it was still available. She wasn't enthusiastic about it, but at least it was something. She could push it from her mind for the remainder of her time here on the island. Once the email was sent, she sat back on the lumpy two-seater sofa that was her favourite place to curl up in the cottage. She flicked down through the other emails and began to delete what she could identify as spam. It was a way to pass the time, to not actually have to think about somehow fitting herself into an office job and starting over again. She was just about to delete a message from the Goat Society when she realised it might not actually be spam. She'd never heard of them, but what harm would it do to open an email? The Parks and Wildlife Service cyber-security systems were surely robust enough to cope with someone whose photo identifier looked like George in a summer hat.

She scanned through the email quickly, expecting it to be some demand for cash for a refuge in some country where goats were more plentiful than people. She read it a second time. And a third. The email was not a request for money, instead it was offering a grant to put in place three goat herders in Ireland to work with the society and manage goat herds in areas of conservation. She must have read that email six times before she looked up the links at the bottom of it and each of them, from LinkedIn to Instagram, seemed to be authentic, although, Ros reminded herself, she was certainly no expert.

Expert or not, she had nothing to lose. She downloaded

the application form for funding and a forty-page booklet about the work of the goat herder and the priorities and objectives of the society.

In short, from what she could see, the idea behind the scheme was twofold. First, to increase awareness about the wild Irish goat and preserve the habitat to protect it in its native environment. The second objective was to allow the goats to go about their business in a way that was environmentally positive. In other words, the goat herder would be responsible for making sure that they grazed in areas that would otherwise be at risk of summer fires, so it would be up to the goats to keep down things that were especially flammable during the hot months of summer, thereby assisting the natural ecosystem to thrive. It turned out that goats had only become a pest in the eyes of the farmer because they had been lured to the sweeter and naturally easier to graze ground of cleared-back land.

Ros sat back on the sofa and the idea tickled her. Jonah Ashe would love this; the notion that someone would be paid to manage the local goat population and save him the hard work of mending fences quite so regularly.

She scanned down through the paperwork once more. They'd need a local management committee if they were going to draw down the funding, but that wouldn't be a problem, she could imagine plenty of the local farmers would be enthusiastic about the idea, and they were offering a decent annual salary to the person employed as the goat herder.

She started to fill in the form, noting the final date for applications was drawing close. Then, once she'd filled it in, she popped it into her bag and decided that tomorrow she would get signatures and, once it was in the post, she would go about setting up the committee who would manage the funding. Hopefully she was right and plenty of people would be on board with it.

Later that night she pulled down one of Max Toolis's old wildlife journals, hoping to gather as much information as she could about the native Irish goat. Over the years, Max had subscribed to quite a few. Mostly, these were the old-fashioned types of magazines that came with a giant folder and, every week, Max had faithfully slotted in the latest issue. He had quite the collection. Ros had enjoyed many hours over the winter months thumbing through the pages. She planned to bring them to him when she went back over to the mainland; if he didn't want them, she would hold onto them. She was rather hoping she could keep them, they were a real memory of her time spent in the cottage.

There were more farmers than just Jonah Ashe on the island and Ros decided that perhaps she should go to the local development company before going to the farmers to get help the next morning. The development company on the island were always looking for projects to get involved in. They busied themselves with the tidy village competition every year and ran what approached a chamber of commerce, but really only consisted of the hotel owners and a few of the locals who had self-catering cottages to let out to tourists.

Mai Boland, who was the chief bottle-washer, CEO and head lackey of the outfit, was completely taken with the idea. 'So, there would be a job in it? I mean, they would pay your wages and you could stay on the island?'

'That would be the plan and for that, we might actually

do some good in staving off forest fires, stop the farmers from complaining about the goats and maybe even make a bit of a thing for the tourists around the presence of the goat on the island?' Ros had hardly slept a wink all night thinking of the project. 'But we have to submit the paperwork by the end of the week and I have no idea how many other places will apply for the funding, so...'

'Well, let's call the management company the Pin Hill Island Goat Society for now and then, if we're successful in getting the funding, we'll put directors in place for governance and...' Mai rhapsodised on about the possibilities for the project, but Ros just wanted some signatures and she figured they could sort all of that out later, if they were successful in the application.

This was what Ros was still thinking about as she pushed in the back door at Ocean's End that afternoon. Her mind was full of the possibilities that she might be able to afford to stay on the island after all. It would mean staying with Constance until she got sorted, but she knew that in actual fact that was the very least of her worries.

Constance was just as excited as Ros when she told her what she'd been up to.

'It's early days, but at least we'll get the application in and see what's to become of it,' Ros said then, realising she was actually far more enthusiastic about this than she had been about applying for the ranger's job. 'So, I might be staying with you for a while after all,' she told Constance.

'Oh.' Constance clapped her hands in delight. 'That would be just lovely. Mind you, it's going to mean you'll have clean out another bedroom,' she said apologetically.

'No problem, I'm very easily pleased...' Ros listened to what sounded like a chime coming from the hall.

'God, is it that time already?' It was the clock in the office sounding out the half hour. It had sat dormant for years, now it was working perfectly again. 'Heather found the key, she found a tray of them tucked away in my mother's desk. She's spent half the morning slotting them into various cupboards all over the house to match them with their locks. I think she has most of them figured out at this stage,' Constance said. 'How on earth did I manage all these years without that lovely clock?' she added as she took down the sandwich box that held an array of tablet boxes that seemed to be never very far away. 'Silly really, Heather said it was only a case of finding the key and giving it an extra wind-up!'

'It's a lovely sound, all right,' Ros agreed. There was something comforting about it. She stood at the window looking out as the sun fell heavy in the sky across the water. It was an incredible view; you could lose yourself in it, really, if you weren't careful.

Back at the ranger's cottage, the inventory was going slowly. Ros had picked up a few boxes from the local supermarket and, so far, she'd only filled one with items that belonged to her. Constance had told her to put anything she wanted in one of the spare rooms and so all she really had to do was walk out of the cottage with a weekend bag when the time came to leave.

'Hello, hello...' A tap on the door startled her and she turned to see Shane standing there. He looked every bit as delicious as the first day he'd arrived on the island. This time, he walked into her little home with a purpose that underscored the fact that this would be his cottage soon. Ros shook off the notion; it was silly, after all, being so precious about a place that had never actually belonged to her to begin with.

'Hey!' She smiled at him, it was impossible not to, he was one of those people whose eyes always crinkled as he spoke, making you feel as if you were bringing out the best in him, without even trying. 'You're eager, fancy doing a bit of clearing back around the willows down at Wilson's Banks?' She was joking him, but there was no point having hard feelings, even though she'd bawled like a baby when she heard he'd gotten the job of her dreams.

'No, I'm really not that eager,' he said and he drifted towards the edge of the kitchen table, leaning against it. 'No goat?'

'No, I'm afraid George didn't make it.'

'Ah, well, that's the way. I wouldn't have expected him to anyway, but sweet that you did your best for him,' he said and he looked around the cottage as if taking in an inventory of his own. 'Packing already? I'm not due here for another week.'

'I don't have much to pack, but I just thought…' There was no point putting it off.

'I suppose I'll be left with all this junk.' He looked around again, his eyes moving from the well-thumbed periodicals that had been Max Toolis's to the enormous old throw that Ros had made from old blanket ends she'd found in the back of the hot press. It was another of her winter projects and she thought it had turned out quite well, considering it was her first attempt at anything like that.

'No, some of it belongs to Max, I'm going to ask him if he wants me to bring it over to him and…' she said, looking around the room. It was full of bits and pieces left behind by rangers and their families who had lived here over the years. 'Actually, yes, you probably will end up with quite a bit of junk, but it's homely, don't you think?'

'I'm a lot more minimalist in my tastes, I'm afraid. I'll be looking at a good-size skip for most of it.'

'Oh,' she said and somehow the idea made her a little sad, which of course was ridiculous; every dog had its day, after all. 'Anyway, what can I do for you?'

She assumed he'd come to get the measure of the place. God, would he be replacing the old double-lined plaid curtains with Cape Cod–style shutter blinds? She shivered at the notion; maybe it was just as well she wouldn't be here to see that.

'No, not a thing, it's more what I can do for you…' he said and he headed out to the porch and brought in a medium-sized shopping bag. 'I thought, maybe we could have dinner and…' His eyes crinkled again and, in spite of herself, Ros felt her knees almost buckle with a sort of nervy excitement she hadn't felt in quite a while.

'So, you came all the way over here just to cook me dinner?' She wanted to ask him if he'd checked the tides for his return journey, but she supposed he would stay here. After all, this cottage was halfway between being her old home and his new home.

'I did, but not just any dinner.' He placed the bag on the table and proceeded to empty it. 'Steak, red onion, a very nice merlot, a frozen – well, it was when I was leaving Ballycove – chocolate pudding… and…' He reached into the bottom of the bag, which seemed to be empty at last. 'What's this...?' He made a face as if surprised. 'Oh my, it's another bottle of merlot!' And again, that irresistible smile.

'You really shouldn't have gone to all that bother.' And a little part of her wondered at his supreme confidence; what if she'd had other plans? What if she had a boyfriend already? What if... but of course, she didn't have anything else to do and nowhere else she really had to be this evening and it niggled her a little that perhaps he already took that for granted.

'It's no bother, I've been tidying up work contracts all week, not that there were many. Between us, it's not the most lucrative of locations for an environmental engineer, which is why I needed to apply for something with an actual weekly wage, but anyway... I've pretty much closed everything up and I thought, I definitely deserve a little downtime and where better to spend it?'

'Ahh?' So, Ros couldn't help but think, not *who* better to spend it with? 'Well, the frying pan is under the sink, if you want to get started...'

'Do you fancy a glass of wine first of all and maybe we could sit outside, enjoy the view...' He reached out, pulled her to him and started to kiss her. Oh, God, but he was a great kisser. So much so that when she became aware of the sound of an engine roaring into the back yard, she pulled back from him and only then realised he'd begun to unbutton her shirt.

'Hey. Ros, are you about...?' Jonah's familiar deep growl filled up the porch.

'Yeah, I'm here, in the kitchen,' she said hastily, putting herself back together again. She turned to see Jonah standing in the doorway, filling up the frame, his expression inscrutable.

'Oh, I see you're...' He stood there for a moment and went to turn, but she spotted a bottle of wine in his hand. Had he been about to pay her a social call, too? And for a moment, they all stood there in an uncomfortable silence.

'Come in, come in, Jonah, I think you've met Shane before.' She nodded towards Shane, who was suddenly standing too close for comfort, although he'd been a whole lot closer thirty seconds earlier.

'No, no, I can see it's a bad time, I...' Jonah edged backwards, turned, stood for a moment. 'I thought...' Then he turned to face her, his eyes searching hers for a moment, as if trying to convey something that his voice would never manage. 'Anyway.' He walked to the table, placed a bottle of white wine on it. 'I just called in to give you this. Mai Boland was in touch with me this morning. I told her I'd be on board with that other project you were thinking you might get off the ground, of course... I can see it's not the time, but...'

'This is so nice of you.' Ros moved forward, placing her hand on the bottle, brushing against his as she did so, but he pulled back, as if shocked by her very touch.

'It's only a token, I had it in the fridge and I'm not much of a wine person,' he said gruffly, and she imagined him, maybe with a great big pint of Guinness in his hand, but the idea of him holding a long-stemmed glass just seemed all wrong. 'Well, I must be off, I've left a...' he nodded towards the porch, 'something to mark where George is a...' And then he turned and in two long strides he was out of the kitchen and stalking across the yard to his jeep.

'Well, he's a bit of a Farmer Fred, isn't he?' Shane picked up the bottle of white from the table. 'Although, he's certainly able to produce a decent bottle of wine for an occasion.' He held up the bottle. 'This thing must have cost the guts of forty quid, he's got expensive taste for a man who doesn't much like wine.'

With that, Shane's phone rang. He'd left it in the porch and Ros had not meant to look at the image of the person calling him. But she did. *Izzy*, her name appeared at the top of the screen. She was a blonde beach babe wearing little more than a flimsy bikini and Shane's arms wrapped around her. Ros didn't have to be a genius to work out that Izzy wasn't his sister from the way his hands were hovering across those huge boobs.

'Don't worry about that, I'll ring them back later,' Shane said lazily from the kitchen, obviously not realising that Ros had seen the image. She couldn't un-see it. She stood for a moment, looking out at the yard at the back of Jonah's retreating jeep. In the kitchen, Shane was going about taking down glasses and mansplaining the fact that more expensive wine did not actually mean a better bottle.

Ros was only half listening to him. She walked to the corner of the porch. Jonah had left a black refuse bag there. She bent down and peered inside. It was a small rose bush, lavender in colour, absolutely exquisite. The scent was grapefruity and she wondered for a moment at where he could have picked it up. Blue Moon. She was pretty sure that was what it was called, not something he'd cut from a wild climber on his farm, that was for sure. It was so thoughtful, just for George, and suddenly, she felt a little overcome with the kindness of the gesture.

'He's…' Ros suddenly felt as if her appetite had deserted her. 'Actually, do you know, I completely forgot, I was meant to go visit my friend Constance this evening, sorry…' she said, grabbing her coat and stumbling out the door. 'Make yourself at home, help yourself to anything you want,' she called back but already she had decided, whatever else happened, the last thing she needed now was to find herself falling for someone she couldn't trust. She had far too many other things to sort out in her life.

36

1974

Dotty

A baby, what on earth did Dotty know of babies? More to the point, she'd never wanted a baby, never even liked children. And at the worst possible time too.

'There will be other parts,' Bobby said to her and he made it sound like a promise.

'It's taken me years to get offered this part and it's…' She felt it, her first big break, slipping away from her. How pregnant was she anyway? She wasn't sure. Too pregnant to do much about it but go through with it, that's what the doctor said when she turned up looking to see if there was any way out of it.

'Look, we'll get married, I'll get a proper job, it'll be fine, really,' Bobby said and he tried to pull her close, but at this moment, Dotty hated herself for ending up like this. She was far too upset to even try to pick apart her feelings for Bobby. 'We can live with my aunt, once we're married, she's...'

'In Fulham? Bobby, I might as well move to the other side of the world, it's miles from the West End...' But she didn't have much of a choice, because without work she couldn't pay her own rent and she knew she should be grateful that at least she hadn't been knocked up by some fella who didn't want to stick around. Everyone knew that a respectable marriage was a million times better than a mother and baby home – she would have to keep reminding herself of that.

Their wedding was small, a half-hour affair in the registry office with one of her friends from the chorus line of her last job and Bobby's brother for witnesses. Constance would have liked to be there, but the baby was already showing by the time they'd gotten that over with. In her letters, Constance was so excited about Dotty's baby. Life wasn't fair at all. Constance would have given anything to have a husband and a baby and a future that revolved around them. It still felt unreal to Dotty that her friend's husband had drowned the previous year. Oisin and Constance hardly had time to settle into married life, much less set about having a baby.

It seemed that before she knew it, Dotty was lying in the maternity ward with the main event happening to her, rather than feeling she was in any way in charge of things. She tried to switch off the sounds of other women in labour, the constant wails of newborn babies and nurses' shoes clacking on the polished tiles. The contractions were nowhere near as bad as everyone said and for the briefest of moments, in the flurry of it all, maybe Dotty convinced herself that she could do this, in spite of all that had happened in the past. Maybe she would be able to make something more of her life than just pretending she was living a life that meant something.

And then she heard the sound of her own newborn baby and it felt as if something tipped over deep inside of her, like a glass filled to overflowing, its contents warm and potent, escaping and contaminating everything that had until now been arid.

'She's beautiful.' Bobby's eyes were moist when he held their child.

'I never realised you were such a sop,' Dotty said. She couldn't bear to look at the kid for fear she'd be overcome with such emotion she might just drown beneath it all.

'I have to get back to work now.' He seemed reluctant to hand the little bundle of cream blankets over to her, but he'd managed to get a job in a small factory. It had dawned on her a few weeks earlier that she'd fallen for the next Richard Burton and ended up with Richard Baker. He was trying to do the right thing, Dotty could see it, but somehow the more he tried, the more it diminished him in her eyes. If she wasn't sure she loved him to start with, now she resented him more with every passing day.

'She's so perfect,' he said again and this time Dotty looked at him and, suddenly, something unexpected rose within her. A memory, or maybe a foreshadowing, she couldn't tell which, but it felt like a shadow, cold and tightening in her stomach.

'Give her to me,' she said sharply. Fathers and daughters. It set her nerves on edge.

'Of course, darling.' He had only started calling her

darling today. That unravelled her too. She'd never imagined herself as the little wife someone would call darling. He put the baby in her arms with the greatest care, as if the very passing of the child between them risked damaging her in some way. Dotty looked down at the little face in her arms. She examined her, for a moment. She didn't notice Bobby making his way out of the ward, because suddenly it felt as if they were the only two people on the planet, her and this strange little person who had come about to alter things so unexpectedly.

'I suppose I should say hello,' Dotty whispered, but actually, she was hardly capable of saying very much at all. Instead, she felt overcome with a compulsion she'd never experienced before, or maybe it was an emotion she couldn't remember feeling. Love. It was pure and utter, undiluted love for another living thing. This little baby was perfect, so innocent and unblemished, so easily hurt and broken. Dotty felt a surge of protectiveness rise up within her, so vast she couldn't put a name on it, taking her breath away until she had to prod herself into forcing air back out of her lungs and in again. It was overwhelming. Love. Making her head spin, her heart race, her pulse quicken; in those first moments, she felt she would kill to protect this child, she would die for her. Tears raced down her cheeks, propelled from her by a lifetime of pent-up emotion.

It was too much.

Too much.

She couldn't cope with it. She was drowning under it.

'Nurse,' she called. 'NURSE.' She began to scream and then two nurses came at once, perhaps expecting some terrible calamity. 'Take her away, I can't... I can't...' She was heaving, her body throwing itself about in the bed as if she'd been overtaken by a demon. Too much. She couldn't cope with the unbearable rawness of it all.

'It's going to be all right.' One of the younger nurses tried to comfort her, but even then Dotty knew she was incompatible with the sort of emotion required to be of any use as a mother. Something inside her had already been broken, perhaps she had fractured it herself or maybe it began with her father; it might even go back further to her mother's family – who knew what was coming down the bloodline there. Indeed, her own mother had failed her and she had been a practical woman, far better equipped for motherhood than Dotty. She'd been out of her depth with Norman Wren, but then, wasn't that why he'd married her?

The vastness of it all frightened Dotty, as if it could drive her to a sort of hell all the alcohol in the world couldn't block out, and she knew she had long ago lost any ability to survive beyond the shallows of life.

37

Constance

It was almost a decade since Constance had been to the mainland. She hadn't thought about it until all the arrangements had been made and then, she remembered. The last time she'd come across there had been an event in the library in Ballycove and, somehow, they'd convinced her to attend. It was a lovely evening, with sparkling wine and finger food and even a local girl playing a harp. Her mother would have really enjoyed it. Two writers had read from her mother's work and Constance had said a few words. She'd travelled back to the island filled with softness in her heart that came only from the company of good people and their generosity of spirit.

Today, there wasn't going to be any sparkling wine. She had been fasting since the previous night. Instead, there would be a battery of questions and tests and then perhaps a CT scan depending on their results.

Already, some of the blood tests had returned what Avril called raised biomarkers. Apparently, something called CA 19-9 was misbehaving. Not that Constance felt any different for some rogue numbers playing havoc with her bloods, but Heather and Ros both wore expressions that told her she probably should be slightly more worried than she was. She tried to reassure them – how sick could she be, really? Hadn't she made the most divine gingerbread the day before, certainly far too good to be on her deathbed just yet!

The hospital was unrecognisable from the last time she'd been here. They'd built on a whole new wing and the entrance was completely transformed by a glass atrium which warmed her to her bones as she passed through it. Ros led the way, following blue and yellow lines into the bowels of the place, so within a short time they were standing in a lift being whooshed up to a section of the hospital that sounded like it should have her in and out and processed quicker than if she was a Christmas card going through the post office sorting room.

'Two days, that's all,' Ros said gently as the doors glided back. 'They'll have you checked out and sent home with a clean bill of health within two days.' But Constance had a feeling that Ros was trying her best to convince both of them.

'Don't worry, Ros, it'll be fine,' she said and she smiled at this girl who had, by her mere presence at Ocean's End, brought her such unexpected joy.

'I know it will,' Ros said and she reached down and squeezed Constance's hand but she looked away then and Constance wondered if she wasn't on the brink of tears.

Hospitals. They did that to you and Ros probably had sad memories of supporting her own mother through her final days in a place not unlike this very ward.

The tests were run as efficiently as Constance could have hoped for in her best reckoning.

'It helps when you're scheduled in,' one of the nurses said two days later when Constance mentioned it. 'It's the emergencies we struggle with here.' And of course, Constance had seen it too many evenings on the news, winter vomiting bugs could send everything into chaos with numbers on trolleys reaching double figures at the worst of times. Thank goodness she was here in summer time.

'Well, you've all been very nice,' Constance said. She was still glad to be going home to the island today. Heather had already brought her overnight bag to the car and, for now, all she had to do was sit here and leaf through a magazine until the doctors came round to discharge her and tell her their verdict on her tests.

'Ah, here they are,' the nurse said now, pulling back the curtains around her bed as if it would somehow give a level of privacy that stretched some ways beyond the appearance of it. With that, three young women all with stethoscopes hanging about their necks, and an older man with the attitude of one used to having all his mundane tasks done for him by others, appeared at the entrance to the ward. In their wake, Heather and Ros. Constance called them over just as the nurse did her best to shut them out.

'Ros is my carer.' It was a lie in the sense that nothing had been fully sorted, but it was the truth in every real way. 'And Heather is family.' Another lie, but who was counting?

'Fine, but...' It was a tight squeeze.

'So, Mrs...' The older man peered at the name tag at the top of her bed, probably to make sure he was giving the correct prognosis to the right patient.

'It's Constance,' she confirmed.

'Of course, Constance,' he said and something in his expression softened and he leaned closer to her and, somehow, she had a feeling that he wouldn't be doing this if he was telling her that things were simple and straightforward.

They weren't.

'I'm sorry,' he began and she knew then for certain that this would not be good news.

Pancreatic cancer. She'd heard of it of course, someone on the island must have had it at some point. A quiet killer. There had been no pain, no aches to speak of, but in hindsight, there had been niggles. A constantly dickey stomach, falling appetite, weight loss, but only recently – nothing huge, but it turned out, it was the little things that all added up to something much bigger. Of course, that day, as he spelled it out, none of those things occurred to her. Instead, all she could hear was the squeaking wheels of the lunch trollies being pushed down the corridor outside. The aroma of a dinner she wouldn't have enjoyed reaching her before she had a chance to shoo them away with it. Savoury mince. She was fairly certain that was what they'd said earlier, although it didn't smell anything like savoury mince to her.

Pancreatic cancer. There it was again and now, to give her thoughts a chance to catch up, she looked towards the windows, but of course, the drawn curtains had blocked them out, so instead she imagined huge grey clouds rolling back outside to reveal the bluest sky and sunniest day she'd seen in years.

Pancreatic cancer.

'Constance?' Heather was holding her hand now. 'Constance, are you listening?' She knew it was Heather, but she couldn't bring herself to meet her eyes, not Heather's, nor Ros's.

'I understand. Weeks, months...' she repeated, because she had been listening. 'Probably not months, though, less... yes?'

'I'm so sorry.' There was a mumbling from the wall of trainee female doctors and Constance was sad that they'd gotten the rotten job of being here for this.

'It's okay,' Constance managed eventually, but she felt tears roll down her cheeks, although the wherewithal to wipe them clear had completely deserted her at this point. 'I've had a good life. I'm lucky, I've got a little notice, to put things right...'

She tried to smile, but she knew it was a wobbly attempt. She waited while the consultant spelled it all out, had he said something about his name being Richard? She wasn't sure. It hardly mattered. She wouldn't be seeing him again. The cancer had been there for quite a while, apparently, silently eating her up from the inside out. That was how it worked – who knew? It turned out, for a long time, she might have been walking about like a mutely ticking time bomb, just waiting to implode.

It would be fast. In the end, she could go about her business; if she moved quickly, there was time to get her affairs in order – if she could figure out where to start.

'Oh, Constance.' It was a gasp more than a sentence,

and when Constance finally looked at Ros, she thought her heart would break because she could see it, right there in Ros's eyes. There was such love for her and this news was breaking her heart as much as it was Constance's.

'Ah, now, come on, I'm not gone just yet.' She opened her arms and Ros moved forward and they hugged each other as if Ros would never let her go. 'Can I go home now?' Constance looked towards the consultant. 'Home to Ocean's End?'

'Of course. I've written prescriptions for painkillers and the nurses here will organise for palliative care and…' His words began to race away from her then; Constance began to shake her head slowly. They would deal with it as they needed to, but today they had heard enough. She knew Heather, silently standing there, was trying to be strong for all of them; Ros was only just holding it together and, as to herself, she really wasn't sure. Everything felt unreal, as if it was happening to someone else.

'Yes. Let's go home,' Heather murmured. She smiled at her with so much love and kindness that in spite of the devastating turn Constance's life had so sharply taken within the space of a few fragile minutes, she knew she was lucky. She really was very lucky indeed.

38

Heather

Heather's phone began to fire off notifications at around three o'clock in the morning. At first, she had no idea what the constant beeping was as, sleepy-eyed, she reached for the bedside light and switched it on. Disorientated at first, she thought she was back in London; despite the net curtain billowing in the open window, she assumed it was a fire alarm going off somewhere in the old flat. She threw back the quilt, her feet touching the floor finally waking her up properly. That was no smoke alarm, Heather wasn't even sure if there were smoke alarms in Ocean's End. She looked across at the old sideboard that sat snugly in the corner of her room. It was a squat affair, with an aged mirror that had blackened round the rim. Her phone, sitting at its edge, vibrated and rang out once more.

Bleary-eyed, she picked it up, expecting it to be some random advertiser, taking the worst moment to sell their wares. She was wrong. It was a new group, set up and including her in it. The Daisy Pickers. What on earth? Who had added her to this? It took another minute to figure out that the members were all familiar, all ex-employees of the flower shops she'd owned in London with Philip.

Bloody Charlotte, she'd mentioned this that day in London. Heather immediately tapped the three dots at the top of the messages to extricate herself from the group, but then something made her hesitate. She knew all of these people, could she just...

But she hadn't spoken to most of them since they'd sold the shops. Their lives had simply pedalled on as before: she had left the shops behind her, but as far as she knew, the people who had worked for her had been content to work for the new owners.

Her finger hovered over the icon for a moment. She knew what this was, opening it would only be confirmation of the fact. Already, there were fifty notifications, another now, from Dawn who had started out with them in the Camden Road shop. Heather smiled, she'd always liked Dawn, a middle-aged woman who could have been bitter about losing her daughter, but somehow remained a kind-hearted soul who always went the extra mile for every customer she dealt with.

Heather took a deep breath, pressed on the conversation that was ongoing, that she had not asked to join and that she knew already would shake her world in a way she'd never expected it to be shaken.

It was exactly as she expected. A line of photographs, downloading to her phone. A gorgeous newborn baby, pink-faced, wrinkled, eyes closed, mouth pursed – beautiful. It was the most beautiful baby, just as every baby Heather had ever seen was beautiful, and for a moment she caught her breath. Philip's baby had arrived; her ex-husband was now a father. All their lives forever changed and she felt once more that familiar yank at her heart – it was the feeling of change, wringing its way through her body, not bad change, but change all the same. *So many photographs*, she thought, as her thumb moved them up the screen of her phone. A baby girl, proud father, exhausted and Charlotte, beaming at the camera, looking down on her daughter as if she'd just managed to do something no other woman had ever managed before. *Stop it.* Then there were the comments, the *oohs* and *ahhs*, the *isn't she gorgeous* and *she's the image of her mother*. Who knew there were so many emojis for *congratulations, it's a girl?*

Heather thought for a moment she might be sick, her back resting against the pillows, crouched over her phone, her body filled up with an unfamiliar tension that threatened to throw her whole insides upside down. Was it jealousy? Could she really not be wholeheartedly happy for Philip's good fortune and wish him well in the way his life was panning out? She started to type, her fingers racing across the phone keypad. *Well done, so thrilled for you both, she is absolutely beautiful.* For what felt like eternity, her finger hovered over the screen. Then she took a deep breath. Felt the air exhale from her lungs as if she was releasing every stress and tension she'd ever felt in London, in the business and in her marriage to Philip.

No.

She would not play along with Charlotte's cruel games. She had moved on with her life, finally. It had taken too long, but now she was here, in Ocean's End, surrounded by people she truly loved. Perhaps it was the news that Constance was dying, but everything in life seemed to have fallen into perspective suddenly. She tapped the three dots, made her selection. Exited the group and exhaled. My God, that felt good. She would let Philip know tomorrow that she wanted no further contact, he could tell Charlotte. They were welcome to each other. She fell asleep smiling, feeling somehow liberated anew. It was a beautiful baby, though, she thought, a really beautiful baby.

Although she certainly didn't expect to, Heather slept soundly for what remained of the night. So soundly, in fact, that she woke the next morning to the aroma of freshly brewed coffee and frying bacon wafting up from the kitchen below. The sun was beaming in through the window so brightly that it lit the room up with a pristine yellow that reminded her of how things looked here when she was a child and it felt as if summer could last forever.

'Oh, you're still here? I assumed you'd gone out earlier. I'll just add some extra to the pan, we can sit together then when Ros arrives.' Constance nodded towards the kitchen window, where she'd probably already spotted Ros making her way across the fields in the distance.

'I can't remember the last time I slept so late,' Heather told her as she leaned against the sink, looking around the kitchen with fresh eyes. God, she loved being here; it was shabby and worn out and everything was dated, but it felt as she was tethered to something that felt right for her. When Ros arrived she told them both about her divorce from Philip and how he'd moved on so quickly with Charlotte and, now, news of their baby arriving in the night.

'And you're okay?' Ros said.

'I'm okay,' Heather said, passing her phone across to Constance to see the baby pictures.

'Are you sure? I mean, it's such a big part of your life, you'd be well entitled to feel a little out of sorts today,' Constance said. She had turned positively gooey-eyed at the sight of the baby.

'It feels weird, in a sort of I-can't-believe-Philip-is-a-father way. I mean, I can't help wondering how he feels now and imagining his life spooling further away from mine than I'd ever really played out in my mind when we were going for the divorce. But at the same time… I have no regrets about it.'

'Charlotte sounds like an absolute cow, if you don't mind me saying so.' Ros made a face.

'She really is, but it doesn't matter, it's nothing to do with me any more.'

'Well you did the right thing, cutting it out straight off, better for everyone in the long run,' Constance said.

'I suppose, the only thing is, it makes me wonder about where my future is going to fit into the world and what it's going to look like,' Heather said and that was the truth of it. That was exactly how she felt right now. A week ago, she thought she'd stay here with Constance indefinitely, certainly she'd had no intention of booking a flight back to London. But now, Constance wouldn't be here any more, and Ros might be leaving too – what was left for her?

'You don't want to go back to London, do you?' Ros asked.

'I mean, it's where I've always lived, I'm not sure I'd know how to live anywhere else.'

'Well, I don't think that's right,' Constance said and she put her cup down deliberately on the table. 'I mean, you seem to be happy here, living here, working on the books and walking the beach and...' She reached across the table. 'You know, you're welcome to stay for as long as you want?'

'I know that, thank you, Constance, but I can't stay on holidays for the rest of my days...'

'So, why have it as a holiday? Lots of people go to other countries and then retire there, you hear about them all the time – that couple we were watching the other night on TV, Constance, remember, in their castle in France, they just sold up everything and moved. You could do that... if you wanted to?' Ros said.

'I'm not sure I'd be up for buying a chateau.' Heather smiled. It was absurd; she couldn't just stay here on her own.

'I'm being serious. You could buy a house here, open a flower shop or any sort of shop you wanted. I mean, if you have enough money to get started, why not?'

'You are actually serious? But what would I do...' It was fairly obvious that there was no great market here for fresh flowers or for much of anything else that wasn't already being catered to.

'You could work on the Maggie Macken Foundation,' Constance said and her cheeks reddened as if it had taken a lot of courage to say it.

'Oh, Constance, what I'm doing for you with the books isn't so I'll have a job at the end,' Heather said. 'It's because I want to help you and I loved the books – I want to make sure that other people get to enjoy them too.'

'It doesn't mean it couldn't be your job, if we managed to make some money on them.'

'You need that to fix up this place,' Heather said quietly, except, now, it turned out that Constance wouldn't be here to see the roof repaired or the house secured.

'What good is this place if the whole estate is gone to pot? It needs to be properly managed, that's just common sense.'

'Oh, Constance, you are so sweet, but really, I can't see how there could be enough work to keep me busy for much more than a few weeks every year.'

'And so, what if there wasn't? Aren't there other things to be doing, couldn't you sit back and take it easy for a while, walk the beach, get a dog, maybe join the local women's group…' Constance paused. 'Look, I'm just saying, if you want to stay and work on the books, I can't think of anyone else I could ask…'

'Thank you, I'll take that as a huge compliment, but I suspect there will be plenty who'll want a few hours every week to help out.' It wasn't real of course, Heather knew that, Constance must surely know it too. They would be lucky to secure the house with whatever royalty payments were made; she couldn't imagine the income stretching much further than that.

'Live for today, that's all you can do, that's all I could do when the very worst happened in my life all those years ago,' Constance said and Heather thought about all that Constance had lost when her husband had drowned. Of course, now, as they all sat here a little shellshocked with Constance's terrible news of a few days earlier, living for today resonated on the air between them in a whole new way. 'That's my experience, just live for today and tomorrow will look after itself.'

It was with these words ringing out in her mind that Heather slipped out a little later to get some groceries in the village. They were like a balm, giving her a relief she didn't know she needed. When had she last just lived for the present moment? On the way back, she turned down towards the pier, intending only to sit on the wall for a while and watch the trawlers return with their catch for the day.

The pier was as busy as she'd ever seen it. Most of the boats were back for the day, moored quayside, three abreast in places. She supposed some were holiday makers, spending their leisure time on the water, making the journey across from the mainland and perhaps having lunch in the hotel and a ramble about the island for a change of scene. It would be a lovely way to spend a holiday, she imagined. Among them, she spotted Finbar's boat. It was easily recognisable with its Mayo flag, but smaller than the other island boats. He kept it as clean as if it was just out of the yard, even though she had a feeling it was a working boat as much as any of the other larger trawlers on the sea.

'Penny for them.' Jake sat next to her and handed her a cup of coffee.

'Ah, that's really nice, thank you,' she said, because for all the time she'd lived in London, there had never been a coffee shop that knew exactly how she liked her coffee, much less one that gifted her as many as she purchased.

'You're welcome. I'm closing up for the day, I was just making one for myself when I spotted you walking along the path.' He looked at her now. 'So, what's up? You look as if you're lost in thought?'

'I suppose I am,' she said.

'You are what?' Finbar said, hopping over the wall from behind and sitting on the other side of her.

'Lost in thought,' she said, but suddenly, she did not feel quite so alone as she had earlier.

'Hope they're worth it,' he said and she saw that he too had a coffee, made in his own mug, but it smelled as strong as the best coffee Jake had ever made for her.

'Oh, I don't know...' She told them both about Philip and the baby and the fact that it had made her feel even more as if she was drifting without anchor.

'What do you mean drifting, aren't you one of us now?' Finbar looked at her in a way that made her stop. 'What's wrong with you at all, if there's a job with Constance and you have a place to stay and you're happy here, why on earth would you be even thinking of going back to England?'

'Why indeed?' Jake shook his head.

'But there is no job with Constance. Not really. I mean, there's some work, but...' Heather didn't want to say out loud that she could afford to drift, in financial terms. There was a sizeable nest egg on which she could live for some time to come, plenty to buy a little cottage with and live out her days here, if she felt like it. The problem was, she'd always been driven. She'd always gone to work, from when she was fourteen and she'd helped out in the little corner shop at the end of the road.

'You could take this place over...' Jake said tentatively. 'I mean, for the winter months. I go back to the real world, it's only sitting here locked up. You'd have to put in your own stock and pay the electricity, but you know you could...'

'Seriously?' she asked. 'I can hardly make a straight cup of Americano. I think you're overestimating my practical skills as a barista, Jake. But thanks for the offer, it's really nice.'

'No problem, let me know if you change your mind, yeah?'

'Ah here, come on now, let's stop beating about the bush.' Finbar sighed. 'You're happy here, aren't you?'

'As happy as I've ever been anywhere,' she said, but it was less than the truth because she'd never been happier anywhere in her life.

'And there's a place to stay, there's work you're enjoying, you can manage to live on what you have for the foreseeable and Jake here is giving you the chance to earn a few bob on the side?'

'Well, yes, but...'

'There's no buts about it. You belong here, you have friends, people who care about you – what have you got in London to bring you back there?' He had turned to look at her now and she had a feeling he was saying a lot more than he was putting into words.

'Oh Finbar.' She knew this, somewhere in her bones, that he cared for her and she supposed, now as she sat here between these two lovely men, she cared for him too, for both of them. They had become her friends since she'd arrived, as good as any she had in London, probably. 'Thank you.'

'Okay, okay, less of the sentimentality, are you staying on or not?' Jake coughed next to her.

'Sorry,' she said, suddenly embarrassed, because she was absolutely going nowhere while Constance was alive.

She wasn't going to abandon her, certainly; the truth was, she didn't want to miss a moment with her. 'I'm overthinking things.'

'Don't be,' Finbar said. 'Just stay until the end of the summer at the very least. I haven't brought you out to see the rest of the islands yet, that's a day that'll make you choose Pin Hill Island over any other place in the world, for sure,' he added.

'Right, I'm getting us more coffee.' Jake stood up and took their cups into the van.

'Well, between coffee and boat trips, I suppose it's very hard to leave just yet…' Heather said, but deep in her heart it was decided. Pin Hill was home now, she'd found what she was looking for after all.

39

Ros

The email arrived just as Ros was leaving the cottage to pop down to the chemist. It was good news, she supposed, although it really didn't feel like it. She was too numb to feel anything vaguely resembling happiness about anything at the moment. Constance's diagnosis had knocked her for six. Since she had heard it, Ros felt as if some tethering line that held her in place had loosened and she was somehow at a remove from everything around her. Nothing felt fully real any more.

They were officially offering her the maternity leave and the hourly rate was even slightly more than she was being paid on the island. It was a stroke of luck that the woman she'd be replacing was employed at the same administrative level as a ranger in the field. Perhaps the cottage had been taken into account as a benefit in kind. At least the maternity leave didn't kick off for another month and, in the meantime, she had enough holiday entitlement days to tide her over between finishing up on the island and starting in Ballycove.

The second email of the morning was one she'd been expecting. Shane McPherson would be taking up the position of ranger at the start of next week. They were happy for Ros to stay in the cottage until she could organise a new place to live. It was very businesslike; there was no inkling in its tone that they were dismantling her beloved home. Still, nothing lasted forever; if life had taught her anything at this point it was that much. She'd known this was coming, at some stage, and she'd known that she would have to give the cottage up when the time came. She was ready for it.

Max Toolis wanted nothing from the cottage and so she'd boxed up everything she owned and a few bits belonging to Max that she liked; the rest she'd offered to the bring-and-buy sale to raise much needed funds for the repairs on the Church of Ireland roof. The local WI were thrilled to take every knick-knack they could lay their hands on. She had a feeling that she had probably supplied them with ninety-five percent of their wares on the day. By the end of it, the cottage was pretty much cleared out and she had the satisfaction of knowing that everything had been donated to a good cause rather than ending up in landfill. Her own bits and pieces were stored safely in Constance's spare back bedroom; perhaps she'd be pleasantly surprised and fall into somewhere charming on the mainland, if their application to the Goat Society didn't succeed.

One thing she was sure of, she couldn't imagine staying in the cottage with Shane when he arrived. Not after that last night. Whatever he'd had planned, with arriving and bottles of wine and cooking together and perhaps watching the sun go down, she'd completely messed up. She still wasn't sure why she'd bolted out of the cottage that evening like a mad woman. That call from a blonde had thrown her certainly, but there was no guarantee it wasn't his ex – it could be, couldn't it? Certainly, her running away had nothing to do with the arrival of Jonah – after all, there was nothing between them, well, apart from a dead kid goat and enough bickering since they'd first met to launch a minor international conflict.

She would mention it to Constance. There would be room for her at Ocean's End. It felt as much like home now as the almost empty cottage that she'd wanted so desperately to hold onto until that day when Jonah had arrived and looked at her as if he was trying to figure out if he knew her at all.

Ridiculous. She muttered it under her breath, but perhaps she was confirming it for George as she passed by the rose bush she'd planted over his resting place. It was a nice gesture, she had to give Jonah Ashe credit for that.

She was trying to jolly herself along, but she was damned if she was going back up to Ocean's End with a face as long as a fiddle. Constance had enough on her plate already.

Constance was fast asleep in a garden chair when Ros arrived. Ros lowered herself into the seat next to her and sat watching the clouds scuttle across the sky overhead. Sometimes, she felt as if she could sit here all day, but unfortunately, each time she did, she spotted some other little job to do to keep the place in check just a little more. To stop herself from whipping out the lawnmower and destroying the peacefulness, she looked across at Constance and felt her heart break just a little more at the thought of how little time they had left together. In this light, the old woman looked even more jaundiced than she had the previous day. Ros suspected she had lost more weight too and dark shadows ringed her eyes, making her face look gaunter in the grey light.

'Oh, dear, I must have fallen asleep, you should have woken me. Are you here long?' Constance said, stirring in her seat, and for a moment Ros wondered if perhaps she should have brought out an extra blanket to tuck around her and stave off any rogue breezes or chills.

'Not long,' Ros lied. She had found it strangely comforting, just sitting here next to Constance as she slept. 'They say an afternoon nap is good for you.'

'In that case, perhaps they've got it wrong and I'll live to a hundred at this rate,' Constance cackled.

'Let's hope so,' Ros said softly. Now that she was awake, Constance seemed so much brighter today. Ros knew that had to do with Heather, who had decided to stay on the island. She was full of plans to buy a cottage and help out with the Maggie Macken estate for now. Of course, Ros suspected that her only plan was to help out with Constance. She would need help, near the end. The thought of her being here alone was unbearable. Heather wouldn't be getting paid, but that didn't seem to bother her too much. Well for some, although Ros couldn't feel envious. She liked Heather too much to feel anything other than happy that life seemed to be panning out well for her. It was good news for Constance too. Heather would keep a good eye on her. With that thought, Heather arrived out and plopped down next to them.

Ros told them about the email confirming Shane McPherson's arrival on the island the following week.

'The hunk?' Heather giggled.

'I think I've gone off him a bit now,' Ros said and she was surprised to find that was true.

'Well, he'll have his work cut out for him to do half the job you have over the last few months.'

'Ah, thanks, Constance.' She was so sweet, but Shane knew the job inside out, he'd probably wipe her eye ten times over in his first week.

'Finbar says he knows someone with a flat over in Ballycove. They might let it out to you for the winter months, just to get you started. It's over the bakery, at the very top, but you'd have fresh coffee and scones every morning. He says he'll ask if you'd like him to, but it probably won't come up for about a month, not until the holiday season is over anyway.' Heather was trying to make things easy.

'But you're not going to stay there with that auld yoke in the cottage for a full month, are you?' Constance asked.

'I'd rather not, actually I was thinking that if you didn't mind...' Ros said a little sheepishly. She'd miss having a place to call her own, but she adored Constance; living at Ocean's End would be like sharing with a favourite grandmother. It'd also be a chance to make the most of the time left to Constance and, perhaps, she could be of some help about the place. 'I could take the back room, give it a good airing and...'

'What about the cottage, in the kitchen garden, Constance?' Heather tilted her head to the side. 'I mean, I know we'd have to do a bit of cleaning up on it, but it's in good nick, even if it's a bit dated. There's water piped in from the house and I'm sure we could run electricity into it until we get an electrician in to look at the old wiring.' She stalled for a moment, perhaps fearing she'd overstepped the mark. 'I mean, if that was something that you both thought could work?'

'Oh, that's such a lovely offer,' Ros gasped. 'I mean, I couldn't possibly, it's much too generous.' It was the answer to her prayers, but then she realised she couldn't just say yes, what about Heather? 'Surely you'd like to stay there yourself, Heather, after all, you have the history with it?' Ros said, although she'd love it. The cottage was such a quaint place and she could really imagine it being very homely. There was everything she'd need, a main room that was kitchen and sitting room combined with a stove at its centre, a bathroom, two tiny bedrooms and gorgeous cast-iron beds, which looked as if they could be as comfortable as anything if they were given a good airing.

'Ah no, I'm very happy where I am and I'm settled in, you know, hat on a hook and all that...' Heather said softly, but Ros saw how she looked at Constance and it confirmed for her that Heather just wanted to be on hand to help out if she could.

'I'd love to have you. Imposition my eye, sure, this place is crying out for people. Heather's right, I can't quite believe it, but the cottage is in great shape, well, apart from needing a bit of a scrubbing and a good freshening up.'

'Come on, Ros, you know you want to,' Heather cajoled.

'Well, that's true, I really do want to. I'd love it, but still, it's too much, too kind...'

'Stop it, it's a tiny house and you'd be doing me a favour,' Constance said, folding her arms.

'How's that exactly?' Ros felt her heart fill with even more love for Constance in that moment.

'Well, at the moment, because no-one has lived in it, it might be considered derelict.'

'It's far from derelict and you know it,' Ros said.

'Maybe, but the fact that no-one has lived there in ages… well, you'd put a bit of life into it, wouldn't you? If you did half as much to pull the place together as you have on the gardens around the house, I suspect I might be the one coming out with the better end of the bargain.'

'She's right,' Heather said.

'And you'd have a base, here on the island, you know, a reason to come back on your days off, I know you'd love that…' Constance smiled at her and reached out and took her hand. 'Say you will, it'd be good for everyone if you did.'

'Oh, you had me at running water – of course I'd love to move into it.' Ros reached across and threw her arms around Constance. She wanted to cry with happiness, but instead, she just hugged her so close that it felt as if they might never let each other go.

'Right, well, I don't know about you pair, but I think there's a cottage in the garden that needs to be cleaned out and aired,' Heather said eventually and handed a basin filled with washing-up liquid and bleach to Ros. 'It won't take as long as you think,' she said to Constance, who looked fit to burst with happiness.

40

1981

Dotty

The ferry crossing had been horrendous this time. They had been thrown around the bunk beds in a cabin that had neither a porthole nor easy access to a toilet. Heather was sick so many times Dotty lost count. Indeed, she felt sick herself, but somehow, she'd managed to soldier on. It had been hours on end of holding a bucket before the child's head and then scrambling to wash it out before the next wave of nausea hit. '*Summer swells*,' an old man muttered in the corridor and even he looked green, although he wore a uniform and his complexion told of decades on the sea.

    Bobby had booked it, the cabin at least, for them. Perhaps he thought that it might make her change her mind, but Dotty had decided a long time ago that their marriage was not worth saving, or maybe that *she* was not worth saving. He didn't love her any more. How could he? At some point the penny must have dropped. She wasn't quite whole, you see. In spite of the glamour and appearance of being someone who could love, she fell very far short of that particular mark. In the end, it was all about Heather, she knew it, even if Bobby couldn't admit it to either of them.

At least their divorce was one thing her mother wouldn't have to bear. Sylvie Wren had died the previous summer. Being Sylvie she picked the most convenient time, a week before Dotty and Heather were due to arrive for a summer holiday on the island. Constance told her she'd walked to the end of the vegetable garden to pick some berries for a fruit tart and keeled over. *Dead before she knew it. A blessing.* Dotty had survived years living half a life and she was only too painfully aware of it. But then again, Sylvie deserved an easy death, she'd done nothing wrong. Naivety is not a crime.

'Come, come, come.' Constance was standing at the pier waiting for them when they finally arrived on the island, her smile as wide as it had been when they were children. 'I can't believe you're here, was it a terrible crossing?' She grabbed Dotty first, pulling her close in a tight grip and holding her until Dotty unfurled from her friend's embrace. 'You must be dead on your feet, both of you.' She looked down at Heather and her features instantly softened. 'Oh, my God, look at you, you're even more adorable than last year.' She swept her up into her arms, nuzzled her neck while Heather screamed with delight.

'We're worn out, if I'm honest, I've never had such an ghastly journey.' Dotty took their bags from the old guy who'd brought them across. 'Come along, Heather, look lively.' She poked her daughter gently with her bag.

'I'll take that.' Constance reached out her free hand for

Heather's suitcase and clasped the kid's hand tightly so they swung arms all the back to Ocean's End.

'For goodness' sake, Constance, all that swaying, you'll make her sick again,' Dotty snapped as they walked.

'But I like it Mum, really.' Heather looked up between the two women.

'I'm sure a few days' rollicking about on the beach will be enough to put the colour back in her cheeks,' Constance said softly and she pulled Heather close to her so her arm wrapped around her as she walked. 'You look good, Dotty,' Constance ventured then, although they both knew it was a lie. She looked wretched, thanks to the long journey, but also, her eyes had started to show the first lines of age, her mouth, once one of her best features, turned down at the corners now, even when she smiled. Not that there was very much to smile about these days: a life in Fulham in a house that had once belonged to Bobby's aunt and a humdrum existence of helping out at the local corner shop between putting meals on the table for both of them.

'No, Constance, you look good,' Dotty answered flatly. 'Widowhood suits you.' She'd said it without thinking, but the fact was that you could see the only wear and tear on Constance was loneliness and maybe a slight fondness for Victoria sponge cakes over the years. 'Sorry, I didn't mean it,' she said quickly, 'I shouldn't have said that.'

'No.' Constance sighed, then she looked out towards the bay, turning her attention to Heather. 'I think we should go rock pooling today, if you're up for it? You can have a rest, Dotty, you're probably just exhausted from all the travelling.'

'Maybe.' But they both knew that wasn't what was wrong with her. The fact was that for as long as Dotty could remember, nothing seemed to make her happy. She could see there was joy all around her, people laughing and making the most of life, but for years it was just beyond her grasp. 'I'll sit with Maggie for a while, catch up, maybe she can tell me stories from the good old days,' she said then, because for Dotty that was always the highlight of coming back here; hearing about the glittering London publishing parties that had been a part of Maggie's life when she'd been at her most successful. She'd even dedicated one of her books to Dotty and Constance. They had been best friends, but like everything else in life, it felt as if someone had bubble-wrapped their friendship up to keep it for best wear only – and Dotty had a feeling that she would never be good enough to take it down and enjoy it.

Maggie always had a decent bottle of brandy on the go.

'Medicinal purposes, dearie.'

'I'm definitely in need of something.' Dotty sank wearily into the deep sofa and downed half the glass in one thirsty gulp. She could swear, the room still tilted around her after that ferry crossing.

'Here.' Maggie topped her up. 'Is everything okay with you, you seem…'

'It's just hunky-dory.' But Dotty felt huge tears well up in her eyes. She couldn't talk to anyone about how she felt, maybe that was half the problem, but Maggie was watching her now: these people, Maggie and Constance, they knew her too well to hide very much from them. 'I suppose, I just needed a break.'

'Sure we all need a little break now and again.' Maggie replaced the top of the bottle and stood it on the edge of her desk.

'My marriage is over, Maggie. When we go back, Bobby will have left the house, it'll be news to Heather, but…'

'Ah no, you don't say.' Maggie made all the right noises.

'We both know I wasn't cut out for marriage, Maggie, I'm more like you that way than my own mother.'

'Poor Sylvie, she liked having someone to look out for her.'

'She did.'

'A pity she ended up…'

'On her own?'

'I was going to say married to your father, but…' Maggie looked away, another of those things about Dotty's childhood probably better left unsaid. But they both knew, she was too young, too naive for a man like Norman Wren – which was of course precisely why he married her.

'Indeed.' Dotty felt the reassuring wave of alcohol go to work at fogging up her brain. Soon it would wash across her nervous system, take the edge off everything. Peace. She loved sitting here, this room, with the bookcases, the open fire, the sun streaming through the windows across the gently fading rug. On the coffee table next to the sofa sat the elegant Edwardian letter box that Maggie had received as a gift from one of her publishers, long ago. Strange, but it looked smaller than she remembered now and she picked it up in her hand, examining it with fresh eyes. It was exquisitely made, with a hand-painted design along its smooth polished finish.

'It's extraordinarily beautiful, isn't it?' Maggie said. 'So much craftsmanship and I've never actually used it.'

'You should,' Dotty said softly.

'I think it would suit you rather well, here. There's a key here somewhere, two of them if I really look.' Maggie shook her head; she was as disorganised now as she'd ever been. She went to her desk, rifled through the drawers and pulled out a slender golden key. 'Ah, here we are.' She held it up and walked back to the chair, handing the key to Dotty. 'Well, go on, open it.' She sipped her drink, sat back in the chair, basking in the comfort of it.

'Really?' Dotty felt like a child, opening up the box. Silly, really, because it was, after all, just a box. Inside was a simple wooden finish curved into a silken-covered ravine, in which sat a gorgeous old pen.

'Mont Blanc,' Maggie said and even though Dotty wasn't sure what that meant, she had a feeling it signified something important. 'Well go on, take it out,' Maggie urged. She was sitting forward now. 'I've always thought every woman should have a place to store her secrets. You can lift out that casing and underneath hide love letters or maybe just your secrets.' She threw her head back and laughed.

'Oh, Maggie.'

'It's yours now. You keep it, it's worth a bit, if you need cash, but I hope you hold onto it and think of me occasionally,' she said softly.

'It's too much, I can't, I really shouldn't.' She'd always admired it and Maggie Macken too. She'd wanted to grow up and become Maggie Macken. Funny, but along the way, she'd forgotten about that. When they lived here, she'd run around the island with the wrong crowd. Eddie Ryan and his mates, none of them would ever amount to much. Last she heard, Eddie was living on the streets in Dublin. His recklessness led him to drugs in the end. *A lost cause*, Maggie had said sadly, because no-one would wish a life like that on anyone.

It was always going to be easier to tell Maggie about the divorce than admitting it to Constance.

'I can't believe it.' Constance dropped down to sit on a huge rock as if someone had taken the air from her. 'Are you sure it's over, is there no hope...?'

'There is no chance,' Dotty said firmly. The problem, she knew, was not that her marriage was over so much as the fact that Constance felt she was throwing it away. Constance, who had gone through life trying always to be good and kind and giving to make up for what they did, had finally made amends with the death of her own husband, the wiping out of the future she had banked on. Constance would have given anything to have Oisin back again, she had adored him. Theirs would have been the sort of marriage that could have made it to the golden wedding anniversary, if fate had not stepped in the way. God, what would Dotty have given if her demons could be so easily put aside with the snatching from her of just one thing instead of this all-encompassing misery?

'But maybe if you talk to him... go back, sit down and have whatever it is out with him...' Constance stopped and looked out to sea, biting her lip in that way she'd always done as a child when she was trying to figure something out. 'Look, what about if I take Heather? Just for a while until you get things sorted...'

'It's not something we can sort out in a while...'

'I'll take her for as long as you want, forever, if you'd let me, you know that.' For a long moment, in spite of the fact that the waves were crashing beneath them, it felt as if the whole universe had fallen into a deep silence.

'I know you don't think I deserve her,' Dotty said quietly. The searing anger that constantly brewed deep within her finally splintered. Her heart raced with it and words tumbled through her brain – awful words, things she should never say, never think, threatened to escape now. She took a deep breath, needed to keep the darkness buttoned in, it always felt as if her very survival depended on it. 'I know you think you'd be a much better mother and I know you're probably right, but she's mine, do you understand, Constance, Heather is my daughter and I'm not going to just hand her over to you.'

'I didn't mean it like that. It was just an offer of help, that's all, plain and simple, one friend to another.'

'Are we still friends?' Dotty hated that her voice sounded so bitter, even to herself. Did she always sound like this? She couldn't bear it. 'Look, Constance, it's not my fault your husband died. It's not my fault that you haven't got any kids. It's not even my fault that you were there that day when my father came into Mr Morrison's garden. I never asked you to follow me or to…'

'Oh, Dotty. Stop it, it's all so long ago. Don't you think it should make us closer, not make us feel as if…'

'Well, it doesn't bind us in some eternal friendship like we've always tried to pretend. It's guilt and murder and we'll never wipe that from our conscience.'

'We should have come clean, long ago, we should have told the truth. We'd both have been far better off for it.'

'NO,' Dotty screamed. 'No bloody way, we made a promise, you promised me, no-one ever knows what happened that day, that's what we agreed...' Dotty thought she'd be sick, right there on the rocks. 'What good would telling people do? It doesn't change any of it.' She felt more nauseous now than she had when the ferry had been rollicking over waves that were thirty-foot high and bashing against their cabin.

'I'm just saying, we were kids, that's all, we were just kids. We shouldn't still be carrying the guilt of it, Dotty.' Constance reached out to touch Dotty's arm, her hand cold, but Dotty shook it off. 'Perhaps if we came clean, gave your father the chance of a proper burial, what's the worst they'll do to us?'

'Listen to yourself, will you? What do you know about what they'll do to us or what my father deserved?'

'I still think of him in that well. Dotty, you didn't go down there, you didn't see.'

'Oh, God, here we go.' Dotty felt as if her blood pressure was about to explode in her chest, drive its way out through the top of her head. 'You have no idea what it was like, what it's like now. My father got exactly what he deserved, we might not have planned it, but I've never been sorry. Look at me, Heather, do you really think I wanted to end up living like this?' Her breath caught in her chest, she hardly knew what she'd said, not able to stop herself from saying more. 'I never wanted to get married, I never wanted to live like this... I wanted...' She wasn't even sure what she wanted any more. Did she want what Constance had? To live at Ocean's End and teach in the local school with every kid on the island adoring the ground she walked on?

Did she want to come back here and live a life that she'd yearned so badly to leave behind?

'Tell me then, go on. If your life is that bad, why don't you tell me? Maybe I can help, I want to help…'

'You can't help,' Dotty snapped, getting up.

'No. You're probably right,' Constance called after her. 'No-one can help you, Dotty, you need to help yourself, you need to stop drinking and grow up and be grateful for what you bloody have already.'

'Oh yeah of course, you were always going to throw that in my face, weren't you? It's a cheap shot, but I'm not an alcoholic, if that's what you're trying to imply. I don't need a drink…' She was shaking, so angry. She might believe she didn't need a drink, but she wanted one so badly.

'Someone has to say it. It's always been there, for years. And no-one has said it and we both know, you're only hiding from the past, but you're killing the future and maybe I could stand back and watch you do it to yourself, but I can't bear to see you do it to Heather.'

'How bloody dare you?' Dotty was livid. She ran at Constance, lashed out with a violent swipe that only just missed her face. It shocked them both for a second, so there they were, the world as they'd always known it suddenly rupturing beneath their feet. Dotty took an unsteady step backwards; she could hardly see what was before her eyes. She wanted to make Constance stop saying these things. For one terrible moment of madness, she wanted to kill her. She wanted to throw her over the side of the cliff, hear her scream, watch her horrified expression as she went down into the waves below. She imagined herself doing it too; no remorse. She wanted to shut her up forever. Somehow, she managed to keep herself in check; but only just.

'I hate you, Constance. I absolutely hate you and this place and everything about us,' Dotty screamed and she felt tears rush down her cheeks.

'Maybe I hate you too,' Constance said softly and when she said it she looked almost as horrified as if she *had* been thrown over the cliff. 'Maybe I hate what happened all those years ago and the fact that I've had to carry it with me ever since. Every time I look at you, I think of it, I can't help myself. Having you here, now, makes me think the only thing I can do to be free is to tell the truth.'

Something in her eyes changed and Dotty knew she was deadly serious. She could march down to the local garda station this minute and tell them everything.

'Maybe you're right, maybe you were never worth the bother. If I never see you again, it'll be too bloody soon,' Constance said, then she stomped off, leaving Dotty standing there with nowhere to put her anger. She couldn't risk Constance going to the police. Who knew what would come of that? Prison maybe and a whole lot of questions to be answered and memories dredged up. There was nothing else for it, but a firm decision that she would never, *could never*, come back here again.

41

Constance

Constance couldn't say she was at peace with it. Far from it. She might only have weeks to live, but rather than tick off a bucket list as she might have imagined she would, instead, the two words that rolled around at the back of her brain were simple. Pancreatic cancer. It was silly. She was an old woman. She'd long outlived many of her contemporaries, she knew that by a country mile, and yet, she thought too, she'd never be properly ready to go.

Sometimes, she found herself looking back across the years and wondering where the time had gone. It was more like a whisper than a roar back to the mostly blissful days of childhood.

And those days, when they'd first come to the island, had been perfect. Constance remembered that first summer, tailing out into autumn when every day had been an adventure. Once she'd got her bearings – which didn't take too long; Dotty led the way, of course, the cat trailing after them –they'd gone tramping along the cliffs and then later down to the village where she and Dotty met other children and played rounders and football and sat on the side of the pier with their legs dangling over the water. That first year here, it felt as if everything had been left behind, as if they'd gotten away with it. But you never really leave the past behind. Not really.

A light wind was beginning to whip in from across the sea. It moved like fingers stroking the grass in the garden. It would be good to have life in the housekeeper's cottage again. It wasn't Buckingham Palace, but Ros was delighted to have a base to call her own at last. Maybe, if Wesley McVeigh managed to get enough money for her mother's books, they could make it into a proper home for her, modernise it a bit – it would be the best gift she could make to Ros, who had brought her so much joy these last few months. Maybe. Although, honestly, Constance still didn't actually believe anyone would want to spend very much money on books that had gone out of fashion years ago.

She blinked; she had to stop worrying about it. There was nothing to be done now but put a little faith in the idea that it would all fall into place after her.

Constance was making tea when Heather threw open the back door, with Ros hot on her heels. She was holding the phone up in the air, her face flushed, the look in her eyes unmistakable. Good news.

'Yes, Wesley,' Heather said. 'I'll put that to her and see what she thinks. That sounds good though, thank you, I'm sure she'll have lots of questions. We'll get back to you in a day or two.'

'What is it?' But of course, with Wesley, it had to be about her mother's estate.

'That was the agent.' Heather was beaming. 'Ros, you got the gist of it?'

'It's unbelievable, I mean, it's very good news.' Ros was nodding her head as if it had loosened beyond her control.

'Well come on, I'm bursting to know?' Constance lowered herself gently into her chair. It was good to have a distraction. Tea could wait until after she heard.

'They've made an offer. And it's a very generous offer, according to Wesley. He's really pleased with it, but...' She paused, hardly knowing how to put it into words.

'But what?' Constance asked.

'There are other publishers interested. It's going to go to auction. You have a few days to see if you are happy with what they are offering and if there's something you feel they are missing out on, then Wesley has said he'll put it on the table so all of the publishers will have a shot at it.'

'Like what? I mean, are they actually going to pay to take on the books?' Constance wasn't sure, because Heather hadn't said anything about money.

'Oh, yes, they are going to pay, plenty. Enough to do the roof, enough to do the whole house and build another right beside it if that's what you fancy.'

'How much?' Ros breathed.

'Six figures, but that's only for the island books. You still get to sell the other series separately and you hold onto all the other rights. Unless you want them to take them too, then, according to Wesley, they'll have to pay more.'

'Six figures?' Ros repeated.

'So, that's...?'

'A hundred thousand, just for the first six books, Constance,' Heather said softly. 'You've done it. You've made enough to start off the Maggie Macken Foundation. You can secure the house and, more importantly, with further deals you can secure her place in history.'

'*You've* done it, Heather,' Constance said softly. 'You've done it. You've saved Ocean's End.' She felt tears of relief well up inside her.

'Don't be daft, I didn't do much at all.'

'Well, that's the biggest load of cow manure I've ever heard, Heather Banks.' Ros roared with laughter. 'Of course you did: without you, we'd never have thought of the idea that the books could be sold again.'

'There'll be enough money to do all those things?' It was still sinking in, Constance had to ask again, just to be sure. 'To fix the roof and secure the place so it'll go on after…'

'I think by the time Wesley has finished selling up the estate, you'll be able to fix the roof ten times over, if you want,' Heather said.

It was the strangest feeling, to think that a huge chunk of worry that had gnawed at the back of Constance's mind for so long had suddenly evaporated. That was what it felt like. She had no idea when the money would come through or how things would work. Heather would have to sort all that out, but soon, Heather could ring up a builder and fix the metal railing that had fallen from the roof a few weeks ago, knowing that there was the money to pay him when it was done. Constance took a deep breath; it felt almost miraculous.

★

'I think I'm too excited to cook dinner tonight,' Constance said when they came up from working on the cottage later. How could she possibly serve up leftover bacon and salad from yesterday after such an amazing day? 'I rang Finbar and asked if he'd like to come for dinner with us at the hotel.'

'Oooh, really?' Ros looked so excited, but then suddenly, that familiar glint of concern crossed her eyes. 'Are you sure you're up to it?'

'Are you trying to matchmake, Constance Macken?' Heather said then to cover over any mention of the fact that things had changed. The fact was, Constance thought there was a spark between Heather and Finbar, even if Heather hadn't actually realised it for herself yet.

'Moi?' Constance said as innocently as she could manage. 'Not at all, I just think we deserve to celebrate. I've booked the hotel for seven, so we could maybe have a glass of wine before we go and that gives you both a bit of time to tidy yourselves up first.' Not that Constance had exactly been preening herself for the evening, but she took down her mother's brooch and pinned it to her best cardigan. Maggie would have been so happy to know that her books were going to keep on going long after they were both gone.

42

Heather

'*The Bookseller* is the publishing industry bible,' Heather said, as she pushed her phone across for Constance to read the article. 'Well, that's what Wesley says anyway and we'll have to take his word for it.'

'Oh my, they've made quite a thing of it, haven't they?' Constance breathed. She was still scanning through the article. Even though she'd read through the press release already, somehow seeing it all there in black and white made it seem more real. 'Oh, my…' Constance said and it was only then that Heather realised she was about to faint.

'CONSTANCE!' she screamed, jumping behind her to catch her as she fell. Just in time, she saved her and managed to half walk, half carry her to the large chair near the old stove. 'Constance, are you okay, can you hear me?'

But Constance was out of it, her eyes rolling in her head,

a filmy rash of sweat seeping from her pores. Her skin had turned almost yellow. Heather took her hand, tried to feel for her pulse, but there was no point. Heather knew next to nothing about taking a pulse or a temperature or any of the basic skills most parents managed to gather when they had young children. She stood for a moment, total panic threatening to engulf her.

'Constance, oh, Constance, what will I do?' There was nothing to give her, no emergency medication to fix this. All they had on hand were painkillers. An awful thought, was she dying? Was this is it? *Oh God, no.*

Out of the corner of her eye, she spotted the card Avril Duignan had left on the dresser with her mobile number and an email address. Heather grabbed it, tapped the number into her phone, her fingers shaking so much she wasn't sure how she managed to get through.

'Come quickly, it's Constance, she's... I'm not sure what to do...' she said and she realised she was out of breath.

'It's okay, don't panic, stay calm, that's really important, just for Constance's sake. I'll be there in ten minutes.' Avril hung up and, somehow, even just knowing that she was on her way made Heather feel as if everything was a little more under control.

'Heather, what happened?' Constance breathed next to her.

'I think you fainted, Constance, I think it was the excitement – it was overwhelming.' Heather managed to smile; she hoped it was convincing. She hoped it was the truth, that Constance would be fine, for now at least, just for a little longer.

'I don't know what happened...' Constance's voice sounded so pathetic and weak and Heather wanted to cry, but she couldn't, she needed to be strong.

'It's okay, Constance.' Heather gripped her hand and held it tight. 'It's okay, we were looking at the announcement in *The Bookseller* and I think it was all too much.'

'Ah, it's better than I could ever have dreamed of, I suppose I was overcome with it all.' Constance murmured then. 'What a complaint, eh?'

'Yes, it's a very good reason to be off your feet.'

'And you here and Ros too. And knowing that Ocean's End is going to be okay...' Constance closed her eyes and Heather wondered if she wasn't drifting a bit, almost as if she was losing a grip on the present moment.

'It's all good. I'm here and Ros will be along soon and so will Avril and you'll be fine by lunchtime.'

'I'll be fine by lunchtime,' Constance repeated in a soft whisper, then she closed her eyes and, for a moment, Heather wasn't sure if she was sleeping or unconscious.

'Constance, maybe I should get you a blanket?' Heather said, more to keep her awake than because it was cold.

'No, no, don't go to any trouble, I'll just sit here and catch my breath, I might have a little nap,' she said as if on the verge of sleep.

It felt as if Avril was on the doorstep far more quickly than was humanly possible, but Heather certainly wasn't complaining.

'Let's take a look, shall we?' Avril said with a tone of confidence that Heather was grateful for. She went about checking Constance's pulse and her blood pressure and looking into her eyes. She asked Heather what had happened and checked that Constance had in fact taken her regular medication for the day.

'I'm all right, really, just overcome with excitement,' Constance said weakly.

'I can see that. Even so, maybe we should get you into bed for a few hours,' Avril said and Heather could see Constance was as likely to slip off the chair as she was to stay on it if left there for any length of time.

Ros came through the back door just in time to help them move her into bed.

'Oh God,' she said; there was no mistaking the fear in her eyes that things might have progressed far more quickly than any of them were ready for.

'It's fine.' Avril placed a hand on Ros's arm and Heather marvelled at how good some people were at putting you at ease.

They managed to get Constance into bed and by the time her head was resting on the pillow, she was already drifting off to sleep. Heather watched as Ros slipped the pins from her hair and it tumbled down around her face. She looked so peaceful and for a moment Heather thought, *at least she's happy. If she slips away now, she's happy, she knows we won't let her down.* The problem was, neither she nor Ros were ready to say goodbye to Constance just yet.

43

Ros

It all felt so hollow now. Ros came down to the little cottage in the garden after she had settled Constance in for the night. Heather offered her a glass of wine before she left, but the truth was, Ros couldn't face anything at this stage.

She'd been there when her mother passed away, holding her hand, praying for something like a miracle. Her mum had slipped away as if someone had opened a side door one day and let her vitality leak through it bit by bit so, in a matter of weeks, she was little more than fractured fragments of the woman she had once been.

That's what Constance had reminded her of tonight.

Ros had been here at Ocean's End first thing in the morning. Constance was her usual self, fussing around her, insisting that she have something to eat before going to check on a curlew nest on the other side of the island.

How could the whole world turn over within the space of an hour or two? That's what it felt like, as if someone had altered the dial on everything, draining life of its most essential essence. The silence was almost claustrophobic. Ros wasn't a religious person, but she found herself praying that Constance would rally quickly. She looked around the cottage now. It was her first night to stay here. She should be over the moon.

The cottage was still lovely, lovelier than Ros could have imagined or dreamed of ever living in. It was tiny of course, possibly that was half its charm. The entire place could fit into Constance's kitchen and sitting room. They'd found an antique rose paint and covered the walls, rolled cream paint across the low ceiling, giving the whole place a lovely soft and feminine feel. Heather had helped her drag the mattresses into the garden on days that were so warm and windy it felt as if the heavens had decided to play along with them. The place felt and smelled as if it had been freshened by the sea air.

Of course, there were no mod cons. She would be handwashing her clothes and heating the place with firewood in the stove in the winter, but when Heather set a huge jug of wildflowers on the tiny windowsill and Ros straightened the throw she'd picked up months earlier across the fireside chair, it felt as if she had truly come home.

'It's lovely,' Constance had said when she'd come down to survey the work a few days earlier. She'd brought with her gorgeous antique linen sheets that had been freshly laundered and dried in the afternoon sun. They smelled of cut grass and washing powder and Ros loved everything about them. 'I'm just happy they're going to be some use.' Constance smiled. She had already sent down a multicoloured circular rug for the centre of the kitchen and told her to take anything she needed in the way of crockery or glasses or pots and pans from the old pantry. Ros loved the sheets most. She imagined folding herself between them and feeling blissfully content in her snug little corner of the island.

Ros yawned. The day had drained her, she knew she had to get to bed. She was due to meet Shane McPherson the following day and it was anyone's guess what time he'd arrive. She had already decided he would have to wait until she checked on Constance and organised anything she and Heather might need for the day.

Shane had brought across his boat. Of course he had brought across his boat, so by the time she got to the cottage he was already waiting for her. He'd managed to get Jay Larkin to bring up his belongings in the back of the post van and was sitting on the doorstep waiting for her when she arrived at the ranger's cottage.

'Good evening,' he said a little cynically.

'If you're hinting at the hour of the day, I've already done my rounds. There's still a full day ahead of us, if you want to start watching the clock,' she said without looking at him.

'I'm sure you have, but don't you carry some sort of mobile phone on you?' They had given Ros one to go with the cottage, but no-one ever called her so she rarely used it, preferring instead to use her own.

'Come on, I've cleared out my stuff, you can get yourself settled in.' She pushed in the front door, leading into the tiny porch and from there the main room of the cottage.

'So, you're not staying on?' he asked.

'No. No, I'm not. It's all yours,' she said and even though she loved the cottage Constance had given her, and she knew it was completely irrational, she couldn't help feeling a little peeved that he had somehow managed to take this place which had been so happy for her.

'So all the old crap that was here?' He was looking around the cottage.

'Donated. The Church of Ireland ladies send on their gratitude, it'll go some way towards repairs to the church roof in St Michaels.'

'Hmm, so everyone wins, it saves me having to drag it across to the mainland on my boat.' And it was hard to know if he was actually happy or not about it.

'I've stripped the bed; you'll have to make it up for yourself.' She wasn't his servant, just so he knew.

'Listen, I'm sorry that...' He stood before her, obviously uncomfortable in this space that had been hers last time he was here.

'Sorry that?'

'You know, my getting this job, well, it means you're out of the cottage and that last night it was awkward... I really don't mind you staying on until you're sorted with something else, yeah?'

'I'm already sorted, thanks,' she said. She didn't owe him any explanations.

'So you're moving over to the mainland to take up the admin post?'

'Probably, yeah, in a few weeks.' She filled the kettle, flicked the switch; it was automatic: in spite of the emptiness, the place still felt like hers.

'And you've got a place there?' He obviously knew how hard it was to find somewhere to live in Ballycove in high season.

'I will have, when the time comes.' She looked at him. Was he actually concerned on some level that she had something sorted and she wasn't going to be living in a doorway somewhere? 'There's a flat coming free above the bakery, apparently. It's let out to tourists at the moment, but the old guy I spoke to said I could have it, starting the week before I'm due to move across.'

'But that's in a month, surely...'

'You don't have to worry. This cottage, as much and all as I loved it, it's yours now. I've got somewhere else to stay,' she said and she dropped instant coffee into two mugs and set about stirring in boiling water with a concentration that didn't brook any more questions.

She went through the various things he needed to know about the cottage. The hot water system was still a bit of a mystery to her, even after a year here, but she did her best.

'So, if there's nothing else you need, I'll be getting back,' she said, leaving him to drag in his belongings from the doorstep. 'Generally, I start on my rounds at six in the morning, if that suits? Better to do as much as you can in summer, because winter days are so short, well, it's making hay while the sun shines.' She turned to let herself out the door.

'Ros?' he called after her as she made her way down the path.

'Yep?' she said, half turning. She was itching to get back to Ocean's End to check in on Constance.

'You wouldn't fancy going to the pub later, just for a pint

you know, to...' He broke off, perhaps realising that the last thing she wanted to do was celebrate his arrival on the island.

'Ah, sorry, no, I can't tonight, I have plans, so... sorry,' she said and she felt a tiny sliver of guilt shave across her because she remembered her own first week here when the students had returned to the city and Max Toolis had left her to stay in the cottage alone. Even for Ros, who considered herself an independent sort, it had been a bit daunting to have only the sound of the wind in the chimney for company.

'Of course, sure, no problem,' he said, bending to pick up his bags.

'Maybe later in the week, lunch? In the hotel? My treat to welcome you to the island?' she said.

'Okay,' he said and he turned back into the cottage, allowing the door to bang closed behind him. Ros found herself instantly regretting the invitation when she saw his reaction. Under the clear blue skies of the summer's day, she knew that the loss of the job she had loved and the cottage she had adored was hardly the end of the world, not when she thought of Constance that morning. She seemed to have aged overnight and she was so weak, hardly able to sip the tea that Ros had held to her lips.

She would have to let go of this simmering resentment towards Shane; after all, she knew, he had not set out to upset her lovely life, and if it hadn't been Shane who had come along and taken the post, there was no guarantee it would have been offered to her anyway.

Ros's step was heavy as she approached Ocean's End. She couldn't shake the feeling that soon everything would change again, she could feel it in her bones; Constance was slipping away from them far more quickly than any of them expected.

When she walked into the house, Heather was sitting at the table, poring over old diaries that belonged to Maggie Macken. Her eyes looked as tired as Ros felt, she too had hardly slept all night worrying about Constance.

'Any change?'

'No, she's been sleeping most of the afternoon.'

'Can I check on her?' Ros didn't want to disturb Constance, but still, she wanted to see her, to make sure she was okay.

'I'm not in charge, Ros,' Heather smiled at her, 'but I will make us both some coffee, if you fancy it?'

'I'd love some.' Actually, she'd take anything that would put a bit of life into her at this stage. With that, her phone pinged. Mai Boland. She showed the text to Heather.

'Ring her, you have to ring her. If they've got the funding, it's going to really give Constance a great boost,' Heather said and Ros wondered if she wasn't more excited about the prospect of it than Ros was. It was a funny state of affairs, when this impending sense of loss managed to steal from you any joy for yourself but still allowed you to be happy for the people you cared about; she knew she'd have felt exactly the same for Heather.

'I've just got the word in,' Mai trilled with excitement on the other end of the line. 'We have funding for five years. Congratulations, you're officially going to be the Pin Hill Island Goat herder!'

'That's great news,' Ros managed, but she knew her voice

was lifeless. Still, she managed to carry on a conversation and promised she'd call into the development company in the next day or two to get the ball rolling.

'"I"s to be dotted and "T"s to be crossed,' Mai said and it was obvious she was really excited about the whole project. 'It'll be so good for the island, everyone will be really pleased.'

'That's good news,' Ros managed.

'And, Ros,' Mai said softly. 'People are going to be especially pleased that you're not leaving after all.'

'I guess I have to be pretty happy about that too.' And she caught Heather's eye. She looked as if she might burst with happiness for her.

It was a nice feeling to knock on Constance's bedroom door and know that she had good news to tell her at last.

'Ah, Ros, you're here.' Constance tried to sit up in the bed a little.

'Don't move on my account,' Ros said, pulling in a chair. 'Heather's making coffee, do you fancy some?'

'No, no, I don't think I could face anything at the moment.' Constance smiled.

'How do you feel? Any better?'

'Oh yes, miles better, I think I might go dancing later.' At least her sense of humour was still intact, but she sounded feeble. Ros thought her heart would break at any moment.

'We might all go dancing tonight...' She smiled at Constance. 'It looks like I'm staying on the island...'

'Oh, you got the job? With the goats? Oh, Ros...' And Constance's face lit up with a strange joyfulness that made Ros think, *this is how she must have looked as a girl.* She was truly beautiful and then, a huge tear ran down the old lady's cheek. 'Oh, don't mind me, I'm so happy for you…'

'Constance,' she reached out, stroked her arm, 'you mean so much to us, to me and Heather.' Ros felt a huge ball of emotion at the back of her throat. 'You know, I don't remember my grandparents, but since I've been here, I've come to think of you as…' Her voice was breaking, she couldn't help it. 'Well, you know, you mean a lot to me and I needed you to know that before…'

'Are you leaving after all?' Constance was making fun of her. But then, she turned her face towards the window for a moment and closed her eyes gently. 'Dear, dear, Ros. You know, if I'd had a daughter or a granddaughter, I'd have wanted her to be like you. I can't imagine any granny on the island having their hearts as full of love for a child as I have felt for you these last few months.'

'Oh, Constance.' And that was it, the floodgates were about to open, but Ros took a deep breath, she would not cry, she would not upset them both now.

'So, since neither of us are going anywhere just yet,' Constance sighed, took a long ragged breath, 'I have things I need to organise, I can't leave without doing those first.'

'What sort of things?'

'I…' she looked at Ros, 'don't laugh, but I need to get my affairs in order and I need to… I need to wipe clean a slate that's been dirty for far too many years.'

'Okay, well, can I help you do those things…'

'Oh, if only,' she sighed now.

'By your affairs, do you mean your will?'

'I suppose.'

'I could ask Surfer Dude, you know…'

'What – now which of us is going barmy?'

'You're not going barmy and neither am I. You know, Surfer Dude – Jake – he's a solicitor with some big practice in the city, he takes a few months off every summer to surf and run the coffee shack on the beach.'

'I never knew that.'

'Ah, there you go, it takes a blow-in to know these things.' Ros smiled at Constance.

'Okay, will you ask him to call up here to me, today, sometime, if he can?'

'Of course. You know, Constance, I'd do anything for you.' She wiped a tear from her eye and leaned across and kissed her on her head.

44

Constance

Somehow, time had drifted from Constance. Now, burned-yellow sun fell through the windows and the ceiling took on a coral hue with occasional silver flashes reflected from the water in the distance. She longed to walk to the window, stand there for a while as she'd done so many times before, but she hardly had the energy to lift her head from the pillow. Each time she turned it felt as if she was rolling over a huge old vessel that had seen the last of its days at sea. She'd woken during the night, convinced that she could feel her body slowing down to a deliberate grinding halt. She had opened her eyes and standing there, at the foot of her bed, were Dotty and her mother, smiling at her. At their side, darling Oisin; she reached out to hold his hand, but he just stood there, smiling shyly at her, and she longed to go and stand next to them.

She woke early, still with that warm feeling that they

were all very close by and waiting just beyond the doorway to take her on a new adventure.

But she had things to do, to make sure that all would be well when she drifted away from Ocean's End.

At four o'clock, Ros finally arrived back at the house with the man she called Surfer Dude. Constance had not known what to expect, but probably she had not expected a forty-year-old in a shirt that belonged in a bad 1970s detective show. The man wearing it was called Jake and Constance thought he could have been Tom Selleck's brother. Constance always had a soft spot for *Magnum P.I.* – perhaps it was the moustache?

'Thank you for coming, I'm sorry about...' She wasn't sure which she hated more, the fact that she had to meet this stranger here, in her bed, or that she sounded so weak. It was as if, somehow, her vitality had deserted her overnight leaving her with barely enough energy to be little more than a spectator on what remained of her life.

'No problem, what is it I can do for you?' Jake smiled, taking the seat that Heather had left only moments before he arrived.

'I want to make my will and they said you were... you see, I've never had a solicitor. There's never been one here on the island and I rarely leave, so...' She needed to breathe, it was a struggle now, almost a confirmation if one was needed that time was running out.

'I'm not sure that I'm...' He looked at her and maybe she knew what he was thinking.

'I'm compos mentis, if that's what you're wondering about, ask either of...' She sighed wearily, because that was no good. 'The district nurse, she'll tell you, she's taken bloods, I know exactly what I'm doing and I want to set things straight, before I... well, I should have done it years ago, probably.' She smiled sadly now. Of course, years ago, there was no-one to leave this house to.

'Okay, well, we can set something out, I have...' Jake pulled out his phone, 'something here, but I...' He looked around the room.

'It won't take long, I promise...' A tear rolled down her cheek. Pathetic, perhaps, but she watched as his expression changed. He would help her, she knew it then.

'Okay,' he said, reaching into his bag and pulling out a pad and pen. Soon, she was telling him exactly what she wanted. There wasn't much, not when you really thought about it. Ocean's End, the little cottage, her mother's papers and books and, of course, her desire to be buried in the plot next to Dotty. They belonged together; perhaps even Dotty had seen that at the end. 'That's all fine, sure there's nothing else?' he asked when they'd finished.

'Not a thing.' And she sighed with a deep relief, as if she'd just folded away half her troubles and there was satisfaction in knowing that the creases would ease out after she was gone.

'I'll need to get it witnessed but it'll have to be by people outside of the beneficiaries.'

'Of course. We can ask Avril to call up before she finishes her rounds and Finbar is coming across in a little while to help Ros move some of the old barrels under the downpipes on the cottage.'

Constance smiled. There was something pleasing about knowing that when she was long gone, the rain would continue to fall and Ros would then use it to water the garden in the height of summer. Everything would go on, just as it was always meant to, trees would bear fruit and maybe, at some point, the old vine in the glass house would be revived.

Avril and Finbar arrived together and both were happy to oblige and witness her will, although Constance caught the look that passed between Jake and Avril. But any questions about her ability to make a decision were put to the side when Finbar opened up the topic of the forthcoming local elections. Constance always enjoyed their little sparring discussions about how the Green Party candidate seemed to completely forget about the fact that protecting the ocean was as important as planting trees or saving energy. Her knowledge of local politics was enough to push any question of her mental capacity to make her will to the side.

'Well, it seems to me that everything here is in order,' Jake said. 'I'll be off, so.' He gathered up his phone and the various pieces of paper that they had put together.

'Do you need a lift?' Finbar asked Jake, perhaps realising that it was getting late and maybe it was time to let Constance rest after the day.

By the time it was done, Constance was exhausted. Once Heather settled her back down on her pillows, she felt as if she could just disintegrate into the sheets. Her bones felt light as dust, her skin soft as if it was as flimsy as tissue paper. The pains and aches of the last few years that she had grown so used to were noticeable only by their absence.

She slept for hours, although it felt like five minutes, and once more, her mother came and this time she sat beside her bed, taking her hand and rubbing her fingers gently, warming her right to the very core of her. *You know, there is one more thing that you must do before you can rest*, she said and Constance's eyes shot open. She felt an extraordinary vigour steeling within her for what she always knew she would have to do one day. It seemed she couldn't leave Ocean's End just yet.

45

Nine Months Ago

Dotty

It came as a surprise to Dotty, but she realised on their second meeting that she actually liked Chipo. The counsellor she'd been assigned (thanks to the platinum level of cover on the health policy Heather had paid into for her for years) was originally from Zimbabwe. She spoke with an accent that strangely reminded Dotty of the west of Ireland, even though she knew it was nothing like.

'So, how did we manage this week?' Chipo raised her eyes from the plant she was watering. There was no fooling Chipo, she'd been through addiction herself, she'd lost a child, lost a husband and had to pick her life up off the floor to take care of four more kids and a mother she'd brought to London from Harare.

'Don't look at me like that,' Dotty snapped at her. Old habits died hard and Dotty had lost the habit of chit-chat, thanks to having cut herself off from everyone who would want to listen to her.

'Have you been to your meeting?'

'Yes, I have. Actually, I went to four different meetings this week,' Dotty said a little proudly, and maybe a little surprised with herself, because at the start of all this she'd never have imagined attending AA.

'Good, that's good. The meetings are always going to be important to you, Dot.' She didn't say any more, but Dotty knew Chipo still attended regular meetings too. Everyone did, as far as Dotty could see. 'And so now you're almost...'

'One hundred and ninety-two days sober.' Yes, she was counting, but only because it gave her something to do.

'It's time to think about more than just...'

'I have and I can't see any way of making things right, not now, not ever... Too much has happened, I've...' Dotty wiped a tear from her cheek. She wanted more than anything to have Heather in her life, properly, but the fact was, she'd pushed her away from the day she was born; she had no right now to try and claw her way back into her daughter's life.

'She'd want to know that you are sober.' Chipo put down the watering can, took a box of tissues from the narrow desk that faced a wall filled with Post-it notes and scraps of paper that must all be important in their own way.

'I'm not so sure she would,' Dotty said and then she put up her hand to stop Chipo from saying any more. 'Look, she's not a child, she's a grown woman with a successful business, and even if I'd been a half-decent mother, the way I've treated her these last few years has been...'

She looked to the floor, examined her shoes as if they were the most interesting thing on the planet. She'd been a horrible drunk, that was the truth of it. On the one hand, waiting for Heather's call each week – the highlight of her week, if she was honest – and then, once they started to talk, she'd find something to fault about her daughter. Anything, it didn't really matter what it was; on one occasion, she remembered starting an argument about The Beatles, on another, she'd gone on and on about the fact that Heather had never given her a grandchild. God, she wanted to die now with the stabs of guilt that pushed into her stomach at the memories of those times.

'Dotty, she might not be a child, but she'll always be your child,' Chipo stated. She poured two glasses of water from the jug between them and placed one before Dotty and one on the small table next to her own chair. 'And I don't want to upset you, but none of us will go on forever. How do you think she'll feel when you're gone?' Chipo had a way of being direct but somehow her words were softened by the kindness in her eyes. 'You see? She will carry this gulf with her that you could easily fill by reaching out and talking to her. You can fix it now, before it's too late... if you're brave enough...'

'Easy for you to say.' Dotty bent forward for a sip of water; surely she was not the only one who occasionally wished that someone would substitute the water in the jug with a splash of vodka and white.

'You are getting the chance to make things right, here, take it, Dotty,' Chipo said softly.

'I...' Dotty waited for a minute, tried to regroup. She'd said it all before and Chipo had an answer to every single reason why she shouldn't contact Heather. She pushed even more for Dotty to make her peace with Constance, but at this stage, it was far too late for that. Constance could be dead for all she knew now and, even if she was still alive, Dotty was probably the last person she'd want to hear from. 'I just can't...'

'You can, I know you can.' Chipo sighed, but she was not someone who could be thwarted easily. She'd told Dotty once about how she had made the journey from her home in Zimbabwe to the United Kingdom as if to warn Dotty that she would not be put off if she set her mind to something.

'They won't want to hear from me,' Dotty said simply, because maybe, aside from blaming herself and burying the guilt of a lifetime wasted, maybe that was her biggest fear now.

'Maybe they won't, but unless you actually knock on their doors, how will you ever know?'

'I can't just...' She took a deep breath. 'Look, it's all very well for you here, telling me I need to do this or I need to do that, but you don't understand what went on... all those years ago and now...'

'Okay, good point, I don't know what went on and I've asked enough times to know you're not going to tell me anyway, but maybe...' Chipo sat back, as if wracking her brains for some way round this impasse. 'Maybe you could write them both a letter.'

'Both of them?' Dotty felt a little indignant now. She hadn't mentioned Constance today, maybe she'd hoped that Constance had slipped through the cracks somehow.

'Yes, both of them. I have a feeling that your friend, Clarissa? Was it? No, no, that's not right...'

'Constance,' Dotty said in defeat.

'Yes, it all began with Constance, I think. If you can just put it into a letter this week, you don't have to post it, but you need to set it straight somehow, will you do that much for now?'

'I suppose...' Dotty said, because it wasn't as if she had anything else to do during the day anyway.

Outside the clinic, Dotty spotted a taxi. She was about to call it over, because really, the buses at this time of day, you couldn't depend on them. And the bus stop nearest her house was just outside the corner shop that had once been where she'd bought most of her off-licence supplies. It was expensive avoiding passing by it, but Carmelita, who knew a thing or two about these things, said it wouldn't be forever.

It was Carmelita who'd eventually talked her into rehab. Twenty-eight days in a place that was little better than a hostel with mandatory one-to-ones and a group hug every other day. Dotty chuckled every time she thought about it. God alone knew how she made it through it. Liver disease, it wouldn't kill her, but that wasn't the point, was it? It was a wake-up call, too close to home to ignore it.

Just as she was getting into the cab she spotted the stationery shop across the road. She stood back, let a very pregnant-looking woman with far too many shopping bags have the cab and walked to the nearby crossing.

She hadn't been in a stationery shop in years; actually, before now, she'd thought they weren't a thing any more. This place was very posh. It smelled of fresh lavender and citrus, as if someone spent their whole time rubbing leaves and rind together. There were biros that cost over a thousand pounds and the fanciest notepaper that looked as if it belonged on the walls of Kensington Palace rather than folded up in an envelope. She settled on a set of long pages and matching envelopes. She'd definitely need long pages, she wasn't so sure that she needed a watermark with puffins and sea moss, but it couldn't hurt. She liked the colour, a silvery blue; it reminded her of the mottled skies above Pin Hill Island. The assistant wrapped up her purchases and took a good chunk of her weekly pension for what was, at the end of the day, just paper after all. As she walked towards the door she saw a stand with a beautiful golden pen. No price tag. Never a good sign.

'Ah, the Mont Blanc...' The assistant almost trotted from behind the cash register. *Must be on commission*, Dotty thought. 'An investment piece. The perfect gift.' She eyed the paper bag in Dotty's hand. 'Do you think, maybe...' She was leaning towards the cabinet, taking a little silver key from her pocket, when Dotty felt as if a tiny copper penny dropped through a slot in her brain.

'No. I already have one of those at home, thanks,' she said and, suddenly, she knew exactly what she was going to do with those letters for Heather and Constance.

46

Heather

'Heather,' Jay Larkin called from the hall and then pushed open the door to the kitchen. He'd called to enquire about Constance, probably. Heather wasn't sure she'd be fit for visitors at this hour, she'd only just opened her eyes for a few minutes earlier when she'd drifted off to sleep once more.

'Hi Jay, oh, you're bearing gifts, I see.' She nodded to the parcel in his hand.

'Oh, yeah, for you.' He placed the oblong box on the kitchen table.

'For me? Strange, I wasn't expecting anything,' she said, lifting up the box and inspecting the packaging for a second before turning back to switch on the kettle. 'Fancy a cup of tea?'

'No time today, I'm afraid,' he said. 'I just wanted to ask about Constance, the missus is going to burn the house down at home with all the candles she has lit for her, is she any better at all?'

'I'm sorry, Jay. I don't know how much better she's going to be, you see...' They wouldn't have Constance for much longer; even if Heather couldn't quite put that into words for herself, it didn't change what they knew to be certain. She was drifting from them as surely as if she was a small boat without anchor on the horizon.

'Everyone on the island will be devastated to hear that,' Jay said and he sniffed loudly to cover up his own sadness. He had dropped into a kitchen chair for a moment, as if to gather himself up again. 'Constance has been a part of Pin Hill for as long as most of us can remember. She taught me at school, did you know that?' He shook his head sadly. 'She was always a treasure; I don't think there was a child went through that school that didn't adore the ground she walked on.'

'I can imagine.'

'I won't disturb her now, so...' he said, getting up and wiping his hand against his cheeks, but he couldn't quite cover over the tears that had welled up in his eyes.

'Are you sure, I can check if she's...'

'No. Not now, I'd want to be in better shape to see her if she's... I wouldn't want to upset her, you know...'

'I understand,' Heather said. Grief, was it worse before or after the event? She wasn't sure, but it was heavy, like a weight bearing down in the kitchen around her.

After walking Jay to the front door, Heather turned back to the kitchen. What on earth had been sent to her in the post? She grabbed a kitchen knife and slid it along the edges, cutting open the tape and paper covering the parcel.

'How on earth? I can hardly believe it,' she breathed when she realised it was the antique letter box her mother had mentioned in her will. God alone knew how it ended up being posted on – she was certain she must have either packed it up in storage by accident or, worse, lost it somewhere along the way in transit.

This had been meant for Constance, her mother had wanted her to have it, and while Heather had pushed the idea of it from her mind, occasionally it bothered her, the regret that it was lost forever. An attached note from the estate agents explained what had happened. One of the people who came to view the house had noticed it on the floor beneath the hall table. It must have fallen when the movers were clearing the place out. They'd handed it over to the agent showing them the property, who'd sent it on to Heather. Relief flooded through her. If she could have reached across time and space she would have gladly hugged those honest buyers.

Funny, but it looked different here. Now, she examined the keyhole and wondered if the little golden key that fitted nothing else in Ocean's End might fit it.

She brought it into Maggie's old office, laid it carefully on the desk. In the slimmest drawer she'd placed the tiny key, with intricate leaf fan design iron work on its end. It slipped easily into the lock, springing open the mechanism with a tiny metal click.

Inside the box was a beautiful Mont Blanc pen, laid in repose on silken printed fabric that looked as if it was from a similar era to Ocean's End. It must be worth a fortune. How on earth had her mother managed to have this in her possession? She traced her fingertips along the edge of the pen. It was cool and smooth and when she picked it out of the folds of fabric, she saw a tiny tab beneath it. Pulling on it gently, she found herself holding her breath. There was a flat compartment underneath. The letters her mother mentioned in her note to Heather? Of course. There were two envelopes. One addressed to Heather, the other to Constance.

With shaking hands Heather quickly tore open the envelope addressed to her. She noticed the beautiful paper, expensive, elegant; puffins and sea plants in plumes across the grey-blue paper. She held the page to her face, breathing it in, but it smelled only of the cedar box in which they'd been stored for... she checked the date on the top right-hand corner of the page. Six months before her mother's death. Heather closed her eyes, suddenly overcome with a sense of loneliness she'd never felt before. When this letter had been written, she'd been in the process of taking apart the life she'd built up for years, her marriage, her business, her flat, her purpose; she had felt particularly alone on those days. At that time, she had tried to be pragmatic about it all. It was simply time to move on, not that she had a choice, she couldn't go on living a life that felt as if it didn't fit her any more.

She took a deep breath, as if readying herself to dive into bottomless waters that held within their depths darkness as much as promise. Her mother had wanted to say something to her, perhaps it was something vile? God knew, they'd had more rows over the years than any other family she knew, but this was her mother's final chance to speak, was it too much to hope for some trace of love for her? Probably. She straightened her back, flattened the letter out on the desk before her. It was just one page, but the writing was dense, as if her mother had taken time to plan it out, maybe even rule it out on the page.

Dearest Heather,

I know, if this letter is one begging for forgiveness it should be a lot longer than I can possibly fit in one envelope. It's too late for me to hold out for any of that. I know now, as I'm writing this to you, it's too late to make up the time I've thrown away in bitterness and anger over the years. But I wanted you to know that I've come to the point in my life where I deeply regret the way it all turned out. Most of all, I regret the chance that I missed out on you, on being your mother, on maybe – don't hate me even more – on being your friend.

In February of this year, I made the bravest decision I've ever made in my life. I entered a rehabilitation centre for addiction treatment and finally faced up to the life I've led and, more importantly, the chances I've allowed to slip away.

I'm proud to say that today, I am one hundred and ninety-six days sober. I won't lie. It has not been easy. It turns out, going without a drink every single day wasn't even the toughest thing; the hardest part of all was facing up to the fact that I failed you. I failed you and everyone else who meant something to me in life: Bobby, Maggie, my mother and, of course, Constance. All of you who expected and deserved so much more, I let you down and, I see now, I let myself down also.

A few days ago, I sat in a taxi and travelled to your shop in Covent Garden. I stood across the road for almost half an hour (until my kidneys got the better of me and I had no choice but to dash home again!), I stood there and watched you. You looked so absorbed, making up a bouquet of some sort, you hardly knew there were other people on the planet, much less that I was across the street.

Here's the thing, I wasn't brave enough to tell you then, even though I'm hoping I'll work up to it one day soon. I'm thinking if I can make it to another one hundred and sixty-nine days sober, I might just be brave enough to say this to you instead of taking the coward's way out in a letter. I'm trying hard to be a better person. To be the sort of person who belongs in your life.

You've been the best daughter, in spite of all the times I've pushed you away. A better daughter than I deserved and that's for certain.

None of that changes one essential thing. I love you, Heather, with all my heart and every fibre of my being, always have, always will. No matter that I didn't know how to show it over the years, I wanted you to know this now.

I was broken a long time before you came into my life, far too broken to even think of how to go about fixing things, but my heart disintegrated into a thousand tiny pieces of love the first time I saw you and today, sober but with some small amount of growing hope for the future, I feel the very same.

Stay safe, my darling girl, I love you always.

Dotty xx

Oh, Mum. It was all Heather could say when she eventually looked away from the letter before her. She had read it over many times, trying to make sense of the woman she thought she knew her whole life and this other voice that had slipped into Ocean's End unexpectedly from beyond the grave. There was so much to take in. Forgiveness? She wasn't even sure she could get her head around the idea of her mother in rehab. Surely, this could not be the same mother she thought she knew so well. But, she had done it. She'd managed almost twelve months sober. Heather pulled out her phone. Quickly checked the date. *Oh no. No. No. No.* She was just two days away from the full year when she'd passed away. She'd almost made it. Poor Dotty – she only just ran out of time.

47

Ros

Ros spotted Jonah Ashe immediately, leaning against the side of that horrible old jeep he drove. She dodged behind a boat that had been overlooking the ocean from the path since she'd arrived on the island. Up close, she noticed there were scratches to the hull; no-one would be taking *Bertha's Breeze* out any time soon. She was bloody freezing. Bloody typical. She'd been for a quick dip. It was early afternoon, the sun was high in the sky and, for once, the tidal pool at the end of the village had filled to a reasonable height. She'd known the water would be warmer than it had been all year and she'd brought along her swimsuit and a towel in her bag with hopes of decompressing for a while in the calm water before returning to Ocean's End.

And it was lovely, just the ticket to dampen down this overreaching sadness that bundled up around her about Constance. She'd just lain there, in the water on her back, eyes closed, thinking of nothing for a few minutes. Perhaps she'd cried, but even so, she felt better now, ready to go back to Constance's bedside and pretend that everything was just fine.

Except it wasn't, because Constance was dying and all the tears in the world weren't about to change that. She would have to put on a brave face, for Constance and for Heather too.

It was only when she'd emerged from the water that she'd realised her clothes, moved probably by some overly helpful local to make sure they didn't get wet, were in a bundle on the path next to that damn jeep. It looked as if Jonah had no intention of going anywhere, any time soon. That was when Ros had darted behind the boat. Now, she was beginning to shiver in the summer bikini that she'd picked up years before for a holiday she'd never managed to make with her own mother. She caught partial bits of conversation from across the pier, Jonah's voice, familiar to her, seemed to travel in a straight line to her ears. Do her a favour and leave? Far from it, he was leaning back, chatting away to Astrid Murphy, a boho hippy newcomer who made jewellery and lived in a tiny cottage in the village that had once belonged to some relation.

She could hear them from here, laughing and joking, not a care in the world, while she stood there shivering with only one desire – to get back to Ocean's End and sit with Constance for a while. There was nothing for it, she would have to brave it before she turned completely blue. She picked her way up along the cobbled path, avoiding where she could those loose stones that somehow were far sharper now than when she'd run unheeding towards the water earlier.

'Hey?' Astrid spotted her coming and smiled widely, pushing back long blonde curls from her face. She was impossibly glamorous, even here, in cutaway shorts and what looked like huge designer sunglasses.

'What on earth...' Jonah stared at Ros, tried but failed to hide a smile. 'Here,' he said, moving forward to pick up her towel and hand it to her. Hastily she threw it across her shoulders, feeling more like a yeti as she shuffled away from them. No doubt Astrid, in the same situation, would have resembled Brigitte Bardot far more than some prehistoric creature bent over beneath the dubious cover of a near threadbare towel that had once belonged to Max Toolis.

'I'll just, ah...' Ros nodded towards the public toilets where most people changed into dry clothes after a dip. Of course, the toilets smelled as if they hadn't been washed out in weeks, but that wasn't the worst of it, the worst thing was, she could hear Jonah and Astrid's voices on the breeze; not what they were saying exactly but Jonah's deep laughter was enough to let her know that they were getting along like a house on fire and, for a moment, Ros wondered how on earth a woman could have that effect on Jonah Ashe. *Stop it.* She managed to pull herself together, although one look in the mirror was enough to confirm she more closely resembled a scarecrow than she did a boho babe.

'Right well, that's me... must be getting back to Ocean's End,' Ros said when she emerged, self-conscious; of course, she wished dearly she'd brought sunglasses to hide behind.

'I'm going your way,' Jonah said and she actually thought she heard him sigh wearily.

'Ye're grand, I'm looking forward to the walk,' she said, but time was marching and every minute counted because when Constance slept now, she could sleep for hours and Ros badly wanted to spend a little time with her. 'Okay, so...'

'Yeah, don't do me any favours, it's just a lift.' Jonah rolled his eyes and then waved goodbye to Astrid, who strode off back towards the village, bringing her long, long tanned legs along with her.

'You're a dark horse...' Ros said and she wasn't sure why she was mad at Jonah or if she was just upset at the thoughts of Constance being so sick.

'What's that supposed to mean? I was only talking to her...'

'Hmph, I'm sure that's what you told your wife too...' They were just past the village, heading out onto the main road.

'Excuse me?' He slammed on the brakes.

'When she came home and found you in bed with your girlfriend? Oh, come on Jonah, don't play the innocent, nobody believes it here.'

'You have no idea what you're talking about, I never...'

'I really don't care... it's nothing to do with me, but Astrid is...' Ros wasn't sure what Astrid was; she looked like a woman well able to look out for herself. At this moment, the only thing she knew was that she was angry, with Shane McPherson for taking her lovely job and maybe with Jonah for no good reason apart from him being Jonah. Most of all, she was simply devastated by a life that would take away people you loved just as soon as it felt as if things were on an even keel.

'Astrid? Astrid who?'

'Oh, dear God, you really are a piece of work...' He was obviously even worse than old Mrs O'Brien knew about.

'Look, I have no idea what you're rambling on about, but if this is some other crazy scheme like picking up a half-dead goat and making me take him around the island in the back of my jeep, well I don't want any of it,' he said and he pulled the van to a halt, leaving her with no option but to get out and walk the rest of the way back to Ocean's End.

It wasn't far, not really. Less than a mile from where he'd unceremoniously dropped her off, but by the time Ros turned in the gates, it felt as if she'd cried more salty tears than the whole bloody ocean beating against the cliffs beneath the house.

'Ros? What is it? What happened?' It seemed Heather had now begun to take the briars at the front of the house in hand. She was kitted out with long sleeves, heavy-duty gardening gloves and sharpened shears to tackle them.

'Oh, I'm fine, don't mind me.' Ros sniffed. There simply could not be another tear left to shed, really, if there were, she would consider herself a medical marvel. 'It's just that awful bloody Jonah Ashe again, that's what's upset me, if you want to know, he really is...' there were no words, 'un-bloody-believable.'

'Oh, no, what's he done this time?'

'Nothing.' And against all that was natural, Ros began to cry again. 'It's not him. It's me.' Then she began to laugh, because that was the truth. 'I'm going mad, that's what.'

'It's grief.' Heather put her arm around Ros's shoulder

and immediately Ros felt a little better. 'Come on, I could murder a cup of tea.' They went inside.

'How is…?'

'Sleeping. Soundly, last time I checked, perhaps there's some healing in that…'

'Hmm,' Ros said, but she remembered those final days in the hospice with her mother. She'd slept a lot too and Ros had hoped against all hope that maybe when she woke, things might get better. 'What's this?' She picked up the letter box from the table.

'It's from… Here, take a look, I'm trying to get my head around it, but really… what are the chances at this point?' Heather handed her the envelope. Ros read the letter slowly, giving each word the solemnity it deserved. At the end, she just looked at Heather and they both began to cry.

48

Constance

'Will you sit with me for a while, I need to talk to you,' she asked Heather when she arrived into the room with a fresh glass of water and news that Jake had delivered a copy of her will earlier; it was propped up on the table next to her bed. Constance had smiled at the news and sighed: it was another thing done.

'There's something I need to tell you. It's something that we've kept a secret for nearly seventy years.'

'We?' Heather looked at her now, smiling, perhaps unsure what to expect next.

'Your mother and I... you know, we had a very special bond?'

'I know, when I was little I was rather jealous. She seemed to love you so much more than me but then when we came here, I could see why and sometimes...' she traced her finger along the back of Constance's hand, 'sometimes, I wished you were my mother instead. Isn't that a terrible thing to say?' It had been a harmless childhood thought; there was no malice in it.

'Dotty found it hard to show her feelings for anyone, Heather, that's the truth of it and there was a good reason for it.'

'Oh?' Heather said. She was humouring Constance, because Heather had always believed her mother was an alcoholic, pure and simple, and maybe she'd never wondered what it was that all the drinking was trying to cover over.

'It's a long story and I hope I have the energy to get to the end of it...' Constance took a deep breath. She was so tired, so very tired.

'Please, don't wear yourself out, not for me, keep your energy, just rest for now...'

'I need to tell you this.' Constance tried her best to smile, but it was hardly a flicker on her lips. 'Heather, your grandfather was a bad man. A very bad man, do you know what I mean?'

'I... I suppose so, my mother never mentioned him, so I never really knew about him.'

'He did things to her or at least he tried to do things, terrible things. Things that we never knew grown-ups would want to do with children. I don't know how long it went on for, but I know it went on for a while, until one day he came after her, blind with rage, and I was there...'

'Oh my God, my mother, that's why she was always... I never knew, I never even thought it could be something like... Oh, you poor things.'

'No, no, I was okay, I mean, I wasn't... At the time, I was

beside myself, I didn't know what to do, but... you see, I thought he would do something terrible to her.' Constance closed her eyes; she could see it as clearly as if it had happened just hours ago.

'Don't upset yourself, not with something that happened so long ago, you really don't have to.'

'But I do, I want you to see...' She hadn't the energy to add that she wanted Heather to see that Dotty might have loved her, if she'd ever had the chance to love herself properly first.

'Well, at least have some water.' Heather held the glass to her lips, but Constance could hardly taste it.

'He came after us. He came after me, in the garden. He was going to...' She shuddered, even now to think of it made her feel sick. 'I don't know what he'd have done, but Dotty knew and she tried to save me. We tried to save each other.' She closed her eyes to gather all her strength. 'There was one terrible moment. That was all it took and that changed everything.' She shivered, remembering Mr Wren in her mind's eye, his expression – complete and utter disbelief. 'He fell into the well, at the end of a garden that no-one ever really went near.'

'Accidents happen, Constance. Don't upset yourself now, it's a long time ago.' But in spite of her words, Heather's expression had changed. She knew this was serious.

'He didn't fall exactly, there was a skirmish, he would have... I don't know, it felt as if it was either him or us and...'

'Ah Constance, stop it, you were only kids. You can't blame yourself if you were trying to...'

'Listen to me, Heather.' She tried to catch her breath,

but it was wispy now, as if it floated just ahead of her and the effect made her light-headed. 'We didn't run for help. Afterwards.' With her words, it felt as if a silence so heavy fell on the room that it blocked out the whole world from them. 'We covered over where he went in.' She closed her eyes, remembering it all so clearly now. 'We threw his bag in after him, I mean, we really set out to make him disappear, Heather, we didn't *want* to save him.'

'Constance, listen to me, you were *children*, children in a terrible situation, no-one can judge you for that.'

'You don't just forget something like this. Heather, your mother saved me that day, but it changed her. Inside, I mean, you couldn't see any difference, not on the outside, but it does something to you. It did something to your mother. She spent her whole life wanting to run away...'

'Away? But she did run away, didn't she?'

'She wanted to run away from life, to escape the memory of it, Heather. She wanted to run away from the truth of what we did; maybe more than that she wanted to run away from the truth of what he had done to her before that.'

'Oh.' Heather let out a huge breath and, with it, she became in an instant a smaller version of herself, right before Constance's eyes. A tear raced down her cheek.

'I'm so sorry.'

'No, no, don't be sorry. I get it now, the drinking, the distance, the whole bloody thing...' Heather was crying now, crying as if her heart might break, crying far more than she had after they buried Dot. 'Thank you, Constance, for telling me, you didn't have to...'

'I did.' Constance was crying too. 'I felt she wanted you

to know, for so long, and then last night, she was here, Heather, and she's so happy, but she needs you to forgive her, you know, just to understand what it was like, why she...' That final time, their final argument, she had tried to convince Dotty to get help, to stop drinking, to wake up to what she had in life, but it had ended up with falling out so badly there had been no going back.

Constance closed her eyes, it was emptying her out, just remembering that final time.

'Rest, Constance, you can rest now. I know, you don't have to worry now, all we have to do is get you strong again and then...' But maybe Heather already knew what Constance had known for almost two days.

'There's something else I need to tell you,' Constance said and she smiled, because probably it seemed as if things couldn't get much worse. 'We were very young, we thought that we might be sent away or worse for what we'd done. We were so scared, when they thought of looking in the well...' She sighed.

'Oh, Constance, don't; it doesn't matter now.'

'It really does.' Constance looked at her, tried to squeeze her hand but she hadn't the strength to pull her fingers closer. 'I offered to go down and check if he was there. They trusted me, lowered me into the well...'

'The same well that my mother rescued you from?' Heather shook her head, fresh tears filled her eyes. 'Oh, Constance, you were such a brave little thing.'

'I was tiny, the lightest of all of us to lower down there safely anyway... But that's not why I went, I went down to save our skins, it's very simple, nothing to be proud of. Not brave at all, as it turns out.'

'Constance Macken, you went down to save my mother's skin as well as your own. You were brave and fearless and, maybe, my grandfather deserved what he got.' Heather's voice was strong enough for two.

'It was so dark. He was under the water, just, there had been floods, such heavy floods so the water had risen a few days earlier. I saw his hand, reaching up the side of the well, as if trying to pull himself out of the water...' She began to shiver now and cry as if her heart might break. 'He was there, dead and buried in the dirty flood water, and I called back up to tell them that there was no sign of him. I looked down, tried to see his face beneath me as they pulled me up, but the water was too black. He's still down there, Heather, in Mr Morrison's back yard, rotting all these years without so much as a headstone.'

'Oh, Constance, it's all so long ago.' Heather reached across and placed her head on the pillow next to Constance's. 'Constance?'

'Yes?'

'I think my mother would have come back and put things right with you...'

'I don't know. I'm not sure she could have forgiven me, I said some terrible things.'

'No. She changed, at the end. She almost made it too, I think. She sent us both letters. Here...' Heather held out the most beautiful envelope that Constance had ever seen. It was like looking at the ocean and the sky, like drifting off to heaven.

'From Dotty?' she breathed. With some difficulty, Constance managed to angle herself on the pillows; Heather perched her reading glasses on her nose and held the sheet of paper so she could read it privately. A trace of a smile played at the corners of her lips, it was as if Dot was right there next to her, come alive in those precious words that had been kept until this late hour.

Constance's eyes swam with tears for the most part as she read the letter silently, once and then a second time, holding it to her chest because it felt as if it was the most precious thing in the world to her now. It was a beautiful letter, perfect, love palpable in every simple stroke of Dotty's pen; heartbreaking. Even if Dotty's timing had been terrible on the one hand, by some miracle it had arrived just in time for Constance. 'I'll read it to you, tomorrow,' she promised Heather just as sleep encroached upon her.

'Let's close our eyes for a while, all that matters now is that you get a little rest,' Heather said eventually.

'It's not really all that matters though,' Constance murmured, but she felt content in a way she'd never felt before.

'It is to me, Constance, it is to me,' Heather said and Constance sighed. She felt so much better, so much lighter and happy to be here with Heather, knowing that the others were not far away now any more.

When Constance opened her eyes again, the room was at that half-light, just as dawn was breaking. She imagined the sun, creaking over the mainland in the distance, its fingers stretching across the fields, wakening cattle from their night's slumber. The crows outside began to stir from the trees.

Constance smiled. She felt no pain, only a lightness of spirit that might carry her across the room, as if she was a slip of girl, dancing about with Dotty, pretending to be *dolls*, with invisible *guys* on the sidelines. And then, Dotty was standing there, her hand outstretched. She was young and pretty and happy. She was so happy it was contagious. Constance couldn't stay there any longer. Suddenly she was drifting from the bed, following Dotty, towards the open French doors, leading to the garden. The early light was flooding across the grass now; the blooming scents of summer roses filled the air, the dew on the grass was soft and comforting. She hadn't walked barefoot out here in years. A light breeze seemed to carry her along to the bench where her mother, smiling, and Oisin, his hand outstretched, were waiting for her. And she was happy, so happy to leave Ocean's End at last.

49

Heather

Heather had slipped quietly back to her own room in the silence of the night, but she knew before she even opened her eyes the following morning that Constance was gone. There was a whisper of emptiness on the air, something at odds with everything. She'd slept so deeply that when she woke she lay still for a moment, her eyes tracing around the ceiling's familiar cracks and paint blisters. There was an odd feeling in her heart, a loneliness that pushed in against the edges of something that felt as if it could run as deep as the ocean. Grief.

She swung her legs out onto the floor, pulled the heavy cardigan Constance had lent her around her shoulders and tiptoed downstairs as if stealing away in the night.

'Hey.' Ros arrived at the back door just as she was going to check on Constance. 'Everything all right?' she asked, but she never normally came up to the house at this hour.

'I'm just about to check on Constance now,' Heather said.

'I'll come.' Perhaps Ros already knew too.

They pushed the door in together, softly; and for once it didn't creak. The curtain at the window billowed slightly with a faint breeze and the room smelled of the sea but there was stillness on the air despite the open window.

'Oh, Constance,' Ros breathed at her side and she ran to Constance's bed. 'Oh, no, no, no.' She looked back at Heather, tears filling up her eyes. 'She's gone.'

'She is,' Heather said and went to Constance and kissed her gently on her forehead. She looked so serene, so content, as if she'd just drifted off to sleep and had been in the middle of a lovely dream when she decided it was time to step away.

They stayed there for a long time, Ros's head down as she wept on Constance's stomach. Heather stood at the head of the bed, gently touching Constance's hair, patting it into place to keep it out of her eyes as if there was any chance it might annoy her now.

Later, as they sat in the kitchen with a pot of tea between them that was cold in their cups, Heather couldn't remember if she'd cried at all. She must have, because she had that empty feeling that only came when every emotion had been poured from you.

'Did you know? Last night? That she was dying?' Ros's voice was barely a whisper.

'I think, yesterday, I think I did, but I didn't want to believe it. I truly believed we'd have her for a little longer.' She looked at Ros now who was a shadow of herself, her colour drained from her, even her hair hanging limp, as if it had given all vibrancy over to the sadness of losing Constance. 'The important thing is, I think she knew it and she was happy, Ros. She was ready to go. She'd done everything she wanted to do.'

'How do you mean?'

'You know, her business with Jake, she'd set her affairs in order.'

'You really think she was ready?' Ros shook her head. 'And she was happy?'

'I do, she talked about her mother being here with her, she *was* happy, Ros.' Heather leaned across and put her arm around Ros's shoulder. 'You helped to make her happy. I'd say having you here made her as happy as she'd been in years.'

'And you, Heather, she loved having you here. You know, when she heard you were coming across, it was such a panic to get that room sorted for you.' Ros was laughing and crying now, all at the same time. 'I thought it would be a disaster, I scrubbed and cleaned every inch of the place. I don't think I ever worked so hard, but I had to when I saw how much it meant to her.'

'But that's it. Constance knew that, she knew how much she meant to you and you were so very dear to her.'

'She'll always be the closest I've ever come to having a granny.' Ros sniffed again.

'She wouldn't want you to be too upset; I think she'd want to know that you were making the very most of your life.' Heather squeezed Ros's shoulders again.

Heather wasn't sure where the next few days disappeared to. There was a wake and a funeral to organise. Finbar had rolled in to help them do things correctly. 'You're not in the city now, Constance would want a proper island send-off,' he told Heather and she had been happy to let him tell her how things were done. She wanted to give Constance the very best send-off she possibly could. This would be her gift to Constance, her final thank you for everything, but mostly for setting her free from the overhanging calluses of her youth in a way she'd never thought she could be.

The three-day wake and funeral were cathartic in a funny way. Neither Heather nor Ros had much time for sleep and Ocean's End filled with neighbours and stories and laughter about Constance's life and what she'd meant to everyone. There was sadness too; older people who had moved to the mainland years earlier made the journey back to the island to remember her. They sat in small groups and reminisced about times they'd never see again. They told some of the best stories about the two girls who lived in the big house and the many escapades that made them notorious with the other kids on the island.

Finbar's memories were a lot like Heather's.

'She was so kind, but more than that, she had time for all the island kids when our parents were much too busy to pay us any heed. Her strawberry-picking parties were legendary each summer. Every kid on the island turned up and we ate strawberries until we were almost sick. And then, there would be homemade lemonade that was prepared in the house and brought out to the kitchen garden. We all loved the kitchen garden. In autumn some of us would come up and she'd send us home with bags of apples for our mothers to make tarts and crumbles.'

'Are they the only apple trees on the island?' Ros asked.

'As far as I know, they only survive here because the wall is so high, and even then they're not nearly as hardy as if they were on the mainland. I peeped in one day when you opened it all up again and they're still there and, you know, I was right back there, a kid looking forward to bringing home a bag of apples to my mother.'

Finbar smiled sadly. Like everyone else, he was very fond of Constance too. He'd been really good, helping out with the funeral. It seemed he had spent most of the last three days at Heather's side, making tea and serving up sweet memories with pies that had been delivered to the door from neighbours and friends that Heather never knew they had. Jake, too, had played a blinder. For an outsider, he'd certainly managed to fall in step with island life. He spent most of the three days of the funeral ferrying cups of tea and coffee from the kitchen into people's hands and clearing away the empties in time for the next round.

She finally met Jonah Ashe. He called with boxes of food and drink from the supermarket and two home-cooked hams that he had prepared and sliced up especially for the wake. Heather had to admit, she found it difficult to understand why Ros seemed to dislike him so much.

'Oh, he can be a bit sharp, but he's a good egg,' Finbar said as they watched Jonah's jeep turn out of the drive.

The service was beautiful. Heather wrote out the prayers, offering thanks for the gift of friendship and kindness that Constance had embodied in life. The readings were chosen to reflect that same sentiment and, at the end, Ros stood and read a long piece by Maggie Macken that had been written as a poem, but was really more of a meditation on the daughter who had meant the world to her.

There wasn't a dry eye in the church by the end of it. Perhaps it was added to by the lack of sleep, but Heather felt as if she was entirely emptied out and maybe that was how it was meant to be, because she looked across at Finbar and had a feeling that the last few days had been cathartic beyond measure. There was room in her heart for something more now. When he squeezed her hand as they made their way on the short walk to the cemetery from the church, she felt as if maybe he knew this too.

The ceremony at the graveside was accompanied by a local piper. It was one of those things that Constance had set in place herself. She loved the mournful sound of the pipes and had chosen a piece that managed to be both soothing and uplifting, as if she might be raised to heaven on the very air of it.

The whole funeral was beautiful, so much more than what Heather had managed to organise for her own mother and maybe that saddened her just a bit. From the way Constance had spoken about their friendship, Heather had a feeling that Dotty would just be happy to see her again, wherever they might be now.

As they stood over the newly filled-in grave, Heather thought of both women, buried here together, friends for as long as they'd been alive. She felt Ros's arm link into her own.

She smiled across at this young woman who had come to mean so much to her.

'Okay?' Finbar asked. He had linked his arm into her free arm and they stood there, for a little while, watching the clouds cast shadows that moved across the patchy green fields of the island into the distance.

'Fine,' Heather said softly. 'We'd better pay our respects at Maggie's grave too, I think,' she said to Ros. She had already decided to come down here one day next week and clean up both her grandmother's and Maggie's graves. It was the least she could do. Would she go and see if her grandfather's remains were still at the bottom of that well? She really hadn't decided about that at all, there had been far too much to think about these last few days.

50

Ros

Ros woke up the following Saturday morning to blue skies and the sounds of the swallows nesting in the drystone wall that surrounded the kitchen garden.

It was lucky for the birds that Constance did not have enough money to bring in a digger and huge excavation tools to sort out the little garden. Not that she'd ever have done anything to upset her precious birds. Instead, over the last few days, Ros had set to, clearing back ivy by cutting its thick roots and separating the growth from the ground. This at least meant that for this summer, the nesting birds could maintain their cover and it put an end to the ongoing choking growth of the ivy.

It was a surprise to find a long narrow glass house along one wall of the garden. The door had been wedged closed with time, but when Ros finally battled her way into it, she was rewarded with a thick grapevine growing along one wall and, even though the weeds had smothered much of what might have been planted years earlier, she could tell the soil was rich and free of any pesticides. In the deepest corner of it, she came across two ancient chairs and imagined Constance sitting there with her mother on wet afternoons with the rain pelting against the window while they read or sewed or just watched the clouds roll across the skies outside.

This morning, she had to push herself out of bed. It was, for the first time since she'd moved into the cottage, an effort. She knew why that was – it was the day they were to listen to the reading of Constance's will. Ros had already organised with Jake to come to the house before lunch.

Constance had thought it all out and with exceptional kindness, or perhaps with typical generosity, she had secured not only the future of the home she treasured, her mother's memory and a future for both Ros and Heather on the island if that was what they both wanted. Constance had literally given Ros the one thing she'd craved for such a long time: a home and a family to call her own. In the last few months, she'd learned that family was as much about what is in your heart as what was written on your birth certificate.

A knock on the door of the cottage jolted her from her thoughts.

'Hello...' came the familiar voice from outside. Jonah Ashe had taken to dropping by at odd hours. Somehow, over the course of the three-day-long funeral for Constance, the awkwardness between them had slipped past. Perhaps it had been smothered by the overwhelming grief of loss, but it felt as if they'd moved on, without actually moving on, in some fragile way.

'Hey, come in,' she called to him. The door was left on the latch mostly, in fact Ros had to remind herself to lock up at night time or if she left the cottage for any length of time – it was another thing she loved about living on the island.

'This is...' He stood in the doorway, his gaze drifting around the room for a moment and his expression was familiar. It was the same reaction everyone had when they first came into the cottage; probably the same as her own that first night. It was like walking into a doll's house. Everything in miniature and yet, she had the practical conveniences she needed around her; in winter there would be an open fire, a comfortable chair to sit and a table at which to entertain if there was ever someone to invite over for a night.

'I know, I'm so lucky,' she said and she got up to switch on the kettle. It was one of those things she did automatically now, sometimes she felt as if she was turning into Constance, except, of course, she'd never be able to turn out a treacle loaf or an apple tart with such ease and expertise.

'I just, ah...' He paused as if considering what he might say next.

'Go on,' she said, because even though a short while ago she would have enjoyed seeing him struggle to find a word, today she knew none of that mattered. They'd gotten off on the wrong foot, he was who he was and she would just have to rub alongside him now she was taking up her new job.

'I was talking to Finbar,' he said, as if this was some sort of explanation for him being here. 'I was talking to Finbar and he told me what Mrs O'Brien told you.'

'Ah.' So, now, at least they didn't have to pretend any more, perhaps that would be a good thing going forward.

'It's not true,' he said simply.

'What's not true?'

'My marriage, it didn't end because I was unfaithful, it was the other way round. It ended when my wife had an affair, I came home and found them together. It was my heart that was broken. Mrs O'Brien was right when she said I ran away from it all, I came here to get over it.' He looked at her now and she just knew he was telling the truth.

'I'm... so sorry, I thought,' she stammered, felt her cheeks flare up warmly under the misunderstanding. She'd spent all this time convincing herself there was a reason to dislike him and now just as certainly as outside in the garden the season was beginning to turn, she felt that their relationship was moving slowly into new ground.

'The last thing I wanted coming here was to meet someone new – this is Pin Hill Island for heaven's sake, it's the back of the beyond. I...' He rolled his eyes and she could see the funny side of things. 'I get it, I can see why you didn't like me.'

'So?'

'So.' He smiled now, his cheeks reddening too, then, as if he'd almost forgotten, he pulled a small packet from behind his back. 'This is for you...' he breathed shyly.

'For me? Really?' She hesitated: it looked suspiciously as if it had come from a jewellery shop. 'You shouldn't have, really.' Now she thought about it, he'd already been so generous during the funeral. On the first day of the wake, he'd arrived at Ocean's End with two giant cooked hams, sliced and ready to serve. It turned out they were from his own farm and he'd cooked them himself, covered them in honey and apple and stuck cloves in for good measure. The hams were delicious. They were polished off in record time, by mourners arriving at the house and helping themselves to a buffet table that never seemed to empty, thanks to the generosity of neighbours and friends.

'It's not that big of a deal. I was in Ballycove and I-I just – I saw it,' he said, stammering slightly.

'What is it?'

'Open it.' He handed it to her now and she was conscious of him, standing just a little closer than she had ever felt him before. She looked up into his eyes and, for a moment, it felt as if time stood still. He really had the most amazing eyes – how had she not noticed that before? 'Go on, don't worry, it isn't an engagement ring…' It was meant to be a joke, but his face reddened even more when the words slipped out.

'Phew, well that's a relief, because you know, I'm inundated with those every other day of the week,' Ros said in an attempt to break the awkward tension between them.

'Oh, come on,' he said and he pushed it into her hand and took a slight step back.

'Thank you, whatever it is, but you shouldn't have.' She tore open the wrapping paper, excited and intrigued to see what it contained. For a second, she wondered if perhaps it might be something like a whistle to herd the goats with. That would be the typical sort of thing she'd expect from him.

It was strange just hearing the truth of his broken marriage; already she'd begun to think of him quite differently. She looked up at him again. He was not some sort of Lothario, rather he was just like everyone else, coming to terms with what had gone before. He too knew what it was to feel the pain of loss, even if his loss was more complicated than hers. She pushed the thought aside, whatever, it was a kind gesture. She was not prepared for what was nestling on the silk cushion within the box when she snapped open the lid. A delicate gold chain with a gold and silver pendant attached. A kid goat. Long-haired, with tiny antlers, and maybe it was her, but she thought there was a distinct resemblance to George. She couldn't speak for a minute, suddenly overcome with such a mixture of emotions.

'Turn it over,' he murmured softly in her ear and she did. There on the back, engraved in fine script, *George. A very special kid.*

'Oh, Jonah.' Ros heard the waver in her own voice, she was on the verge of laughter and tears. 'Oh, it's so... I don't know what to say...' She looked up at him and realised he'd moved closer to her, so close that she could smell his aftershave. It was light and clean and felt like coming home wrapping around her.

'I...' But he didn't say another word. Instead, he reached out, scooped her into his arms and kissed her, long and lingering so she lost herself completely in him.

Afterwards, she looked at him as awkwardly as he had looked at her earlier. All this time, she'd completely misjudged him, blinded by idle gossip when she should have seen through it. Perhaps she would have, if it hadn't been for all the other things going on in her life.

'Is it okay?' he asked her, his voice much softer than she'd ever heard it before.

'Is what okay?' she said and she liked the fact that he was still holding her in his arms.

'That I kissed you?'

'Kiss me again and I'll tell you,' she said, laughing, and then she reached up on her tippy-toes to kiss him once more and she had a feeling that this was the start of something, very, very special.

Later, Ros looked around the kitchen in Ocean's End. In spite of herself, she found she was smiling at odd moments and she reached her hand up to check that the pendant Jonah had given her that morning was really real.

She still couldn't quite believe it. Nothing had changed here since Constance had sat at that table. Well maybe everything was a bit cleaner, a bit more cared for, but essentially, everything was the same. Constance's cardigan was still draped across her chair, her reading glasses were left in the centre of the table, the chain wrapped carefully around them, and the clothes brush she'd used every day was tucked away on the shelf as if she might pick it up at any moment.

To take her mind off things, Ros took the old brush down and began to clean out random hairs and bits of fluff with a sewing pin that had been popped into the seam of the curtain.

She was lost in thought when Jake pushed the back door in then. He was hardly recognisable from his usual Hawaiian-shirt-and-short-wearing self. Today, he was decked out in what looked like a really expensive suit, linen with a crisp white shirt and a neat leather case in his hand.

He looked every inch the competent and successful lawyer that he was in his city life.

'Perfect timing, Jake.'

Heather set about placing the tea pot on the table. She and Ros had already put out cups and Constance's favourite jug with milk and biscuits just in case they fancied a nibble of something.

'So, then, shall we get started?' Jake said. Ros just wanted this morning to be over. At least then she could continue thinking of Constance sitting here with them, not as she had been in those last few days when she was drifting away.

'Right,' Jake said, taking the seat that had always been Constance's, which Ros thought was maybe for the best on this occasion. 'Now, as you ladies know, Constance asked me here to help her set her wishes in order not very long before she died. She was very clear about how she wanted things to be and she asked me specifically to make it clear that these are her wishes…'

'Of course.' Ros and Heather looked at each other. Whatever Constance's wishes were, they would do their best to make sure they were carried out.

'So,' Jake murmured, opening the ribbon with a little ceremony, keeping his eye on the contents of the folder so none of the loose pages escaped. He took a pair of glasses from his inside pocket and suddenly, he looked like a real solicitor – no-one would imagine he was Surfer Dude now. When he began to read, Ros thought she might begin to cry again – really, it was too much. Hadn't she cried enough before this, she didn't want to cry again now.

'I, Constance Macken, resident and owner of Ocean's End, of Pin Hill Island in the County of Mayo, being of *sound mind, not acting under duress or undue influence and fully understanding the nature and extent of all my property and of this disposition thereof, hereby make, publish and declare this document to be my Last Will and Testament and hereby absolutely revoke any and all other wills and amendments previously made by me...'*

It was too much. Ros couldn't help it: she began to think of Constance that day she had brought Jake to see her. She remembered her, sitting up in bed, so delighted that she was setting everything straight, as she called it. Now, Ros felt her throat begin to close over with emotion and tears filled her eyes so she could hardly see the table in front of her. She hung her head low, willed herself not to sniffle and, instead, settled on just wiping away her tears as Jake continued to get through the legal jargon of the will.

'We will now move on to the disposition of property in the will,' Jake said and he leaned forward, sipped some of his tea and turned over the page. '*I devise and bequeath my property, both real and personal and wherever situated to be shared in equal parts between my closest friends Heather Banks and Rosalind Stokes. This includes both the house and lands at Ocean's End and all rights relating to my mother's literary estate. It is my dear wish that they will set up a foundation in her memory, to help other writers, readers of her books and anyone who feels they might benefit from time spent at Ocean's End. However, this is not set in stone and my bequest has only one string attached – the house in the cottage garden is Ros's for her lifetime, to live there for as long as she wishes for the rest of her life. I hope that the care and maintenance of the estate will provide employment, abundance and home to Heather and*

Ros and that they know they belong on Pin Hill Island for as long as they wish to stay.'

'Ah, Constance...' Ros said, touched once more by her dear friend's generosity. Heather reached across and took her hand. It was settled. They were here for good. Finally, Ros had truly come home.

After they had tidied everything away, Heather broke into the silence of Ros's thoughts. 'So...' she said simply.

'So.' Ros knew, there was much to think about, but not today, neither of them wanted to think about anything much more than letting Constance's final wishes settle on the air around them.

'We'll have to make some plans,' Heather said, taking down both of their coats and handing Ros hers. They'd decided on a long walk across the fields to close off the day in an effort to shake some of the loneliness from their hearts.

'It's going to be good though, isn't it?' Ros caught Heather's eye.

'Oh, yes, it's going to be great.' Heather said, linking her arm through Ros's as they went out into the breezy evening. Ros felt her heart lifting; she couldn't be sure, but she thought she heard, somewhere on the air the sound of Constance laughing and a little whisper in her ear that said, *all is good, all is good.*

Epilogue

London, a year earlier

The words just flowed out of Dotty once she began to write, it was as if there was no stopping them. She would have to go back over it all again, wouldn't she? Words. Words. Words. So many things to tell her after over forty years. Chipo would be pleased, although Dotty had no intention of showing these letters to her counsellor. She would tell her, everything. Soon. But this was just for Constance.

In fact, if she was completely honest, she had no intention of showing them to anyone. She had a plan. If she could just remain sober for another one hundred and seventy-one days, she would take a taxi to Heather's flat and explain everything to her daughter. She would ask for forgiveness, even though she really didn't expect it to be granted. But she would tell her the one thing she should have said over and over to her child many years ago. She'd been practising in the mirror. It felt positively ridiculous, sitting there at the kitchen table with her compact mirror in her hand, eyeballing herself while she said those words. Every morning. Every night. *I love you, Heather. Always have. Always will.*

Dotty took her cup of green tea to the kitchen table. Green tea, strange days indeed in the little house in Fulham. She had written what she wanted to say in an old notebook she'd found at the back of a drawer a few days earlier; this had to be just perfect, Constance deserved her very best attempt. Now, it was a case of transcribing it, or a close version to it, at any rate. Not that she intended to actually send it, not if she made it one hundred and seventy-one more days sober. She would go back to Pin Hill.

The idea had seemed impossible at first. There were so many reasons why she couldn't make the trip, chief among them the fact that she was seventy-eight years old and she hadn't taken a long trip in over forty years. The last time she'd been there, she swore she'd never return. But never, it turned out, was a very long time indeed. She longed to go there now, had yearned for it for years, if she was honest. She had missed Constance, more than she had ever thought it was possible to miss anyone. She had truly, deeply missed her friend Constance Macken, but she would put that right, very soon.

As an alcoholic, she'd always thought that being sober would be too hard to bear; it was a revelation that actually the opposite was true. A clear head, that was what made the difference. She was beginning to make out the individual trees from the woods and it was a cornucopia so rich, it was hard to understand how she could have missed out on it all before this. She'd wasted so many years, so much time and love and kindness, cast aside because she'd allowed the fabric of her life to blend together. Instead of a rich tapestry, she had lived something that was little more than a jumble of ragged ends stitched together hastily between gulps.

The first rule of her new life, accept the things you cannot change. She sighed, there was still time.

She was digging up the courage to change those things she still had the power to change.

Carmelita was a great help. She'd been sent her way quite by chance, by an agency Heather employed to look in on her, to make sure she had bread and milk and eggs in her fridge. Carmelita took her to her first meeting, she'd been the one to help her pack her bags when she went to rehab, the only one who knew she'd gone there. Carmelita would help her book her flight to Knock airport. Dotty had made up her mind; she would leave one year and one day exactly after she had taken her final drink. Even now, so far away in time – but just a whisper really when you were seventy-eight – thinking of it made Dotty's stomach turn in excited but nervy somersaults.

She looked out her kitchen window. Not much of a view, but she could see the sky, just the tiniest patch of blue, the colour of her notepaper, almost. That very same sky looked down on Ocean's End, such a small world really, when you thought about it. She picked up her pen, straightened out the pages on the table before her and breathed deeply the morning silence that she was growing at last to love.

Dearest, dearest, Constance,

I'm sitting down to write this letter to you in some small attempt to make amends or perhaps just to clear the air, because I'm not sure that I can ever truly make amends to either of us.

That day, that last day we spoke, deep down, I knew that you needed to confess – the truth was, I've never been sorry for what we did, but I had no right to stop you from doing what was the decent thing, probably.

Maybe, if I was brave enough, or honourable enough, both our lives might have turned out differently. You might have stopped blaming yourself for every bit of bad luck that blew your way and I... well, who knows, maybe I could have had a happy heart, something worth sharing with Heather and Bobby. Maybe we could have been best friends forever.

Maybe we have been best friends forever in a way – I've never had a truer friend, Constance, I could never replace you. That's what I wanted to tell you more than anything before it's too late. I hope I'm not too late.

If I can manage it, in one hundred and seventy-one days' time, I will be sober for one year exactly. It's important that you know this, because I've felt for a long time that I need to make amends, but what good is the word of a drunk? I needed to be clear and clean, you deserve that, at the very least.

There have been so many times over the years when I've picked up the phone, dialled your number and quickly replaced the receiver. You see, it turns out that I was never the brave one. Real courage is facing up to your deepest fears and I've always run away from mine. You, on the other hand, for all your meekness and modesty, showed your great mettle that day in Galway. You came to save me, even though you thought it might mean facing up to Lickey Gillespie, even though it meant going into Mr Morrison's garden and, in the greatest act of boldness, you went back down that well – you, my friend, have always been the one with a lion's heart.

I simply ran away. I ran first into the oblivion of alcohol, then to London. My dancing career lasted all of two seasons, my job in the local corner shop lasted fifty years. I've lived a small life, made no great difference to anyone, Constance, but I want to change. I am changing for the better every day.

I'm forgiving myself, with the help of a counsellor called Chipo and a cleaning lady called Carmelita, I'm accepting myself. I've finally understood what's been at play my whole life. Tasting poitín in a garden shed when I was twelve years old was the second step on my road to addiction. Drink was in my blood, generations of it on my mother's side and God alone knows what my father's contribution was – it certainly wasn't abstinence or valour of any sort, in spite of the war medal.

The good news is, I'm taking the third step now. Every morning I wake up and put my feet on the floor next to my bed. I am walking in new shoes, sober shoes, at this late stage, dare I say? Courageous shoes.

Chipo, my counsellor, says I have unresolved issues to face up to with my father. I haven't told her everything, but I will. I trust her, you see, even though I haven't told her that yet either, it's another thing on my list of things to do. Instead of getting shorter with each day, my list seems to only lengthen, which is both depressing and invigorating – I'm putting a lifetime to rights, one small day at a time.

So much to cram in to the years that are left to me.

So much to cram in to the years that are left to both of us.

I close my eyes at night with memories of Ocean's End. Of sitting in the bay window with you, looking out across the sea at night, watching the lighthouse in the distance pick out the ever-changing sea. I sleep soundly, thinking of it all, remembering.

I'd like to sit there, even just one last time.

I'm coming back to you, Constance.

I'm coming home.

Wait for me,

Your friend always,

Dotty xx

Acknowledgements

OFF THE mayo coast, here in the west of Ireland the sea is dotted with tiny, mostly uninhabited, islands. I've said a million times, I am so lucky to live in a place that is such an inspiration. Achill (home of the *Banshees of Inisherin*) is a major part of the inspiration for Pin Hill Island. It is wild, unspoilt and the people are the warmest you'll find anywhere. So we have set sail a few miles out to sea from Ballycove this time; it is not alone the location that is slightly different in this story. *The Women At Ocean's End* touches on things that, before now, I've always steered clear of, but some stories are meant to be told and sometimes, we have to be brave in the telling of them.

On the road to telling this one, I am very grateful to have had Vicki Mellor at my side; an editor who really is so much more. I have enjoyed working with you very much, Vicki, and this book would not be what it is without your clear insights and many great suggestions.

Team Aria once again have been truly superb to work with, there are so many names and hopefully, I'll get everyone in but here goes...

Huge thanks are due to Holly Humphreys, Shannon

Hewitt, Charlie Hiscox, Zoe Giles, Yasmeen Doogue-Kahn, Sophie Dawson, Rhian McKay, Nicola Bigwood, Nikky Ward, Jessie Price, Leah Jacobs-Gordon, and here in Ireland – Lorraine Levis, Lana Morrison, Brigid Nelson, Hannah Cronin and Cormac Kinsella.

I am grateful also to Rosie De Courcy, who started out on this journey with me – thank you for spotting the wood among the trees.

This book is dedicated to my wonderful agent – Judith Murdoch, who has been sitting on my side of the fence for far longer probably than either of cares to admit. I count myself very lucky to have her in my corner. Thanks are also due to Rebecca and Nick and all at David Luxton and Associates who handle film and foreign rights.

Thank you to all those who champion my books near and far, booksellers, bloggers, reviewers and booklovers.

I am grateful to you, the reader, for picking up my book: I know that whatever you decide to read is a commitment of your time and I hope you really enjoy spending it with Constance, Heather and Ros and the rest of the islanders on Pin Hill.

Finally, in the real world of actually writing and editing this book there was family Hogan, Seán (electrical wizard), Roisín (fashion advisor), Tomás (technical guru), Cristin (personal assistant and all round girl Friday) and Penny (plate cleaner extraordinaire) – for whom I am grateful every single day.

Thank you finally to James, my one and only, Errol.

About the Author

FAITH HOGAN lives in the west of Ireland with her husband, four children and their beloved chocolate lab. She has an Hons Degree in English Literature and Psychology, has worked as a fashion model and in the intellectual disability and mental health sector. *The Women at Ocean's End* is her eleventh novel.

Aria

Stories to fall in love with.

Thanks for reading!

Want to receive exclusive author content, news on the latest Aria books and updates on offers and giveaways?

Follow us on X @AriaFiction and on Facebook and Instagram @HeadofZeus, and join our mailing list.